Born in Dublin, Orlagh left Ireland after university to break into the film industry in London, working on productions such as *Calendar Girls* and *Ali G* before taking over as Head of Physical Production at Pathé Films, where she oversaw numerous award-winning films including *Breakfast on Pluto* and *The Queen*. Orlagh co-produced the BIFA-winning documentary *Joe Strummer: The Future is Unwritten* and *Mary Shelley*, starring Elle Fanning. Orlagh lives in Somerset with her husband and their two children. *No Filter* is her first novel.

NO FILTER

NO FILTER

Orlagh Collins

BLOOMSBURY
LONDON OXFORD NEW YORK NEW DELHI SYDNEY

Bloomsbury Publishing, London, Oxford, New York, New Delhi and Sydney

First published in Great Britain in July 2017 by Bloomsbury Publishing Plc
50 Bedford Square, London WC1B 3DP

www.bloomsbury.com

A CIP catalogue record for this book is available from the British Library

ISBN 978 1 4088 8451 5

Typeset by NewGen Knowledge Works (P) Ltd., Chennai, India
Printed and bound in Great Britain by
CPI Group (UK) Ltd, Croydon CR0 4YY

1 3 5 7 9 10 8 6 4 2

For Alan, for everything

EMERALD
Throwback Thursday

Is that it?

I manage not to say this out loud but McKenzie stands there, sucking her teeth, like she's reading my mind. 'Before you go, Emerald, there is one more thing.'

The way she presses her lips together it's obvious she's moved on from A level Economics. 'Yes, Miss.'

'I was wondering whether anything more might have come back to you?' There's a dramatic pause here, during which I do a sort of squint, as though I don't know what she's talking about. 'From the unfortunate incident after Inter-house athletics last week?' she continues.

I'm suddenly too hot. I quickly shake my head. 'No, Miss.'

'Even the smallest new detail would help,' she says, leaning back against the desk now, almost sitting. 'While I can't bear to think a Hollyfield girl deliberately locked another pupil into the changing rooms, stealing her clothes while she showered —' She stops now and does a little shudder '— why on earth would Ignatia Darcy stage something so … embarrassing?'

My eyes aren't even closed and it's like I'm back there again, peering in the tiny window at poor, frizzy-haired Iggy, shivering outside the shower cubicle, soaked to the skull and wearing nothing

1

but a pair of sumo-wrestler style knickers fashioned from a roll of blue hand-drying paper.

Iggy is probably the only girl in the Fifth Form that's even close to being overweight. And not like, 'OMG, my thigh-gap is tiny!' crap. She is almost properly fat. I hate that this is significant, but at our school it is. She's also pretty much friendless. I haven't even told Kitty this but when I took Iggy to her dorm afterwards, she told me how she only started comfort eating after her little sister died of meningitis three years ago. Died! I had no idea. I was gripped as she described the aching loneliness she feels at our school. Days went by, she said, without her talking to anyone but our teachers. She said her viola keeps all her secrets because she's got no one else to tell. As we sat together on her tiny bed I wanted to let her know that I too feel lonely. Of course I said nothing, but I did hold her clammy hand in mine for a bit, which thinking about it, was probably kind of weird.

It's like McKenzie senses me drifting. She moves closer. 'You chose kindness in coming to me that afternoon, Emerald. I'm well aware that others close to you chose to turn a blind eye, at best.'

It wasn't a question but her badly pencilled brows seem to arc in wait. Oh God, someone hand her a shovel. I don't know where to look. Truth is, I had no idea Bryony was behind the whole 'incident' when I reported it. The fact that Bryony knows it was me who rescued Iggy and then got McKenzie involved is making my life hard enough already.

I scan the room and my eyes land on the large, industrial clock above her desk. It's almost five past four. My phone vibrates inside my bag and I'm suddenly desperate to check Instagram to see if Rupert has liked my new post. It's just another photo from Glastonbury last weekend but it had forty-two likes by lunch.

More buzzing. C'mon, c'mon. I've got to get out of here. Besides, Mum will be here any minute.

A sharp gust from McKenzie's nostrils makes my arm hairs stand on end. When I look up, her bespectacled eyes squint kindly back at me.

'You were a deserving winner of the Citizenship Award this year, Emerald, but remember, courage is a muscle. We strengthen it with use.'

That's easy for her to say.

'We'll get to the bottom of all of this soon, I'm sure,' she says, smiling at me now. She leans in closer. I don't think I'm imagining it. Yes, the space between us is definitely getting smaller and there's a significant risk that our Head is about to do something drastic, like hug me.

I quickly hoist my bag on to my shoulder. 'Better go.'

'Right oh,' she says, inching back. 'Well, see you at Speech Day tomorrow.'

'Yes, Miss,' I cut in. 'Bye!'

I'm so desperate to get out into the air I tumble straight into a vomit of Third Form girls pouring out from their last class of the day. I lean against a pillar and search for my phone as they swarm around their lockers like flies. I stare at my shoes, unable to shake the image of Iggy's devastated face as I held her heavy hand in mine.

A familiar, high cackle rips through the chatter. I look up to catch Bryony and Kitty squad-strutting across the library lawn. The usual hangers-on trail behind, relishing the general radiance in their wake. They're all backlit by the hazy sunshine and it's as though the world has suddenly gone slow mo. I'm not the only one to notice. The Third Former beside me digs her friend in the ribs. 'Friendship goals!' she squeals, pointing at them.

3

Kitty is out front, expertly distressed topknot and endless tanned limbs gliding along in off-duty model mode. Seriously, my best friend would make a Kardashian look basic. Bryony is pretty too, but she's short and has to work that bit harder.

'Votes flying in already,' Bryony says to Kitty, waving her phone in front of her face. 'Even she's got to admit this is properly funny.'

Kitty grabs the phone and smiles. The girls behind begin to laugh over her shoulder until the smaller of the Spanish twins spots me and her face falls. Kitty looks up from the screen and waves, shoving the phone into Bryony's stomach. It's another few seconds before Bryony stops typing and whips her head in my direction. I watch her try to slide it back into her blazer pocket as she walks, but her hand keeps missing the slot.

'There you are,' says Kit, loosening my tie before offering me some gum. Bryony is less relaxed. 'In McFrenzie's office, again?'

'Yeah, another sermon on A level choices. Lucky me,' I reply, attempting to chew casually.

Bryony eyes me suspiciously.

'Votes for what?' I ask and the twins behind bite their cheeks. When Kit finally grabs the phone and slides it into my palm the most unflattering photo EVER literally leaps up at me. I almost drop it. I struggle to focus on the split-screen image of me with the taller of the Spanish twins wearing the same yellow Ted Baker dress at the Fifth Form Ball. WHO WORE IT BEST? scribbled in pink text between our two pictures. But it's not just the awful dress or the fact that my competition looks like a skinnier Selena Gomez. Bryony has purposely used a horrible shot of me fixing my knickers through my dress. I look like I'm scratching my bum!

Fifty-nine likes!

Twenty-eight minutes ago.

4

Bryonibbgal *same dress same night. You know the drill.*
#tbt #WhoWoreItBest #whowins

What! How could she? I'm shaking my head when the phone buzzes in my hand as someone else votes **@bryonibbgal** with loads of Spanish flag emojis. Bryony snatches it back.

'It was a joke, babe,' says Kitty, taking my hand.

Am I supposed to laugh?

'C'mon, Em. It's funny,' Kitty adds, giving me a playful dig on the arm. I try to smile but really it's all I can do not to push her hand away.

'No point throwing shade at Kit,' Bryony jumps in. 'I posted it. And trust me, there were others WAY more unflattering.'

My mouth is open but there's no sound. Like an airlock at the back of my throat with a faint ticking I'm hoping only I can hear. Bryony is still eyeballing me. Naked Iggy was another joke I didn't get, apparently. And this is what I get for keeping quiet? I can't believe I just lied to McKenzie to save her ass. I can't look at her. I can't look at any of them.

As though sensing I'm about to break, Kit slinks her arm in mine and drags me down the steps towards the car park.

'Can someone explain why we're being dragged back to school tomorrow for Speech Day and a bloody tug of war? Such a waste of time! Don't see why summer can't start after our last exam,' says Kitty to a general buzz of agreement. We're at the main archway when her schoolbag plummets to the ground with a heavy thud. She spins around on her heel to me. 'Um, where's your mum, Em? It's like …' She checks her phone. 'Quarter past four?'

The knot of tension in my gut twists even tighter. Seriously, Mum! Not today, please! 'Um, I might have forgotten to remind her it was her turn to pick up,' I say, rolling my eyes while swallowing a thousand shards of broken glass. 'I'm such a ditz lately.'

Bryony casts a knowing side-eye at Kitty. What's she doing in the car park anyway? Parents don't pick up boarders until after Speech Day tomorrow. I guess she's just relishing her power a little longer.

Just then, in the distance by the tennis courts, I spot Iggy shuffling along backwards, hauling her wares like a homeless bag lady. I realise I'm staring when she glances at me and smiles. I look away quickly but it's too late.

Bryony follows my eyes. 'Oh look, Em, it's your friend,' she whispers loudly, before making the sound of a reversing truck out of the side of her mouth. 'Wide load! Beep, beep, beeeeep.'

Everybody laughs. I want to run across the courtyard, seize Iggy's shoulders, look into her eyes and say sorry. I want to shout it out. I need everyone in the school to hear it.

I open my mouth wide, but still there is no sound.

Kitty takes out her phone with a huge dramatic sigh. 'I suppose I'll have to call Mum.'

Nineteen hours later

I reach for the open door of Dad's car. I think about slamming it, but I don't. Instead the door clunks shut beside me, heavy and final. I slip down the large leather seat and turn my face to watch Mum and Dad through the passenger window. Nick, the counsellor, is standing directly between them, framed by the clinic entrance. He's around the same age as Dad, with a look that says he's pretty pleased with himself. Crisp, pink shirt belted into oatmeal chinos; that kind of guy.

I can tell Nick's whole preppy-thing is making Dad itch. He's folding and unfolding his arms when suddenly Mum takes a step back, leaving Nick closer to Dad and making their little triangle more isosceles than equilateral. I guess our little family is pretty much this shape too: the shortest distance between me and Dad, and Mum increasingly at arm's length from both of us.

I can hardly believe that just twenty-four hours ago my beef with Bryony seemed like such a big deal. Before I got in from school yesterday afternoon I don't think I knew what a real problem was.

Kitty's mum eventually pulled up at the archway, drumming her fingers on the steering wheel as we piled in. Can't blame her for being hacked off. Our lift-share arrangement hasn't exactly worked out for her lately.

As we left the Hollyfield gates behind us, I had no idea it was to be for the last time this year. It certainly wasn't how I'd pictured my last day of Fifth Form. Usually I would have felt way worse about Mum not turning up, but I was so distracted trying the home number and desperately attempting to get enough signal on our country lanes to untag myself from the hideous photo. When we eventually pulled into our drive I wanted to weep with relief at being closer to Wi-Fi!

'See you in the morning,' I said, clambering out of the car, barely looking up.

'FaceTime later, yeah?' Kitty hollered as I opened the boot-room door.

I didn't answer but I waved them off with my best everything-is-fine smile.

As if I didn't already know something was up, music was playing loudly inside the house. I couldn't tell where it was coming from. I called out for Mum but my shouts were dampened by the noise of Kitty's car pulling away on the gravel outside. I traipsed into the hallway, through the breakfast room and into the kitchen, praying my rising dread was all just madness inside my head.

'Mum?' I cried, but there was still no answer. I sprinted up the stairs and heard the faint sound of running water, which got louder as I reached her bedroom. Yep, her bedroom, not theirs. Mum and Dad no longer sleep together.

I peered over the far side of her large, unmade bed as Fleetwood Mac blared out from a speaker in the corner.

'Mum?!' I was still yelling it as I entered her en suite bathroom, where a tap gushed violently into the sink. I reached to turn it off and my legs buckled under the sudden silence. I tried to process the pill packets and empty foil trays scattered all over the floor: Diazepam, Lorazepam, Xanax, Zolpidem – all of which had become familiar to me from the discarded packets twinkling up from the bottom of empty bathroom bins. I tumbled down the narrow hallway, swatting my hands against the walls on either side for support. Then I fell through her dressing-room door.

There she was, on the floor, motionless, just a faint gurgling coming from her open, bluish lips. The smell hit me like a spade and I collapsed beside her face, which was lying in a perfect pool of vomit. I rummaged for her pulse and began trying to resuscitate her, clearing her mouth the way we'd been taught to on that grotesque doll in lifesaving class.

No matter how bad Mum's been lately, I never expected to have to do that.

One – elephant – two – elephant – three …

I was beyond twenty before she began to cough. That's when I allowed myself to breathe.

I immediately called Dad. After that I just sat there gripping her hand, regretting every single horrible thing I'd said to her over the last week. When I began to free the stray, wet hairs that had stuck to her face, she squeezed my hand back and my insides caved. I stared at her, curled up, folded into herself and looking smaller than a mother should be. For a moment I thought about snuggling into her like a little girl, but I felt her hands and legs were cold so I grabbed an old blanket from the closet and tucked it in all round her, neatly pressing in the edges like she was one of Grandma's puff pastry pies. Then I lay on the carpet and trembled alongside her.

The paramedics worked quickly. Dad's PA, Magda, arrived at the same time as the ambulance and Dad wasn't too far behind. Mum spent last night at the University Hospital and was delivered straight here to rehab this morning.

Nick calls it an intervention.

Dad jumps in to the car beside me. 'Christ, that man talks,' he says, slinging his seat belt on. He lays his hand on my right knee and steadies his breath, but he doesn't take his eyes off Mum. I glare at her through the window and slowly raise my fingers to the glass to wave. She does the same and our eyes lock.

The engine roars into life and the car begins to roll away. I too try to get my breath to steady but my heart is jumping around inside my ribs. I try to copy Dad's calm but everything inside me is out of sync. I can't believe this is real. I can't believe we're leaving Mum in a place like this. I want Dad to speed away so I don't have to watch, but mostly I want to open the car door and pull her back inside.

Dad starts to reverse down the clinic's long drive. I have no choice but to stare as Nick leads Mum back inside the large Regency building which, with its wisteria-laden verandah, looks very like our own home not far away on the other side of Bath. Weirdly this similarity makes leaving more awful. Mum doesn't turn around, which helps, but my guts shoot deep down inside me like a lift suddenly summoned to the ground floor. I watch her and Nick getting slowly smaller until the bright July sun hits the windscreen and swallows them up whole.

We're racing through the Somerset countryside towards the airport now and it's like Dad can only drive in fifth gear. I sit up and try to peer over the dense hedgerows, but they're too high and we're going too fast. The throbbing inside my head isn't helped by the overpowering smell of new car. I open the window and gulp in some air.

'Shall we listen to some music?' he asks. His words sound light and new. I try to let them lift me but can only nod as Ed Sheeran begins to pour from the speakers around us. On the rare occasion that Dad listens to music he rarely strays from Thin Lizzy or a bit of old-school U2, so this is strange. I'm also totally sick of this song.

'Is this the radio?'

He takes off his sunglasses. 'It's … a new playlist,' he says, his face softening. I'm not sure my face can hide its surprise. 'Y'all right there, Scout?'

Dad's always called me this.

'Everything's going to be OK, love,' he says now, looking at me with that dad face. Dad's kind of handsome, or so Kitty says, though I hate her mentioning it. 'You were great in there with Nick. And, Em,' he says, putting his hand back on my knee, 'I want you to know how much I appreciate your …' I watch him feel around his mouth for the right word, 'cooperation … on everything. The past twenty-four hours have been horrendous for you, I know that, but Mum's in the best place now.'

I taste the desperate pleas loading themselves on to my tongue and consider how they might sound out loud. I want to beg him not to pack me off to Grandma's. I want to tell him how much I don't want to be in Ireland on my own for the next eight weeks. I want to beg him not to steal my chance of a real summer. But of course I can't.

'It was like it wasn't really her,' I say after a while.

'She's medicated, honey. That's all.'

'D'you think it'll work?'

He exhales slowly and I watch him try to smile. 'Foxford Park is the best treatment centre there is,' he says, without answering my question.

I want to go home. I want to curl into a ball on my own bed but I can't even do that. Dad's court case starts on Monday, miles up the motorway in London, and he's clearly decided I can't fend for myself at home so my

11

summer exile will start in Portstrand later today. We drive under the dark dome of a railway bridge. I want to hide here in the darkness, never to reappear.

Dad clears his throat. 'Look, I know it's hard, but let's try to be positive.'

'Uh huh.'

'Nick said rock bottom is the best opportunity for a lasting recovery. And remember, Em, these are Mum's issues, not yours.'

Dad's mouth seems to have been hijacked. He's never talked about Mum's issues before so even this tiny chink of truth feels awkward but he smiles his toothy grin, which makes it hard not to at least attempt a smile back. 'I'm really sorry you've had to miss your last day.'

I know it's not cool to admit it but I actually like Speech Day. Plus I wanted to be part of all of the end-of-term goodbyes, but honestly, with everything that's been going on with Bryony lately, it's strangely OK to be missing out. The one upside to the whole awfulness is not having to put on my game-face for a day.

I sense Dad turn to face me again. 'Hey, what is it?'

I want to shout EVERYTHING! But I look at his tired eyes and say nothing. I never do. Acres of golden fields whizz by outside my window. 'I'm fine, Dad.' I lie.

He takes his foot off the accelerator and looks over. 'Em?' But he knows me too well.

I open my mouth, genuinely unsure of what's coming. 'Won't it be weird? Me staying with Grandma, after –' I don't finish the sentence; I'm not sure I know how. I've never talked to him about what happened with Mum and

12

me in Grandma's house that Christmas. When I try to remember, it's only ever flashes and the pieces don't join up. What I do know is that until then we spent every Christmas there with her but we haven't been back to Dublin since. Grandma still phones and stuff, but it's not the same.

Dad doesn't say anything and I immediately feel guilty. He leans over and turns the music down. 'You and Grandma always got on a bomb.'

'But it's been like forever.'

'Five years isn't forever,' he says. I sit straighter as he reaches out to turn the music back up. Our hands brush in the no-man's-land of the enormous dashboard and we both pull back. 'Anyway –' he flashes a quick smile – 'Grandma's excited to see you.' He feeds tiny morsels of the steering wheel between his fists without looking at me.

I can't think of anything to say back so I busy myself unplugging my phone from the charging dock. I ran out of battery at the hospital last night and spent the whole time flicking through crap magazines while trying to sleep on Dad's shoulder. I was way too wired with anxiety and Diet Coke to pass out but Dad found a pack of cards in the family room and we spent hours playing Old Maid and Gin Rummy. It was all quite Victorian.

Just two texts; both from Kitty wondering where I am. There are the constant WhatsApps from Bryony about Kitty's party too, but these are to me and eighty-nine of our closest friends. It's so strange to think Mum nearly died and nobody even knows. I'm not sure I can face telling Kitty about this yet, let alone the fact that I'm about to drop off the face of the earth for the next eight weeks.

Feeling reckless, I decide to text Ru. I've spent six months fancying the way-out-of-my-league Rupert Heath, and after weeks of shameless stalking I managed to get with him twice, the last time being at the Fifth Form Ball (the annual cross-pollination of what McKenzie calls 'our nice Hollyfield Girls and the fine Cliffborough Boys' – *ick!*).

Wanna chat later? Xxx

Thoughts of the ball only lead to a horrible flashback to the knicker-picking image. Please God don't let Ru have seen the photo before I untagged myself.

I reread my text and remove two of the kisses.

Ed Sheeran belts out another ballad as we hit the motorway and Dad sings along, bopping his head out of time. While I definitely can't pretend this is normal behaviour, it's impossible not to love him for trying. Nothing back from Ru. I consider replying to Kitty but how do I even begin to explain everything in a text? Can't call though. Not with Dad in the car. With a glance at the clock, Dad turns off the music and switches on the news, which is all about the migrant crisis. The reporter clears his throat and adds that the body of the missing schoolgirl was pulled from the Thames Estuary this morning. His reporter voice rambles on but all I can think about is what would happen if I were to be washed up by the sea. My head fizzes wondering how they would describe me and I can't decide what would be worse: drowning or the world's press photographing me without my editorial control.

Bloody hell, I performed CPR on my mother last

night. Why am I even thinking about a stupid photo? My head hurts. At least I think it's my head. Wish I had a word for this horrible weariness; that feeling like I want to slip under but also like I'm too jittery to even close my eyes.

Dad screeches into the airport car park. He whips his seat belt off and grabs his files from the back seat. 'Dublin here we come!' he announces, sarcasm only thinly disguised. Hopping on a plane is the last thing he needs now.

I lean forward and my damp T-shirt peels off the leather seat. 'Thanks … you know, for coming with me.'

'After the night we've had, love, I'm hardly packing you off as an unaccompanied minor.'

'Dad, I'm sixteen!'

He laughs. 'It was a joke,' he says with a wink. 'Still, it'll be nice to see the mother.'

I quickly dab on some lip gloss and reach for the car door once more.

LIAM

One big, unapologetic anticlimax

'Oi oi Flynn, turn off that porn!'

I hear Kenny snickering to himself outside but I want to finish this line so I ignore him. I reread the lyric I've just written and it's woeful. I'm sure there's a finer word to illustrate just how crap, but I can't think of it now.

'These babies aren't going to drink themselves, Liamo,' Kenny roars again, even louder now. God, he's such a knob. I fling the guitar down and go to the window. There he is, the sorry-arsed eejit, standing on our rain-slicked drive, waving his bag of cans like a raffle winner. I can't help smiling at him.

'I need you, man. I'm just about holding it together here,' he says, clutching his chest. We've been nursing the tragedy of Kenny's broken heart for weeks now, which isn't easy for Fiona, his new girlfriend. 'Come on, ya prick. The night's not getting any younger.'

Years of ginger jibes have done little to dent Kenny's ego. I bet there are few lanky-looking redheads in Ireland with such a high opinion of themselves. I stick my head out. 'Give us a few minutes,' I shout.

'Here wait! I've got one for you: Dany Targaryen or Sansa

Stark? Is that a high-class problem, or what?' He bursts into a wide grin.

Kenny's been my best mate since were kids – three or four year olds – and for as long as I can remember he's been asking me this same question: 'If you had to choose between ...' and here he inserts two choices; it could be people, items, or scenarios. Anything, from which death-metal band you'd be in, to whether Murph's ma's hotter than Turbo's. He's relentless about it too.

'G'wan, you have to pick!' he'll say. If you don't do it in time he'll belt you right across the head like you were asking for it. There's no grey with Kenny; he's a black or white kind of fella.

I shake my head.

'Do the fine women of Westeros mean nothing to you?' His face is a knot of disbelief.

'Is Dany the one with the dragons?' I ask, but he's tutting under his breath now, like I've forgotten the rules.

'Feck's sake, Flynn!' He begins his countdown. 'Five, four, three ...'

'All right then, her, the one with the white hair. Jaysus.'

I've yet to get to the end of a *Game of Thrones* episode but I'm not going there now. Anyway, Kenny is rubbing his hands together gleefully, which would indicate this was the right answer.

And so it begins, another night on the piss. Who knew the summer would hold such pleasures? To think this was supposed to be the big one! The Leaving Cert exams are finally over and we're finished school forever, with almost seven weeks left before the reality of results and real life bitch-slaps us into submission. This was to be the summer it all made sense, the milestone, the one to remember, but so far it's one big unapologetic anticlimax. Even if I get the college course I supposedly want, it's all a lie, but we've had too much bad luck in this house for me to be getting any notions. Just the thought of results and I want to take the edge off.

I poke my head around the door of my baby sister's room. Evie was the accident, as they say; arrived when it was all kicking off and Dad was in the thick of the layoffs. Pregnant at forty-two! Mum was mortified. I overheard her telling the neighbour she felt like an irresponsible teenager, off buying pregnancy tests.

Evie's graduated to a real bed but she can't get the hang of it at all. I scoop her bundle into my arms and lay her back on the soft mattress. After I tuck the sides in, good and tight, I place my cheek on hers to listen to her breathing. Her breath is sweet and warm.

'Goodnight, monkey,' I whisper. Then I'm off down the stairs three at a time. I leap for four on the last rung.

I walk into the kitchen to find Laura pretending to dry plates but mostly being a prima donna. 'Everyone in my class is on holidays, Mam. I'm the only one who never has a tan.' Mam is doing her best to ignore her but my sister is persistent. 'They're all in Marbella or Croatia. Why don't we ever go away any more? It's not fair!'

'Shut up, Laura!' I shout.

Mam drops her scrubbing brush into the sink, making the dishwater splash back up. 'Liam!' She sighs, but Laura's already left, slamming the kitchen door behind her.

'What?'

'Don't speak to her like that,' she says, wiping away the

stray bubbles that hit her face.

'She was being a little cow.'

'Liam!'

'Well, she was, Mam, and it's not right.' I hate myself for doing it, but don't I get up and storm out of the room too?

I find Laura in her usual sulking spot at the bottom of the stairs. 'What's your problem?' I ask, my outstretched hand shaking. I know I'm angrier than I have any right to be.

'I was just asking,' she says, blowing at her fringe. This gets my blood up even more.

'You were just asking why we aren't going on holiday, were you?'

'No!'

'What then? What were you asking?'

'Stop it, Liam!'

'Look at me, Laura. Don't make Mam say it. Because that *really* isn't fair.'

Laura looks at me that way she does, like I'm the meanest person on earth, but there's a glint; a tiny undeniable glint in her eye that knows I'm right and that's enough for me.

'Have you any money?' She whispers this bit. 'I've no credit on my phone. G'wan, Liam … please?'

She says it like she hasn't eaten in days. Cashed my first paycheck from the Metro Service Station yesterday, so I give her a tenner, but I can't resist a quip. 'Snapchat's gonna rob you of your ambition.'

'What do you care anyway?' she says, stomping up the creaking stairs, already forgetting the favour.

I swing around the bannisters and shout up after her, 'Whatcha mean, what do I care?'

'It's true,' she hollers back, with a lash of her ponytail. 'You never tell me anything any more. You never let me hang out with your friends!'

'You're thirteen!'

She storms into her bedroom. 'God, you SO don't get it!' she screeches.

Da's van rattles into the drive. Home late again. He holds the phone in one hand, barely raising the other palm off the wheel to wave at Kenny, who's now kicking a ball against the wall outside. Da's never grasped the concept of hands-free.

I take him in, in his overalls, coming home for his now cold dinner in the beat-up Transit. I can tell he's not talking to a friend. It's the way his shoulders seem higher up, closer to his ears.

As family companies go, Flynn Construction was a hefty outfit once. Between Da and Grandda they built half the new houses in this town, but in three years it's all crumbled to dust. I remember the days when Da left early for work, looking all smart, getting into his blue Beemer, the smell of shaving cream and purpose lingering in the hallway. At one point they had four or five big jobs on at once. Da'd be gone all day; going round the sites checking everything was hunky dory.

The worst thing is Da seems to like putting up flat-pack furniture for gobshites now. It's as though he accepts his fate; sporting his handyman overalls and sorry little toolbelt like it was all a lifelong ambition. The fight's left him.

He didn't get out of bed for a week after it happened. Evie had just been born so Mam had the two of them at home under her feet. Grandda had been buried less than a year at this stage. They had thirty men on the books at the height of it. That's thirty families like us. Only we got hit worst because Da, being the principled eejit he is, insisted on paying his men what they were owed, despite the fact that Horizon, the developer, pulled the plug, leaving him with nothing but a half-built estate and a crew of angry workers. Most of the lads he laid off hit the pub. There was the night when him and John-Joe put a bottle of whiskey on the bar in Moloney's, after a feast of pints, and yer man Moloney, the aul fella, had to call Mam to collect him at two in the morning. Everybody around here knew about the bankruptcy. People were making Mam lasagne and Pyrex dishes full of food were flooding into the house as though Grandda had died all over again.

Da glances up from his call and catches me looking. He squints at me through the windscreen and his eyes shine. I smile back at him. I'm his hope, the chance to make it all better.

I can't bear looking at him any longer so I head into the kitchen where Mam is laying his plate of chops on the table. I'm thinking about apologising to her when Dad comes in and strikes me over the back of the head with a tin of Swarfega.

'Howrya?'

'Yeah, all right.'

'Are you coming with me in the morning?'

I don't answer; I'm thinking. Tonight will be a late one but I love mornings on the boat with Da when it's just the two of us. He's good on the boat: hardy, dad-like and in control again, sailing with his leathery face to the wind, chopping up the waves all the way to the island. It's a chance to pretend he's a king once more; that he's not really relegated to carrying the weekly shop over to Lord Rosloe. Together we are free men, out on a trip, father and son on the high seas of North County Dublin.

Mam plants a kiss on Da's cheek and walks out with an armful of neatly folded laundry. Da looks at his plate and looks at me. 'Is it a bit late after twenty-one years to break it to your mam that I hate peas?'

We both laugh. I love seeing him happy. That he can walk in here, limping, unshaven, and joke about stuff despite all the shite. He's the get-by type. He's not one for picking at the wound. I'd be right in there scratching the scab.

'Who were you on the phone to outside?' I ask.

He's scrubbing his hands in the sink. 'Rosloe's new gamekeeper.'

'What happened to Frank?'

Da shakes his head. 'Didn't get that out of him,' he says, grabbing a tea towel from Mam's other pile of ironing and wiping filthy brown streaks all over it. It's just as well she's upstairs. 'He wants things done proper now.'

'Called you to say that?' I ask, joking, but he looks sombre.

'So that means no more solo jaunts for you. D'you hear me?' he says, picking up his plate and scraping the offending peas into the bin. I nod guiltily. I took Kenny out for a spin in the boat a couple of weeks ago. It was the day we finished our last exam and we went all the way out to the lighthouse and burned our school shirts on the rocks while all the roseate terns and kittiwakes looked on. Kenny was impressed I knew the names of all the birds, but I could have been making them up for all he knew.

Mam walks back into the room. 'Kenny's outside on the wall.'

I nod. 'Sorry for being a dick earlier, Mam.'

'Watch your language, Liam.'

'Sorry.'

'It's OK, love.'

'I will go with you in the morning, Da.'

'Good lad!' Da shouts, without looking up from his plate.

EMERALD

The end of all my summers

My eyes flash open. For a moment I can't remember where I am or how I got here. I feel the cold phone screen against my face and lift my head to slide it out from under my cheek. Pressing the home button for the time, I read 20:07. To the left of that it says Vodafone IRL. Ireland!

I'm on the bed in Grandma's spare room. I stretch out and realise I feel good, which suddenly feels awful. I remember coming up here to unpack shortly after Dad and I arrived, but I must have fallen asleep. It's not even a millisecond before all the grim recollections flood my heavy head.

Dad's mobile rings downstairs and I immediately regret wasting the last of my time with him up here asleep, but I might as well wait for him to finish his call. I reach for my phone again: three more missed calls from Kitty. The WhatsApp group for her party has gone mental. The fancy-dress theme is now 'circus'; vintage, apparently, which just makes it sound better. I move on to Instagram whilst creaming my scaly knees and elbows with some lotion I find beside the bed. It's a serious habit: Instagram that is, not my attention to dry skin.

24

Kitty has regrammed Bryony's #whoworeitbest post!

148 likes
0o_kittykatz_o0 📷 @bryonibbgal
bryonibbgal #MAJORsenseofhumourbypass
view all nine comments — I have to do it
0o_kittykatz_o0 seriously though, awks!
bryonibbgal England v Spain 74% says put it away UK
Rupertisnotabear2000 😃
bryonibbgal IKR @rupertisnotabear2000 LOLZ
0o_kittykatz_o0 Btw party planning. Must.
bryonibbgal YASSSS!!!
0o_kittykatz_o0 👯 👯 👯

What?! I let the phone plummet on to my chest and close my eyes before they leak. Rupert has seen it. And commenting too. He never comments. Kitty? I expect this of Bryony, but Kitty? How can this hurt so much? I try to focus on the wallpaper but its furry swirls are making my head ache, so I scan the room until my eye lands on the crack in a tiny bar of soap sitting on a glass tray by the pea-green sink. I'm trying to distract myself with the whole sink-in-the-bedroom business when the stairs begin to creak with Dad's slow and heavy footsteps.

'Em?' He moves slowly into the room. 'Budge up there,' he says, perching on the edge of the bed. 'How you doing?' His unshaven face looks crumpled. We've been in the country for all of three hours and he sounds more Dublin than he has for years.

'I'm OK,' I lie, hiding the phone and sitting up.

I really don't want to but looking at his face I suddenly hate Mum a little. I hate her for making me yet another problem Dad has to fix. I hate her for leaving me here alone for the summer. Most of all I hate not being able to talk to her. I look at Dad again. He's waiting for me to say something but all I can think about is how angry I am with everybody in the world except him (and possibly Grandma). Hot stinging tears build behind my eyes but I refuse to let them out. 'Couldn't I stay with you?' It flies out of my mouth. It's a ridiculous thing to say considering he's just flown all the way here to drop me off.

He looks out into the orange sky, which has come alive again after the rain and slowly shakes his head. 'Sweetheart, it's this case. It's taking all my time. You do understand?'

Dad never talks about work but I've gathered from the scraps of overheard arguments with Mum that one of his companies is the throes of some major case.

I nod.

'I know it's a blow,' he says, folding me into his strong arms before pulling away and fixing me straight in the eye. 'Magda will be at the house with me tomorrow. Email her a list of anything else you need and we'll have it sent over. It may be hard to believe now, but you might even like it here,' he says.

There are several things I'd like to say now but I take the precaution of keeping my mouth shut.

He kisses me on the forehead. 'Well, it's straight back to the airport for me. I've to catch the last Bristol flight, but I'll call first thing tomorrow. Look at me,' he says, cupping my chin in his hand. 'I love you. Everything is going to be OK. I promise.'

'Bye, Daddy.' I gulp. I can't get up. I don't even care that I called him Daddy. Right now feels like the end of all my summers.

'Goodbye, Scout,' he calls out, his voice fading away down the stairs.

Eventually the chatter downstairs stops and after his final goodbye to Grandma the front door closes. It's just Grandma and me now.

I lie back and watch my chest pound up and down inside my T-shirt. My dad has left and my mum has gone. I start to doubt whether she'll ever come back. I try not to think about how Mum could want to leave me, or what I could have done to stop her.

The whole idea of summer is now just a cruel mirage. The school-free weeks that once glistened in the distance like unopened treasure are now a deluded fantasy: Kitty's summer party and the endless wild nights we'd spend, raving by the lake and laughing under the stars. Not to mention my meticulously crafted plans to get Ru to actually fall in love with me. All those daydreams feel pitiful now; an illusion vanishing before my eyes like a photograph from the Polaroid camera I bought in Urban Outfitters, only in reverse. I desperately want to shake it back to life but it's fading rapidly to black.

I drag myself up and trudge down the stairs.

'Emerald,' Grandma calls from somewhere I can't see. I catch a glimpse of myself in the hallway mirror: greasy hair piled on to my head, bare freckled skin and lip gloss long gone. Without make up I look like I'm twelve. I don't want Grandma or anyone else to see me like this. When I turn around she's appeared in the sitting room doorway. I freeze.

'There you are,' she says brightly, but her soft eyes don't look right. Her delicate face is full of stuff needing to be said but her lips let none of it out.

'Thought I'd get some air.'

'Oh,' she says, her mouth falling. 'I was thinking we'd have some tea.'

I'm about to change my mind when I feel her arms clasp tightly around me like one of those metal bulldog clips. It's the hug I was waiting for; the one I skirted around when we walked in the door from the airport. I wasn't able for it then. I wonder, am I now?

I'm the taller one, which I don't think either of us is prepared for. I don't know when this happened. It's been too long. How did I not realise how much I missed her?

'When you get back then, eh?' she says, taking both my hands in hers. I nod enthusiastically. Then, spotting an old coat to hide myself in, I grab it from the stand and make for the door with a new urgency.

''Twas your grandad's; the overcoat. I keep it there for the burglars,' she calls after me. I look back to find her staring at the carpet.

'Right.' It's all I can manage. 'I won't be long.'

As I step out on to the drive the drizzle dabbles my scorched cheeks. I suck the cool air deep into my lungs. I cross the road and head towards the beach, which magnetises me as though I never left. I scan the length of the dark shore that stretches for miles ahead before looking back at the houses peppered in patchwork pockets on either side of the SPAR newsagent. Square white homes, all with long gardens to the front and further up, a row of golden-bricked terraces built closer to the road. One now appears to be a Chinese restaurant.

Grandma's is one of only two properly old, Georgian-style houses that flank the run-down looking hotel beyond. You can't actually see her house from here, just the entrance gate. It's set well back from the road and the tall trees at the bottom of the drive do a good job screening even its beautiful garden from view. The heavy iron railings and long, dark drive make it seem a bit creepy from here.

Suddenly I'm dialling Kitty, desperate to rage. I take cover under a little ice-cream kiosk as it rings.

'Pick up, pick up!' I swish around underneath the red-and-white-striped roof, peering inside at the old-fashioned looking ice cream machine and the buckets and spades that hang from the ceiling.

'Boo! You know what to do.'

It's a new greeting; they change each week. Even when they're utter rubbish, Kitty still sounds effortless, every time. I think it's timing, or some confidence thing I totally suck at. I consider what to say to her. Of course I want to go off about her regramming Bryony's post but then I might not even get to Mum, or the fact that I'm stranded in this miserable place for the next eight weeks.

Suddenly I'm hanging up and walking down towards the sand. What am I doing? I need to rehearse this call. For once in my life I'd like to say what it is I actually feel.

I'm unable not to stare at the extraordinary view of the sea. The beach goes on forever and tiny stick figures dot the sand in the distance. There is a boat with a tall sail too. Everything looks so still. I stare out across the water and see an island I never noticed before silhouetted against the lilac and pink horizon. I stand in the delicate trickle of rain and take it in. I think about posting a picture. I'm composing the caption in my head when something stops me. I want to feel this instead. It's literally pulling me closer.

I've got to touch the water.

LIAM

Sitting on our cold arses in the half-dark

And here we are, strolling along Strand Road, gearing up for more cracking Friday-night action. Taking the evening at a steady pace, we saunter along, enjoying the sights and the sounds of our patch in full swing. Kenny is jabbering away in my right ear. He's still on *Game of Thrones* but mercifully the noise of passing traffic does a fine job of drowning out most of the harm. Mid-sentence, he stops by the Martello Tower to light a fag. It's then I spot someone far out on the rocks below.

Dressed in a long coat, the figure idly flicks something into the water and it skims over the waves in tiny little leaps, impressively far out. The coat spins around and I see it's a girl, slowly ambling back over the rocks towards us. Then she stops, kneels down and dips her hand into the pool at her feet and fishes for rocks. Suddenly she's up again, taking giant strides back towards the sea edge. Extending her right arm out and then her left, she hurls a smattering of pebbles into the waves. I watch her stand there, arms now by her side, still and silent, her face lifted straight to the sky. Even from here I can tell I haven't seen this girl before. Everything about her shape and how she moves seems new and different.

Kenny is digging my arm. 'Bet you feel like that with me, eh, Flynn? What with the peril of my nobility and all that?'

He's in full flight but I've lost his thread entirely, so I just whip back without answering, scanning each of the jagged black rocks by the tower. She's gone.

Kenny's voice carries us the rest of the way to the shelters – that lair of urban lawlessness beloved of Portstrand's lost youth. Like old-timers we pass through the concrete colonnade and settle into our usual spot on the stone bench, just up from Murph and Turbo. All of us staring out to sea, sucking on our cans and watching the watery darkness fall.

'D'you know, I've reached a point where I am grateful for the hurt,' Kenny announces with an unnaturally serious look on his face. 'I mean, I'm still in love with her, obviously, but I'm stronger now.'

It takes me a minute to register he's moved on from fantasy drama. 'And how does Fiona feel about you still being in love with Ashling?'

'You know, she's all right, man. Think she appreciates my honesty.'

'Me hole she does, Kenny.' I turn my head. 'You didn't seriously tell her that?'

'Fiona's an intuitive woman. I can't lie to her.' He takes a deep breath. 'Looking back, all the pain with Ashling … it was a privilege.'

'Bloody hell, Kenny!'

'Wha–?'

'D'you read that in a book?' I have to ask. Kenny

admitted reading his ma's self-help books after he was dumped. 'It's not a line that's come out of you. I know that much.'

'Cheers, Flynn,' he says, rolling his eyes the exact way Laura did to me earlier. He looks dejected. He starts squirming beside me, his busy fingers sparking his lighter and flicking at the ring pull on his can.

Murph and Turbo move on with a wave. Now it's just the two of us, not including mad McDara, the shelter's mascot, who is sitting alone further up the bench. A couple years older than us, McDara has the look of a fella you'd see on those police photofits: scribble thin, with demented eyes, greasy spiked hair and fists permanently jammed into his pockets. He's examining his phone and twitching. Angry drum 'n' bass leaks out from under his hood and he looks ready to punch someone. It's his usual look though, to be fair.

The sun's beginning to set and what heat there was in it has long left. I stare at the sea and I'm resenting the waves; I'm in that kind of mood. I'm suddenly grumpy about everything and nothing at the same time. I'm pissed off that I've pissed Kenny off. I'm pissed off on Fiona's behalf. But most of all I'm pissed off we're pissing away what was to be an epic summer, sitting here on our cold arses on this half-bench in the half-dark, waiting for something exciting to happen.

Kenny lifts my arm to check my watch. 'Nine forty-three!' He announces it like it means something and he stands up and looks down the beach.

To his left, in the distance, I spot the coat approaching from the rocks. Her figure moves lightly before disappearing into the shadow of the wall. I stare into the murky light until she reappears and her silhouette becomes clearer, bit by bit. She walks slowly along the long concrete passage towards us. Her face is hidden as she floats past McDara but even he looks up. His eyes follow her until she stops just past him and then he returns to his phone.

Pulling the swathes of coat around her, she lowers herself into the damp stone seat where Murph and Turbo just sat.

Kenny opens a fresh can and clears his throat in *way* too obvious a fashion. I can't look at him and I can't look at her, so I gawp straight ahead. Nobody talks. The only sounds are the waves and the distant din from McDara's headphones. Then she starts to speak quietly into her phone, clearly thinking we can't hear. Noise travels within these grey walls, everyone knows that, but you can even tell by how she sits she doesn't know this place at all.

'Hey, it's me. Yeah, I'm fine,' she says, not sounding remotely as she claims. She's clearly rattled about something. There's a long pause and I strain my neck in her direction to hear more. 'Actually, Kitty, I'm not fine ...' she says. I'm admiring her honesty, waiting for the raspy, English-sounding voice to start again when she puts it back up to her ear and takes another deep breath. 'We need to talk –'

I'm listening away when I notice the usual stench of piss has lifted and I slowly fill my lungs with the new salty air. I'm just thinking how the shelters might look different with her in them when the phone starts to ring in her hand! She hasn't been on a call at all; she's been pretending!

I've never seen someone do this for real and I'm hooked. I sneak a glance out of the corner of my eye as the ringing phone lights up her face.

'Hey!' she drawls into the handset. 'Hello? Kitty?'

'C'mere, c'mere!' Kenny blathers in my ear. I know he thinks he's whispering, but he's not. 'Sansa Stark or your one, Hello Kitty, over there? Quick fidget, no strings? G'wan, I'm counting …'

I give him a dig. 'Shut up, Kenny!'

'Shit!' The girl mutters to herself. I can just about see the phone, dead in her palm: all lights out. She looks down at it hopelessly.

'C'mon!' says Kenny.

He keeps talking but his voice has morphed into white noise now. I put my can down and, without thinking, don't I get up and start strolling towards her. I've no idea what I'm gonna say when I get there, but I figure at the very least she can borrow my phone.

Next thing I'm standing at her feet, staring down at her. I'm totally unprepared for the huge eyes that flash back at me, scrutinising me, and in the shortest second they've swallowed me up, just like that. My heart leaps like a trout. She yanks her coat even tighter around her as though unsure of what she sees and as the jaws of the coat snap tight, I get a waft of something chocolatey. It stops me in my tracks. I stand there, silently holding out my phone.

Her dainty fingers reach slowly to mine and I reckon she might be about to say something when we both spot the car driving up the empty beach towards us. A car on the beach, on the actual sand!

'What the fu—?' cries Kenny, reading my mind from ten feet away.

Instinctively, we all turn towards McDara, who, under his hood, is oblivious to the unfolding drama.

The dark car pulls up right in front of the shelters and turns its headlights on, at which point McDara clocks it and rises up like a phoenix from the ashes. He laser-beams in both directions before he pelts past us at surprising speed. As he's running he flings something on the ground and it lands at the feet of the girl. Three Gardai get out of the unmarked car. Two of them give chase and the remaining one, our lad, jumps nimbly up from the sand and approaches us, his short dark figure framed by the graffitied pillars on either side. If I weren't crapping myself quite so much I'd probably admit how cool it all looks.

'Stand up!' the Garda orders, all official in his culchie accent.

I'm already standing but I edge back into the middle. The others push up off the bench and Hello Kitty gently places her flip-flop over the baggie on the filthy wet ground.

'Empty your pockets,' he adds gruffly with a quick scratch of his chin. Kenny roots in his jeans and pulls out his phone, his fags, his inhaler and half a Twix. I fish out some cash, along with my keys and squint over to see she's got nothing but her dead phone.

'Anyone got anything they'd like to declare?' he asks, eyeing each of us in turn. I can see him better now, including the feeble moustache above his lip and the greying hair that sits a good inch and a half off his scalp, still sporting the well oiled course of an earlier comb.

'No,' we answer together.

Christ, what is she going to do about whatever is under her foot? I look at the Garda's face and the horror is rising up through me. I want to shout at him and explain that the drugs are McDara's and he probably meant to throw them at me. I need to let him know none of this is her fault.

'Names and addresses please. You first,' he barks, walking towards Kenny and stabbing him gently in the chest with his pen. He has to reach up slightly to do it.

'Yes, Guard. Paul Kennedy, 4 Seaview Park,' says Kenny, like he's in court before a judge.

'Liam Flynn, 217 Newbawn Lane.' My heart is banging like a Kango hammer but it's mixed with rising excitement as I realise the girl is going to have to speak again and the whole delicious mystery might start unravelling. She clears her throat as he steps towards her.

'Emerald …' there's a blink of a pause, 'Rutherford –'

'And where do you live, Emerald Rutherford?' the guard asks, loosening a bit, like her two words have just greased his rusty gob.

'There!' she says, pointing into the concrete wall behind her. 'Up there I mean, just off the main road, I'm staying there.'

'Emerald Rutherford.' I say the remarkable name silently to myself, enjoying the feel of it inside my mouth.

'You're all aware of the recently passed bye-law prohibiting the consumption of alcohol in this public space?' he asks.

'Just having the one, Guard,' says Kenny, moving to cover the bag of cans on the bench behind him.

'On your way now, lads. There's to be no drinking out here,' he says, as he shunts down towards her. 'Miss Rutherford, you'd best be off home now too. We've had word there was trouble around here tonight.' She nods.

The Garda turns to go but then he stops and tilts his head at me. 'How's your father, Liam?'

His suddenly slow words prick at me like a thousand tiny pins. 'He's grand, thanks.' I hate this kind of pity.

He smiles. 'Tell him Tim O'Flaherty was asking for him.'

'I will, yeah.'

'We're off now,' Kenny shouts after him, like the lapdog that he is.

He waves a salute to the Garda who gets back inside the car alone and drives off up the beach.

'Hole-eey shit!' Kenny cries and then he does a one-eighty to face Emerald. 'I didn't have you pegged for that. Cool as a bleedin' cucumber you were,' he says, draining his can.

She looks puzzled and frightened in equal measure. Kenny starts talking again in his almost-drunk hieroglyphics but I'm not listening, I'm looking at her. Her sad eyes flit around all nervous and she bites down on her bottom lip as she tucks her chin into the collar of her coat. I notice the splay of freckles over her nose and the little crossover of front teeth on her full lips. I'm staring at her now like I knew I would.

She bows her head and as she bends down to pick up the little plastic bag at her feet, her long, fair hair falls in a cruel curtain covering her eyes. 'I guess they were looking for these?' she says, clutching the bag of pills high up by her face. She forces a laugh that's full of panic and her eyes scan ours as though searching for something far more than me or Kenny will ever have to give.

'Whoa!' says Kenny, reaching to take the bag from her.

She takes a step back. 'Shall I leave them here in case that guy comes back?'

'Not so hasty,' says Kenny, taking another stride closer. 'We can stash 'em for McDara down at the dunes,' he says decisively and snatches the baggie out of her hand. 'I don't fancy being the enemy of that lad. Besides, there's a fair few in there,' he says, shaking the bag. 'And you never know when we might have a yen for something lively ourselves,' he adds, with a skip. 'Let's get out of here though. Come on, come on!' He jumps from the concrete ledge and offers Emerald his hand from the sand below. To my disbelief she takes it, briefly, and vaults down. I hurl down after them. 'Woo hoo!' Kenny howls, running along the wet sand.

I look at Emerald, trailing behind him and I too want to beat my chest and howl into the new and promising darkness.

'Who are you?' I ask, managing to catch up so we're walking alongside each other, heading towards the dunes.

'You've a deadly name by the way,' Kenny shouts back, interrupting.

'Oh, everyone calls me Em,' she says, trailing her bare toes along the shoreline. 'Emerald is a bit of a mouthful.'

'It's lovely,' I say, and she swivels her shoulders around to me. The rain has stopped and the surface of the water shimmers as though lit from beneath. She flicks her hair off her face like an elegant pony, which for some reason makes me grin, stupidly.

'It's a bit embarrassing really.'

'Why?'

'My eyes aren't even green.' I watch her not-green eyes glisten. Oh good God, help me.

'Up here!' says Kenny, running up a dune with more athleticism than I've witnessed in our entire fifteen-year friendship. Em slips off her flip-flops and hikes off behind him. I follow them up the steep hill to the back of a grassy mound. 'Let's put the bag inside this.' Kenny says through a mouthful of beer and then he shakes the can to remove the last few drops before attacking it with his keys.

'We could bury it?' I suggest, hoping this might be a useful contribution.

'You might want some kind of marker,' says Emerald. 'All these dunes look the same,' she adds. I kneel down beside her on the cold, damp sand, trying to work out if I'm dreaming.

'Good thinking!' says Kenny, wagging his finger. 'We need ourselves some sticks.'

Together we watch Kenny run off towards the fence by the golf club. I'm close enough to catch that sweet chocolatey scent again. 'You still haven't told me who you are.'

'Who I am?'

'Yeah, like … how did a girl like you get here, tonight?'

She laughs, thank God. 'On a plane!' she says, all smart-arse. 'I'm staying with my – Oh no, Grandma! What time is it?' she asks, searching through her pockets.

I look at my watch. 'Coming up to half ten.'

She stands quickly and brushes the sand from her legs. 'I've got to go.'

I immediately wish I'd lied so I could hold her here longer. 'Really?'

'Yes,' she says, tying her hair back into the little band from around her wrist.

'Maybe I'll see you again?' I shout after her and then I wince; it was more of a plea than I'd planned. In my head it sounded casual.

'Maybe,' she cries from the bottom of the dune.

It might be the light, but as she dips to pick her flip-flops up, I think I see her smiling. Maybe is good, I decide. Maybe is not no. Maybe implies possibility.

I watch her run off into the darkness; coat trailing behind like a giant cape. When she reaches the shelters she turns back, like she knows I'm watching.

I am.

EMERALD
Mikados?

It's completely dark by the time I get back to Grandma's. I go to tap the heavy brass knocker but find myself tumbling inside the opening door instead. She's been waiting.

In spite of my racing heart and guilt at being late, I feel strangely better. For the first time since we arrived, I look Grandma properly in the eye, but now that I do I can't help but notice how fragile she looks, all wrapped up in her flowery robe. She's changed so much. Of course she has, but it's not only the time that's passed; Grandma Annie was never just some tired old lady who smelt of lavender. I never even thought of her as old before. She had gumption and a mischievous twinkle in her pixie eyes, but now she looks wilted, like the sad rose cuttings in the vase behind her. In Instagram filters, she's faded from the fairy-tale brights of X-Pro II to some black and white one no one ever uses. Willow perhaps?

'Sorry, I lost track of time.'

'It's fine,' she says, but the angle of her head says otherwise. 'I was hoping you didn't get lost, that's all. I must get you a key. I'll have a spare cut.'

We stand there examining each other. It's awkward, which makes me sad. I never thought it would be this way

42

with her. I can smell the cold off the old coat and there's a scent of polish in the hallway I must have missed earlier. We both go as though to speak before the silence gets louder.

She gets there first. 'D'you fancy that tea?'

'I'd love it.'

'I've put the immersion on. If you'd like a bath?' she says, sliding the coat off my shoulders and placing it back on the rack behind her.

I follow behind as Grandma drifts slowly around the pastel blue room, which looks exactly how I remember, including the cream Aga and the same row of untidy geraniums by the window. She pulls two teabags from the ancient, striped tea caddy thing before I spot an iPhone charger Dad forgot hanging from an ancient socket by the fridge. I plug my phone in.

'What did I do with that pot?' she asks, opening and closing cupboards. Then, moving on from the teapot, she takes down the shiny brown ceramic chicken from the large dresser and removes a packet of biscuits. I'd almost forgotten that chicken. I pull out a chair and take my place at the round wooden table, which feels oddly like doll's furniture in the large room. I don't remember these chairs feeling so small.

'Aren't these lovely!' she says, handing me a pink marshmallow and jam biscuit, before nibbling on one herself. 'Once I start …' she says and her veiny hand disappears inside the chicken again. She doesn't finish the sentence.

'Thank you, Grandma,' I say, but it's for more than the biscuit. I take a bite and it tastes sweet and stale. 'Haven't had one of these before.'

She makes a surprised face. 'Mikados? I expect they might not have them in England. I got them for your dad but didn't he get stuck on that phone. Sure he'd barely touched his tea when it was time to go.' Her eyes are suddenly wet. I want to take her ivory hand and hold it in mine. She sets her teacup down again without drinking any.

The moment passes, so I just smile. I wonder whether she knows about the sticky crumbs dotting her top lip, but mostly I wonder how long she's been this sad. I drag my chair across the floor, sitting closer to her now. 'I wish Dad could have stayed, even for tonight. Don't you?' I say it without thinking. It was a stupid question.

'I know!' Her hand flies to her heart. 'And that Dublin Hilton Hotel is so awful! It's not even near the airport. Sure we're as close here, but there's no talking to him.'

For a moment I wonder whether she heard me properly. 'Dad's gone back to England, Grandma,' I point out but she looks confused. 'He's not staying at a hotel.' As soon as I say this her face distorts like the biscuit wrapper she's twisting in her hands. Then, just as fast, her eyes go sort of blank and she stares into the distance, as though studying thin air. I pretend not to watch.

'Oh, I do get befuddled these days!' she says, running her nail over the tiny chip in her china cup before getting up and shuffling more of the peculiar biscuits on to a plate.

It's a surreal end to an already way too surreal day. 'Will you have another?' she asks, placing the head back on the chicken and returning it to the dresser. Without waiting for my answer, she is gone.

'Grandma?'

'There'll be plenty hot water by now,' she shouts from the hallway.

For some reason I begin stirring my sugarless tea and as I look over to Grandma's place I see she hasn't touched hers. Apart from my slurping and the strange new ringing in my ears, the room is deathly quiet.

She tiptoes back in. 'I've left a towel on your bed. Goodnight, pet,' she says, kissing my forehead before making for the door again. 'We'll say a prayer for your mam tonight.' She announces it from the corner of the room.

She's still looking at me as I brush away the flecks of dried coconut left on my cheek by her wet lips. 'Night, Grandma!'

It's not like Grandma to leave a room with a pot undrunk. 'It's not blood running in that woman's veins,' Dad would say, when she'd visit us in Bath, ''Tis tea!' I used to count how much she'd drink and in one day, she had twelve cups! Maybe she's cut back. Anyway, I'm not sorry to be on my own now. I want to think. I want to go through everything that's happened. I cradle the hot cup in my hands and glance around.

My eye lands on a large framed photo of Dad and me, hanging on the wall beside the fridge. I get up to have a closer look and smile at my reindeer jumper and earmuffs. It's from Christmas five years ago: that Christmas, the last time we were all here. I'm holding Dad's hand. We both look really happy. I remember Grandma bought me a purple Furby, which I pretended to love, even though I was eleven, and how on Christmas night, Dad and me played Twister Dance in the living room until he fell and bruised his coccyx. But before I can grasp a proper hold, each flash of memory sparks and disappears, leaving only a sick feeling in the pit of my stomach.

I force myself to think about something else. I didn't even give my full name down at the beach. Does that mean I've lied to a policeman? He interrupted before I got the chance, so it couldn't technically be a lie. Is it? They'll hardly be able to trace me back to Grandma. I sip some tea. Dad would be horrified. I'm sure it is just adrenalin but I'm strangely exhilarated. My thoughts are too fast for my brain. Seriously, what was I thinking following those boys down to the dunes? I want to tell Kitty about the drugs and the beautiful wide-open sea. I wonder what she'd think of that guy, Liam, and his stupidly blue eyes.

That's if I'm even talking to her.

It's late. I think about posting a picture with the crazy biscuits. Deciding it would look better with Grandma's old chicken thing in the background, I carefully rescue it from the dresser and place it behind the piled high plate. I open Instagram, hold a biscuit to my mouth and snap! It takes a few goes to get a half-decent shot of my face. I scan through the filters and settle on Lo-Fi, which feels suitably tacky. NAME THIS LOCATION? Scrolling through the list of existing Portstrand locations, I eventually hit CREATE 'Grandma's house Dublin' and tap SHARE. I figure this is one way of announcing my departure.

Of course I'm holding the phone in my hand, hoping for immediate likes and a chorus of 'Where are you, Em?' comments to flood through, but after waiting a whole thirty-seven seconds there's still nothing so

I swipe through my Instagrid at the montage of bright and beautiful squares I know so well: endless blurry pics from Glastonbury – our wellies knee-deep in mud, wrist-banded arms, waving our cider cups, relentless selfies, goofy Boomerang videos of Kitty and me after our last exam, Rupert and his dog by the lake, a team pic on the way to the netball tournament at Charterhouse, my new leopard print Adidas fishnet pink socks. I keep going, scrolling through to the lavender fields behind our house, then on to Mum. There she is, my beautiful mum, with her piercing green eyes, beaming out from our kitchen like a glossy magazine article.

I stop. If I didn't know me, maybe I'd believe I really lived this rosy life with all the doubt and confusion filtered out. Maybe I wouldn't notice the growing space between the me in those lovely images and the me that sits drinking tea in Grandma's kitchen. Guess that's the whole idea.

I'm staring at the screen when it starts clattering around loudly on the countertop: it's Kitty! The nausea is instant.

'Hi,' I say, abandoning my earlier anger. Instead I'm instantly justifying myself, explaining how my phone died when I was at the beach, but she's already talking.

'There you are!' she exclaims, and without waiting for me to speak, she continues. 'Where were you today, Em? You didn't reply to any of my texts and then I get one from you saying to call urgently, BUT THEN I see you're eating biscuits in front of some chicken thing on Instagram. You're in Dublin? Seriously –'

'It's Mum.' I cut her off mid-rant and let the silence happen.

'Oh,' she says. I can sense her shuffle about. 'Everything OK?' she whispers.

'Not really. And Dad's tied up in London, so here I am in Portstrand, with my grandma.'

'Oh God, babes, that completely sucks,' she says, stating the obvious. 'But hey, you got out of Speech Day, which was unspeakably boring. And you'll be back for the party –'

'Actually, I won't.'

'What?'

'I have to stay here for the summer.' Saying it again is like pulling the plaster off a gaping wound.

'That's a joke, right?'

'Nope.'

'But how can they make you stay in Ireland for the entire summer? That's ridiculous.'

'I don't have a choice. Mum's treatment is going to take eight weeks.' I think this is a pretty heavy hint. I start to pick the jam out of the half-eaten biscuit with my finger.

There's a long delay. 'D'you mean like, rehab?'

I can't bring myself to answer.

'Oh shit,' she says and it's obvious I didn't need to. I can tell she's not going to ask any more. Mum talk is one of the few things that has Kitty lost for words. She's the only person I ever speak to about Mum, and even then I hardly tell her the half of it. It's not that I don't trust her; I do, it's just that Mum doesn't get fun-drunk like her mum, Camilla, who after a heavy Sunday lunch has been known to become – wait for it – a bit of a flirt. No, Mum drinks for oblivion now and it's hard to explain that to someone who thinks hardcore drinking is sipping vodka from an Evian bottle at the Fifth Form Ball, and considers being pissed to be *the* most hilarious thing ever.

'Are we OK?' Kit says suddenly.

'You regrammed Bryony's photo!' It just bursts out of my mouth. I count four seconds of silence.

'Em,' she says eventually, 'she's been so worked up about the whole Iggy thing. She's convinced McKenzie knows it was her. I was just trying to be supportive.'

'She was warning me. Like, here's your retribution for snitching. Say anything else and this could get so much worse.'

'C'mon, Bryony loves a beef. You know that. She was sickened when you won that Citizenship Award and she's always been a bit green-eyed about Ru. But seriously, Em, it's not that deep and,' she says, with a little laugh, 'that dress photo *was* funny.'

'You said I should buy it.'

'The dress looked fine, Em. It was way better than the second-hand one you wanted. There was no way Rupert was going to fancy you in that.'

I'm speechless.

'Actually, does Ru know you won't be around all summer?'

'Not yet. Don't say anything.'

I practically hear her brain whirring. 'But –'

'What?'

'He's going to want to know where he stands.'

'D'you think I know where I stand, Kitty? He hasn't even replied to the text I sent ten hours ago.'

She sighs loudly. 'Just saying.'

I glance at the clock above the Aga. It's the RSPB bird one I bought at the garden centre for Grandma's birthday a few years back. It's supposed to play a different birdcall each hour but it's exactly midnight and the Tawny Owl neither *twit*s nor *twoo*s. It's obvious we're both done here. 'I've got to go.'

'Look, I'm sorry. I can see how it could have seemed nasty.'

I really want to believe her. 'OK.'

''K, babes. Night night!' she says.

And that's it.

LIAM
Smooth moves, Sea Dog

When will I ever learn? Late night beers with Kenny and an early start to the island with Da is never a good combo.

'What date did you say the results are out?' Da roars it at me as though a gale-force wind is howling and I'm on another boat altogether. It's breezy, to be fair, but not nearly enough for him to roar like Captain Birdseye over there. I'm at the wheel less than a few feet from him.

'I didn't.'

'Don't nitpick, Liam. When are they out?' His face is pinched against the strong sun. Da's not a man to be burdened by anything as poncey as sunglasses and he has the lines on his face to prove it.

'Seventeenth of August,' I say, with a shrug and pretend to concentrate on the GPS.

'You excited?'

'Nah.'

'You worked hard, son. There's no shame in looking forward to the rewards.'

He actually believes I was up there slogging away. I want to tell him I wasn't always studying, that I was mostly playing guitar, but right now, looking at his smiling, hopeful face, that would be cruel. 'Can we talk about something else, please?'

'All I'm saying is I'm proud of you, no matter what, son.' He booms this back at me through his imaginary gale. 'By the way,' he says, sidling back down the boat towards me like a determined crab, 'Tony Doyle was asking what you were thinking of doing come September so I told him all about the Quantity Surveying course,' he says, taking my left hand from my lap and placing it back up on the wheel. 'He was very impressed. Said he could do with a smart organ grinder up at his place. Worth bearing in mind for your work experience, eh?'

Why can't he let it go? 'I haven't got in yet.'

'You will, son,' he says, patting my shoulder before shuffling back up the boat again, his thin, dark hair blowing gently about his head. 'Isn't it mad to think Dundalk is only up the road now? The one thing they got right back in the boomtime was the roads.'

Jaysus, make him stop! 'Did Mam pack us lunch?'

'She did.'

'Can we eat it by Deadmaiden's Cove?'

He doesn't answer. 'It's about protecting yourself,' he says.

'What d'you mean?'

He sighs, nodding towards the lumps of tarpaulin-covered crates at our feet. 'Save you ever having to do some other fella's shopping.'

'It's not like you couldn't knock this on the head, Da.'

He shoots me a look and I immediately wish I hadn't opened my mouth.

'Wish it were that simple, son.'

I look back at his steely, worn face held high and the shame hits me: this job isn't a choice. Wasn't I berating Laura for her identical ignorance only yesterday?

'Anyway,' he says, recovering, 'with that sort of qualification you could get in with a specialist surveying company, or even have your own practice. You won't end up beholden to anyone. Isn't that right?'

'What?' I ask, even though I heard him perfectly.

'You want to sail your own ship. Don't be relying on any of them,' he says, bobbing his head enthusiastically like he's agreeing with himself.

'Er, yeah. Can I sail over to the cove after we've offloaded?'

'As you wish, Captain.' He smiles at me, satisfied he's been heard and that I'll do the right thing.

We're getting closer now and the island's small, stone harbour wall is visible ahead. A group of birds squawk noisily around us, diving deftly into the water.

'Look, Liam!' says Dad, pointing. 'It's them greedy guillemots again.'

I watch them for a bit, swooping in and out of the water on their white bellies, having the *craic* and I find myself thinking all sorts of mad, ponderous stuff about life. I've to be careful out here; there's something about being deep in the seawater that will do that to me. Before I know it I'll be full of big thoughts, contemplating what we're all doing here – that, or writing lines of embarrassing poetry inside my head.

Da lifts the tarpaulin cover by our feet, dutifully counting up the crates again, looking up and down from his clipboard all the while.

The boat is neatly packed underneath. I've often wanted to rummage through these boxes and see what sort of gear that Lord fella has sent over to his island gaff each week.

'Nine,' Da mutters to himself.

'You know we could be carrying drugs or guns,' I tease him.

He continues ticking off his list. 'Hate to disappoint you, but it's only the usual groceries,' he says. Still, that doesn't stop me fantasising we're really lugging over some sort of contraband that would give the journey some drama. There's not much jeopardy in bog roll and baked beans.

'How's it going at the Metro?' he asks.

''S'all right.' As far as summer jobs go, Deli Assistant isn't the worst way to earn the minimum wage.

'Is that right?'

I know he wants more. 'I'm getting good at the oven timings now.' This is actually true. 'I didn't burn any baguettes this week.'

'Sure then yer laughin'!' he says, tossing his head back. 'They paying you well?'

'Not bad.'

'Anything to deposit at the Credit Union yet?'

'Soon,' I say. I'm saving. I've signed up to do all the available shifts over the summer. Mam and Da are helping me buy a car for getting to college and back each day. They'll match whatever I've earned by the end of this summer, but only as a loan. I'll pay them back after college, along with whatever balance we'll need to borrow from the Credit Union. I hate the idea of taking the money off them but if

I don't have a car then I'll have to live in Dundalk, which would probably cost even more.

'Where d'you get to last night then?' he asks, taking over the wheel.

'Kenny's. I met a guard who knew you.'

He straightens his back. 'What d'you mean, you met a guard?' he asks, peering into the distance. 'Who was it anyway?'

'Tim O'Flaherty? We were down the beach first. He was looking for someone, that's all.'

'Ah, Tim's a decent skin,' he says, studying a bird hovering above. 'Sure his sister is married to John-Joe.'

John-Joe was one of Dad's foremen, his favourite actually. He hit the drink after it all happened. He's sober now but I'm already regretting bringing up yer man O'Flaherty.

'I met a girl last night.'

He drops his pen back into his breast pocket and steps over, shunting me off the steering wheel. 'Is that a remarkable thing of a Friday night these days?'

'Well, I didn't really *meet* her. Her name's Emerald.'

'You serious?' he asks, glancing up at me and twiddling dials on the dash at the same time.

'She's English, I think.'

'Makes sense. You'd be an awful gobshite to give yer daughter a name like that around here. Still though, it's nice,' he adds, steering the RIB in expertly along the wall. 'Yer man, what's his name? You know the actor? That American lad. He did that, called his daughter something mad. Ah, I can't remember now, but he's in that show yer mam loves.

Anyway, didn't he go and call his young wan Ireland, or something.' He scratches his head. 'So where did you meet this Emerald?'

'Shelters.'

He's staring above my head to the harbour beyond. 'She on her holliers?'

'Dunno.'

'How long is she here for?'

'Dunno.'

'Jaysus, son, what do you know?' he says, laughing.

'Not much.' Once again I'm lamenting my choice of chat. Just saying Emerald's name out loud makes it sound like I made it all up.

He shakes his head, 'Good luck with that so.'

I trail my hand along the surface of the water as we slow down. We're close to the private port on the island's western shore now and the silky heads of several silver seals peek up out of the water up ahead. I see a giant of a man I don't recognise patrolling the wall.

'Is that the new gamekeeper fella?' I shout up, but I see Da's already staring at him. In this moment, in Da's look, and the way his right shoulder hangs in apology, I twig something about power and its current imbalance. The reality that is Da's lack of choice hits me again. In fact, it wallops me between the ribs.

'Pull her in here!' Yer man Gerry roars at us like we've never moored a boat.

Da steers in close enough for him to catch the rope. 'Fine day,' Da shouts as he cuts the engine. No response, but this doesn't stop him. 'Any news on Frank?'

'Heart attack,' Gerry says, but the way he barks it's not clear whether he's talking about Frank or whether this is some sort of threat.

'Ah no,' says Da, with a sigh. 'That's terrible news.'

I watch the big man rubbing his beard, eyeing us and the boat in quick succession. Da opens his mouth to speak again but Gerry gets in first. 'You'll be dealing with me from now on.'

I glance at Da and I don't like the look on his face at all, but I start unpacking, hauling crates up the steep, stone steps and stacking them in piles by Gerry's enormous feet.

Da follows me up. 'Grand job, Gerry,' he says, extending his hand towards the fella's belly and looking at him right in the eye. I stare at Da's outstretched palm. Gerry's looking back at Da but he keeps both arms by his sides, unmoving. A cloud must have sailed over the sun because all three of us are now standing in the shade.

Thankfully Da pulls his lonely arm back in, but then doesn't he start patting my back with it. 'This is my son, Liam. Haven't got him for long, he'll be off to college soon.'

Gerry chooses to ignore this too and looks down, tapping his clipboard with a pen. 'I've got ten crates on my list here,' he says.

Da crouches down on his hunkers, scratching his head. 'But nine is written on the inventory from McCabes,' he says, searching his pockets a little too anxiously for my liking.

The black slugs of Gerry's eyebrows tilt and he ogles Da all sketchily. 'I'll call the store. You'll hear from me if there's anything missing,' he says, before turning to his beat-up old Land Rover. I'm *that* close to sizing up to him, I don't care how big he is, but then he pulls a rifle from the bowels of the boot and places it on the passenger seat. What a feckin' mad yoke! In all the years Frank watched over this island, he never found a reason to be packing heat.

Next thing I hear Da, at it again. 'Well, we'll see you Wednesday. Tell Frank I was asking for him,' he says, hopping back down into the boat again.

I follow, a bit speechless now. Who does that gun-toting muttonhead think he is?

Da's completely silent as we head on over towards the island's eastern shore. I know better than to say anything. I imagine it'd be a bit crushing having some psycho ignore you that way in front of your son.

I'm OK with not talking but I want to think of something to make him feel better. My head starts throbbing again so I give up and eventually amuse myself watching a crowd of clown-faced puffins perched on the holes in the rocks.

'I never tire of looking at those fellas parading around the cliff edge, showing off in front of their girlies,' Da says at last. 'Sure, they'll be gone on their holliers again next week. Gone with the guillemots, off for a bit of sun.'

He starts humming away to himself now and I leave him be. I'm relieved; at least the silence is untangling.

'I met your mother down by the beach,' he says then, out of nowhere.

'You did?'

'Sixth of June it was. The Monday after the Whit week-end,' he says, pushing at some controls in front of him that I can't see. 'I was rambling home down by High Rock that evening, when I spotted her sitting over by the old diving board. D'you know the one?'

Everyone in Portstrand knows that diving board. I nod.

'She was on her own.' He's lost in his thoughts. His chest butts out from his body, not unlike one of our neighbouring puffins. 'I walked down and caught a good look at her, side on. Her legs were dangling in the water and her hair fell down her bare back like seaweed, for it was long then,' he says, turning to look at me, as though checking I got this bit of detail. 'She was so still and perfect. And do you know the best part?' But not waiting for an answer, he goes on, 'She was singing gently. Or maybe it was humming she was doing, but truly, son, she was like one of them selkies you read about in fairy tales.'

'Ah, Da!'

'Honestly, she was that beautiful. She didn't look human.'

'What d'you do?'

'Sure I was, what's the word … mesmerised? I think I just swaggered towards her, hoping by the time I got to her I'd have found me balls so as to say something.'

'And did you?'

'Didn't she rise up and dive into the water, just as I got close. I looked on for a bit, waiting for her to resurface, but I was uncertain of what my eyes were seeing on account of the sun. I was beginning to believe I'd imagined the whole thing, when I finally saw her head pop up. She'd swum out fifty metres at least, but eventually she turned around and her tiny head smiled up at me from a distance. She knew I was watching her the whole time. But that's your mam, knows everything.'

'Did you get in after her?'

'Me hole I did,' he says, slowing the engine and dragging the rope from under his feet. 'But I asked around and found her in Moloney's the following Friday night. Bought her a drink.'

'Smooth moves, sea dog.'

'Listen, son, it's not about the moves, you'll learn that soon enough. When love pounces on you like that, it's little choice you have in it at all.'

'G'wan, Casanova!'

'Old dog, long road,' he says, tapping his nose. I hold it in as long as I can but then he looks at me; he's also about to burst. Next thing we're both laughing. I'm not even sure why, but God, it feels good.

'Pass us that bag of sandwiches,' he says, rising up and tossing the anchor over. I fling the holdall down the length of the boat and he fishes out the lunchboxes and hands one back to me.

I've never heard Da talking this way before and I'm trying not to appear as drawn in as I am. 'So was that it? Deal sealed over a Bacardi and Coke?' I ask.

'Ah no, I had to work hard that night,' he says through a mouthful of ham. 'And for a few long months after.'

'Tell me she played hard to get.' Maybe it's the fresh air and Da's mental faces, but I'm giddy now. Any trace of a hangover has lifted and the sunlight on the water is magical.

I look over at him and I'm smiling, thinking about how glad I am I came out this morning, despite asshole Gerry, but then I notice Da's face has changed and his body stiffens like a cold wind has blown through him. His jaw falls loose. I watch as he moves the little plastic tub off his lap and he looks off over the edge of the boat.

'There was another fella with the glad eye for your mam, back in the day,' he says into the water below. Then he turns and stares right at me. 'I used to think on that a lot and then, when everything went belly up, I'd wake in the night with acid pulping through my veins that she'd had to give up everything we had that was nice.'

My heart starts to race. What's he's talking about? He picks up another sandwich and examines its crusts all the way round.

'Had I not led her away from him in Moloney's all those years ago, she'd probably be living the high-life in England now. It's an awful feeling, worse than losing everything to him in the first place.'

It takes me a minute. 'Jim Byrne? Jim Byrne had a thing for Mam?' I say, trying not to choke.

'Don't say the name. Please, son,' he says, closing his eyes and shaking his head into the wind.

The fingers on his right hand uncurl and his crust drops limply into the water. A pair of sleek grey seals goes after it, swimming right up to the boat, but neither of us can bring ourselves to speak.

EMERALD

Looking in the wrong place

I wander into the kitchen, zombie-like. Grandma has laid all sorts of cereal out on the table. Each day there's a new one to try.

I spy the unopened Special K and lazily shake some flakes into a bowl.

'How did you sleep?' Grandma asks, nervously shuffling boxes.

'Not bad, thanks.' I lie, 'cause it's easier.

Really I tossed and turned with total racy-brain, trying *not* to look at my phone ... and failing. It started with some crappy YouTube tutorial on how to curl long hair with a sock, but then Kitty posted a shot of her and Bryony from the changing rooms at Zara. Truthfully, it wasn't even how unbearably close those two have become in my eight day absence or the fact that I'm miles away from all their fun, it was actually Bryony's perfect side boob that got me most depressed. I couldn't stop myself looking; there she was, staring into the lens all coy. What a joke; she knows how good she looks. And like she'd let Kitty post anything where she looked anything less than amazing. Had a major selfie cull at 3 a.m. and went to sleep basically hating myself. *Ughh* … I'll never have a spontaneously Instagrammable body.

Grandma fusses around, now closing up the gazillion cereal boxes with those freezer bag ties. I notice she looks like an older, female version of Dad, which you might think is obvious, but it doesn't always go that way. I look like my mum *and* my dad. Everyone says I have Mum's eyes, but I think they're too big for my face, and they're grey, which let's face it is an eye colour nobody would ever choose.

I should probably start writing that list of stuff to email Magda. I know it's ungrateful, but her impeccable competency just annoys me lately. She's the complete opposite of Mum. Well, maybe she's not. I guess she's more like what Mum would be if she wasn't so … God, my eyes and nose are beginning to run. Maybe I'm getting my period? I can't keep track of it these days.

Grandma stops watering a plant on the window sill and thumbs one of its leaves, shaking her head gently from side to side. 'I've overwatered the poor begonia,' she says, tutting loudly before carrying it outside.

I pick up my phone to check my email when it pings with a text from Rupert. Rupert!

SOZ HAVEN'T REPLIED. HEARD U R IN DUBLIN 4 SUMMER. DUNNO IF I'M FLY WITH LONG DISTANCE? HAHAHA. HOPE UR OK. RU

I collapse against the back of the chair and reread the text, scanning it for clues of something … but there's nothing;

63

lame shouty caps with a question mark, when he's not even asking a question. The phone quivers in my hand. What's just happened? I don't hear from him in over a week and now this? I stare at his name; the very sight of which once set surges of electricity racing through me, but there's nothing. I wasn't even his to dump.

'Asshole.'

'What's that, pet?' Grandma asks, strolling back into the room obscured by her beloved plant. I know she heard me.

I pick at some imagined milk flecks on my T-shirt. 'Nothing.'

'Oh,' she says, before leaving the room by the other door. It's not even Rupert and his shitty text; it's the reality that I'm really stuck here; that this is true and *why* this is true. I put down the phone and push away my bowl; I can't eat any more.

I walk into the living room and Grandma is watching TV. I clear my throat.

'I want to call Mum.' I hadn't even rehearsed it. I'm not even sure I knew it was coming.

'Of course,' she says, pushing herself up from her chair. 'Your dad left the name of the place by the phone. Let me see.' She's up on her feet now, rifling through Post-it pads on the hall table.

'S'OK, I'll google it.'

She shuffles on her feet before disappearing towards the kitchen. 'I'll be in here if you need me,' she calls back.

The phone answers after three rings. 'Foxford Park Clinic, good morning,' says a cheery lady on the other end.

'I'd like to speak to my mum, Eliza Rutherford.' It comes out as a whisper and as soon as I've said it damp patches prickle my underarms.

'Bear with me, please,' she says and she's gone.

Mum didn't take Dad's name when they married. It was, she once claimed, an attempt to keep her family name alive, which is ironic given that she barely speaks to the rest of the Rutherfords now. It's like they've been erased, somehow rubbed out by the reality of never being talked about. Their names, so little spoken of in our house, have faded now and we almost behave like they never existed.

A man comes to the phone. 'Hello, is that Emerald?'

I'm surprised to hear my name, but then I realise who it is. 'Yes. Hi, Nick.'

'How are you, Emerald?' he says in that slow, draw-out-each-word-I'm-really-listening voice. I don't answer. 'May I ask, is it an emergency?'

I want to say yes; I'm falling apart. But no words come out.

'Your mum is doing well and I'm sure she'd love to talk to you, but you'll remember our policy for new patients, which, I explained, is a period without family contact. I appreciate this may be difficult for you, Emerald.'

He's using my name a lot. Perhaps this is something you learn as a counsellor; to make people feel heard or some such thing.

'She'll have an opportunity to call home next Saturday, so I'll let her know you phoned. Is that OK?'

'Uh huh,' I reply, biting down hard on my lip. To be honest, I wasn't even sure I wanted to speak to Mum at first, but now I want her more than anything in the world. My mother, who's screwed up everything so badly she's not even allowed to come to the phone.

'I hope you can understand, Emerald?'

'Sure,' I mumble and quickly hang up. I look in the mirror above the old phone table and watch a fat tear attempt to form in the corner of my eye. For a moment I don't recognise myself, or the strange expression my face is making. I drag a tissue from the table and dab the wet blob back into someone else's eye.

Grandma watches me from the doorway.

'She was busy,' I say quickly. I guess I've got so used to covering for Mum I've become incapable of telling the truth, even when there's no need to lie.

Grandma sees right through me. 'It is difficult, isn't it?'

'I'm going to have a lie down.' I slur the words as I tumble up the stairs.

I flop on to the creaky, old wooden bed. Next Saturday! I can't speak to my own mother for yet another week. I think about getting really angry but I'm actually embarrassed for her. I'm embarrassed *by* her too and the shame of it all rinses through me. I hate how well I know this feeling, but still, I crawl underneath it and let it cover me like a blanket.

My brain's too fizzy for sleep so I pick up my phone and reread every one of the eleven(!) texts Rupert has ever sent me. I file back through his entire Instagram and all I feel is empty. What if underneath the tanned exterior and Hollister hoodies there's nothing but an alarmingly uncomplicated void? In any event, I was nothing to him. We shared nothing. There is nothing to even miss. Did I even like Rupert Heath or did I just like him to be liked?

I go through my feed, which might be the worst idea ever, but I'm on an emotionally battering roll. Only nineteen likes for my selfie with those marshmallow biscuits. One of these is from Magda so that doesn't even count. I hit delete. What's the point? It just looks bad. Might as well have 'loser' as my username these days. I scroll down to see Kitty and Bryony screaming out from the endless sea of people at Glastonbury. There's at least ten new uploads too, each with a gazillion comments beneath, all with excited grammar and extraneous emojis. Why do their smiles make me feel so sad? What on earth is wrong with me?

Bryonibbgal #tbt GLASTO!!! SIKKK START TO SUMMER WITH MY BAE!!!!!!!

0o_kittykatz_o0 SO MUCH LOVE 4 THIS ONE. FKN YASSSS!!!

Hang on! Where am I????? I was in these photos once but I've been airbrushed out of the entire weekend! 114 likes for another photo of Bryony waving the enormous flag that Kitty and me tie-dyed in her garden two years ago: our flag; our special flag! I clamp my hand over my mouth, seized by a painful wave of envy and loss. I hug my knees into my chest and bury my face in the musty pillow.

There's a tiny knock on the bedroom door. I don't know how long I've been out but the sleep felt deep. Grandma pushes gently into the room, armed with a tray. I blink a few times before my eyes slip shut again.

'Banana loaf,' she nods. 'Still your favourite I hope?'

I peel my lids apart once more and watch as she slowly comes into focus. Maybe I'm still half asleep, but for the first time since I arrived Grandma's eyes sparkle a little like they used to. I'd entirely forgotten that banana loaf existed, but as the room fills with its warm, nutty smell, all sorts of powerful feelings wash over me. My chest sinks with gratitude as I sit up.

Then it comes back to me; I ate it here in the kitchen, that Christmas. I remember Mum and Dad driving away, and Grandma was so sad after. I'm pretty sure I told her it was my favourite just to cheer her up. There'd been a fight; I can remember that too. I close my eyes, wishing all the images in my head would stop flying about for long enough for me to actually see them.

Grandma hands me a steaming mug of tea. 'D'you know it's been years since I've done any baking. Can you believe that?' she asks, tucking a spare pillow in behind my back. I sit up straighter and listen. 'It felt good to get the cake tins out again. So thank you, love.'

'For what?'

She taps her hand on mine. 'For taking me out of myself.'

We've gone skiing for the last five Christmases. What was so bad that we left Grandma here for the Christmas holidays alone? Like me, Dad's an only child so there is literally no other family on his side apart from some distant cousins we never see. What if no one came to visit her? No friends have called round since I arrived over a week ago and she hardly leaves the house except to go shopping. I haven't heard her talk to anyone except Dad and some old guy selling aloe vera products door to door. Maybe that's why she seems so on edge? Maybe she's nervous about upsetting Dad? Maybe she's afraid if she does we may never come back here again?

Baking was Grandma's thing. When she'd stay with us, she'd make pies and cakes and all sorts in our kitchen. I suddenly feel inexplicably sad.

I go to sip my tea but it's too hot. 'Why did you stop?'

'Ah, you know ...' she starts and then says nothing more, that way Irish people seem to do. I watch her go to speak again but she just lightly closes her eyes.

'Grandma?'

'Well, it's not the same, greasing tins for one,' she says, thumbing at loose crumbs on the plate.

'But you baked all the time.'

She blows into her cup, her lips quivering as she goes to take a tiny drink. 'Well,' she says, smoothing out her skirt, 'that was usually for the church; coffee mornings and the like,' she says, with her eyes resting softly on mine. 'I tend not to go there much these days.'

'Don't you love a good mass? Dad always says –'

'Things change, Emerald,' she says, brusquely.

'Have you?'

'In some way, perhaps. That is, I assumed the church was the place for me. I never questioned it. I assumed the parishioners there were my friends but one day I realised they weren't true friends at all,' she says, more softly now, twisting her stooped shoulders towards me, her palms cradling each other in her lap. 'I was looking for comfort, Em, but let's just say, I was looking in the wrong place.'

A final nod seems to signal the end of the topic. As we sit together silently I can't help running through everything she's just said in my head. I can't pretend to understand it all but that doesn't stop the flash going off behind my open eyes.

'Have your cake in peace now, pet. I'm here if you need me. That's all I wanted to say,' she says, pressing up off the bed and padding softly towards the door.

'Grandma,' I call after her. 'It smells delicious.'

She smiles back at me and then she is gone. Letting my eyes slowly close, I sit back against the headboard and for a few short seconds my mind is blissfully still with nothingness passing gently in and out. My heart swells as I lift the plate on to my lap but just as I raise the cake to my lips the flash sparks again, almost blinding me.

I sit bolt upright, slamming the plate down and rummaging around the duvet. My hand finds the cold slab of laptop and I flip it open, quickly clicking on Safari. On the top of a deep inhale I hold my breath and open a new tab for Instagram. I look at my username, ladyesmerelda01, in the top right-hand corner. My heart thumps wildly, but I stare straight ahead, my eyes boring into the weird-looking word, determined not to let my focus slip down to the shiny new posts below. I click on EDIT PROFILE, scroll to the end and there right at the bottom I see it: TEMPORARILY DISABLE MY ACCOUNT.

I click again and slam the laptop shut.

Long, slow exhale.

LIAM
The King stays the King

I'm cycling up Paddy's Hill en route to meet Kenny. It's not far from the Metro, nor is it that warm out either, but I've got a fierce sweat on due to my broken gears and a misjudged woollen jumper, so the fine mist of rain on my face feels lovely. The new playground at the top of the hill looks out over the marina and there's no finer lunch spot than those swings.

When I arrive there's only one shifty-looking bloke and his kid on the see-saw. I dawdle over to the swings and sit myself into the rubber seat like it's a throne on loan. Pushing off with my feet, I sail high above the wood chips and the fence in front, watching over the passing traffic and the restless world below.

I'm reflecting on the morning gone, when it strikes me I'm actually beginning to enjoy my crap job. I guess I'm lucky to have it. Lorcan, our old neighbour, got it for me, which was sound of him. Three years on from the Leaving Cert and he's reached the dizzy heights of Duty Manager at the Metro Service Station on Portwall Road.

I shouldn't knock him. That's the deal once you leave school: graft like a knob-end to get up the ladder in a job that just cages your soul. God knows why our school tried to pretend it was any different.

No matter who you are you'll need fuel for your car or milk for your kids. People come into the station for their diesel or the paper or what have you, but they stay for a chat. Not with me, but I see them with Lorcan or the guys on the till. Having a gas about the weather, the economy, their holliers. The Leaving results: oh, the chats have started on that now too. What the kids are going to do, where they're going to college, will they get into the bank? Who's heading off to Australia, Canada or Qatar? I expect Da's having the same conversation: boring people in other shops, any eejit he meets. Dying to tell them all that his son is going to study Quantity Surveying up in Dundalk, and then he'll explain it for them. 'Building site management,' he'll say proudly. I see their concerned faces, looking at his fragile scaffold of hope and they're praying to Jaysus it works out. Nobody around here wants Donal Flynn suffering another blow.

I've a horrible feeling I've done enough and I'll get on to the course. The unspeakable thing is that I don't want any part of that plan. I don't want to build anything. I don't want to manage anyone. I don't want to be in any way associated with, or responsible for, anything in the sorry world of construction. Flash bastards financing even more boxes, ugly little boxes for caged and broken souls.

Da wants me to challenge the Gods. He doesn't say it of course, but I know his strategy and it's doomed. Even if I work my pawny-arse through college and make it all the way to the other side of the chessboard, the best I can hope for is to be the Queen. Developers have the money and will always be King. As Da learned the hard way, the King stays the King and I swear I'm never going to be any developer's bitch.

A snazzy-looking Freelander pulls up by the pitches and I know it's Kenny. He gets to borrow a new motor each week. Come September he'll be working for his uncle in the showroom full-time. 'A born salesman,' as Da says.

I'm getting tired of my own weighty thoughts so the sight of him, hopping out of the car in his cheap suit, is a welcome relief. I watch him for a bit, strolling around on the phone, with his heavy bowl of gingery hair flopping about his face. He starts pacing up and down, all hand gestures and long, dramatic drags on his fag. I'm marvelling at what it'd be like to be in Kenny's head, when I realise I'm smiling. He sees me and hangs up, stomping over urgently.

'All right, man. What's the story?'

Kenny does this a lot. It's important to note he's not actually asking a question here; it's merely an opener to what *he's* got to say.

He plonks himself on the swing beside me and takes out another fag. 'So that was Fiona …' He's about to burst with something else, his lips are tight, like a trouser seam about to give way. 'Party at her gaff Saturday!' he says, grinning at me.

I kick off the ground again and start to swing.

'Where are her folks?'

'Off on a golfing weekend in Connemara, my friend. Woohoohoo!' he roars, joining me in the air now. 'I'll be checking out me honey's new tan lines, I tell you.'

73

As he says this, he does something with his eyebrows, adjusting the knot of his tie, which is pink. He looks like a complete flute. 'Who's coming?'

His eyes are wide and excited. 'Everyone!' he says, biting down on the unlit cigarette.

I slow down and run my feet along the ground. 'Seriously?'

He pulls on the chains and leans in close enough to slap my thigh. 'And a load of her mates from school. ALL of whom are pretty rideable, I might add.'

Fiona went to an all-girl school three stops up on the DART line. Her parents are a bit posh. Not proper posh, but like five-bed posh, which is posh enough around here. 'What's the party for anyway?'

'It's her eighteenth next week. I told you. Total free gaff, man!'

'Nice one!' It's all I can think to say. I have to admit it's the best outlook for a Saturday night we had so far this summer.

'So I was contemplating,' he says, sounding out each of the word's four syllables while looking needlessly over each of his shoulders. 'We dig up McDara's buried treasure and look for our just rewards. Surely even a pirate like him will swallow a small commission for the safe return of his bounty. What do you say, Flynn, my man?'

But I'm no longer listening. I'm overcome with a brave and brilliant notion. Possibly the finest idea I've had for some time. 'Do you think it would be cool if I brought that girl?'

'Who?' he says, grumpy I've ignored whatever he's just said.

'Emerald.'

'Hello Kitty from Friday night?' he shouts out.

A couple of recently arrived mammies flash a glance in our direction. 'Yeah,' I whisper.

'How?'

'Whatcha mean how?'

'I mean how are you proposing to find her again?'

'Dunno. But would it be cool to bring her?'

'Man, yer my best mate and I love you, but I'm gonna be straight with you here, 'cause I know you'd do the same for me. That broad's not gonna come to one of our parties, even if you could find her.'

'How d'you know?'

'I just know, man,' he says, shaking his head. 'And you know it too.'

I pull a mini baguette out of my backpack and start folding rogue skirts of ham back in.

'I mean, did you even hear her?' he adds.

'What's that supposed to mean?' I ask, suddenly standing, but I don't need an answer. I know exactly what Kenny's getting at. 'I asked if I could see her again and she said yes. Well, she said maybe, but –'

Kenny shoves my shoulder, almost setting me off balance. 'Maybe?' He says, sighing. 'So let me get this straight. She said maybe *and* you've no idea who she is or where she lives?'

'I do know,' I blurt out but he's looking at me now like I've lost it. 'She's staying at her grandma's place, I think. And it's just …' I'm waving my arm behind me now for no logical reason. 'Back from the beach. That was what she said, wasn't it?' I'm not sure what more to say, so I take a bite of my sandwich and watch some kid, not much older than Evie, begging his ma to kick back his ball. She doesn't look up from her phone.

'There are a thousand houses back up from that beach, pal. Best of luck with your door to door search, yeah,' Kenny says, with one carrotty eyebrow raised to the sky, but in the briefest moment his scepticism turns to a look of genuine concern, which is disturbing. 'But listen, if you ever do find her and she'll give you the time of day,' he says slowly, 'sure, bring her along.' Then he looks in my bag, which is empty apart from a copybook and a bag of Hula Hoops. 'Eh, where's mine?' He's serious.

'You're assuming last week's sambo is a catering contract now?'

He stands, waving his non-fag holding hand in the air. 'I'll have you know, while you're in your hutch buttering rolls, I'm in the showroom closing deals. I'm making the dough while you're baking it.' He leans in and starts pointing. 'G'wan, give us a bite, will you?' I break the end of my baguette and hand it to him. 'Lavish is what you are, Flynn. I've always said it. Bell you later, yeah.'

Facebook Mammy looks up from her phone and Stoner Da spins around from the see-saw to watch him go. All three of us keep watching as Kenny hops back into the car and drives off over the kerb like an off-roader. I guess you could call it charisma.

I lie back horizontal, staring up at the enormous upside-down sky.

How am I ever going to find her?

EMERALD

Falling off(line)

Grandma announced this morning that she was having her hair done. With nothing better to do, and spotting the opportunity for a magazine binge, I decided to join her.

To say I was unprepared for the silence that comes with going offline is an understatement. It's deafening; like a constant, growing emptiness between me and the rest of the world that I can neither fill nor escape from. Like I wasn't already cut off over here; now it's as though I've fallen into a strange dimension, orbiting a whole new gravity-defying vortex of nothing. There have been moments where I genuinely don't know what to do or how to feel. I keep having this sensation, like those sinking bumps before sleep, where I slip into a soft dark void of blackness before I'm jolted roughly back into the world. I can't say this for sure, but I'd guess it's up there with near-death experience. (Overdramatic? Me?)

BUT, on the way home we stopped at a garage to get petrol. I sat in the car examining my split ends, half watching Grandma as she shuffled in to pay, when a small movement in the distance caught my eye. I looked up and there, just inside the shop doorway, stood Liam – he of the bluest eyes – pinning something to a noticeboard, chatting away to a woman with a buggy. I watched his head arch back as he laughed. Even through the glare of the window, I knew it was him.

I watched him fixing a ridiculous white hat on top of his head and smiling at her warmly. In a stupid, daydreamy way I found myself pretending it was me he was smiling at, and I inhaled and exhaled, relishing the new space in my chest. Seconds later Grandma got into the car beside me and we pulled out of the forecourt. While Grandma bemoaned the increased price per gallon I found myself paying strangely close attention to the route she took home.

Dad rang this morning. I lied and said I was fine. I had to. I didn't say happy, even he wouldn't believe that, but it's one less thing for him to worry about. All the stress with Mum couldn't have come at a worse time, but I guess you've just got to get on with things when you're married. My parents move around each other like magnets; the ones with the same charge that is. No matter how much you try and push them together they repel each other and can never actually touch.

It wasn't always like this. When I was little, Mum waltzed everywhere. She was fun, if slightly hysterical. She'd chat up strangers: workmen who called to the house, or the waitress in a restaurant who brought our drinks. Everyone fell in love with her. Sometimes we'd dance around their bedroom listening to Fleetwood Mac, Amy Winehouse, Everything But The Girl; all that tragic sing-along-to stuff. Tidying up the CDs was my job. I'd fall on to the bed after her and lace her thick, strawberry-blonde hair around my fingers as she slept.

She was always unpredictable, a bit like a teenager maybe, but there hasn't been dancing or door slamming in our house in a long time. I guess all those pills have blunted her performance.

A box of books arrived from Amazon, along with a dongle thing for my laptop. Magda sent them. Obviously, Dad asked her to. At first I thought he might be trying to justify my exile by painting it as one long reading list opportunity, but this theory was out the window once I looked inside. These are definitely not Dad's book choices. Still, it was sweet, even if I've already read half of them. So now I'm on the couch rereading *The Fault in our Stars* and Grandma is watching the news. Grandma doesn't have Sky, like that's even a surprise. Besides, I'm not interested in TV tonight. I've got a plan.

'I'm thinking about looking for a babysitting job?' I announce my half-formed idea.

Grandma stops flicking through the channels and twists in her chair to face me. 'Why would you do that?'

'To … earn money?' It seems like a reasonable answer to me. It may not be the real answer of course, but it's a convincing one I reckon.

'Your dad will look after what you need. And if there's something in particular you're after –'

'And it'd be a good way to meet people?' This bit is actually true.

'Your father would never approve,' she says.

'Why not? It's entrepreneurial; that would impress him.'

79

'Oh, I don't know. Besides, there are thousands of teenagers around here. I can't imagine anyone is struggling to find a babysitter.'

Her answers are so frustrating. I don't understand why she's so down on the idea. I think about getting up and leaving the room but instead I sit there, seething silently. 'I'm the only teenager around here with nothing better to do on a Saturday night. That's got to be a marketable benefit?'

Unfortunately this comes out a little petulant. Grandma turns up the volume on the news like she's actually really keen to hear something about falling dairy prices. OK, I get the hint! I pretend to read my book for a while before disappearing up to my room.

Well, even if Grandma's not behind it, I've decided to press on with my venture. I know Dad would be cool with it. Besides, I need something to stop myself sliding into an abyss of melodrama and self-pity. I finish cutting out another card from the lid of an old green shoebox and I add it to the pile of little flower cards I made earlier. The Metro place, where Liam works, will be my first drop obviously, but I've spied a couple of other shops around here, and I'm nothing if not thorough. I set off to ask Grandma for the home number.

I only get as far as the landing before I hear her. She's whispering on the phone, to Dad! I slink down the first flight of stairs to listen.

'She's got it into her head she wants a job ... babysitting,' she says. 'I told her you wouldn't like it ...'

Arghhh! Why is she doing that? I get that she doesn't want to upset Dad in case the cold war starts over, but I am seventeen in September. I am not a child. I watch her fan out her fringe in the mirror, and consider going down and interrupting them.

'She'd like to meet people.' She says this suddenly and I notice the tremor in her voice.

Hang on! Is Grandma trying to persuade Dad?

'It's not much fun for her being at home with me all the time.' This bit's a whisper but I hear it clearly.

So she is on my side. Dad is clearly in his irritating over-protective mode and I've got this the wrong way round.

'Well, think about it, please,' she adds.

I listen to her hang up and go back inside. I pretend I didn't hear a thing and breeze back into the living room, armed and determined. 'Can I use the home number? I've made some small ad cards but my English number might put people off. What d'you think?'

'Could I see them, Emerald?'

'Here!' I hand her my sample. 'Flower shape too girly? I could make tweaks?'

Babysitter available any time

– Responsible student –

Please call Emerald on 8560989

'It's lovely,' she says, in a drifty sort of way. 'Why don't you put up a few and we'll see what your dad says? I can't see the harm.'

I can't work out what's going on between Dad and Grandma, but this is definitely progress and I'm taking it.

LIAM

Twenty seconds of insane courage

I've worked two extra shifts already this week so it's as though I've hardly left the place. From my deli counter I can see over the whole shop, out beyond the forecourt and on to the main road. There's nothing much to see right now though. The rain is coming in sideways under the Metro canopy and a poor aul fella is getting himself soaked filling up outside. Some young wan has forgotten her PIN number paying for fags and she's getting shirty with Lorcan at the till. There's little trace of grace today. The good news is I managed to wangle Saturday night off so I'm free to go on the lash at Fiona's party.

I took Evie for a stroll on the beach when I finished work yesterday and hung around the shelters with her until gone teatime. Course, I could lie and say something about how my baby sister loves to paddle, but I had this now embarrassing optimism that Emerald might turn up, like she had that Friday night. It's daft I know, but I can't seem to accept she could just disappear.

Lorcan is legging around with his clipboard now, ticking off deliveries. I'm thinking about making myself another espresso when I clock him heading towards me. I start shuffling the paper baguette packets.

'Howyra?' I'm doing a Kenny here. It's not a question.

'How's your station there, Liam?'

'Er, grand, I think.'

'Are you up to speed on the rota?'

'Everything's clean and I've loaded up all the sandwich filler tubs that were running low.' I study him for a minute. 'That is what you meant?' I ask. I hate sounding thick but I don't understand Lorcan's jabber half the time.

'Listen,' he says, leaning in to the counter on his elbow, 'I've got the Area Franchise Manager coming in after lunch and Seamus didn't show up to work today. I'm a man down.'

'Oh, right.' I hope this didn't sound as smart-arsed as it did in my head.

'You couldn't do us a favour and help to unpack some of these?' he says, motioning with his thumb to a row of trollies laden with half soaked deliveries piled up inside the doorway. 'Now I know you haven't had the training for that module yet but I'd really appreciate it if you could ... muck in?' He does something funny with his hands as he says this.

Quickly contemplating what training could possibly be required for unpacking cartons of biscuits, I open my little gate and I roam on to the shop floor, feeling all free-range. 'I'm on it,' I say.

'You'll need this,' he says, handing me a little Stanley blade and pointing to a cardboard tower of chocolate fingers by the confectionery aisle. I crouch down and start. I reach in and pull all the dusty boxes from the back of the aisle first and put them at the front, the way Mam does with the new milks in the fridge. It doesn't take long before I'm through them all and on to the Hobnobs. I've got a nice little rhythm going when Lorcan swoops back in.

'Hold it! You'll have to do it all again,' he says, rifling through the cream crackers I've just stacked. 'I forgot to tell you about the date rotation!'

'It's cool, man.'

'Liam!' he practically shouts, 'the Area Franchise Manager isn't coming in for a casual chat, you know. We could be on the line here. All of us!' I notice the pearly beads of perspiration dotted along his hairline.

'I moved all the shortest dates to the front. If that's what you mean?'

He stops and mops his brow. 'You did?'

I nod. 'Yeah.'

'On all of them?'

'Yeah.'

He fixes his hawkish eyes on me and his thin, sweaty face tilts solemnly down. 'You're wasted behind that counter, Flynn. D'you know that? Wasted is what you are.'

I think that was an actual compliment. Out of the corner of my eye I spot the aul fella from outside, leaning up against my coffee counter. I can see him properly now; I've served him a few times.

'What can I get you?' I ask, strolling back into my hutch, wishing I could remember his order. I love doing that; it makes people smile. I guess we all like to feel memorable. What's more, I might have found one of my first real regulars. His scant wet hair is stuck to his shiny scalp and

84

his eyes twinkle out from under their heavy, fleshy lids. But that's not what's mental about this guy; it's his brows. They're like whiskers: long, white, wiry whiskers keeping his eyes warm.

'Cappuccino, please, with none of that chocolate dust, mind. And just a tea for myself,' he says in a gravelly voice that's much bigger than his tiny frame suggests.

'Gotcha,' I say, grinning back at him. I stand there, frothing the milk and watching as he counts out sachets of sugar from the silver container I packed to the brim earlier until four packets sit in a neat little stack on the counter beside his car keys. I hand over his drinks. 'Sweet tooth?'

'That's herself,' he says, handing over the exact change before placing cardboard rings around the cups and disappearing back into the shop floor.

When I get back I find Lorcan has promoted me to the magazine section: piles and piles tied up with plastic cord. I scan the old copies coming out and the new editions going in. I swear it's all the same; Cara's turmoil! Kim's meltdown! Some actress puts on weight! I hope Laura's not reading this shite.

A woman taps my shoulder. 'Sorry, love. Where's your noticeboard?' she asks. I point to the shopping baskets by the door.

'Ah here! I walked right past it,' says the woman as her cheeks flush red. She gives a little laugh before vanishing off and I get back to reading about some star's 'surgery hell!' This guff is properly mean.

''Scuse me.' It's yer woman, shouting over at me again. 'I forgot to bring some of them tacks,' she says, looking all flustered now. I walk over and scan the board, which is packed with little white cards advertising everything from lost cats to mobile hairdressing and buggies for sale.

Then I see it: *Donal Flynn, general maintenance and DIY. No job too small!*

I hear the woman's voice but her words are a blur. I've actually lost my tongue. Maybe I've swallowed it in the shock of seeing my da's life's work reduced to a tiny post-card on the small-ads noticeboard. I read the ad again and the blood rushes from my head to my feet and I wobble unsteadily. I notice only two of the ten little horizontal tags with his mobile number have been torn off. I look to where he's cut carefully in between the number flaps and I picture his large, gnarled hands struggling with Mam's good orange scissors. A wave of fury rises up through me and I drop the pile of *Grazia*s. I want to kick them back out of the automatic doors and into the rain.

'It'd be all right to nick a tic-tack yoke off this babysit-ting one, wouldn't it?' says the woman, holding a brass thumbtack high in the air. 'It had three on it. Look!' she says, flapping a flower-shaped notice in my face. I'm afraid I might scream something at her when I clock the card she's holding. I grasp it from her hand and read:

Please call Emerald on 8560989

Emerald! I stare at the swirls of loopy handwriting. I'm fixed on the bends and curves of each lovely letter, my ears filling with the unmistakeable *click-clack*ing roar of a heavy roller coaster carriage, groaning, chugging up its track, defying gravity to finally reach the highest point of the Malahide Mega Monster Ride. Suddenly I'm nine years old again, a hundred feet high in the air, surveying all of the Velvet Strand before me. My stomach is doing back-flips. It's real!

I look up at yer woman. 'It's bloody real!' I cry out, closing my eyes as my carriage whips off down the track at ninety miles per hour. I clutch the card tight to my chest and smile like Charlie Bucket with his golden ticket.

'Lorcan, I'm going on me break!' I shout, as I run off into the staffroom loos.

I slam my arse against the door, shutting it behind me. My hands find my phone in the vast plains of my apron pocket. For a split second I doubt whether I can do it. I watched a movie once and this guy was telling his son that twenty seconds of courage could change his life. This suddenly feels unbelievably relevant and I'm dig-ging deep, mining my guts for the mettle this moment requires.

My hands shake as I punch the number into my phone. 'Get it together, Flynn!' I crash the toilet seat down and stand on it so I can keep an eye on the exit.

It's ringing!

'Hello?'

It's her. Be cool, it's her ... 'Hiya, Emerald?' I'm picturing her beautiful, sad, not-green eyes.

'Hi.' She sounds jittery.

'It's Liam,' I say. 'From the other night, at the shelters.' I know she knows it's me. I don't know why, but I do.

'Yeah, I remember,' she says, a little flatly and my heart drops low in my chest as I crumple back down on to the seat.

'You sound … disappointed.'

'Do I? I'm sorry,' she laughs. It's a gorgeous laugh, quick and free. 'I thought it might have been about the babysitting ad, that's all.'

'No babies, yet! None that I know of anyway …' Oh, man, did I just say that? 'Sorry, that was a joke. A bad one, obviously,' I add, jumping off the loo and attempting to pace forward and back in the tiny cubicle while eating my fist. 'Actually, it is about the ad. I found your card at the Metro. I work there, I mean, I work here.'

'Really?' she says. 'Small world.'

Now, I don't know if it's because I so desperately want it to be true, but I get the feeling she's just smiled. And then, like I'm expecting a buzzer to go off and the flowery card to disintegrate in my hand, that twenty-second-bolt-of-whatever, fires up from somewhere. 'Would you like to come to a party with me on Saturday night?' I hold my breath in the silence, which feels very long.

'A party?' she asks, saying the word like it's the first time she's heard it.

I hear a voice getting louder outside the toilet door.

'Flynn, you in there?' Christ, it's Lorcan!

'Yeah, a party,' I whisper as quietly as I can.

'OK,' she whispers back.

'OK? Did you just say OK?'

'Yeah, OK.'

I slide down the wall and on to the grimy floor. 'Magic. Thanks.'

Next thing Lorcan slams his hand against my cubicle. 'I've a queue of mammies out there looking for lattes. Would ya c'mon!' he shouts.

I scramble to my feet. 'On my way!' I call out, happy-dancing on the other side of the locked door.

EMERALD
Truth is, I lie all the time

I've been in Portstrand exactly two weeks today. How can fourteen days feel a whole month long?

I don't think I've uttered so few words in one week, ever, and that includes the six days before we came here, when I was blanking Mum for turning up to Prize Day both late *and* drunk.

There was a presentation for all the prizewinners and we each had to have our photo taken with McKenzie. It was bad enough I'd won the Citizenship Award, for 'notable friendship and leadership skills', a day after I'd covered up the incident with Iggy Darcy, but then Dad had some business drama and couldn't come at the last minute. The other three prize-winning girls from our year were flanked on either side by a doting, presentable parent and when it was my turn I had to stand there alone with McKenzie's icy fingers gripping my shoulders way too tight. It was like she too was willing me not to cry as I looked out at the entire school with their shiny, happy families.

Then I caught a glimpse of Mum at the back of the marquee. She was wearing the prim blue shirt I'd left out for her but she'd tucked it into these weird too-tight white jeans, but it wasn't even that I'd tried to dress her like someone else's more conservative, more middle-aged mother: it was the lipstick. Bright, London Bus red lipstick. I could see it smeared on her teeth from where I stood. She hoisted the gold handbag chain further up her shoulder and waved up at me, crying out my name.

Who does that? Everybody looked at her and then at me, their faces frozen, mouths gaping, suspended somewhere between pity and horror. It was wrong, all wrong. I knew it and it felt like everybody in the marquee knew it too. I wanted the ground to swallow me up. My guts churned and my mouth filled with liquid like I was about to be sick. I fantasised about fainting but I had to get rid of her. She was a bomb about to go off and I had to stop her. I walked down off the stage and kept going forward, looking straight ahead. I eventually intercepted her, staggering towards me from the back of the tent, I linked her arm and dragged her all the way back outside to the car park. Once I got her in the car, I bent over double, hoping to puke, hoping for some release, but the waves of nauseating pressure refused to crash.

As though we hadn't endured quite enough shame already, Magda was dispatched in a taxi to drive us home. At the junction with the main road, I watched one of the thundering quarry trucks approach and I swear, I honestly thought how much better if would be, for all of us, if Magda were to simply drive out into the road in front of it.

It's awful to admit I once had this thought. I can't bear to think about it now.

★

But today is different. I've woken up knowing I have something to do that's not a trip to the shops with Grandma or a decent programme to watch on TV. I pretty much aced the whole babysitting set-up and now I'm off to a party with garage-guy, Liam. I'm not sure it's right to feel this excited, though as soon as I gave Liam Grandma's address on the phone, I knew it was a mistake. Given how much she grappled with the idea of a babysitting job, the idea of a party, with boys and alcohol, might finish her off altogether. Also, if Liam called to the house she'd only interrogate him, probably call Dad too. In fact I wouldn't put it past Dad to get Liam on the phone and ask him his intentions there and then. Together they'd get the wrong idea and I'm not up to that level of humiliation just yet, so we've agreed to meet at the stripy kiosk by the beach at eight. It was the only landmark I could think of.

Of course I couldn't tell Grandma about the party so I needed a watertight cover story. I'd spent hours thinking when one fell into my lap while I was out for a run yesterday afternoon.

I must have been running for half an hour when I found myself in a new estate of houses on the edge of the town, well outside the circuit I'd driven with Grandma. I took my headphones off and sat down on the perfect, fake-looking grass beside a large rock with *The Glenn* carved into it. Clusters of happy kids milled about and I lay back and watched the houses glistening in the sun, listening to their chatter. A blond boy with a dirty face wearing a dinosaur onesie rode up beside me on his bike.

'Hi!' I was just being friendly but he didn't answer. He was sizing me up like I was an outlaw when my attention switched to a girl, cartwheeling elegantly nearby. Her long, slim legs suddenly stopped and she looked over to the open hall door behind her. 'Jack! Dinner!' she called out, spinning back around. Both dino-onesie and another much older boy, who was kicking a ball about nearby, turned in the girl's direction. 'Jack DUGGAN,' she shouted by way of qualification. 'Dinner!'

Older Jack returned to his keepy-uppy and Dino-Jack rolled his eyes before pedalling in the direction of number 18. When I got home to Grandma's I googled 'Duggan, 18 The Glenn, Portstrand' and discovered Mark and Sinead Duggan put in for planning permission in May.

My fantasy babysitting family took shape before my eyes. Truth is, I lie about Mum stuff all the time so I know I can pull this off.

I practically bounce into the kitchen. 'Morning. D'you sleep OK?' I ask Grandma, who's engrossed in a magazine.

'Good morning,' she says, flicking a look over the top of her reading glasses. 'I did. How about yourself?'

'Fine.' I busy myself with the new coffee machine Magda sent over, twirling the long box of coffee pods between my fingers. 'Cappuccino, latte, espresso?'

'No thanks,' she says, nodding towards her pot of tea.

There's a nervous flurry rising in my belly. Perhaps it's the massive lie I'm about to tell. Then again, I have agreed to go out with a total stranger tonight, to a party full of even more strangers, which may be contributing to the jitters. I realise I've done a lap and a half of the room holding the milk.

'There's a film on with that DiCaprio fella later. *The Times* gives it four stars.'

I expect she's been saving up this little nugget all morning, dying to tell me. There are literally five channels on her TV so there is never anything good on. I should probably engage here and at least ask which film it is, but I'm kind of desperate to get on with my plan. 'I've got a babysitting job tonight. Forgot to say.'

I say it like it's no big deal, but her eyes dart back up at me. 'You do?' she says.

'I had a call yesterday. You were in the garden.'

'For whom?'

'Family called Duggan. His name is Mark. They've got two kids, a boy and a girl. Said they wouldn't be too late. Midnight.' I blurt it all out, just like I'd rehearsed in my head.

'Duggan?' Her little eyes fire and I watch them scan several random objects in the room in a matter of seconds. 'Where do they live?'

My palms sweat and I can't believe the *boom-boom* inside my chest isn't loud enough for her to hear. 'Er, I've written the number on a piece of paper upstairs, but it's The Glenn. Near the train station.'

'Oh, quite a way away,' she says, loosening. 'I'll drop you off.'

'Don't worry, I'll walk. I know exactly where it is. I've passed it on my run,' I say, turning around and clamping the milk-frothing gadget into its little slot to avoid looking at her. 'He said he'd drop me back after too.' I leave it a few seconds before I twist back towards the table with a smile.

'Well, that's cheered you up,' she says.

I pop a coffee pod in and hit the button. Part of me is weirdly pleased with my scheming and I wonder if winging-it is a legit talent. I watch her return to the magazine I know she's now not really reading. I look around and stare at the dark, creamy liquid dripping into my cup.

'Pet?' she says, after a few minutes. 'You'll give your dad a call to let him know, won't you?'

Can't say I wasn't expecting this. The only consolation is how much worse it would be had I told her the truth. 'I'll do it now,' I say carefully, clutching my over-full coffee as I push back into the hall.

I park myself on the bottom stair. I'm about to dial Dad on the home number when I spot the curled up old Post-it note still stuck to the front of Grandma's well thumbed address book. I put the handset down and examine the other relics of Grandma's life neatly ordered on the hall table: a crystal golf ball paperweight, a faded block of Post-it notes from one of Dad's companies, a bowl of dusty pot-pourri and a half-empty bottle of holy water. I place my hand around the plastic bottle of the Virgin Mary and she feels nice and warm from the sun. I slowly punch the number from the Post-it note into the phone.

'Hi, this is Emerald, I'd like to speak with my mum, Eliza Rutherford, please.'

'One moment, Emerald.' The woman's voice drags each syllable out, painfully slow. My bare foot taps against the leg of the table as I try not to think about what I'm doing. 'Putting you through now.'

Before I can thank her, I recognise Mum's breathing on the other end of the line. 'Em?' She sounds shaky.

I panic. For a moment I genuinely consider saying nothing, but then I did call her, and I'm a week late. 'Hi,' I say, a little bluntly. The image of her face lying in vomit flashes before my eyes.

'Thank you for calling, darling.'

The foul smell from her dressing room hits me again and I almost retch. 'S'OK.'

Mum and I aren't practised at being honest. Neither of us is comfortable saying things as they are. She could be dead had I not found her. Despite what Nick said about it being a cry for help, I can't but wonder whether dying was her actual plan. How do we know she even wants to get better?

She sighs deeply. 'It's so good to hear your voice.'

Even though I know Foxford Park isn't like this at all, I picture a dark corridor with a line of inmates behind, all waiting for the one phone like in some old TV prison show. I think about saying something, but it's difficult to talk about anything else when she still hasn't addressed what happened. One of us has got to bring up that afternoon, but surely that's up to her. I wait.

'How's everything in Portstrand?' she asks.

It sounds so absurd I almost laugh. 'Fine.' I can't pretend this small talk isn't ridiculous.

'Darling …' She sounds like she's going to cry. I know the face she's making now: the one where her nostrils flare and her lips press together like she's trying to hold the tears in. I'm ashamed to admit it but I want her to cry. I want her to bawl at me. I want her to break down like I want to.

'Yes?' I press hotly.

'About everything, I'm –' But she stops.

Go on! Say it! I wait with Grandma's heavy receiver clamped against my ear but there's nothing more.

'I miss you.'

That's all she says. I want to tell her I miss her too. I want to tell her that I've missed her for years, but I can't and I just wait, hoping she'll continue. She doesn't and now I don't know how to respond, or if I'm even meant to. We both exhale into the long silence. Oh God, Mum, is it really so hard to say it?

'Are you eating all right? Is Annie … looking after you?' she asks.

I'm thinking about her choice of words, the weird hesitation in her voice. Something from somewhere blazes inside me. 'Yes! Of course she is! She's my grandma!'

'I'm just concerned.'

'You've got a funny way of showing it.' My heart is pounding.

'Emerald!'

I stand up. 'I've got to go.'

'Wait, Em, please!' But I stay silent. 'You can come and see me, you know. As soon as next week they said. Will you?'

Oh yes, Family Days. Nick told us about those. Apparently we sit around with all these other families and they get you to cry and then everyone promises to change and then nobody does. OK, he might not have said exactly that, but I know I'm right. Sounds like a total waste of time. 'I dunno.'

'Think about it? Please?'

'OK, maybe.'

'I love you, Emerald.'

'Yeah, OK. Bye.' I hang up the phone too quickly and scrunch myself up on the last step like a crumpled tissue, cradling my head in my hands. I immediately want to pick the phone back up and say something different. I want to start the call all over again.

Why was I so harsh with her? Why couldn't I be nice? I didn't even ask her how she was. It must be awful to be there with those psychiatrists and only allowed to call home when they say so, but I can't understand why she can't just say sorry. Or if she can't say that, I want her to tell me that she didn't really want to leave me. Or at least that it wasn't my fault.

LIAM

It's a promise, and sometimes that's enough

I've ants in my pants, as Mam would say. I've been like this all day. I've been on clock-watch the whole afternoon and now there's only twenty minutes to go. Kenny was in earlier, sorting out what booze needed buying. Him and Murph were making a trip to the offie. I put in for a naggin of vodka for Emerald. She doesn't look like a girl who drinks beer, but then maybe she is. Kenny suggested white wine so he's getting a bottle of that too. I hope she won't think I'm a presumptuous tool but I figure it's best to be prepared. Dib, dib, dib, 'n' all that!

I'm beginning to think the face I remember is one I made up and not hers at all. Da was out last night so I spent hours playing my guitar. Words kept coming. I started to record another song for SoundCloud: just a Johnny Cash cover, but I didn't get round to uploading it. I haven't the balls to put any of my own stuff online yet. There are now fifty-four likes and four reposts for my first cover of 'When the Stars Go Blue'. I bet that Ryan Adams fella is shitting himself.

'Who's Emerald?'

These are the first words I hear stepping out of the shower. Laura is poking her nosy head around the bathroom door and grinning at me. I don't have time for this.

'Get out!'

'She your girlfriend?'

I grab a towel and flick it at the door. 'Get OUT!'

'I was just asking,' she bleats, all wounded.

'Yeah, well, don't.'

I hear her fall against the other side of the closed door. 'See! You never tell me anything.'

'There's nothing to tell.' I towel dry my hair and consider the sad reality that this is one hundred per cent true.

'Liar. I heard you talking to Kenny.'

I open the door straight into her devastated face. I lower my voice. 'Stop sneaking around me, Laura. Please!' I close the door again.

She jams her foot inside the room. 'Or what?'

I lift her foot out of the way with my own and she growls through the flimsy timber. 'I'll tell Da about all your online guitar stuff –' she says.

I yank the door open, but she's holding it shut on the other side for self-protection. 'Laura!'

She suddenly lets go and I fly backwards against the sink. I'm standing there, glaring at her. I don't need to say anything; this is a matter of loyalty. Her flushed red cheeks confirm as much. To be fair to her, she's kept this secret until now. God knows I've done it for her, countless times, like last week when Turbo saw her swigging from a bottle of Jägermeister down the beach. She promised me it wouldn't happen again and I haven't breathed a word of it to Mam or Da.

Laura's silence on the music thing is the only favour I've ever asked of her. She knows Da would flip if he thought I was entertaining the notion of 'throwing it all away'.

Mam knows of course; she knows everything. When it's only us at home during the day, I'll play with my door open. Sometimes I play Adele or Joni Mitchell just for her. I'll hear her singing along downstairs, with Evie. It's our secret; she's way too wise to ever go there with Da.

Laura is scowling at me now. I'm watching her bottom lip quivering, like a thousand things are trying to get out of her mouth at once.

'*Arghhhh!*' she blurts eventually, storming off in an unjustified huff.

I dry off and I pick up a bottle of some Calvin Klein aftershave I got for Christmas the year before last. Does this stuff go off? I quickly slap some on anyway and head into my room to find something to wear. I finger through the four items of hung-up stuff in my wardrobe and pull out a checked shirt I've never worn, then I hang it back up and grab a long sleeve navy T-shirt from the folded pile underneath. It smells clean. I put my jeans and boots back on. No point doing anything with my hair, it is what it is. I pop into Evie on the way down and give her a kiss, for luck, and then take the stairs three at a time.

'I'm off out!' I shout back into the house from the hall door.

'Don't be late!' Mam cries out from the kitchen.

I slide open the porch and step into the fresh evening air. I have to squeeze between Da's van and the blue hydrangeas Mam loves as much as the four of us put together. As I hit the road I feel the heat of the sun on my back and the smell of washing powder wafts up from my T-shirt as I walk. Or maybe it's the aftershave. I shake my watch down to my wrist; nearly ten past eight! But she'll be late; girls always are.

I pass Dessie's newsagent and turn the corner into Brackenbury, and there it is: the sea, glistening away, all shimmery at the bottom. This view stops me in my tracks some days. You've to get to the end of the road to get the full beach panorama. From here it's only a glimpse, but it's a promise and sometimes that's enough. The water is perfectly still, like oiled glass. Two kids in pyjamas play football on the green. Laughter and music spill out from a garden close by. The happy-chatter gets louder as I pass and a marvellous smell of sizzling sausages wafts over their side gate. The taste of cold beer suddenly hits the back of my throat. Despite my meddling sister, it's a fine evening to be alive.

I walk on past Kenny's old girlfriend's house, cross over by the doctor's surgery and hit the SPAR on the corner of the main road. Cars still line the beach side and there's a queue of kids milling around outside the kiosk. I get a flash of long blonde hair sitting on the wall behind: a mirage rising up through the heat. I try to look again, closer, but the kids are blocking my view. A white van speeds past as I go to cross, forcing me back up on to the path. I can't see anything now. A caravan tootles along behind a long Volvo and I jump out into the road and wait for a break. After a group of motorbikes spurt past, I dart over, finally hitting the safety of the other side. I look down to my right and there, behind the gaggle of kids with their ice creams, I see the golden mane sitting alone watching the sea. As though sensing me she slowly turns into view.

It's not her.

EMERALD

A total operating system upgrade

It's not easy to dress for a party *and* nail the girl-next-door-about-to-go-babysitting look. Grandma will definitely suspect something if I come downstairs in anything other than the jeans or baggy track pants I've been wearing all week. I've got that fluttery sensation in my tummy again. It's been there since I hopped out of the bath. I'm slathering myself in more of the cocoa butter I found in the bathroom when the blankets in front of me start to pulse. I assume it's another text from Dad, and I flip up the covers with a greasy hand where my phone is vibrating underneath.

Watching the phone *ping* away in my hand I realise it was a mistake not to shut down my WhatsApp account as well as Insta. It is going off! Kitty has posted a load of selfies of her wearing the exact showgirl outfit she put on Pinterest weeks ago, complete with enormous turquoise feather headpiece. She's holding a champagne saucer and slaying it as only she can. It's hard not to marvel at her, but as I do, it suddenly strikes me as kind of weird that someone so gorgeous needs to invite all of us to remind her just how off-the-hook gorgeous she really is. The whole thing is sort of YAWN.

Kitty: Roll up. Roll up. Let's get this party started!!!!!

Despite everything I thought a minute ago, I start to punch out some stock compliment, the like of which I've typed a thousand times and never really mean. Actually, it's not that, but there comes a time when all the compliment trading gets a bit meaningless. I'm side-swiping for an underused emoji, still pondering whether all this fawning is some kind of compulsion, when someone else gets there first.

Bryony: MY GURL BE ON FLEEK TONIGHT!!!!!

Ugh! Bryony giving it all that, like she's not from Bradford on Avon.

More photos come in; *ping ping ping*. Everybody's at it now. I scan through my friends dressed in a variety of amazing outfits: a sad-looking clown and even a strong man with inflatable weights. Bubbles … I see Bryony is typing again.

Bryony: On my way!!!! With THIS ONE

I stare at the photo of Bryony, dressed as a sexy ringmaster, kissing a furry lion. What? I look again and although I can only see one side of the lion's face, I'm sure it has Rupert's eye and nose and mouth too. I shake my face to get my eyes to focus. Yes, it's Ru in a lion costume! Rupert and Bryony are in the same picture, together, lips touching and his giant furry arms slung around her neck. WTF? I collapse on to the bed and scan all the new photos again. There's no preamble. No warning. No reveal. It's like it's not even a thing. I knew Bryony liked him and he liked her, hardly unusual for two uber-popular people, but not like this. Have I been seriously deluded? Is that why she posted the ugly picture of me? I lie back and stare at the ceiling expecting something intense and urgent to engulf me … But nothing, only a faint winded feeling like my chest is losing air.

Seriously, how can they even pretend this is cool? Everyone knows Rupert and me kissed. Kitty has been pushing us together for months. It's been like an entire squad assignment. Unless … of course Kit, Bryony and EVERYONE ELSE already know about the text he sent the other day and they've moved on already? I consider typing something cool back, but I have no words. I don't know what to feel. Between this and the nonversation with Mum earlier, I am OVER today.

Then it strikes me, clean, like a mallet over the head: I'm not upset about Ru and Bryony. Well, I'm hurt and possibly quite angry but not sad. Truth is, it's humiliating. It's that horribly familiar sense of shame, only made worse by the reality that their cute little revelation has been shared with the whole WhatsApp group.

I thought coming offline would do it, but still I feel like I can't get away. I'm not even there and it's all still stalking me.

How did I once believe that this summer, with my endless exams over, I could go for a total operating system upgrade and morph into a new, improved version of myself? I try to reject all the superficial crap, but then I can't cope without it either. I've barely known what to do with myself, or my suddenly way-too-empty hands this past week. Without the endless side-swiping and scrolling, my fingers knit themselves together obsessively, like Grandma's.

Perhaps I have Obsessive Comparison Disorder. Seriously, I read somewhere that this actually exists. I almost reactivated my Instagram last night, but I closed it and … considered Snap Chat. But I held firm.

I look at my phone again, not to pour over the trillions of comments that jolt the handset every few seconds. I just want the time. 8:21p.m. I'm late for my own lie! Next thing Kitty texts me that photo of her! Was the post to WhatsApp not enough? God, I want her glass of champagne. I want *something*. Maybe it's recklessness, desperation or massive FOMO, but I need to get out. I need to escape my brain. I pull on some jeans and grab my bag: phone, lip gloss, euros? Check, check, check.

Maybe a quick revenge selfie before I leave? A quick WhatsApp won't hurt, will it? Remind them all I'm still alive. Let them know Bryony's photo hasn't actually finished me off. I tie my hair up and stand over by the window, sucking in my cheeks and head-tilting exactly like Kitty taught me. Angles and a flattering light source is everything, she says. Chin drop is a bit severe, but it'll do.

TURNIN' UP IN DUBLIN TONIGHT.

I punch the words into caption, not quite resisting the urge to add unnecessary shamrock emojis. I reread it and cringe; I sound just as try-hard as Bryony. Delete! I'm staring at the shadows under my eyes, thinking I need some kind of filter. I'm ruminating on the skin-bleaching merits of Instant over Fade when I hear the front door. OMFG. It's loud! It's only the second time I've heard Grandma's doorbell ring.

'I'll get it!' I holler, pounding down the stairs, literally racing for the door. I figure it's best that Grandma stays rooted in front of the TV this evening. If she gets up out of that chair she's likely to insist on driving me to babysitting and I can't take that risk. I start to drag back the heavy wooden door.

I hear him before I even see him.

'Howrya!'

It's Liam! All sparkly Levi-blue eyes, leaning on the other side of Grandma's porch, leaning like he's holding up the door, the house, the trees and the whole world; not the other way around. Oh my God, I'm so late. He's come to get me! Clueless to the house of lies I've built around tonight, why wouldn't he? He automatically steps inside but soon his wide smile fades. It takes a minute for me to twig that the look on his face is a reaction to the abject horror stamped all over mine. I can't let Grandma see him. This could blow everything.

The chair creaks in the living room and I picture Grandma rising up out of it. 'Who it is, Em?' she shouts out excitedly.

I immediately want to push him back down the drive, or hide him behind the wheelie bins, but I just stare straight at him, wordlessly ushering him back, away, anywhere but here. How do I begin to explain this? I don't remember him being so tall. His eyes work hard, examining my face but he's not telepathic so next thing I'm literally shooing him out of the porch.

'Emerald?' She's turned the TV down and the whole world goes quiet. 'Who's there, love?'

Jesus effing hell! 'Um … just the aloe vera guy again, Grandma,' I shout back before moving out on to the front step myself and marshalling Liam silently back down the drive. His once confused face sets to something harder and he turns around and walks off. I immediately want to call out to him to explain, but I know I can't risk it. I'm praying he'll stop by the rose bushes, or duck down behind the car but he keeps retreating towards the road. An invisible rock slams into my chest as I watch him walk away.

Do I follow him? Do I go in and see to Grandma? I quickly stick my head through the living room door. 'Hey,' I say, sounding anything but normal. 'I'm going to head off now.'

She scans me up and down. 'Right so, Em,' she says. 'Did you get the spare key from the hall table?'

'I'll grab it on the way out. Thanks.' I'm trying not to sound agitated but I'm not sure it's working.

'And you definitely don't want me to run you down there?'

'No, no, I'll enjoy the walk,' I say, edging backwards out of the room, guilt writhing further along my spine with every step.

She blows me a kiss. 'OK, best of luck.'

'Enjoy the film!'

'Oh, and Em?'

Ohmygod, he's probably half a mile away already. I grit my teeth. 'Yes?'

'You won't mind if I slip off to bed later? I find it hard to keep my eyes open after ten o'clock these days.'

'No, God, of course not. I'll be fine.' I give her a final wave and scurry back out of the door.

LIAM
Dream, Liam, dream!

I hear her footsteps behind but I don't turn around until I'm past the gate and well into the neutral turf of the main road. Only then do I stop walking. She's wearing these high blue jeans and I try not to look at the thin band of flesh between her waist and the bottom of her cropped T-shirt. Her hair is tied in a loose knot on top of her head and a couple of long strands fall down around her face. She looks exactly like I remember, which doesn't help. My heart is going like that Kango hammer again.

'The aloe vera guy?'

She's looking at me with that intense, spring-loaded stare, logging everything I haven't yet said. I feel see-through. It's like at any moment she could take flight, like a bird. I almost wish she would.

'I'm sorry,' she says.

'For what?' I'm goading her to say it.

'For being late … and you know –'

'Lying about me?' She does this tiny nod. 'Don't worry,' I say, stomping on ahead. 'I get it. Kenny was right –'

'It's not like that,' she shouts, chasing behind me now. That she understands my half-finished sentence just confirms

Kenny was spot on. It's obvious she thinks I'm not good enough for her. Don't know what I was thinking at all.

'Liam!' she shouts again. 'Wait. Please.' I turn back as her hand reaches up and yanks at her knot of hair and I watch hopelessly as it cascades down. I'm not being dramatic; cascade is the only word to describe how it falls loosely around her shoulders like water. 'It's not you ...'

I turn around and begin to walk slowly on again past the entrance to the beach. All of its earlier promise feels unbearable now. I don't want to look. 'It's not me then, no?'

'No!' She's gathering pace and marching along beside me; her body wired with fitful energy. 'No. Honestly, it's nothing to do with you. It was just easier not to say where I'm going tonight. My family is kind of complicated.'

'Aren't they all,' I say it under my breath, but I slow my pace and allow her to fall into my rhythm. The beach exodus traffic passes steadily, practically brushing the pavement where we walk. Em lurches as a giant green bus whirrs past her on the outside so I move around to her right, shielding her from the road. It's not a big deal. It doesn't mean anything.

She stops and bites down on her newly glossed lip. 'So where's this party?'

I notice the crossover of her front teeth again. For some reason this token imperfection makes me happy. The evening sunshine drenches her face in warm gold. I can feel myself thawing. 'D'you remember Kenny?' I ask. She nods. 'It's his girlfriend Fiona's birthday – her eighteenth. Her parents are away so it's a free gaff.'

'A house party?'

'Yeah, like a house party,' I say, thinking this is indeed a finer term.

'Should I have brought a present?'

'Nah, you're all right. I doubt Kenny's even got her one.' Her mouth laughs without her eyes. 'It's just down here, about halfway to the village. Won't take us long. If you're still up for it?'

'I'm up for it,' she says quietly and we continue along by the golf club, slowing to a calmer, more manageable pace now. She looks up from the pavement to me. Her eyes are a kind of colour I've never seen; like stones.

'So what are you doing in Portstrand then?'

'Staying with my Grandma.'

'So I see. I've always wondered who lived up that dark drive. Never see anyone coming or going. We used to call it the haunted house. Well, you know … when we were younger.' She's looking at me strangely. 'How long you here for?'

'Been here two weeks, which means I've got … six to go.'

'Serious?'

'Yep.' As she says this, her hands stop trailing the railings and she does something with her hair, taking it all over to one side.

'Where's the rest of your complicated family then?'

'In England. Dad's super busy. He's mostly in London and my mum is doing a course. So I'm … here,' she says, shrugging her shoulders.

'You don't seem too happy about it?'

'I wasn't at first, but –' She stops and we linger on this as a determined dog-walker weaves in between us.

'Can't say I blame you.'

112

'Sorry … that didn't come out right. It just wasn't how I'd imagined my summer.' I'm thinking about what to say when she continues. 'It was thrown at me, I guess. I had other plans. You know?'

'Sure,' I say, not knowing at all, but immediately I'm trying to imagine what her other plans may have been. 'How old are you?' I blurt it out of nowhere. I've been dying to ask.

'Sixteen.'

'You seem older?'

'Do I?'

'Yeah, you do.' I'm not sure where to go with this. She hasn't asked anything about me, so it's a bit awkward. 'D'you live in London?' I ask eventually, just to stop myself from humming.

'No. Somerset.'

I don't know where this is but I don't want to sound thick. 'It's this way,' I say as we wait to cross the busy road.

We hike up the steep bit through Elm Park, which is a little estate Da built ages ago, and then we cut through the lane at the back and walk together in silence for a bit. We're walking in time now and I turn and smile at her. She smiles back. Despite all the confusion and anger I felt ten minutes ago, my heart sinks as we get close to Fiona's. Feels like we're finally getting somewhere. I'd have more of a shot at getting to know her roaming suburbia than at this party, that's for sure. I try to slow down but we've already reached the bottom of the hill by Fiona's estate: hers is one of six big, red-bricked houses in a little cul-de-sac. Music pulses up the pavement from the garden.

Em turns to me. 'I might not stay too late, if that's OK?'

'Anytime you wanna leave, just shout. I'll walk you home.'

Kenny flings the door open before we even hit the drive. 'Well, howrya, Flynn, ya big ride, ya?' Clearly Kenny didn't wait to get stuck into the booze. He's got a big skeezy head on him already.

'All right.' I grunt it. I want to deck him, but I can't and the prick knows it. 'You remember Emerald?'

'How could I forget,' he says, and he does this funny bow thing like a complete spanner. Then he stands there for a bit, gawping at us.

'You gonna let us in?'

'Sorry, yeah, yeah, in yis come now. Looking foxy there, Emerald, if you don't mind me saying,' he says, pushing me behind her. I elbow him in the ribs as we hustle through the hall and into the enormous kitchen that's lit up like a showroom. Everything is expensive-looking: cream walls, cream table, cream chairs, cream cupboards: the glass ones with the lights behind them. There are tasteful black and white photographs of Fiona's family on the walls. I've never been past Fiona's front door before, but still none of this is a surprise.

A load of familiar girls with very long hair, in very high heels and in very tight dresses, are stationed by a giant kitchen table, every inch of which is covered in bottles. Their chatter stops as soon as they see us. There's an over-powering smell, like a mix of sticky peaches and weed. Nicky Minaj, or one of those, is blaring out from speakers in the roof.

Fiona comes running across the room. 'Liam!'

'Happy birthday,' I say, immediately thinking how nice it would be to have a present to give her now. I'm only thinking this because Em mentioned it earlier. I'm crap at that sort of thing.

'Yay, you're here,' she says, with her wide smile of super-white teeth. Then she goes ahead and plants a big kiss on my cheek, not a bother. 'You must be Emerald!' she says, looking Em up and down.

'It's just Em actually.'

'Oh, cool. Kenny's told me about you. He was right – you *are* gorgeous! You're from London or somewhere?' She laughs. Em hardly has a chance to answer because Fiona's jabbering away again. 'Here, we're all doing vodka shots. D'you want one?'

Fiona takes Em's hand before she can answer and drags her towards the harem of identical girls. Kenny was right: they're pretty good-looking, to be fair. But Em's a different thing altogether.

I feel Kenny's arm slink in around my shoulder.

'Fair play to you, Flynn,' he says, thrusting a can into my hand. I open it with one eye on the girls. They're all looking at Em. You know that way: smiling but still scanning everything, trying not to look like they're looking. Fiona hands Em a shot and they clink their glasses. I watch as Em throws her long hair back, downing it in one. All the smiley girls cheer.

'Just hope you can handle her,' Kenny says, slurping away beside me.

Fiona gives Em a paper cup and she stands there, clutching it with two hands as the girls introduce themselves. I have an urge to get her out of here and away from them. I'm leering at the back of her head when she suddenly turns around to me. No, I've been caught! But she raises her cup, as if to say 'cheers'. I raise my can and we smile at each other. For a brief second it feels like no one else in the room can see her.

Kenny knees me in the back of the leg and we lurch towards the garden. 'C'mon!' He reaches in front of me to open the double doors and together we fall on to a large wooden deck and over a couple of enormous terracotta flowerpots, which are dappled with fag butts. All the lads are here, sitting around on the patio furniture looking awkward, like they're trapped in a page of the Argos catalogue. There's even one of those outdoor heater yokes. Billy Gilhouly is trying to light his fag off it.

Red-faced and sweating he turns around. 'All right, Liamo. How's it going?'

'All right, Billy?' I smile because it's impossible not to smile at Billy. No matter who you are, or what fecking stupid thing you just did, you never, and I mean never, look as thick as Billy Gilhouly. He's sporting some new hipster beard, which isn't working for him at all.

'Sweet as, bro. Sweet as …' he says, fag in his mouth, somehow still unlit despite the raging furnace next to him. He resumes his efforts and I look back in through the double doors to see if I can spot her. Turbo and Murph are here too. It feels a bit like Maths class all over again. The girls are yakking away through the open window and I try to pull out Em's voice, but it's all screechy noise. I lean up against the shiny barbeque and crane my neck further towards the kitchen.

'So how d'you know Liam?' I don't recognise the girl asking.

'Oh, I don't,' Em replies, 'not really –'

I hate that this is true and I'm afraid to hear any more. Kenny and Billy are opening the patio doors up full so the music cranks up even louder now. Kenny struts in and out as if it's his fancy gaff.

'Ah, here, Fiona, give us that Spotify,' he shouts, reaching for her phone.

I've a good mind to ask him how he's feeling about Ashling now, but I swig from my can and savour the last of the evening sun on my face instead. Turbo is ripping Billy to pieces beside me. I wanna hear this.

'Did yis all hear what Billy told Cliona when she caught him with his arm around that bird in Moloney's last week?'

'Feck off, Turbo!'

'What was that, Billy? I can't quite hear you?'

'Shut up, I said.'

'I'll go in and ask Cliona what it was? Back in a tick, lads,' says Turbo, plonking his can down and setting off towards the kitchen.

Billy grabs him back. 'It's a sorry mouse …' he says into the funnel of his hoodie, biting down on one of the little toggle yokes.

'What's that, Billy? Speak up, man.'

'It's a sorry mouse … that has only one hole,' says Billy, staring at his feet but his tomato face is plain for all to see.

Turbo slugs greedily from his glass before wiping his mouth. 'There's a line for yis, boys. Fecking genius!'

It continues this way for a while with fellas taking the piss out of each other because it's the only thing we know. We don't ask each other how we are, or how we feel about things. Well, if we do they're questions we don't really want an answer to. I'm thinking about all of this when I hear Kenny.

'You're very quiet tonight, Liamo.' He's just stirring.

'Yeah?'

'All cerebral in your thoughts again?'

'That's it, Kenny. Bang on.'

Despite being such a talker, Kenny somehow manages not to say anything, not really. He's not one of life's listeners either. Maybe fellas don't listen to each other the way girls do. I want to talk to Em. I want to be alone with her again. I want to make all the earlier awkwardness better, but I don't know how to get her away from Fiona yet, so I move over beside Turbo and settle in.

By the time it gets dark almost everyone has moved outside; there's at least twenty of us dotted around the swishy-looking deck. Between the beers and whatever Ibiza-shite Kenny's put on, everything feels better. I'm gathering the courage to wander in to the kitchen when I spot Em and Fiona toppling through the patio doors.

'You're in there.' Kenny slobbers it in my ear.

I shove his shoulder to get his face out of mine, watching her all the while.

She leans against the table between Turbo and me. 'Hey!' I know Turbo's trying not to stare at her, but he is. Thankfully she doesn't seem to have clocked him or his efforts.

118

'Y'all right in there?' I ask, trying not to smile.

She leans back on to the table to get her balance. 'Yep.'

'Sure?'

'Yep.'

I'm enjoying her economy: no fat, no blather. 'I'm gonna head in for another can.' I want to get her away from Turbo before he starts laying into me next. 'Coming?' I ask. She doesn't say anything, just gets up and follows and together we weave through the bodies and into the brightly lit kitchen. The once immaculate room is now strewn with bottles, cans and all manner of cocktail-making wreckage.

'Bought you some booze earlier. Just in case, you know.' It's hard to read the look on her face but then she sways. At first I think she's putting it on, but I look into her eyes and I can tell: she's drunk. She's properly drunk. 'Eh, seems like you're already on your way.'

She glares at me.

'No offence, like.'

'Fiona's been looking after me,' she says, swallowing a hiccup. 'We did a few more shots.'

I watch her tilt again towards the table. I grab a four pack from the stash and unhook a can from its plastic ring. She holds out her hand and I reluctantly slot one into it. As we move back outside her body drifts from mine, walking in the opposite direction from the others and finally sitting down on a low wall near an oil tank on the far side of the garden. I'm trying to work out the significance of this move as I follow behind and sit down.

'Got a cigarette?' she asks.

For some reason this shocks me. I shake my head. 'D'you want one?'

'Nah, don't worry about it. I was only going to have a drag.' She sounds even more English now through the slight slurring. She looks me up and down, not even trying to hide it. 'Fiona's told me a lot about you,' she says, idly blowing loose strands of hair off her face.

'Has she now?'

She cups her chin in her hand, looking up at me with those eyes and nods. 'You've just done your A levels ...'

'It's called the Leaving here.'

'Whatever,' she says, waving my words away. 'You're already eighteen. A Gemini! And ... you're the nicest of all Kenny's friends, apparently.'

I try to swallow a smile. 'Generous.'

'I've just finished exams too. GCSEs though.'

'Yeah? How'd that go for you?'

'As expected, I guess. You know ... ?' she drifts off. 'Anyway, what's it like?'

'What?'

'Being finished with school and ... out in the world?'

'Dunno. Doesn't feel like I am, like any of us are. I mean, look around you,' I say, nodding over towards the shower of hopeless, showboating eejits who haven't even grown into the patio furniture. She smiles. I try to think of something to say now she's got her chat on. There's so much I want to ask her but I feel panicky, like I'm wasting time. We look around each other for a bit, almost like we're trying to avoid our eyes finding each other's again.

'So then ... Bob the Builder?' she says, out of nowhere.

For a second I think I've misheard, but no, she's looking right at me, smiling. Does she think it's funny? I can't tell what this expression means. I'm not sure I want to. I clench my teeth, hoping the anger doesn't jump out of my mouth.

I hurl my empty can into the bush. 'Fiona said that?'

'It was a joke.' She jumps in. 'She said something about you joining your father's building company. Maybe I got it wrong?'

'You did!'

She leans towards me. 'Sorry.'

I search for words but can't find any that are right. I'm embarrassed now and I feel bad for tossing the can into Fiona's lovely garden. For the second time tonight I've made us both uneasy and I don't even have a drink to busy my hands with. 'You don't need to be sorry,' I say finally. 'Can we talk about something else though?'

'Of course.' I can see she's concentrating, like she's trying not to look drunk, but she does, which I have to admit makes me feel a bit less self-conscious about the questions I'm desperate to ask. It's as though I've nosed ahead in a race she doesn't know she's running.

'Were you serious, you know, about being here for the whole summer?'

'Yes.' She sounds briefly sober, like I've forced her to recall something awful.

'I forgot. You had plans.'

'S'OK,' she says, taking out her lip gloss. She reapplies it and takes a long swig of her beer.

'Suppose there's things neither of us want to talk about?' She doesn't comment so I stare at my feet. I'd go and get another can but I want to keep talking. 'I wasn't sure whether you'd drink beer.'

'What did you think I'd drink?'

'Kenny thought white wine.'

She laughs at this and rolls her eyes. 'I'll drink anything,' she says and she knocks back the rest of her can by way of a demonstration. We're silent again and I notice the music inside has upped a gear to something bassy and loud. I never know how to describe dance music but it's a long way from Fiona's chart stuff now. It's all pounding beats, deep and dirty. I peer back through the dark and study the familiar faces dancing in the kitchen, which looks lit up like a spaceship from here. Then I clock the tall hood moving through the edge of the crowd. Bodies part to let it pass. It must be him.

The hooded head presses up against the glass doors, staring out into the blackness. I'm already picturing his mad eyes across the garden when the door opens and his lanky hooded shadow lurches towards us. How did he even get in here? I stand up; it's instinct.

'All right, Flynn!' he bellows as he gets closer.

I can't even feign enthusiasm. 'McDara.'

He sidles up close to Em, rubbing his nose. 'Is that yer one?'

She throws me a glance before she looks back at him and this small gesture makes me feel good.

'Not bad,' he says, gawping at her, head to toe, and then he winks at me. He actually feckin' winks! I make what I hope is a reassuring face at Em. 'Kenny tells me there's gravy owing,' he says, sniffling. 'Only the ginger blouse called it a dividend. That suit's clearly gone to his head.'

He's going a mile a minute. God knows what he's just put up his nose. 'Em, this is McDara. From the shelters last Friday.' Feels unnecessary to point out they were his drugs she stashed from the Guards.

'Hi.' She smiles at him, which strikes me as an impressive thing to be able to do under the circumstances.

'Here, for yer troubles,' he says, pushing something into Em's hand. She flashes him that smile again and my stomach clenches. 'Never let it be said I'm not a reasonable man, yeah?'

She nods and he turns around looking horribly satisfied, swaggering back over the Lego-looking lawn, punching his fist in the air to the music. The state of him.

Em pokes at the two brown heart-shaped pills in her palm. I'm waiting for her to fling them away when she looks up at me with twinkling eyes, reaches down to pick up her can, and then, without breaking her stare, she pops one of the pills in between her teeth and drains the beer before I can blink. Just like that! OK, I was not expecting that. 'What the … ?'

'*Eughghhh!*' she cries out at the taste, before looking up at me.

I want to shake her. 'McDara's trouble. You wouldn't know what the –'

'Everyone's doing them!' she cuts in before biting at the mouth of the can.

'What?'

'Fiona said.'

I know my head is shaking. 'Have you even taken a pill before?'

'Er, yes,' she says.

I'm pretty sure she's lying. 'And did you take it in one go the last time too?'

This annoys her. 'Are you taking yours, or what?' she says, holding out the other brown heart between her fingers.

I pinch it out of her palm. 'Dunno,' I say, quickly dropping it into my pocket. I know it's safer there than with her. I'm watching her, waiting for something, but now I'm not sure what. This wasn't the direction I'd imagined the evening to go in. I've no idea what's in this girl's head.

'D'you wanna dance?' she asks eventually, getting up from the wall and fixing her jeans in a way that makes it hard not to watch.

'Can't we just talk for a bit?' I feel like a tool asking her this but I know if we go in there I'll lose her again.

She sits back down and lands that look on me. 'What d'you want to talk about?'

It's that look I can't predict. I think about what to say, but as I'm thinking don't I only go and burst out, 'D'you have a boyfriend?'

She looks around like she's thinking.

Ah, Christ! I've blown it. Haven't I? Have I?

'Funny you should ask,' she says and then stops. 'Rupert …'

I feel a bit sick. 'Oh.' It's all I can manage. 'Rupert?' I say then, like a total fruit. I hadn't planned to say it out loud. My brain's trying to picture this Rupert fella and all

I can think of is yer man from those *Twilight* films years ago, even though I know that's not even his name. Now I can't shake the image of that good-looking prick from my mind. Obviously, she has a boyfriend. I was asking for it.

'It's Ru actually. Everyone calls him Ru.'

'Course it is.' It was only a thought. It wasn't meant to drop from my mouth like a rock.

'As of eight o'clock this evening, I'm pretty sure he's moved on,' she adds and begins tapping her foot steadily against the wall.

'Yeah?' I ask with too much enthusiasm. Judging by the look on her face the moving-on lark she's just mentioned may well be one-sided. I stand up.

'Oh, yeah,' she says, getting up too and fixing those jeans again. 'He was kissing one of my supposed best friends on WhatsApp earlier, which was nice.'

I'm about to go in for more questions but she's already walking back towards the house.

'Come on. I'm freezing!' she calls out.

I follow her, obviously. We step back into the warmth of the kitchen and the place is hopping and thick with smoke. I spot Kenny, Murph, Billy and Turbo in the swarm with the girls. Everyone is dancing and grinning at each other. Em takes my hand and leads me in to the crowd beside Fiona and then I feel her slender fingers fall away. I stand there like a lemon. I'm not drunk enough for this. I don't dance, as a rule, so I look around, nursing my beer. The music is pretty good now, I'll give Kenny that. I begin to shuffle so as not to look the complete walnut, but my feet get stuck on some sticky drink that's been spilt all over the floor.

Em is dancing now. Just small movements: her hips sway gently with her arms bent halfway in the air, letting the music in, slowly. Her face tilts down and her hair falls over her face, then she looks up and thrusts a triumphant arm in the air. She moves easily, effortlessly. I see her beam at Fiona who beams right back at her. I'd be warmed by this if I didn't know it was just the drugs beginning to work. She swirls around and fixes her gaze on me, transformed from the girl on her grandma's step earlier.

I want to join in. I want to do what she's doing and I consider the pill in my pocket. My thumb searches over the outside of my jeans to feel if it's still there. It is and that's enough. I start to dance: nothing showy. My feet aren't even moving, but I am. I'm moving with the room. Emerald and me, dancing with my mates and man it feels good. No one's feeling not-good-enough now. No one's casting bitchy glances. Everyone is happy, drunk and lost. I feel a tap on the shoulder and one of Fiona's friends passes me a bottle of vodka. I seize it and stare at her.

'Drink it!' she orders and for some reason I do. The vodka fills my mouth. I gulp it down and the smell shoots up my nose, sousing my whole head in the flash of alcohol. I keep dancing. The whole room is moving, arms and eyes, giddy and alive. Two girls in front are dancing together, doing stripper moves like you'd see on some music video. I can't not look. I see Em is watching too. I feel her breath on my ear as she leans in.

'It's like you're all at different parties.' She's shouting, but still I can barely hear her. I must look confused because she tilts back to me again. 'The girls are so dressed up,' she says, motioning around the room, 'And look at you guys.'

I survey the lads and she's right: we're in T-shirts and bad jeans and the girls look like they're about to go clubbing in Miami with Kanye and Drake. I laugh and lean back over to her. 'I like how you're dressed.'

'I'm supposed to be babysitting,' she says, nodding to her jeans and the flat canvas shoes on her feet.

'That's what you told her?'

She starts dancing again. 'Yeah.' She laughs.

'But –?' I'm trying to work out how she can possibly get away with rocking up to her grandma's house in her condition but she's twirled off again, sashaying towards the other girls. I decide it might be an idea to have another can while I worry about how she's going to pull off her plan.

I'm wandering to the fridge when I feel someone take my hand from behind. I know it's her.

'Grab one for me.'

'Here,' I say, 'let's share this.' I hand her the newly opened beer but she doesn't take it.

'Think I might need some air,' she says, stumbling a little before heading towards the door. I follow her, my mind in overdrive. As soon as we sit back down on our wall by the oil tank, I hit her with it.

'Seriously? Babysitting? How does that story work, what with you necking pills and all?' For a second it's like I'm talking to Laura and I know I've got to back off.

'*Ssshhhh!*' she says, waving me away. 'It was pill, singular. And …' She fingers a thick strand of hair against her cheek. 'I have until midnight.'

'Midnight?' I blurt. Man, she hasn't a clue.

She leers up at me like some sort of fallen angel; shivering now. 'I'll work it out. I'm quite smart actually!'

'Are you indeed? All coming out now, isn't it?' I can't help but smile at her.

'Grandma goes to bed at ten, it won't be difficult.'

'Still,' I say, 'you'd want to be brainy for all your lies.' I sink another mouthful of beer.

She looks back at me, all serious, and it's clear I've said something wrong. Her long fingers rub roughly at her neck and into her hair. I've no choice but to watch her in silence. I don't know what to say.

'It was one lie, Liam,' she says, without looking at me. 'Just like it was one pill.' Her stare flicks back at me before darting towards the trees at the end of the garden again. It was only a glimpse but enough to catch the hurt in her eyes.

'Em?' She takes a shaky breath and turns back around. Her pupils are black saucers and her hair has matted to her head. There's no lip gloss now, but her pasty Bambi face is somehow even more gorgeous. 'I was joking.'

'Forget it.'

I want to put my arms around her to stop her shaking. 'For what it's worth, I'm borderline remedial.'

A reluctant smile breaks from her pursed lips and my guts settle. 'You're borderline funny too,' she says, softly pushing her hand into my shoulder, her body not quite returning to where it started. Her face stays closer to mine and for a

128

moment I let myself imagine what it would feel like to kiss her. It's not the time though. Not like this.

'Everything is funny here,' she says, inhaling deeply and looking up at the sky. I follow her eyes up to the sky but really I'm just wondering whether that Rupert fella goes to her school when she goes to speak again. 'I didn't mean there was anything wrong with being a builder, you know, earlier?' She looks deep into my eyes before taking a drink from our can.

'Don't worry about it,' I say, more gruffly than I planned. 'It's a load of bollocks anyway, all of it.' She looks back up at me, like she's really thinking and then she closes her eyes.

'What does your da do in London?' I ask, deciding it's a bit late to freak her out about the whole pill-come-down-timings.

There's no reply at first but then her eyes flash open. 'Stuff. Deals. Loads of things,' she slurs. Her eyes close again and I'm about to ask something else when she adds, 'He's in the middle of this case, this court case. So that's taking up most of his time because it's …' And then she drifts off. Her eyelids fall again and her hair dangles in front of her face. I reach over and fold a strand back behind her ear. She doesn't seem to notice.

'And your mam?' I'm trying to keep her focused now.

'Huh?'

There's no point pretending she's not wasted now so I ask, 'You feeling anything yet?'

'What?' she asks blankly, and I feel bad.

'Nothing. What course is your mam doing?' She looks up at me and suddenly I know how she must have looked as a child. I have an urge to shield her from everything that's happening to her, but I know it's too late. 'I'm just chatting. Don't worry about it.' Don't want her to think I'm fishing from her in this state.

'Interiors!' She kind of barks it and then she moves her right leg over to straddle the low wall and her hands slide slowly down her long thighs. She breathes deeply in and out through her nose a few times. I've seen this before.

I stand up and tilt her chin to look up at me. 'I'm going to get you some water,' I say. 'Don't move!'

I run through to the kitchen, which is now rammed with people, half of whom I don't recognise. The place is trashed. I reach into one of the tall creamy cupboards and grab the first clean glass I find and I fill it up at the sink. The cold water runs all over my hands, then I race, half soaked, through to the hallway and hunt in the jacket pile with one hand, snatching what I hope is her coat and her cherry bag trails along with it. I shove my way through the sea of bodies dancing in the kitchen and back out into the garden.

The small sound of her giggle in the distance freezes me. What's she laughing at? I'm about to smile at her madness when I see she's left the wall and the sound is coming from the barbeque where she's standing next to his unmistakeable hood. She laughs again, taking a cigarette from the pack he holds out to her. When he raises his other hand to her face, she lifts her hand to meet his. I can't look.

My fingers shake and water spills out on to my boot. I'm afraid the glass is going to smash, I'm squeezing it that tight. My head is spinning and my stomach churns at the thought of his filthy hands. I twirl around and trudge back into the house. Sweaty bodies gyrate everywhere I look, but I force my way through them into the hall, where I bump straight into Kenny.

'What's up, man. You winning?' He's plastered. I try to brush on past him but he drags me back. I'm about to tell him I'm off: that I'm leaving. 'Hey?' he says, ramming his shoulder up against mine.

'I don't know what her game is at all,' I say, using the banisters to hold myself up.

He's staring at me, confused and drunk. 'What?'

'She went off to talk to that … germ. She's out there laughing with him now. I mean, what –'

'Who?' Kenny barks.

'McDara. Emerald's out there with Mc-feckin'-Dara!' Saying her name and his name out loud together unscrambles my brain. Even Kenny's too, judging by the look on his face. What the hell was I thinking leaving her out there, alone, with him! 'Here, hold this,' I say, shoving the water into Kenny's chest as I reach into the kitchen for her stuff. I grab the water off him again and race through the dancing mob where the lads' wasted heads turn as I pass them for the third time inside three minutes. I only stop running once I've burst back into the cold. Most of the water from the glass is now on my jeans. Taking a second to catch my breath I move quickly past the swarm of huddled bodies smoking spliff by the barbeque, but she's not there. Nor is he. When I look over to the wall I can't see them either. The garden is properly dark and I have to squint into the blackness, but there's nothing. I break into a run. All sorts of horrors have hijacked my head. 'Emerald?' I cry out.

It's not long before I find her body slumped over the wall, decorating the flowerbed on the other side. I scoop her up and brush her down. 'Hey! You're OK, you're OK,' I say, turning her face towards the light so I can see her. Her body is warm and heavy and her hands are clammy. Her beautiful face is scarily white. 'Emerald! It's Liam, are you OK? Em, Em?' I want to shake her but I hold her close to me instead, as I panic about what to do next. Jesus Christ!

'Someone shut off my ears,' she slurs.

Relief spills through each of my ribs. 'What?'

'Can't open my eyes. Everything's … I'm spinning.'

'You're rushing,' I explain, as gently as I can. We both take a few deep breaths. 'Please tell me you haven't taken anything else? Emerald!'

She shakes her head.

'OK, but you've gotta tell me if you start to feel any worse. D'you promise? Turbo's sister is a nurse and I'm calling her. I don't care if you're supposed to be babysitting. OK?'

She nods.

'What did you want with that scumbag anyway?'

'I just asked him for a cigarette.' Her breathing goes heavy again and I take the broken unlit cigarette from her palm and dispose of it in an empty can while I think about what to do. 'Liam?'

'Yeah?'

'Can you hold me?'

'I've got you.' I sit behind her and fold my arms around her, rocking back and forth on the wall gently, together. I can't believe I nearly left her. The bass from the kitchen pulses through the trees around us as her heart thumps

132

steadily inside her chest. I listen closely to her breath and I feel something adjust inside me. I want to keep my arms around her forever, but not this way. I don't want to feel this kind of fear again. This happened to me the first time, but I'm not telling her that.

'Liam … ?'

'Yeah?'

'Think I'm going to be sick.'

'I know,' I say, getting up. 'Come on, let's move you over here.' We shunt around the corner by the shed where I spot an old bucket. I turn it up so she can sit on it. 'Have you got that hair yoke you had earlier?'

'What?'

'Your bobbin?'

She stands up. 'In here,' she says, jutting her hip towards me. I slide my hand into the deep pocket of her tight jeans and quickly pull out the elastic before she can think I'm getting any ideas. Not that she's having any thoughts, other than the fact she's about to puke. I bunch her hair into my hand and attempt to tie it into the elastic but it's not as easy as it looks and she plummets forward. I manage to scrape most of it off her face before I crouch down beside her, gripping the fist of hair in my hand gently. Her breathing tells me it's close.

'How you doing?' I ask, rubbing my hand on her back and trying to reassure myself it's OK. It's OK that I didn't leave her, that she's gonna be OK and that it's also OK for me to have my hand where it is. I try not to think about how it felt to put my hand in her pocket …

'It's coming!' she blurts.

'You're beside the drain, which is handy.' I'm not expecting a laugh. I only want her to know it's gonna be all right. Her breath gets heavier and I watch loose strands of hair fall from my half-arsed ponytail and into her eyes. I'm tempted to rescue them but her whole body swells up from the bucket and heaves. She reaches out to the wall, swatting her palm against it. She's snivelling and I shift towards her, still holding her hair back. Her body surges once more and she vomits clean into the drain. I look away, feeling it the decent thing to do, but it's not easy to turn around and keep hold of her hair.

I let the minutes pass. 'You OK?'

'I want to die.'

'Better out than in,' I say, but she looks up at me, glazed and haunted. 'You'll feel better soon. Honest.'

She just stares, saying nothing and then she drops her head between her knees again. We stay this way for a while, quite a long while in fact.

Finally she takes a breath. 'Will you stay with me, Liam?'

'Sure.' She smiles a thank-you. 'Can you make it back to the wall?' I'm thinking it might be good to get away from here. I spot an outside tap further along and when she gets up I fill the bucket and slosh it at the drain, washing away the remains of her boozy puke. By the way, I'm not normally like this. Under normal circumstances I'd be drunk in a corner with Kenny and the lads.

'Water!' she pants, stumbling to the tap like a dying man in the desert and guzzling straight from the gushing stream. It sprays all over her face. Guess it won't do her any harm. She refills the mug and cradles it carefully as we walk back to our wall. 'I think I'm gonna be OK.' I don't reply. I'm watching her flop back down when she says, 'Tell me about yourself.'

I look at her. 'Me?'

'Yes, you!'

'Er ... well, right now, I'm worried about you.'

'You are?

'Yeah!'

'That's sweet,' she says, sipping from the cup. 'What time is it?' she asks, taking my wrist and attempting to read my watch upside down.

'Around midnight. You're supposed to be home, Cinderella.'

'When am I going to ... ?'

'Come down?' She bows her head for yes and I think this through for a minute. 'Properly?' She nods again. 'Three a.m., ish.'

'No!' she grunts through her clenched teeth. 'I'm too high ... I can't ...'

'I know.'

'Could we maybe just walk ... ?'

'Well, I wouldn't say you're quite ready for Grandma.'

She pushes herself up off the wall. Last thing I want is to have to go back out through that kitchen. I scan the passage where she vommed and I spot the side door. She clocks it too, grabs her coat and we amble towards it. I reach for the handle but it's locked. Then she shoves her bag into my hand and places her foot up on the lock.

'You sure you should do that ... ?' I start, but without me finishing she hauls herself up and vaults over the wooden door. I hear her land cleanly on the other side. After picking my jaw up from the ground, I follow, copying her moves, but my whole leg-swinging operation is shambolic in comparison and I tumble clumsily down the other side.

She sprints up the drive with a giggle. 'I take it you've never been to pony club,' she shouts back.

I run after her. We're well beyond Fiona's estate when she eventually stops to put on her coat. 'Got everything?' I ask, trying not to sound out of breath.

'Yeah,' she says, feeling for her little bag. Then she slides her hand under my arm and links it, pulling herself in close to me. 'C'mon … you were going to tell me about you,' she says again.

'You feeling better?'

I see her jaw go that way it does on the other side of a pill. 'I'm definitely feeling better now,' she says.

'So what d'you wanna know?'

Her vast, dilated eyes light up. 'Everything!' she says.

Now I know she's hardly straight but she doesn't look sad any more and besides, this interest in me is heady stuff. I'm deliberating where to start my hopeless life story when it hits me that unlike everyone around here, Em doesn't know about college, or Da, or the whole bankruptcy thing. I could tell her anything. I could be anyone. But I say nothing. I just draw her in closer. Feeling her grip my arm like this might be the greatest feeling in the world. 'D'you want to walk back by the beach?'

'Just keep talking, I love listening to you.'

'Jaysus, you are off your nut! C'mon then,' I say, trying hard not to break into a skip as we weave through the lanes, huddled up together like we were born for it. We walk fast.

Suddenly she stops in the middle of the road and drops her bag. 'If you could be anything in the world, Liam Flynn, what would you be?'

I look at her standing by the derelict phone box in the moonlight, still sporting my dodgy ponytail, and I stand a foot taller realising she's remembered my whole name. 'Anything?'

She throws her arms out wide. 'Yes, anything!'

I think for a minute. 'Maybe a Guard. You know, a cop?' It's true; the nine-year-old in me would happily settle for it, but it's not only that; it feels like a respectable fallback, one that Da might accept.

Her extended arm drops. 'What?'

'You know, like yer man in the shelters last week. Ripping up the sand in an unmarked car mightn't be the worst way to spend –'

'Seriously?' She strides towards me, her face folded into a parcel of disappointment. 'A policeman? For real?'

From the look on her face you'd swear I'd said fish-gutter. 'Might not get the grades though. Five Ds at Ordinary level. Could be tight. I'm not even messing.'

Her head swivels back to me. 'OK, very funny, but I asked you if you could be *anything*. Come on,' she says before giving me a gentle shove. 'Dream, Liam. Dream!' she shouts.

She marches away again and I stare at her back, contemplating exactly what it is about her flyaway charge to dream that I find so outrageous. What exactly is making my chest feel tight and my heart beat faster? I think hard, but it's not about what to say, it's more finding the guts to dare say it at all. I look at her face with her crazy moonlit eyes and suddenly I'm opening my mouth. 'I'd like to write songs.' The newborn words tumble out, like they can't find their legs. I've never admitted this to anyone, not even Kenny.

I watch her spin around a streetlight a few times, with one arm outstretched again, like a child. 'Now, you've got it,' she says slowly, still spinning. Then she stops and turns to me, deadly serious. 'You're going to be an eminent songwriter one day.'

Eminent! God, she's a gas. I laugh. Maybe it's relief or maybe because it's funny. She's funny. This whole night is like something I'd never even dare to dream. 'You know this for a fact then, do you?'

'I know things,' she says, even more slowly. Her eyes locked on mine.

That she might believe, even for one tiny, twatted, pilled-up second, this could be possible feels feckin' deadly. I ask her the same question back.

'A writer,' she says, tipping an imaginary hat from her head. I've no idea why. 'OK, forget I said that.' She waves one hand in front of her face like she's rubbing out her words. 'I mean it's so … predictable,' she says, scrunching up her face, before curling herself back into the streetlight once more.

I keep staring as she does another whirl out from the pole, her face staring up at the stars. Then she joins me on the road and takes my arm again. She's on a roll now, jabbering away, describing her best friend who it turns out is this Kitty girl and she's raving on about some fancy party

138

she should be at with her in England tonight. She lets slip that she nearly took her first pill at the Glastonbury festival three weeks ago. I knew it! I'm about to have a go at her but then she seems upset, talking about some other friend who's been making her life miserable. She's full of chat now, about some school ball and a lake where they all hang out during the summer. I could listen to her forever. Her world sounds like *Skins*, but at Hogwarts, and all a million miles from here. I'm glad she's taken over the talking because whatever's coming out of her, I'm gripped.

'Not that any of it matters now I've ended up in this place.'

I have to hide what happens to my face as she says this. We cut through the car park and scrape along the hedgerows, our linked arms never coming undone. Finally we find ourselves standing on top of the huge sand dunes, staring out. From here, I have to catch my breath and I can feel her do it too.

'OK ... so this is kind of mind-blowing,' she says.

'What?'

'This!' She motions to the moonlit sea, stretched out before us like an explosion of possibility, glistening in the velvet night as far as our eyes can see.

My heart swells; I love that she loves this too. 'Guess it is.'

We drop on to the soft sand, marvelling in silence. We don't need to speak. I turn to look as her blonde hair blows gently around her face and those large, unnaturally dark eyes hook on to mine.

'Tell me more stuff,' she says. 'Go on.'

I wish I could fascinate her like she fascinates me. 'There are wallabies on that island,' I say after a while.

I hadn't planned to reveal this local factoid, it just came out. Maybe because she reminds me of one of them: an exotic creature washed up on the wrong shore.

She knocks me over playfully with her shoulder. 'Shut up!'

'I'm serious. Almost two hundred of them.' I'm pointing needlessly towards the great shadow of rock several miles out in the sea. 'It's true, although not many people around here even know.'

'You mean like kangaroos?'

'From the marsupial family, yes.' For some reason I adopt a woeful Australian accent as I say this.

'On that island?' she asks, indicating across the water and looking at me like I'm the one who's lost it.

'Yeah, on the island.'

She digs me with her elbow. 'I'm not *that* off my face!'

'I swear! They came from Dublin Zoo in the Eighties.'

'Er, why?'

'An uncontrollable baby boom! They go at it like rabbits, apparently.' As I say this, my cheeks start to burn.

She smiles and stares out to sea. 'Let's go and see them?'

I check her face but she doesn't flinch. I wonder whether she realises what she's said and then, without stopping to think, I just say it. 'I'll take you.'

She laughs. 'In a canoe?'

'No, we could take a trip. You know, if Rupert wouldn't mind?'

'Yes!' she squeals, ignoring the question part of what I said.

I don't know how to describe it, but something extraordinary is happening in the tips of all my nerve endings.

She fumbles in her little bag and takes out her phone. 'It's nearly two,' she announces.

I listen to the sounds of the sea in the dark, hoping for something: a sign, or anything to help me know what to do right now. What do I say, how do I stop her slipping away? 'D'you think you'll ever be allowed out again?' I'm terrified she's going to be locked up for the summer and my, as yet, unarticulated plan to spend as much time with her as is humanly possible is already foiled.

'She'll be asleep.'

'Grandma?'

'Yeah. I mean, she would have called, wouldn't she? If she was awake, she would have, right?'

'Er … ?'

I'm thinking about this pretty seriously, when she holds out her phone in front of us. 'Smile!' she says, placing her head softly against mine. The phone makes that digital shutter *click* sound. She stares at the picture, her thumb hovering over the filter options below it.

'Can't see much,' I say, examining our two barely recognisable faces, silhouetted together against the night.

'Watch this,' she says turning to me.

She hits a small square at the bottom of the screen and I watch our faces burst out of the dark. 'Hey, I like it now!'

'You do?' she asks and I nod. 'Hail filter, bringer of light!'

'I love it,' I say truthfully.

'I love it too.' She pulls her coat around her. 'You know I've got to go now.'

I lean my hand into the spiky grasses and push myself up. 'Here!' I reach out my hand to drag her up. 'I'll walk you back.'

'S'OK, I can see those shelters from here.'

'I'm not letting you walk home alone.'

'Watch me then. You can see Grandma's house from here.'

I'm about to object when she goes to kiss my cheek, but don't I move and make our faces crash. My lips hit up against hers, the wrong way, and for at least three unbearably long seconds I'm sure I've ruined everything. I pull back in panic but she quickly throws her arms around me and draws me to her. I'm just beginning to sense the warmth of her body through her coat when she pushes herself back and tears off down the dunes.

I can only stare as she disappears into the night once more.

It's like I'm standing in cement.

EMERALD

The last of these lies

Shards of sunlight pierce the badly drawn curtains, stinging my eyes. Utter *ughh!* I roll over to have a fresh wave of panic take hold and I try turning to the other side but there's no escaping the realisations flashing behind my eyes in quick succession. I've no choice but to face the me of last night in the realness of this brand new day. My head hurts. My jaw aches. Even my teeth are in pain. What the holy effing f★★k was I thinking?!?!?!

Liam? Liam! Liam, Liam, Liam, Liam, Liam. Suddenly I'm reliving the feel of his warm hand on my back and I physically retch a little, like I'm there, vomiting over that drain again. But why am I almost smiling now when I could as easily die of shame? He held my hair back. He tied it in a ponytail and held it back!

Something feels strange. I reach under the blankets and pull my phone out from underneath me, where I also find my headphones, which are somehow tangled up with the toes of my left foot. Then I remember: Grandma! Grandma? It takes my fogged brain several seconds to recall what even happened when I got in last night. Or more accurately, this morning. I get a flash of her bent over asleep in the living room and me creeping silently past the open door and upstairs to bed. Oh, good God, did I really leave her there, crumpled up in the armchair?

Felt like hours later when I finally got to sleep. I glance at the bedside table where the rusty old carriage clock reads 11:41. My tongue feels like my school jumper and my throat is cracked and dry. I need to check Grandma's OK. I need to know I haven't been caught. I need to see Liam. I need to thank him for not leaving my side. I need to convince him I'm not a total tragedy. I need a shower.

I try to sit up. Shit, I am dizzy.

The water is hot. In fact I'm probably burning, but the steam feels good. I grab a tube of some antique-looking shower gel and begin to wash my face. I scrub my neck, my chest, my stomach, my thighs, my arms, my legs, all over me, in an effort to scour away the embarrassment of it all. I let the water run over me as I play-back all my lines from last night. Lord knows there were plenty. *C'mon, Liam, dream!* Like what the actual f**k? Who says that? Who was that mouthy girl, prattling on endlessly? I hang under the water for ages, contemplating how I managed to say more to Liam in one night than I have to Rupert in the entire two years I've known him. Oh no … Rupert! Was I banging on about him too? I'm not sure I'll ever be done cringing, but the water is starting to get cold.

I fling back the shower curtain and grab a towel, which is damp and far too small. What is it with Grandma and her tiny towels? I dry my face and see two dark black patches on the towel from where I've rubbed my eyes. How can

144

there possibly be any mascara left? I stand in front of the mirror, rub away the steam and look at myself through the streaks – it's not good. The remainder of last night's make-up casts long grey shadows under my eyes. My lips are dry and my face looks fallen. I pick up the HD foundation I pinched from Mum and begin to smooth it across my freckly skin, but even that's not doing its usual magic. The fact is nothing can hide the feeling creeping up through me: that I'd never have taken that pill if I hadn't been so wasted. My eyes look funny but I can still see Mum in them, and that's the worst feeling of all. It's one thing to look like my mother, but I don't want to be a drunk like her too.

'Emerald?' Grandma's voice explodes into the silence and I automatically freeze. Panic thunders through me like a second heartbeat. I replay her voice in my head and decide it sounded normal so I allow myself to exhale cautiously. Maybe everything is OK. Why am I so jumpy?

'In the bathroom!' I say it with as much energy as I can but this takes it out of me and I have to sit back down on the loo. I'm convinced my guilt is obvious even behind the closed door.

'You all right, darling?' she asks gently.

What does this mean? What does she know? 'Fine. I'll be out in a minute,' I reply, as chirpily as I can before collapsing back down on the floor.

'Grand. I'll be downstairs. I'll get some sausages on.' I hear her voice fade off down the stairs.

I lean my head against the door. It's OK, I think. It's OK. I stand, wrap the towel around me and lean up against the

145

sink, glowering sternly at my reflection. I feel a soliloquy coming on.

'Emerald, what were you thinking? *Were* you even think-ing, letting your guard down like that?' But it felt so good to talk. And he held my hair back. 'STOP IT, EMERALD!'

Even from the top of the stairs I can tell it's a beautiful day. The tiny glimpse of sea from the landing window is the bluest blue and the hallway is bathed in sunlight that lifts everything, including the carpet dust. Stepping into the kitchen I take a deep breath, hoping to somehow inhale the optimism of it all, but I'm immediately hit by wafts of frying pork. I swallow a gag.

Grandma is hovering over by the window sill, moving the begonias. 'They don't like too much sun,' she says, like I actually need this detail.

'Sorry I slept so late.' I search around for my charger, try-ing not to look too frantic about it.

'Sure you probably needed the rest.'

I can't think of anything to say. Besides, it's taking all I have to stay upright. I wish my heart would stop pound-ing. I also suspect my face is letting me down so I decide to plonk myself by the kettle in the corner and hide.

'What did they pay you?' she asks, flitting lightly around the room.

I start filling the kettle. 'Forty euros.' I'm desperately try-ing to remember the exchange rate? I think I've got it the wrong way round, but she doesn't say anything. I turn around and watch her crack an egg into the pan one-handed.

She twists her upper body back to me. 'He was very good, wasn't he?' Her right hand holds the egg flipper, and

I watch tiny droplets of fat fall on to the shiny floor. It takes a minute for my blunted brain cells to realise she's talking about Leonardo Di Caprio, from that movie she was going on about last night.

'I finished my book.' The words stick in my throat. Her eyebrows raise as she takes this in and if it's possible I feel even worse. I can't look at her. I vow this is the last of the lies. My phone *ping*s back to life on the countertop and I lunge for it. Then, as I stare at the dark apple bursting from the bright white screen, my drunken 3 a.m. Google searches come flooding back to me. Please God say I didn't go on Insta. No, no, no, please, no! OK, account still disabled. Hallelujah. I hit Safari and I see my long history, trawling through every Liam Flynn in Dublin and not one of them him.

I'm reading a jolly text from Dad, asking how the baby-sitting went, when I realise Grandma is talking again. 'Oh yes,' she says. 'Someone called for you not long ago.'

I have to grip the countertop to keep myself upright. 'Yeah?'

'A young man from the Metro Service Station. Said his name was Liam.'

Here? He phoned here? I watch her laying strips of bacon into the hot fat, letting each one sizzle before lowering it slowly down into the pan. I pivot on my bare foot to hide my face from hers. 'Did he say anything else … you know, or … leave a message?' I ask, clearing some imaginary dirt from the sink.

' 'Twas about the babysitting ad, he said. He wanted to know whether you'd like it to go in the newsletter.'

I can feel my shoulders melt from around my ears and I allow myself a smile.

'I'll take a walk up there later,' I say, biting my cheeks inside my mouth to stop the ridiculous grin breaking out all over my face.

She looks up and out into the garden. 'Nice manners,' she says, almost to herself.

Right, last lie, I promise.

LIAM

Skinny latte, no sugar?

'Where d'you get to, Romeo?'

It's Kenny. He's standing in front of me, brandishing an open can of Red Bull and a packet of Tayto. If that wasn't bad enough, he's still sporting last night's clobber and there's a manky bang of drink off him too.

'Have you even been home?' I ask. I lean over the counter to get a good look at him in his full walk-of-shame glory.

'On my way now,' he says, practically skipping up and down between my neatly stacked baskets of freshly baked baguettes. He's grinning like a muppet. I know he's desperate for me to ask him, but I won't, not yet. 'What time were you in here this morning?' he says, fishing noisily into his crisps.

'Eleven.'

'How's the head?'

'Grand.' Then I start smiling. I try to hold it in, but I can't help it. We're grinning at each other like two happy kettles about to hop off the boil. The smug head on him; I can't bear to look. I spot one of Mam's friends by the till and I wave over.

'Ah, here, Flynn, you're killing me. What in the Jaysus happened?'

'What?'

His kettle's beginning to whistle. 'With yer one!'

'You mean Emerald?'

'Yeah, yeah. C'mon, man. Did ye? You know … ?'

'Did I what?' I ask, leering at him over the glass counter the way Mr Gallagher used to do to us over the desks in Geography.

He rolls his eyes in frustration. 'Did you –'

I can tell he's about to burst. 'Have *you* something you'd like to tell *me*, Kenny?'

He hustles in real close. I breathe through my mouth to avoid the ferocious whack of cheese and onion. He motions to me to lean in closer again and I do. I swear I'm faint from the fumes, but I hang in there.

'Unbelievable!' He mouths it, before looking around like some hammy spy in a film. 'UN-BE-FECKING-LEEVIBLE!' he goes again. Then he stands up all straight and gawks at me.

'Those were her words I take it?'

'I'm serious, man,' he says, taking a long slug from the can, clearly delighted with himself. 'Phenomenal is what it was!'

I hit him a playful thump on the shoulder. 'Good for you. Milestone moment and all that!' He rolls up one sleeve and I can tell he's about to start again. 'No more details though, yeah?' I say, holding my hand up. 'I get the picture.'

'Sound,' he says. 'I've got to run but I'll bell you later.'

I look up and he's off. I'm not sure if I even answer him because that second, literally that exact second, I see her by the bank of newspapers outside. I follow her as she passes the flower buckets and then, there she is, standing in the doorway, that same fallen angel, only wearier. I wave over but she doesn't see me and scans the shop, looking lost. I want to run out there, but I'm cool. Finally she clocks me and shuffles over. Her chin is dipped, tucked apologetically into a scarf that's looped around her neck. I focus on the tiny stars dotted all over it, unsure where else to look.

'Nice!' she says, pointing to the top of my head.

I fix the stupid-looking hat. 'How you doing, madser?' I'm incapable of not smiling wildly at her.

'There are no words for what I feel right now,' she says, dragging one of the tall stools towards her and slumping elegantly into it. She rests her head in her hands and her long hair spills on to the countertop. I discreetly move the sugar and the container of plastic stirrers.

'Scarlet!' I whisper it in her ear. Her head smells like clean washing, which is a welcome let-up after Kenny.

'Sorry?' she says, peeking up at me through her laced fingers.

'That's what we'd say … as in, I'm scarlet!' She looks at me. Not getting it at all. 'Ah, I'm just messing with you. You're alive anyway, I see.' I turn to pour more beans into the grinder. 'Coffee?'

She nods. 'I left Grandma asleep in her armchair!' Her voice is even more raspy than usual.

'Just now?'

'At half two this morning!'

151

My coffee-holding wrist falls limp. 'You what?'

'Don't!' she says, closing her eyes. 'I've already bathed in self-loathing this morning.'

'And she seemed so nice –'

She shivers and then makes this noise: a bit like a getting sick sound.

'Was it all right that I –'

'Phoned my grandma's house? Yeah. Wouldn't make a habit of it though.'

'Hadn't planned on it.' It bursts out of me defensively, like an emotional airbag.

'Sorry, it's just … we haven't been here for a long time. Grandma's afraid to put a foot wrong with me in case it's another five years before we're back.' She's rolling up a packet of sugar, not looking at me. 'I'm pretty sure boys constitute a wrong foot. I think she liked you though.'

I move over to the coffee machine so she doesn't see me beaming to myself. 'Let me guess … skinny latte, no sugar?'

She sighs. 'I'm not that predictable?'

I shrug back, confused.

'Flat white, extra hot,' she says, like she's given this request countless times. 'Can I have it to take away?'

'You'll find we only do paper cups in this fine establishment,' I say, hoping I've done a good job of hiding my disappointment, but then I can't help it; it just comes out. 'You've to leave already?'

She jumps down off the stool. 'Yeah. I just wanted to drop by and …' She flicks her hair from her eyes. 'You know … say thanks.'

I've got that happy-kettle grin thing going on again, but I don't care. 'Thanks for what?' I ask. I'm pushing my luck.

She looks right at me and I can see she's doing everything she can not to smile. 'For the coffee of course.' But then, like she can't hold it in, her teeth bite down on her lip and she smiles her beautiful crooked smile. I'm weak.

She lifts the cup to her mouth, stops before taking a sip, but as she goes to speak, Whiskers, the aul fella with the eyebrows, appears from behind the magazines. He approaches us and leans in, gently placing his elbow on the countertop. He looks to Emerald, studying her for a moment before greeting me with a slow, deep nod.

My eyes flick between the two of them and I'm struggling to hide my frustration with his untimely interruption. I decide to serve him, if only to get him gone. I lean into him like an impatient barman from Moloney's and bark, 'Cappuccino, four sugars, no dust, and a tea?'

One of his majestic white brows scrunches up the top of his lined face and he winks at me. 'Good man,' he says, but as he's talking I'm sensing Em pull back from her stool and I'm panicking she's going to leave. Before I know it I've already slid down the length of the countertop towards her.

'Could we maybe … do that again?'

She takes a plastic lid from the pile and carefully fixes it on top of her cup. 'I'd like that.'

I feel Whiskers watching us but I don't even care. 'I'm off Thursday night?'

She takes a slow sip and there's a long pause. 'I think I'm free.'

'Same place? You know, the kiosk by the beach where you didn't show up last night?' She smiles and shrugs a yes so I lean over and whisper, 'Shall I have the paramedics on standby?'

'Oh, that's kind!' she says, pushing me away. Then she turns towards the door. I'm waving at her back when suddenly she spins on her heel and raises her cup. 'It's delicious by the way.'

I watch her leave. Whiskers is watching her too, both of us, what's the word … mesmerised?

EMERALD

I'm good with complicated

When I got back from the Metro, I decided to tell Grandma all about Liam. I was bursting to tell *someone* and I was too cross with Kitty to tell her anything. Besides, I knew it would mean nothing to her. Grandma was doing the crossword when I walked in. I watched her in silence, before announcing that I'd made a friend.

'What's her name?' she asked immediately.

Her assumption caught me off guard and when I opened my mouth Fiona's name fell out.

'And her surname?'

I didn't know.

'Where does she live?'

I knew this of course but that would be weird, so I just shrugged. 'We … just met, up at the service station. At the notice board. She teaches piano, you know … part-time.' Oh God, more lies.

'Oh, right,' she said, tapping her pen against the paper like she was thinking of the answer to a difficult clue. 'She's also sixteen, you say?'

'I didn't. She's just finished her exams. More like seventeen, I think.'

'Was she up in St Joseph's?'

I swear it was like she was running through a checklist. 'Is that a school?' I asked, even though I knew it was. We've passed it on the road lots of times; you can't miss it.

'D'you know anything … about her parents?'

I laughed out loud at this. 'No, Grandma, I don't! She just asked if I wanted to hang out with some of her friends on Thursday night.'

She put down the pen and lifted the glasses from her nose. Finally her face softened. 'You'll tell your dad all of this, won't you?'

About this fantasy friend! 'Yes!' I said, unable not to roll my eyes. Not even Dad is this bad. It's like she really believes I'm still eleven.

Every day since Sunday I intended to tell Dad about '*Fiona and her friends*' but there was never room in our texts, and somehow it's already Thursday. I glance at the grandfather clock in the hall: it's 7:58 p.m. 'See you later,' I say, poking my head around the living room door.

The gardening show Grandma likes is on TV. She's in the zone. This is good. 'Oh … bye, love. And you'll be home before eleven?'

'Yes!' I say, jokingly shaking my head. I walk further into the room and kiss her on the forehead. This affectionate gesture takes us both by surprise.

She smiles up at me. 'Have a nice time,' she calls out to the closing door.

As I step out on to the drive, the warm evening air wraps itself around me. I'm taking my shirt off, knotting it at my waist when I realise I haven't even changed my clothes. I'm still wearing the leggings and T-shirt I've been wearing all day. I reach into my bag and feel for my lip gloss. I just like to know it's there.

A gentle wind carries the scent of Grandma's gorgeous roses from the other side of the garden. An intense rush rinses through me, like excitement only with a vague queasiness. I'm halfway down the drive when I stop to marvel at one of the heavy yellow roses. These were Mum's favourites. Dipping my nose into its soft, velvet petals, I close my eyes. I breathe in slowly and my head fills with a memory, sudden and vivid.

She sings quietly beside me. We're sat side by side and I'm looking up, swinging my tiny legs underneath the dressing table, watching as she puts her make-up on. Music's playing and I make out the sound of ice clinking loose in a glass. I'm staring as her long, blonde lashes become darker with each stroke of her magic mascara wand. She takes the glass to her lips, smiling at me as she slowly comes alive. I play eeny, meeny, miny, moe *with the perfume bottles clustered on her antique table, rearranging them like chess pieces, opening the lids and inhaling their scents of tuberose, fig and jasmine …*

My head goes heavy. I bury my face deeper into the flower like I'm trying to hide there in the smooth folds of Mum's skirt. I inhale again urgently. *'Mum?'*

The scent is dizzying and sweet, but it was only a glimpse. She's left with the breeze.

A tiny stab of pain shoots through my fingers where I've gripped the yellow rose too tight. A trickle of crimson runs into the large outer petals. I suck my punctured thumb as the remains of the stained flower scatter on the drive behind me and all I'm left with is a sudden chill. I put my shirt back on, berating myself. I can't let myself be seduced by these memories, not when I know there are others, lurking just below, which could as easily tear me apart.

I reach the gate and turn right on to the pavement. The sun is still strong over the water. As soon as I cross the main road I can see someone leaning against the kiosk in the distance. I know it's him; I can tell by the languid stance and the swell of dark-brown hair, swirling proud of his forehead like a Walnut Whip. I walk towards him, head down.

'Punctual this time, I'll give you that,' he says, reaching into his backpack without taking his eyes off me. He hands me a container and takes one out for himself.

'What's this?'

'A flask.'

I examine the One Direction sticker stuck to the front of it. 'You don't say.'

He laughs and jumps over the low wall before setting off towards the water. 'C'mon,' he says, beckoning me down the grassy hill.

'What are we doing?' But he takes my hand and I try to hide my surprise as I place mine in his and we hike down the steep slope together. There's hardly a ripple on the shimmering sea before us. He brushes his thumb against my palm as we amble over the grassy mounds. His skin feels rough but his grip is reassuring and strong.

The shelters are empty, apart from a few empty beers cans. 'There's never anyone here this early,' he says, like a mind reader.

We sit down at the nearest edge of the bench. Despite the warm evening, it feels cold down here in the shelters. Perhaps dank is the word. In fact, it's hard to imagine a more desolate place to spend a summer's evening than this concrete tunnel and I wonder why something so bleak was built somewhere so beautiful. Even on a dry night like tonight there are unnatural puddles on its uneven floor. Shards of bruised purple and silvery grey sparkle out from its slate coloured wall.

I reach over to look at his flask and see his also has a sticker. I nudge him. 'Which one was your favourite?'

He elbows me back. 'They're Laura's, my sister,' he says, leaning into the wall and setting his backpack between his legs. 'She was mad about that Niall fella. She's gone off him though – far too cool for all that now. But once you put those yokes in the dishwasher, that's it, stuck for life,' he says. 'That's real commitment for you.'

'So I see!' I say, picking at the shiny worn sticker with my nail.

He peers over and twists my flask around to have a look. 'Yeah, look, there he is!'

He smiles and I smile back at him, for a bunch of reasons really, one of which is that he's beautiful. Not upfront hot, but like that guy in a band (some band much cooler than 1D), who you don't notice at first, because you're trained to be distracted by the Harry Styles type frontman. As I look closely at Liam's cheekbones and chalky complexion, I realise he's definitely the cute one – a drummer maybe?

I hold up the flask. 'Gonna tell me what this is?'

'Open it!' he says, twisting the cap off his.

The air fills with the rich, unmistakeable smell of cocoa and without taking anything to my lips I drink in all the easy, unfolding loveliness of Liam Flynn. As if he can feel me watching, his nose twitches and with one long swipe he wipes at the rim of the flask with his sleeve before taking a drink. I slowly unscrew the cap off mine and hold my face over it, gratefully drawing in its warmth. 'That smell ...' I say, closing my eyes.

'Mam was making some earlier. Made me think of you.'

I'm pouring the steaming liquid into the lid just like I watched him do, but I stop before it's full. 'Hang on. You're saying I smell like ... hot chocolate?'

He leans over. 'C'mere, let me check,' he says, sniffing at my neck.

Suddenly I know what it is. 'Oh God, it's Grandma's cocoa butter cream.'

'That's it! You smell like an old lady. Hard to resist.' He laughs. 'Cheers.'

We *chink* our warm cups and I take a sip. Feeling the delicious, sugary heat slip down my throat, I quickly take another. '*Mmm* ... D'you know, I see a bright future for you in hot beverages.'

Liam's smile falls. 'It's no worse than my current plan.'

'Aren't you going to work for your dad's company?' I rest my cup on my thigh, but taking in his new, tight expression, I squirm. Something passes through him and I suddenly remember all the awkwardness the last time we talked about this. 'I got that totally wrong, didn't I?'

He sighs. 'My da doesn't have a company any more. I mean he works, obviously, but …' He places the flask down on the bench and stares out at the waves. 'Nothing's like how it used to be.'

Liam speaks fast. I need to concentrate when he talks. His accent is so much thicker than Dad's and it takes a second for the syntax to rearrange itself inside my head. I have to watch his mouth to check that the shape matches the words I'm hearing, but my eyes won't play along and they keep flitting back up to his eyes, which are open and easier to read. He's uncomfortable now, pressing his tongue into his cheek. 'Sorry,' he says, shaking his head. 'I shouldn't have got weird about it at Fiona's. It's just … complicated.'

'Hey, I'm good with complicated. Remember?'

'Actually, it's not even complicated. It's just shit,' he says. 'Dad had to go bankrupt. He was badly exposed. In it up to his neck, he says, but how do you legislate for a ruthless prick who screws you over, smiling at you all the while. Now, it's like the rest of the world's back on its feet, but Da can't seem to get up. What's worse is that I don't think he even wants to.'

'I'm sorry,' I say, inching my hand across his leg.

'S'OK. It was over three years ago now. Only problem is he expects me to go into the same business. Not start up the old company, but more than anything in the world he wants me to do this building site management course 'cause he thinks that'll fix it. If I succeed then all his and Grandda's work won't have been for nothing.'

'That's not exactly fair.'

161

'It's the way it is.'

I want to make him feel better. 'If it helps, I don't really remember you getting weird.' He turns his shoulders and raises one of his eyebrows. 'I mean, a few parts of the evening could do with some … unravelling.' I'm no longer sure what to do with my hands.

He dusts down his thighs. 'But you had a good time?' he asks, flicking his gaze back to mine.

I wish he didn't ask like this. It implies he doesn't know, or worse, that I don't know, which is of course somewhat true, but it's a dreadful thing to admit. 'I think so.' I know I enjoyed the walk home, but the party is a blur with only bursts of unbearable clarity. I sit on my hands now, trying to think of something to say. 'People were nice. There was no backstory required. That was kind of cool, you know?'

His face twists.

'Like, no one asked where you go to school, or who you know, that sort of thing,' I say. 'It was just like, hi, I'm Em.'

'Well, they wouldn't ask you.' He says 'you' in a way I don't think I like. 'You're English. It's a catch-all; it covers everything.'

I realise he's smiling and I swing my leg like a pendulum against his shoe. 'Hey, can I ask you something?'

'Sure,' he says, wrestling his jumper over his head and for a second he's lost in a storm of grey cotton. His T-shirt rides up his chest and I try not to look at his bare stomach, but I do. His skin is pale and creamy, a long way from the covers of those *Men's Health* magazines I saw in Rupert's bedroom. I never remember wanting to reach out and touch those, the way I want to do to Liam now. I quickly lose all grip of my thoughts and for only the second time in ten minutes I feel myself blush.

'Go on,' he says, pulling the soft folds of his T-shirt back down to his waist. I turn towards him, but can't meet his eye in case he'll read the longing in mine. 'Weren't you going to ask me something?' He whispers it.

'Oh, um. I was wondering, did I bring up Rupert? You know, the other night?'

His knee starts to bounce up rhythmically from the stone bench. 'You may have mentioned him.'

'I was afraid of that.'

'Don't be,' he says, but he's not looking at me.

'I'm totally OK with it, just to say.'

'With what?'

'With him going off with my friend. Just in case I may have indicated differently.'

'D'you wanna talk about it?' he says, flashing his face back to mine.

'Not really. She's a cow and he's a bit of a shit.' Did I just say this out loud? I look at Liam's face, registering these words in silence. I'm marvelling at how clear that whole situation suddenly looks, from this distance, when I see that Liam's smiling.

'Listen, don't hold back on my account.'

'She sent me a photo of them kissing. When I say to *me*, I mean to our entire WhatsApp group. Did I tell you that?'

He smirks. 'I believe you mentioned this also.'

Ick! I can only imagine how much I prattled on about an ex who was never even mine. The bench suddenly feels

163

too hard. He takes another drink and leans his body into mine. I feel the tightness in my shoulders dissolving as he gets closer.

'I'm OK with it too,' he says, pulling away from me.

Missing the feel of him against me, I sit up. 'With what?'

'With you being OK with it. I especially like the part about him being a shit. I'm particularly OK with that bit,' he says, grinning.

Watching his lips move I wonder how his mouth would feel against mine. I almost lose myself in this thought, but I'm compelled to keep talking.

'I thought everything was supposed to look more perfect from a distance and only up close do we see the cracks, but I'm beginning to think it's the opposite. Looking back on it now, I was on edge the whole time with Ru. I could never relax when he was around. But I can't blame him, it was me. Everything back home has been so draining lately. It was all such hard work.'

He doesn't answer and for a moment we both stare ahead. I watch a dog race along the shoreline in the distance but inside I'm madly processing how I let all this truth slip out so easily.

He smiles back. 'Equations should … balance themselves.' I stare at him, trying to figure out what he's on about. 'They should stack up. Like, you get back what you give in.' He takes a drink. 'But it sounds like you've got a dodgy X or a Y in that formula of yours.'

I'm losing myself in the pools of his pale eyes, concentrating on his words when, for the second time this evening, he takes my hand but he just lifts it to his lips.

He sort of holds it there, gently, for a moment and it's the loveliest thing. The back of his hand moves slowly down the length of my cheek and my heart rushes so violently I have to grip the concrete bench between my fingers until it passes. I look at him and realise for the first time in days, maybe even weeks, I am happy.

'Well, howrya, Flynn!' The shout comes from the bottom of the beach steps. I make out three figures way beyond the shelters, the far-off *clink* of their bottles ringing as they walk.

It's Kenny and two other guys I recognise from Fiona's house. 'All right, Emerald!' Kenny again, introducing unnecessary syllables to my name as only he sees fit. I feel Liam's fingers slip away and he slowly releases my hand. It's difficult not to read rejection in this tiny movement and my heart drops. Patches of Saturday night flare like flames in the blackness: my dancing, stuff I said to those girls, stumbling through the crowd to ask that awful guy for cigarettes. I don't know what they saw or what they heard. I hardly know half of what I said and right now, despite all the loveliness of earlier, I want to crawl into one of the dark puddles on the ground. I get up and hand the flask back to Liam. 'I better go.'

His smile fades. 'Already?'

I try to think of a clever excuse but my brain's not cooperating and I stand there nodding. The sound of their jingling bags and footsteps gets closer.

It's like Liam reads my panic. 'Saturday night. Dinner?' he says. There's a mischievous look in his eye. He hasn't acknowledged the others and they're almost upon us. 'I

165

won't let this go until you say yes,' he says, tugging at my shirt sleeve. 'C'mon.'

'Yes. OK, yes,' I say, desperate to leave, but also desperate not to.

'Same place?' he leans in and whispers.

'Our wall?' Oh God, why did I just say it like that? 'By the stripy kiosk, I mean.'

'I like that. Our wall it is,' he says, smiling.

I nod and turn away, the tips of my fingers still tingling where his just touched them.

LIAM

One-at-a-time kinds of eyes

I was feeling pretty good about tonight until I saw her.

'Seriously!' she roars, trying to lift my backpack from beside my feet.

She's wearing some class of a shirt-dress and a pair of sandals with jewels on them. She looks stunning, but my Saturday night dinner invitation clearly got lost in translation. Thinking about it now, who'd blame her? I feel like I've dragged her here under false pretences and the night is about to nosedive.

She winches the bag on to her shoulder. 'What's *in* here?'

'Supplies.' I can't bring myself to call it dinner now.

She stares at me and I can see the synapses in her brain fusing. There's an uncomfortably long pause and then she leans forward, her eyes impossibly wide. 'Are we … having a picnic?'

The way she says picnic confirms I've made a bad call. 'I just thought –'

'Brilliant!' she says, cutting in before I can finish. Next thing I know, she pumps her fist against mine.

'You're not disappointed?'

Taking her fancy shoes off, she turns around and gives me this look that's hard to describe, but I feel better. 'C'mon,' she says. 'You gonna show me where we're going?'

'Here, gimme the bag.' I reach for it, but she ducks and weaves past me, hunching the bag further up her back and stomping off along the beach.

Eventually we reach a deserted spot, high up on the dunes about a mile beyond the golf course. She spins in a circle and collapses on to the sand, bag still on her back like a turtle's shell. 'This is perfect!' she says.

It is perfect: a bunker of velvety sand, scooped into the top of a tall dune, with the sinking sun melting into the navy sea behind. The long grass shields us from the wind that's been blowing our hair into knots. It's calm and protected; our very own tower with views from Howth almost as far as Portrane. I take the bag from her back and start unpacking.

She leans in, fishing Mam's woolly rug out of the bag. 'Here, sit up a second,' she says, nudging me as she lays the stripy green blanket beneath us. Slowly smoothing out a corner, she looks up. 'This feels warm. Like hot?'

'That'd be the chicken.' She's eyeing me now like I might have been dropped from the pram. 'There's a new rotisserie machine at work now. Lorcan, my boss, is beside himself!'

She shakes her head, but in a nice way. 'What else have you got in there?' she asks, peering inside.

I pull the bag away. 'Let's have a drink first.' I fish out a miniature bottle of white wine and hand it to her before taking another one out for myself. She cracks the lid and quickly lifts the bottle to her lips. 'Hold up!' I say, lowering her hand back down.

I pop the red and white striped straw I pinched from the Slush Puppie machine into her bottle. She sucks up a long drink before biting down on the straw. 'Why, that's the finest, warm –' she turns the bottle in her hand and examines the label – 'Chenin Blanc I've ever tasted.'

'You're welcome.' I pop a straw in my own and watch it bob about for a bit before taking a sip. 'It's the *only* Chenin Blanc I've ever tasted. Would ya like to hear our special tonight?'

She leans back on her elbows. 'Go on.'

'Bird à la baguette,' I say, sliding the bread from its wrapper and brandishing the two halves; it was a necessary move what with the size of the backpack.

'Ooh la la!'

Jaysus, I feel like a plank. Her eyes are on me the whole time as I tear off sections of the baguette and hack at the chicken with a little plastic knife that isn't up to the gig. I should have brought some butter.

She reaches over for the packet of Kettle chips but doesn't open them. Then she lifts up one of the sandwiches I've made, takes a bite and chews delicately. 'D'you really want to be a musician?' she asks, out of nowhere.

'What?'

'The other night, you said if you could be anything, you'd be a songwriter.'

'You weren't supposed to remember that.'

'Well, I did,' she says, trawling a net of Babybels out of the bag before rummaging further and lifting out fistfuls of kindling. 'Er, wait a minute!' She drops the cheese. 'No wonder the bag was so heavy!'

I shift my arse to reveal the hunks of firewood I'd removed from the bag then I start to assemble them in a stack.

'Wow!' she says, taking her phone from her pocket. 'A real-life boy scout!'

I chuck a Babybel at her. 'Shut up!' I begin flicking the lighter in my hand but it takes loads of goes before I get it to flame. Her phone shutter clicks behind me. I spin around. 'Oi, don't post that online or anything.'

I was only messing but she looks serious all of a sudden and drops the phone into her lap. 'I won't,' she says. 'I just wanted a photo of you.'

I stop what I'm doing but I can't look up. It was such a simple, honest thing to say, it takes a minute for it to sink in. I get back to poking the fire, not wanting to embarrass her. Anyway, I want to smile, privately.

She recovers quickly. 'So d'you sing?' she asks.

I roll up the bread wrapper and stick it into the flames. 'Only to myself.'

'Oh, come on.'

'What?'

'I'd love to hear you.'

'We've nowhere near enough of this …' I twist the bottle around in the sand to read the label again. 'Anyway, what about you?'

'Do *I* sing?'

'I meant write, but hey, sing for me if you like.' I'm beaming at her, but it's all nerves. The notion of letting my voice out so close to her ears is intoxicating. I can't think of anything as terrifying as letting her know how much I feel for her now. Every vein in my body is hopping around giddy.

'I've never written anything … significant,' she sighs. 'I mean, I'll spend hours on the perfectly crafted Insta comeback, but no stories or anything clever like that. Embarrassing for a wannabe writer, right?' We both laugh. 'I guess it's just a dream for now, but maybe I'll follow it some day.' She looks up. 'You should follow yours too, you know.' She hands me her phone. 'Here, check this out.' It's the photo of me on my knees beside the tiny fire, the pink evening clouds behind my head and the last remnants of sun sinking underneath the grassy dune.

'*Mmm* … not bad,' I say almost coolly. Of course what I really want to say is, '*Wow, that's an amazing photo and I'm thrilled to bits that you took it.*'

'You were right, you know,' she says. 'Usually I would upload it, but I'm having a break from all that stuff.'

I lean over to add a little more kindling. 'What stuff?'

'Insta, Snapchat … I'm in the dying gasps of WhatsApp but even those seem to be fizzling out. Online me is missing, presumed dead. Not that anyone has noticed.' She looks down after she says this and sifts the sand through her open fingers.

She looks so earnest I can't help laughing. 'I don't do social media anyway.' For a minute she stares, like she's working out whether she heard me right. I turn around.

'At all, ever?'

'Never bothered with it.'

I shake my head and her expression changes. 'That's like saying you don't do the internet. In fact, that's kind of preposterous, Liam,' she says, like I've wronged her somehow.

'I do "do" the internet.'

'So you google stuff. Wow.'

'No, smart-arse. I'm always on YouTube and that, *and* I have SoundCloud, you know, for my music. Just not all that social stuff.'

She shoots me a look and then throws the end of her baguette towards a seagull, impressively far ahead. 'That's almost as pretentious as wanting to be a writer.'

'OK then, so if Instagram or whatever enhanced your life so much, why d'you come off it?'

She goes to say something and then stops. 'I'm having a break, that's all.'

'Whatever! Laura, my sister –'

'The Niall fan?'

We both roll our eyes. 'She's on Snapchat all day long, like it's an oxygen tank she carts around. All her mates, slating each other, like proper bitch-offs, and man, the selfies! She compares herself to her friends' pictures the whole time. I mean she'll put her phone down and I swear she's actually depressed. I've told Mam she should ban her, but I guess you can't do that.'

Em sucks up the last of her wine. Her face looks like it's thinking as she spins on to her front, propping herself up on her elbows. 'SoundCloud?'

'Forget it.'

'Not a chance,' she says, flinging another Babybel into my chest before standing up. 'You can't hide on the internet, Liam Flynn,' she says, punching at her phone.

'You won't find me.'

Her hand drops to her side. 'C'mon! You put your songs on SoundCloud to be heard. That's the general idea, right?'

'Not by people I know. That's what the alias is for. Anyway, it's all …'

'Yeah?'

'Ah, it's just sad, heartfelt stuff. Only covers anyway. For now.'

'What sort of covers?'

'Songs with a story.'

She leans over on to her right side now, propped up on her elbow. 'For real?'

'Low-life poets, I'm a sucker for those.' I can tell she's biting her cheeks, like she doesn't want to laugh. I finish my remaining crust and flick bits of chicken grizzle into the fire before lying back down. I wish I'd brought more wine.

We're side by side again and I take in her whole face. It's a face that improves the more you look at it, if that's even possible. When she looks up my eyes land on hers. I can tell this unnerves her, but she just flicks tiny grains of sand at my chest.

The sun has long gone and the light has faded. I can't trust all that I'm thinking not to spill out on to the rug between us. She smiles without opening her lips, but she doesn't look away and we lie there, looking into each other's eyes. Hers are dark now, like they've soaked up the night. I look from her left to her right and back again, but it's her right that I settle on. It's too much to take in both; they're one-at-a-time kinds of eyes.

Then she bites her bottom lip and that's it. I close my heavy lids, steal a breath and lean in.

EMERALD
Wham, wallop, kapow!

It's been fifty-nine hours and I'm still smiling inside. This is the third morning in a row I've woken up like this, quietly happy. It's an entirely new experience and I want to lie here and think about Liam before any bad thoughts have a chance to enter my head. It wasn't only the physical feeling of his soft, warm lips on mine, but the way it made me feel inside. Whenever I'm alone, I close my eyes and relive the touch of his hand, pressed into my back and I retrace in my mind the delicate dent at the side of his bum and how it felt through his cold jeans as I ran my hands along his side. Even the hard skin on the heel of his hands and the fine line of dirt underneath his index fingernail are precious, important details. I've memorised the feeling of our fingertips touching as we walked home, hand in hand, along the sand. And how, as we said goodbye outside Grandma's, those rough fingers found my face and held it up under the street light like a prize.

So far, I've found one hundred and forty-three Liams from Dublin on SoundCloud and none of them are him. I've now set myself a wider, more forensic task, given this whole alias thing, but it'll have to wait – I'm meeting him in an hour. He hasn't told me where we're going. All he said was he's lending me his sister's bike to get there.

Does this even happen? From my experience with Ru, I'd assumed you had to fancy a boy from afar for ages, break down every single one of his physical attributes, psychoanalyse the four words he's ever grunted at you, try desperately to get him to follow you and then endure some torturous DM rigmarole back and forth for weeks, only to inevitably discover that, surprise surprise, he prefers your better-looking friend.

The phone rings downstairs. I think about getting up to answer it but it stops and my brain slides happily back to Liam. I've just worked out he's only the sixth boy that I've kissed – like properly kissed. Hardly a difficult calculation, I know, but our kiss was totally and completely different to the ones with Rupert, or Kitty's cousin, Tom, or that humourless French guy in Val d'Isère last Christmas. I'm not sure the relentless slobbery pecks that feely-Felix-from-the-village and I shared as twelve-year-olds even count. I've decided to edit those from my burgeoning sexual history, thank you.

No, this felt like my first real kiss. I knew how to do it. Every nerve ending fired into life, but still there was no panic. It was easy. It was like we fitted. I keep thinking there must be something wrong. Surely I must have something to feel bad about? It can't be this easy. He can't really just like me. It's the strangest thing.

I've spent my whole life saying what I think people want me to say, hoping that if I just try harder, one day I'll do, or say, or find the right thing to stop Mum getting drunk, to stop Bryony being a bitch, or whatever. I worried I'd forgotten how to say what I actually think, but talking with Liam on the dunes last Saturday night it hit me like – *wham, wallop, kapow!* I want to tell him stuff. He makes me want to say the kind of thing I usually only admit in my head. It doesn't matter how hard I try to lie or say something I don't believe when I'm with him, because it's like he sees inside my brain. I'm convinced of that now. There's no point in covering stuff up. Besides, with him, I don't even want to.

Grandma is standing by my bedroom door. I'm not sure how long she's been there. I rub my eyes and try to look like I haven't been lying here for almost an hour. 'Morning!'

'Can I come in, love?'

I'm probably still grinning, but I don't care. 'Of course.'

'That was the hospital,' she says.

My smile falls away. 'Is she OK?'

'Not your mum, love. Twas only Beaumont, about my appointment.'

I sit up and swing my legs out the bed. 'What's wrong?' I ask, reaching for her hand.

'It's a routine check, pet. They're doing a scope. Nothing at all to worry about but I wanted to let you know as I'll have to stay in overnight next Friday, while they run a few tests.'

I exhale a little. 'Oh.'

'Will you be all right? It'll be less than twenty-four hours, they said. I'll let your dad know.'

'Grandma! I'll be fine. But you, are you OK?'

'I'm grand. Like I said, it's routine. I hate leaving you here alone, that's all.' She's up again, walking back across the room.

'Just routine?'

'That's all,' she calls back from the doorway. 'I'll pop down and put the kettle on.'

I snatch my phone from the bedside table and dial Dad. It goes straight to voicemail. 'Hey, it's me. Call me back, please.'

We cycled north along the coast road and then followed the estuary for miles and miles until we arrived here in this tiny, remote village, a world away from the bustle of Portstrand. Liam signals and I follow him up a steep single-track lane.

'Where are you taking me?' I shout up at him.

He steers left into a gravel drive. 'We're here!' he says, freewheeling over to a couple of cars parked on the hill. I follow him, staring at the back of his neck, which is now sunburnt between his hairline and the top of his T-shirt. I have an urge to place something cool against it. He hops off the bike and reaches for mine and props them against a wooden fence.

I look around, catching my breath. 'OK, still no idea.'

He nods to a break in the bushes. 'This way,' he says, moving in front and pulling back the branches so I can pass through. And then I see it: acres of rolling green countryside. The village we just passed is nestled into the hills behind and the church steeple towers in the distance. It's beyond beautiful. Looking around, I notice that the sloping hills are covered in row after row of perfectly spaced bushes.

'C'mon,' he says, heading towards a tiny, white, single-storey house. A hand-painted sign above the door reads *Kelly's Berry Farm*.

'We came in the back. I wanted you to see it from the hill.' He smiles and takes my hand. 'Wait till you taste the strawberries – they're around here.'

'I prefer raspberries.'

'You're for turning, you'll see.'

We walk into the sparse little shop. With its bare walls and concrete floor it feels deliciously cool. A portly woman in a flowery apron sticks labels on to large punnets loaded with perfectly ripe berries.

'Scorchin' out there today,' the lady says, without looking up.

I'm watching her methodically peel and stick each label when my pocket starts to vibrate. I glance over at Liam, gesturing towards my phone as I reverse out into the warm sunshine. Leaning against a fence, I close my eyes from the strong sun. 'Dad!' I say, sliding down it to the dusty ground beneath me.

'Hey, what's up?'

'Did you know Grandma's going in to hospital for tests?'

'Yes. It's nothing to worry about,' he says calmly. 'Should have told you. I've been so up against it, it completely slipped my mind.'

I stretch my legs out in front. 'Oh, OK, cool. Actually, Dad, can you talk?'

'Uh huh.'

'It's just … she doesn't seem herself sometimes. I mean, her old self. D'you know?'

'In what way?'

'It's like she's nervous around me, like she's afraid –'

'C'mon!' He sounds almost cross, as if I've said something crazy.

'I'm serious, Dad! I've been meaning to tell you stuff, like the night I first arrived she was saying things, mad things …'

'Darling, she's seventy-six!'

'But this other time, after she baked me this banana loaf …' I stop here. I can't hear his breathing and I wonder if he's still listening and whether I should go on. I hold the phone away from my ear and check whether I've hit mute.

'Yes?' he says suddenly. I sense irritation and picture him checking his watch.

'Also, she treats me like a child. Could you, you know … talk to her? I honestly think it's because she's afraid. You know, that we won't come back. I've been thinking about all those Christmases –'

'OK, honey, that's enough!' He sighs. 'She's been having digestive issues. That's all.' I can hear him say something to someone who's walked into his office. 'There's nothing to worry about.'

'But –'

'I promise, Em. It's all fine. I'm going to call her now.' Neither of us says anything for a minute. 'How are you getting on anyway?' he asks, but not in such a way that he wants an answer, at least not a long one. I don't let this stop me; I'm dying to tell him.

'Good, actually. I've made a friend, well, more of a –'

'That's great, sweetheart,' he cuts in. 'Listen, I've got to go now but you can tell me all about her soon.'

Her? *Aghh*, it's maddening how he does this. 'Sure.' I harrumph through gritted teeth.

'Love you, Scout.'

'Yeah. Love you too, Dad.'

I hang up and blink into the bright sunshine. Liam is standing before me holding an empty punnet. It takes a second for my kaleidoscope eyes to focus. He holds out his hand. 'Your da?'

I grab it and pull myself up. 'I was about to tell him about you.' I dust off my jeans a little too roughly. 'But he had to go.'

He slinks his arm around my neck and we set off amongst the strawberry beds. 'Probably just as well,' he says with a smile and together we take in the lines of the luscious green all around us.

We've been picking for twenty minutes now, competing with each other to select the plumpest, most succulent-looking strawberries. Liam is straddling the rows with quick-fire picks; I've gone for the hunched over, on the knee rummage, which I think is giving me the edge. He still hasn't let us eat any, which in this heat is beginning to feel torturous. Our punnet is almost full. 'OK, nearly there,' he says eventually.

I dip my hand in. 'Finally!'

'Nearly!' he says, tapping it back. I follow as he grabs the punnet and walks to the end of the row where the grass rises into a bank bathed in full sunshine. 'OK, lie back,' he says, smiling. He sits down beside me and gently pushes me back into the soft grass. 'Go on!' I do as I'm told. 'Close your eyes.'

I know what he's about to say next so I open my mouth slightly.

'Wider,' he says, placing a large berry between my lips. The smell hits me first and then I bite into the warm flesh and my mouth fills with its sweet juices. 'Now, tell me that's not the best taste in the world.'

I grin up at him. 'Not bad,' I say, reaching my hand back in. His shoulder shoves mine and he digs me gently in the ribs until we're both laughing. Then he leans over and kisses me full on the lips: so soft and easy, like something we do all the time. Then he lies back and we eat together, listening to the chirping birds and the distant roll of the church bells. God, I want him to do that again.

We quickly devour several layers and our mouths and fingertips are stained lipstick red. 'Everything OK, with your da?' he asks.

I nod, taking in his new pretty lips as he expertly de-husks another berry and adds it to the pile in his lap. 'He's fine. Grandma's going into hospital for some tests. I was just worried about her.'

'But she's OK?'

'Apparently. She was more concerned about leaving me, you know … overnight?' Without thinking I look up at him and his eyes examine me carefully, almost tenderly. I wonder whether he's looked at other girls like this. What's happening between our eyes is so intense it's like I've somehow made a suggestion I hadn't intended. I put my arm over mine to shade out the sun, which has climbed even higher in the huge, cloudless sky. I lie back and attempt to bask casually in its heat, but large drops of sweat run around the back of my neck and I'm damp between my legs. I'm terrified there'll be wet patches on my shorts. I shift position but it's hard to hide from the unease I've managed to create.

'When does she go in for these tests?' he asks, searching around amongst the berries.

I'm certain my face is crimson now. 'Next Friday, until lunchtime Saturday.'

He plucks a strawberry from the basket and looks away. He's still looking away when he starts to speak. 'D'you know, I was thinking, even before, you know ... whatcha said about your grandma and all, that maybe we could go and see those wallabies?' He turns to me now. 'Only if you want?'

My mouth falls silently open. I thought I'd dreamt the bit about his Australian marsupials.

'The thing is ... and I guess this is why I'm only saying it now –' He stops. 'We'd have to go at night.' He sits up. 'It's the boat. I'd have to like, borrow it – without asking. You see, it's not Da's, he's only a skipper, so I'd have to take it when it's not being used and that's why Fridays are best, or Tuesdays, but actually, Em ...' he says, taking a long breath and rolling on to his front again, 'I've been thinking about it a lot since the night of Fiona's party and I've been trying to work out how we'd do it, and ...' He takes another deep breath. 'I'm really sorry that it took your grandma being in hospital to make it possible, but it's just ... the timing could be perfect.'

I can't look at him now. Even eye contact feels illicit. Just the thought of the shared darkness makes me tremble inside.

'Emerald, say something, please.'

'Can you talk me through this plan? Is this even a plan?'

'Well,' he says, plucking at the grass with his fingers, 'I tell my folks I'm staying at Kenny's – that's easy. If your grandma's not around then that part could be easy too. The boat is moored at the marina, but I know the gate code and can get the keys. We could time our arrival just as the sun sets. I'll check the exact times, but if we leave around half eight that should probably –'

'Where's the tricky part?' I jump in.

'We can't be seen arriving or leaving the island.'

'OK …'

'And I can't sail in the dark. So,' he says, dropping his head into his hands, 'we'd have to stay there, until it gets light enough to leave again.'

'Hang on. Stay where?'

'On the island.'

'Is there a hotel?'

He finally looks up at me. 'No. There's nothing! It's private land. Just a big old house where the lord fella sometimes lives. There's no phone signal either. Nothing but wildlife where we'd be going. We'd need to leave again at sunrise, before Gerry gets up.'

'Who's Gerry?'

'The bollix who looks after the place. He's new,' he says, shaking his head. 'As long as the boat is back in good time for Da to do his ten o'clock supply run that morning –' he stops talking just as I'm beginning to doubt whether it's possible this trip could get any dodgier. 'We'll have to wade in a bit from where we anchor. You can swim?' he asks, as though this might be the flaw in this whole crazy plan.

'Of course I can swim. But, hold on ... so we're not even allowed on this island?'

'Strictly speaking, no. But I know my way around like the back of my hand, every cove and every cave. I can turn off the navigation lights as we get close. If it's not fully dark we may not even need them. There's an amazing remote bay on the eastern side and it has a little shore and we can moor there.'

He's clearly thought about this a lot, which feels like the kind of glorious thing that happens in someone else's exciting life. I let him go on, but as I watch his mouth move around his Dublin words, in that way I still can't predict, I start to wonder what would happen if I was to swoop in and land my lips back on his.

'Em, I can't tell you how unbelievable it would be to wake up there at sunrise,' he says. 'With you.' He leans back to pull his phone from the front pocket of his jeans. I bite my cheeks so they don't give me away. 'I'll check the forecast now,' he says, busying himself with his thumbs.

'Where will we sleep?' It seems as good a question as any.

He's distracted by something on his screen. 'A tent,' he says and rolls on to his side. 'Weather looks OK,' he says, tossing the phone down on the grass. 'So tell me, are you in?'

I'm too thrilled and panicked to answer. 'Let me get this straight – you're suggesting that this Friday, we ... as in you and I, the two of us ... steal a boat and trespass on to a private island in the dead of night so you can show me some wallabies that are stranded on the wrong side of the world?'

'Almost,' he says, staring at me. 'But you forgot the sunrise,' he adds.

I suck air into my chest and hold my breath.

'Are you in?' he asks, leaning against me now. He takes a strand of my hair and hooks it gently behind my ear.

Oh God! I scrunch up my face and cover it with my hands. I can't open my eyes.

'Please tell me that's a yes?'

There are a hundred reasons why I shouldn't do this. Still, I peek out from behind my fingers and exhale with a slow but definite nod.

He tosses a berry high into the air, catching it cleanly in his mouth. 'Yes!' he shouts, lying back and folding his arms behind his head. 'Yes, yes, yes,' he roars again at the open skies.

LIAM

Dancing in the moonlight

I've been creeping around all week; scheming and skulking, but mostly dreaming. Tonight's the night and I've a head full of lists and a savage longing raging through me, distracting me from even the most simple task. Laura caught me talking to myself in the bathroom yesterday and I had to pretend I was on the phone and now Da's standing in the corner of my room in a ferocious-looking hump. It's not easy getting private thinking time in this house.

'Who's been on the computer?' he says, as if being on the computer was an unusual, shocking thing to be doing. 'There's all these pages open on the machine below.'

It takes me a minute to cop what he's on about, but then I remember, it was me. Last night it felt possible to dream alone in the dark as the house slept, Google throwing up results to all sorts of questions I'd never before dared to ask. I dreamt how easy it would be to sit down and talk to him and Mam rationally, and explain that I've found a music production course, a proper degree. But now, as he stands there in his stained overalls, holding a piece of half-eaten toast an inch from his lips, I don't know what madness had come over me.

I look at the clock – it's only nine minutes past seven and I'm not even working today. 'Good morning to you too, Da.'

He just scratches himself, blind to the interruption. 'It's taking me ages to shut them all down. Who's been looking at all those …' he waves his giant hand in the air dismissively, 'music playing courses anyway?' he says, before taking a bite and chomping away loudly.

'You know you can open a new tab?'

'I know that,' he says, glaring at me. 'But who's planning a move to Galway, or bloody Manchester, is what I want to know?' He's clearly been through all the sites. There's a horror in his voice that makes us both go silent. His face twists with confusion. ''Twas hardly your sister?'

For a second I genuinely consider shunting it on to Laura, but even I know this is raving. 'I was just having a look …'

His arm falls by his side. 'I'm not sure this family needs a deluded idler right now. D'you?' he asks, the toast crust hanging loose, like it's about to drop from his fingers.

'It was … for Em,' I stammer. 'She's talking about coming over here for college in a few years.' I add this on as casually as I can.

'Jaysus,' he says, not even trying to hide his disgust. 'You've only known the girl a couple of weeks.'

He walks out leaving the door wide open. What was I thinking, expecting a rational conversation with that man?

I've checked my list twice now. Everything's packed neatly under the tarp, exactly like it is on Saturday mornings with Da, but this time instead of supplies from McCabes, the

188

boat is packed with our own smaller cargo. Everything we need: tent, sleeping bags, torches and enough drinks and snacks to see us through the night. I've even got extra petrol to top-up the tank after, 'cause Da will deffo cop the drop in the gauge.

Apart from the gentle *clack* of the sails on the neighbouring boats, the evening is still and silent. My stomach is flipping. I couldn't eat my sausages earlier; I swear Mam could tell something was up. I don't remember being this nervous ever, even throughout my exams, or before I read at Grandda's funeral.

Her shadow emerges from the dark corner by the dinghy supply shop before she does. Her silhouette is long and thin, like a cartoon. I glance at my phone: 8:29 p.m. On the button! She stops to punch in the code I gave her and I watch as the metal gate opens and she walks down the slipway towards me. All going well we'll be pulling into the island's eastern bay in darkness, just like I'd planned.

'It's eerie down here,' she says with a little shiver.

As she stands there looking at me I'm consumed by an urge to kiss her, but I don't. I stare back. It's like we're both thinking: are we really gonna do this?

'Y'all set?' I say, reaching for her bag and slinging it into the RIB.

She takes my hand. 'As I'll ever be.'

This is about the extent of our words as we follow the estuary out, into the enormous sky. The sea spreads out before us like miles of silvery tinfoil. I'm desperate to tear off into the vast horizon, but I'm careful to keep to the marina limit of four knots. I know better than to attract attention.

The half-sun that's left is the deepest orange and I'm concentrating hard on reading the water in the waning light. I can see the black shadow of a yacht's mast in the distance. Da says controlling the boat is like riding a horse. 'Coax the beast.' He says it all the time, like it should mean something, but I've never been on a horse in my life. I focus instead on what he calls a delicate touch and maintaining that is challenge enough right now. Em is quiet but I'm happy to leave her to her thoughts. The *clanks* of the pier boats and the squawking gulls are soon behind us and the only sound is the *whirr* of the engine and the *slosh* of the RIB cutting up the waves as we go.

I'll feel better when I've got her there in one piece. I'll talk then.

We start out slow and steady but in this wishy-washy half-light even fifteen knots feels fast. I'm completely focused as I steer our course, making sure we're riding across each wave, never contouring, just like Da taught me. I look over at Em sitting in front, so beautiful and still. I notice her life jacket is open.

'Zip it up!'

She shakes her head from behind but does it anyway. I bet all the little fishes in the Irish Sea can hear the thunderous pounding of my heart.

The journey took almost twice as long as I'd planned, but at 9:24 p.m. I steer the boat into Deadmaiden's Cove. It's the only bay on the island's coast with an actual shoreline, apart from the short beach by the harbour of course, but that'd be looking for trouble. For a brief moment I consider risking it and pulling the RIB in closer; I've seen Da do it, but I'm worried about the rocks underneath, so I cut the engine and we drift for a bit. It takes a few deep breaths before I'm steady enough to speak. 'You OK?'

She tries to stand up but the boat is still swaying 'Think so,' she says, sitting straight back down again and tying her hair up into a messy knot. 'So this is the swimming part?'

The more time I spend with Em, the more I reckon she's a swan: unruffled above, but paddling like a mad yoke beneath. I'm not convinced by her calm cover. I shuffle along the boat and plonk myself down on the wide, inflatable edge beside her. I want to take her lovely head in my hands. I want to kiss the face off her. I want to scream out – hallelujah, man alive, we made it! But I don't. I'm in survival mode, focused on the dry land before us. I grab a tent pole from under the tarp and plunge it into the water. My hand is fully submerged before it hits the bottom. 'I'll take her in a little further and we should be able to stand.' I edge in closer to the shore and drop the anchor. I haul the two boogie boards out from under the tarp. I take the pole and twist myself over the side again.

'That should do it,' I say, packing up our supplies into their waterproof bags.

'Shall I drag one?' she asks.

I shake my head. 'Pass them down to me. That'd be great.'

I start taking off my jeans, shoving them into the top of one of the bags. Standing in front of her in my shorts, I've to work hard to convince myself this is no time for feeling mortified. I lean over the side and begin lowering myself into the dark, cold water. *HOLYMOTHEROFDIVINE*

JAYSUS, it's FREEZING. I suck the shock back in, but my teeth start chattering like those joke shop ones you wind up.

'It's pretty shallow from here to the rocks. You OK to make it over?' The words are clattering out of me and my breathing has gone mental but I'm so desperate not to put her off.

She too is breathing in ripples as she hands over the boards. 'Uh huh.'

'Want me to take your backpack on this?' I ask, nodding at one of the boogie boards floating behind me. At least it's what I meant to ask, before the clanking of delph inside my mouth chewed up the all the words.

'I'll manage,' she says, somehow understanding and she begins passing the heavy bags over. Then she starts to unbutton her shorts so I turn away, wading through the icy water and dragging the boards behind me and towards the shore.

I steal a look back and catch her long white legs clambering out of the boat.

'*Aghhh!*' she squeals as she hits the water. I'm moving backwards now, watching her. I can't help but stare at the impossible vision of her in her dark knickers and denim jacket, backpack held high on top of her head. Seeing her stride through the subzero water so determined, makes me think of what Da said about those selkies in fairy tales, except this one here's a total badass.

'I can't believe we're here!' she says with a shiver, shunting further down inside her sleeping bag. The air is cold now as we sit outside our newly erected tent. We're drinking sweet tea with straight vodka chasers to warm us up – it's working.

'I won't pretend I'm not impressed at how you pitched that tent. You should see us at Glastonbury. It's tragic.'

I want to ask her more about Glastonbury. I've dreamt of going to that festival since I was kid, but I expect it involves yer man Rupert, so I'm not going there. 'It's not that impressive. If it wasn't so dark you'd see.'

'It's vertical,' she says, her eyes travelling up and down, taking it in. She turns back and rests her chin in her hands. 'How do you know your way around this place so well?'

'Used to come here with me da. Frank, the old game-keeper, would let us come over and explore. We'd have lunch together up on these cliffs. This is the wilder side of the island. There's nothing much around here except the hardy old wallabies and a few mangy cormorants. Even the sheep and deer prefer to hang out down by the "big house".'

'Do these wallabies like … ? I dunno … are they danger-ous?' she asks, pulling on a thick pair of socks and arranging them in neat, precise folds down her shin.

'Nah, they're pretty shy. They'll be in the bushes now. We'll be lucky to see any in the morning if I'm honest.'

'Oh,' she says, placing her newly socked feet back inside the sleeping bag. She pulls her knees in close and stares out at the endless moonlit sea poured all around us, like she's drinking it in. I close my eyes, listening to the sound of the waves flailing about in the dark.

'D'you get on with your mum, you know … like –?' she stops.

My eyes spring open. 'Like what?'

She takes a cookie from the box in between our legs and delicately picks off the chocolate chips. 'Like you do with your dad.'

I have to think about this. 'Dunno. I mean, I don't know if I *know* her, like I do me da.' She nods like she understands. 'She's just my mam. Guess I'm a bit more like my aul fella anyway.' I've never said this out loud and the words 'like my aul fella' spin around inside my head and it feels like the ground under me is moving. I'm suddenly desperate for this not to be true. 'I've been having a look online,' I say, trying to ground myself. 'You know, after we spoke about the music stuff …'

'Yeah?'

'But Da went to check the shipping forecast this morning and found all the pages about production degree courses open on the computer.'

She looks up at me from under her hair. 'Now he can find out about what you really want … without you actually having to tell him.'

'Said it was for a friend.'

Her hair whips around her face. 'Why?'

'I had to!'

'Oh, come on. It's not like your dad is really going to stop you following your dream,' she says, looking at me, her dark, excited features tied up in confusion.

I pull away, bristling. 'You wouldn't understand.'

She sits up, looking genuinely hurt. 'What wouldn't I understand?'

'Forget it.' I snap and the air sours. It's me. I can't help it, but I instantly want to make it better. 'Are you like your mam?'

'I hope not,' she bursts out. An uncomfortable smile takes over her face. It's like she wants rid of it now but it's taking too long to fade and we both have to wait for her mouth to slowly return to normal. 'Mum's kinda messed up,' she says. Although she hasn't moved, I feel her shift away from me. She looks up, taking the bottle from my hand. 'I've already lied to you about it. It's a horrible habit of mine. I'm usually better at covering it up but I suspect you might have noticed.'

I want to see into her eyes but the light is so bad now.

'She's not on a course, Liam.' She gives a short sniffle before taking a deep breath all the way up from her toes. 'You see, she doesn't really fall around or any of that obvious drunk stuff.'

Her face looks unbearably tense and I suddenly wish I hadn't asked.

She looks away and holds her breath before letting it out slowly. It's all shaky.

'Sorry … if you don't want to talk about it –'

She lifts her head. 'It's not that, it's just –' she breaks off and begins to pick at the remains of the dark varnish on her thumbnail. 'Apart from Kitty and maybe Magda, nobody really knows. Because we live in a certain type of house and I go to a certain school, people generally assume we're this perfect, happy family. And I guess I play along. In fact, I do more than play along,' she adds quietly. 'I practically engineer it, like the more messed up things get the harder I work

195

to pretend how idyllic it all is,' she says, pushing a sharp burst of air out through her nose. She stops and crosses her legs inside the sleeping bag, leaning her body forward into her lap, burying her face.

Unsure what to do with myself now, I reach for the bottle between us. I'm thinking about taking a drink when Em goes to speak. 'I'm not used to talking like this.'

'You're doing great,' I say, bracing as the neat vodka bob-sleighs through my insides.

She grabs the bottle and takes a long slug, wiping her nose with her sleeve. I can't work out whether this drink is a deliberate defiance given what she's just told me about her mam but I can see a tear bulge in the corner of one of her dark eyes. She tilts her head back, refusing to let it out. I reach over and thumb the tiny swell of hurt from her soft cheek.

There's a loud sniffle. 'She might only be in the next room, but she'll have slipped away somewhere. Usually I'll just get on … do my homework, forage through the fridge and go to bed. On the rare night Dad's not in London, I'll cook dinner. Sometimes I even pretend Mum made it – it's not that big a deal. But,' she says, letting out another shaky breath, 'the day before I arrived here, I found her on the floor. She'd tried to disappear and be gone, like … forever gone. She tried to die, Liam.'

I take her hand, holding it in mine, where it flutters, delicately like a frightened bird. It's cold now. Neither of us says anything but we move together silently. As she shivers next to me, I'm suddenly feeling her pain like it's my own.

'I've never been scared like that before. I honestly felt like I was fighting for both our lives.'

'You saved her?'

She nods. 'I had to resuscitate her. It took twenty-two elephants before she started to breathe. But once I saw she was alive, I wanted to shake the life back out of her. I swear, Liam,' she says, covering her mouth with her hand and moving her head from side to side. There's a tremor in her breath and I squeeze her other hand, not knowing what else to do. 'I know it's so bad, but it's like I still can't shake the anger.'

I gently press her head on to my shoulder and wait for her breathing to calm. After another sniffle she lies down, flat on her back and I notice the quivering slowly settle.

I jolt when she pulls me down beside her. 'C'mere,' she says. 'Check out the stars.'

Despite what she's told me about her mam, I'd be lying if I said I wasn't excited by this closeness and by the truth and possibility of our whole adventure. Maybe I'm a little drunk too. 'You're not gonna ask me if I can see the bloody Big Dipper?'

She elbows me. 'D'you mean you can't see it?' She leans in, pointing furiously upwards. 'Look, up there! It's the Plough.'

For a second she has me. 'You can see that?'

'The big twinkly ones, left of the black hole?'

I dig her back and she dissolves into giggles beside me. I smile broadly into the darkness. 'I don't understand astronomy. Sometimes it's nice not understanding stuff though,' I say, looking down at her. 'Like you.'

'There's no real mystery, trust me,' she says, moving in closer. We lie like this: Emerald and me, side by side, looking up at the night. I can safely say, between the twinkling sky above and the swell of contentment rising in my belly, this whole night is a feckin' mystery.

Her hand pats at the ground until it finds the biscuit packet. She props herself up on her elbow and picks chocolate chips off another cookie.

'Why d'you do that?'

'Helps this go down,' she says, taking the vodka bottle to her lips, but she lowers it without drinking and disappears off into her thoughts – that way she does.

'It's all so exhausting,' she announces, from miles away inside her mind.

She's looking at me now like I should somehow understand what she's on about. 'What is?'

'All that … look-how-good-my-life-is thing. You know, that front. Basically pretending to be someone else.'

'Is that what you're doing now?'

'No!' she says, slamming her hand on to the trampled grass between us before slowly straightening a few of the individual blades she's just squashed. 'S'what I usually do though. I'm that over-edited photo, the one you'd never upload without softening the edges and filtering out the flaws.'

'Those flaws and edges are what make you you, you eejit.'

She rolls her dark eyes at me. 'I don't expect you to understand. You are who you are. That was obvious about you, instantly.'

'What?'

'You've no idea what it's like, Liam. What I look like, what I say or what I do – everything is judged. It's like at any moment of the day or night I can see a live, up-to-the-second barometer of how much people dislike or like me, which, according to my best friend's Instagram, was 148 people the last time I looked!'

'D'you really care what some bitches from school –'

'I am one of those bitches,' she says, pulling her legs out of the sleeping bag and hugging them tight to her chest again. 'That girl, Iggy, the one I told you about who was left naked and humiliated a few weeks ago. I had a chance to stand up for her, to uphold her story, and I didn't take it. I was the only one who could do it and I didn't. And Iggy knew,' she says, pausing to catch her breath. 'She knew I knew and still said nothing, that's the worst of all.'

I'm sucking my teeth thinking of what to say back. There is something in her eyes I recognise. I'm not sure what it is but I know it.

'I couldn't stand up to my closest friends.'

She shakes her head like she thinks I'm about to tell her it's all OK, that anyone would have done the same in her position, but I know she doesn't want to hear that and besides, it's not necessarily true. 'Guess you understood the consequences.'

She sits bolt upright. 'That's not a good enough reason not to do something.' I'm looking at her now, leaning her left cheek on her knee and staring at me sideways. 'He calls me Scout, you know?'

'Who does?'

'Dad,' she says. 'When I was little we'd spend Saturday mornings together at the library on top of Waitrose. We'd stretch out on our old green sofa afterwards, him reading the FT and me acting like I was immersed in my new books. Mostly I just chewed Percy Pigs and daydreamed.' She stops and looks at me straight on. 'I was ten when I pretended to read *To Kill a Mockingbird*. I didn't understand half of it, but I got why Atticus Finch was the most courageous man alive. From that day he was Dad and I was supposed to be Scout, the little girl unafraid to speak out. Part of me believed I'd really grow up to be like her. But I haven't, have I?' She eyes me warily. 'What are you staring at?'

It's not that I haven't been listening. I have, but I've somehow managed to lose myself in her face while doing so. I opt for the truth. 'The tiny freckles, dusted over your nose like icing sugar.'

As she shakes her head her hair falls out from behind her ears, hiding her face.

'And,' I say, lifting her chin, 'the way your front teeth kind of cross and your canines are really pointy.'

'Liam!' she cries.

'It makes my stomach flip to see that smile of yours.' She tries to stop it happening, but her lips part and the sides of her mouth crawl upwards against her will. 'There it is! I'm getting pretty fond of those flaws, just so you know.'

She laughs now, nice and wide but then quickly it's over. 'You know, I watch my friends and everything they do seems so easy and natural and I feel so far away, even when I'm right there with them. It's like sometimes I don't even know how to do normal stuff.'

'Like what?'

'Like having fun and –' She doesn't say any more.

I look at the moon bouncing on the water and listen to the waves tug at the edges of the cliffs below. For a few minutes I allow the energy of their magnificent roar to propel me forward and next thing I'm pushing myself up off the ground, extending my arms out to her in one glorious swoop of mad motion. 'Stand up!'

'What?'

'Give me your hand.' I take her into my arms and hold every inch of her that I can against me.

'What are we doing?' she says through clenched teeth, like a ventriloquist, hardly opening her mouth. I push her gently back, still holding both our hands together and swing them, and us, from side to side.

'We're dancing,' I say, jiving in and out now. She moves with me but of course she can't hear the music playing inside my head. We sway there under the moon, just us, dancing in its spotlight. I start clicking my fingers in 4/4 time, doing the bass tabs of amazing percussion like I'm Phil Lynott himself. Letting go of her hands, I move around her the way Da does around a dance floor at a wedding, or around the kitchen table if he's had a few.

She's staring at me like I'm a total mad yoke but I can't stop myself. I'm blissfully murdering the incredible song, half wondering whether I should wrap it up, when I realise she's begun to move, twirling around me, lost in her own song too. I'm watching her pat out a drum beat on the arse of her shorts when I catch the lyric she's singing into the vodka bottle. Fleetwood bloody Mac, I'm sure of it. Sacred heart, there's no holding back. I raise my imaginary guitar to the sky and music flows out of me, only Thin Lizzy has finished and it's my own words pouring out now.

> *'I wish you could see you the way I do,*
> *Your all-knowing look cuts right through,*
> *You see the truth when I've no clue ...'*

I slowly open my eyes to discover she's no longer dancing and it's just me, dribbling out the last words alone. I never got further than the third line so I stop and stare back at her: she's watching me with that exact look, the one that rearranges planets, gravity and all earthly reason.

'I like it,' she says, pulling me down to the ground and leaning back on her elbows. 'What's it about?'

'The first time I saw you, flinging fistfuls of angry rocks into the Irish Sea –'

She sits up before I finish. 'You saw that?'

'Guess I'd something of a head start.'

She thumps my chest.

'How the first time your eyes searched mine, at the risk of sounding like a complete spanner, I knew.'

She's picking at the grass underneath us again and scattering it over my sweaty head.

'You do this thing, where your eyes linger for a split-second longer ...'

She looks up at me, on cue.

'Like they're doing now! It's like you see under my skin. But it's not just me – it's how you watch the whole world. Does that sound mad?'

She shakes her head.

'You're real, Em, and that stuff surrounding you is fake. It's just the distance in between you're struggling with.'

She's thinking; I can see it in her eyes.

'Since that first night,' I say, placing the heel of my hand gently on the curve of her left cheek, 'I've wanted to find out –'

'What?'

'– what it is you're searching for.'

A flock of dark, indistinguishable birds swoop down into the rocks from the dim sky and she huddles her body into mine, whispering something I don't hear. Suddenly my limbs and lids feel heavy. I turn to look at Em but her eyes are shut. I close mine too, just to feel how good it is to lie here, curled up against each other.

EMERALD

It happens so quickly

Something is buzzing under me. Where am I? Where are we?

'Liam, Liam,' I say, shaking him. 'Your phone's ringing!'

He sits up and rubs his eyes. 'Huh?'

We both fumble around under the sleeping bags. I notice he's only searching with one hand, he is holding mine with his other. He throws his head back and laughs. 'It's only the alarm!' he says, clamping his hand on his chest. 'Must be half four. C'mon, sun's gonna rise any minute.'

'Ohmygod, I thought it was your dad or something,'

Still holding my hand, he pulls on it. 'D'you sleep OK?'

This is only the earliest I've opened my eyes ever! My teeth are chattering and my right hip hurts from where I've been lying on the lumpy, hard ground. 'Not sure, really.'

I remember the night draining to its last few per cent. Sleep, once it hit, was instant and absolute. Liam reaches for the zip in the tent floor and gradually peels it open. At first all I can see is the light: bright and holy, puncturing our darkness. Then I feel the air, cool and new, recharging my cold, limp limbs and sleepy head.

'It happens so quickly,' he says, pulling me to the front of the tent. We lie on our bellies and watch as the tip of the yellow sun cracks the horizon. As it rises steadily, burning into the navy sky like a fireball, I almost forget about how badly I want my duvet and something resembling a toothbrush.

A tunnel of light carries across the water to us, flooding our faces with its honeyed hue. I don't know whether I'm half asleep or dreaming but I can only watch as the perfect, circular sun reveals itself. I steal a look at Liam's pale skin, which looks like it's been ironed in the night and next thing I'm tilting his face towards mine and despite everything I feel about morning-breath, I start to kiss him, slowly.

He suddenly breaks away, breathless. 'Feels like I'm under a spell.' I know what he means. Everything about this morning is sprinkled in a fairy dust I don't believe in, but for some reason I don't answer. 'Say something, Em.'

I feel his eyes on me as I close mine, relishing the healing heat of the sun on my face. 'It's so nice.'

'What is?' he asks.

'The silence. It makes me feel new.' I open my eyes. 'I just mean it's honest. Real.'

'It's making me nervous,' he says.

'The silence or the honesty?'

He laughs. 'Right now, probably both. And then, as though this moment couldn't get any dreamier, he starts to hum, soft and indistinguishable at first, but then louder; slow, deep and beautiful. It's another one I know. It's that Elvis one about the wise men. Suddenly he stops, turns and looks at me, like he's watching the realisation unfold. I'm expecting him to laugh again but his brow is all furrowed, bottom lip clamped under his top teeth. I think he's holding his breath.

'That's another one of my dad's favourites.'

A smile explodes all over his face. 'Serious?'

I nod. 'Elvis is legit punk-rock in his book.'

'We're gonna get along, so,' he says, nudging me.

I can't meet his eye but I roll over happily like I'm in a chocolate advert and all newly caramel-centered. 'You were right, you know …'

'About?' He loops his middle finger around mine and pulls me closer. 'Right that I'll get on with your da?'

I shake my head. 'No. I mean yes. For sure you'll get on, but not that …' Our eyes fuse. 'You were right that it happens so quickly. I never knew.'

'OK … please tell me you're not talking about that sunrise,' he says, pointing his finger back towards the horizon.

I take his hand and circle it, between us. 'I mean this.'

We never got to see the wallabies this morning, but I didn't mind. It was, without doubt, the loveliest waking-up of my life. We made it back to the marina on time. We left the boat moored in the same spot as if nothing had happened. We'd been gone less than ten hours but it may as well have been a week. Watching the sun rise like it did this morning made me feel that anything is possible.

When I got back to Grandma's I climbed straight into bed and pulled the heavy blanket over my head, hoping to re-dream what had just happened. As I drifted off, I thought of her waking in the hospital, oblivious to how my world has changed. I slept soundly until the phone rang. I was sure it was Grandma but instead a cheery-sounding woman asked to speak to me and now I appear to have my first proper babysitting job at seven thirty tomorrow night.

I got back into bed after, bringing my laptop in with me. It took only one search before I was on to him. The Elvis song was there in my head as soon as I crawled back under the sheets. I opened SoundCloud and typed it in. Only the most covered song of all time. I had to scroll through a gazillion other Elvis covers to find him, but there he was: Undercover Cop, Dublin, singer, songwriter, musician, ninety-six followers, four tracks. A Lego man in an American police uniform and handcuffs as his profile pic.

Undercover Cop, Between the Bars (Elliot Smith cover). 1 year

Undercover Cop, Sweet Thing (Van Morrison cover). 1 year

Undercover Cop, When the Stars Go Blue (Ryan Adams cover). 1 year

Undercover Cop, Can't Help Falling in Love (that Elvis guy). 4 days ago

Four days ago! The night we were on the dunes. I thought my heart would detonate when I hit play. His voice! Hearing him sing again, I was right back there, dancing in the moonlight.

Liam sings like he talks. All low and scratchy and drinkable like water. It's all him, laid bare. The hairs on the back of my neck stood tall and I felt my whole face and body burn like the sun was rising from the wardrobe in front of me. His Elvis cover had ninety-four plays when I started; it had one hundred and seventeen before I'd even got out of bed. I listened to the other tracks after that, none of which I knew. Great as they all were, he'd recorded those last year, not the same freaking night that he first kissed me!

I decided to bake a cake for Grandma. Just a basic Victoria sponge but I had to put my insane joy into something solid, something I could touch and share.

'Welcome home!' I said, taking Grandma's suitcase and heaving her weighty plastic bags into the hall. 'You've been shopping?'

Without answering, she turned to me. 'You've been baking?'

'Don't get too excited.'

'Oh, Em!' she cried, barely inside the door and hugging me to her so tight. When she pulled away I saw her eyes were all teary, that way they go. We moved into the kitchen and sat down, me wearing her stained apron and her with her damp anorak still zipped. 'What brought this on?' she asked, unfolding her glasses as I poured the tea.

It was simple really. I wanted her to feel how I felt when she made me that banana loaf. 'I want to thank you, like you had thanked me, for taking me out of myself,' I said, handing her a plate. 'That's all.'

'Well, it's wonderful, is what it is,' she said, before making light work of the slice of sponge on her plate. On her last bite Grandma stood. 'I picked something up from the shops,' she said, rummaging in her bags on the counter. She handed me a DVD of *The Fault in our Stars*. 'It was on offer by the checkout.'

'Grandma!'

'You've seen it?'

'No!'

She practically jumped. 'Well that's it, we'll watch it tonight.'

Tonight? I was hoping to see Liam tonight but I knew I couldn't say that now. 'But you don't have a DVD player.'

'When I recognised their faces from the cover of your book,' she said, sliding a small DVD player out of its box, 'I decided it was the perfect excuse for me to join the twenty-first century.' She looked so pleased with herself. I hadn't the heart to tell her no one buys DVDs any more, hence the bargain buckets by the supermarket till.

'You sure you're OK, pet?' It's the third time Grandma's asked since the credits rolled. She's followed me out to the garden and we're sitting together on Granddad's bench under the apple trees.

I'm not sure if I'm OK. I'm not sure at all. I was expecting to cry movie-tears of course, but I didn't expect to feel like this. I can't stop the tears coming. I'd been preparing for the beauty and the pain of Hazel's story to come alive on screen, I was ready for that, knew I'd bawl my eyes out, but still, I wasn't prepared for this.

Grandma shifts in her skirt. 'It'd take a heart of stone not to sob at that,' she says, inching closer to me. 'Of course you must have known from the book.' She taps her hand lightly on my leg, glancing up at the sky before eventually turning to face me. 'Still, you do seem so very upset, love.'

'Does expecting a blow make it less painful?'

Grandma shrugs.

'Sorry, I'm fine. It's just ...' I break off and blow my nose as I consider whether or not to keep going. I don't know what I'm really feeling, or what I'm crying for. 'I guess I wasn't expecting –' Oh God, can I do this? 'What I mean is ...' I say, choking up, my breath now emerging as scrappy sobs. 'I hadn't expected to feel like the mum.'

She sits forward on the bench, facing me. 'Whatever d'you mean?'

I grab another tissue from my pocket and sniffle into it. 'You know the scene where Hazel gets a reply from the writer guy?' Grandma nods again. 'She's so excited and she shouts out from her bedroom, "Mom!" And her mother comes racing up the stairs in a total panic, fearing the worst for her sick daughter, thinking something dreadful has happened?'

'Yes,' she says, 'I do.'

She puts her hand on my knee. I must have skipped over that part in the book because I was totally unprepared for the landmine that was buried in this scene of the film. I can hardly recount it for Grandma now. I'm afraid I'll disintegrate into tiny wet lumps, small enough to slip through the cracks of the hard wooden seat beneath us. But now I've started, I can't hold anything in. 'Do you remember the mother's face?'

Grandma slowly bows her head.

'I knew her expression because it was mine. That's how I feel with Mum. That's how I run upstairs. That's exactly how it was when I found her after school. That dread, my palms slamming against walls to get there quicker without falling over. That was me. That's how I felt. That's how I feel, Grandma.'

And that's it, my weeks of stoicism blown. Every orifice on my face is leaking and every limb trembles. I didn't know I had this many tears trapped for so long. Surges of pain erupt out of me in violent, crashing waves. I dab my running nose with my scrunched-up tissue. Grandma leans over to me and holds me in her arms.

'I don't want to be like the mum any more.'

She pulls me closer, burying me in the folds of her woollen shawl. 'I know, sweetheart.'

'I don't want to be her mother.'

She rocks us back and forth 'Shush … shush, darling,' she says. A steady stream of cars glide past in the distance, as though nothing is happening. I stare up at the stars and imagine the sky slowly falling, covering us like a blanket.

LIAM

Trying so hard to hold back

'Hi, it's me,' I say, sitting my arse down on a trolley and kicking my feet up on to a crate of Monster energy drinks. There's nowhere else to sit in this poxy stockroom. Suddenly I'm all in a panic about the potential for another 'me' in Emerald's life.

'Hi, you,' she says.

I allow myself to relax down into the uncomfortable plastic seat. 'Where are you?'

'In my room.'

'Whatcha doing?'

'Nothing,' she replies cagily, as if she's afraid I'm going to pop out from behind her bedroom door or something. Then I hear her laugh.

'Sorry, I'm trying to picture you.' I instantly wish I hadn't said it like this. 'OK, forget that came out of my mouth.' She doesn't say anything. 'How was the film?'

'Oh God,' she sighs. 'I can't even …'

'Did you have a boo-hoo?'

'Don't!' she says. 'I feel better though. As therapy, I'd give it five stars.'

'And as a movie?'

'Devastating! Even Grandma cried.'

I'm struggling to picture Emerald really crying. Maybe it's easier for her at home with her grandma than on a dark windswept cliff in the middle of the sea? 'So whatcha doing tonight?'

'Oh, you know … YouTube, probably. You asking?'

'Yeah, I'm asking.'

'Go on then.'

'Kenny, Fiona and the lads are going to Moloney's. Wanna come?'

'Wait,' she jumps in, 'I'm babysitting, I almost forgot!'

'Oh?' My heart drops. I need to see her. I get up and pace the dusty floor, desperate not to let another night go by. 'Is it an actual real-life family this time?'

'Yes!' she says and I picture those eyes of hers turning to heaven. 'Her name is Helen. Just one little girl, who's three –'

'Let me guess. Number 11, The Briars?'

'Yes! How –'

'She's Turbo's sister, the nurse. The one I nearly called for you the night of Fiona's party. Helen's cool. She'll laugh when she sees me.'

'Hang on, are you … planning on joining me?'

'If you'll have me?'

'I'd love it, but … you don't think she'd mind?'

'Nah. Sure, I know Lily well. You watch your carpool karaoke, I've got this whole child-minding thing down.'

She laughs. 'OK, let me ask her when I get there. I'll call you.'

'Oh, and Em?' I say, taking a deep breath. 'I've missed you,' I whisper before quickly hanging up.

★

213

Despite the fact this is now the third time inside of a week I've joined in the whole babysitting lark at Helen's house, I still can't get used to being on Turbo's sister's couch with Em. Turbo held court at the beach last night, telling us all how Helen's been cooking up any excuse to leave the house so she can have Em mind Lily. Told us all she hopes if they spend enough time together Em's classy accent will somehow rub off on her daughter. Her latest ruse, he said, is a night class on decluttering, in Italian. Em took the slagging well, to be fair.

It seems impossible to find time alone with Em, so to be able to kiss her like this on the soft, warm couch again feels amazing. She feels amazing. I've worked a shift at the Metro every day this week and even though we've hung out at the shelters together practically every night, we're surrounded by the lads every feckin' minute. Lily's conked out upstairs but, as usual, Em's refusing to have the TV or any music on, in case we don't hear her crying, so it's only us and the sound of our increasingly urgent breaths.

I can't stop myself. I'm afraid of what I want to do with her now. I'm panicking I'm ahead of her. The way she flows underneath me; I'm sinking into her. Is she afraid too? I hope she is. I'm terrified. I've never felt desire like this. I'm not sure I've even understood desire could feel like this. I definitely never suspected the pain that comes with trying so hard to hold back.

'Stop, Liam,' Em whispers. I hear her voice but it seems far away. I'm trying to work out where it's coming from. It's only when she pushes her hand into my chest that it really registers. 'Liam! I hear the car. Helen's home,' she says, pressing my body off her and sitting up. She fixes herself and quickly stands up, shuffling the cushions around. Then she looks at me. 'Y'OK?' She's smiling.

I pull my T-shirt down. 'Uh huh.' It's all I can manage.

Now we're huddled together, stomping up the hill towards the village. The pace is partly to do with the cold and partly to do with a shared ambition to hit the chipper before the pub crowds. We pass the Scout Den where kids spill out on to the street after some kind of junior disco that's just ended.

'It'd be good to go to the island again,' she says, out of the blue. I stop in the middle of the road. 'Sorry, forget it,' she says, shaking her head. 'It's a terrible idea ... I just thought –'

I pull her back to me. 'No, hold on. Wait! It's not a terrible idea.' A car beeps us out of the way and I shunt us both to the footpath on the other side. 'I'm ... surprised, that's all.'

'It's just that it's, you know ... nice,' she says, leaning against a lamp post now and sucking in her cheeks for some strange reason. 'Being alone. Just us.'

I almost laugh but I'm suddenly deadly serious. 'That's something of an understatement, but yeah, it is.' I can't help but lean in to her, desperate to feel the length of her body against me again. We stare at each other for a few seconds, silent under the strange bright light. 'How though?'

'I could sneak out,' she says, eyes all earnest. 'Grandma's always asleep by ten thirty. Friday nights are no different, and she doesn't get up until after seven. She's like clockwork. I'm pretty sure I could pull it off. I've been thinking about it –'

'You have?' I ask and she nods. 'OK, that makes me happy.'

She smiles back. 'But could you?'

A wave of adrenalin takes me and I'm riding it with only instinct. Logic has long left. 'If we wait till your grandma's asleep, we're talking proper darkness, which I'm not supposed to sail in at all, but then, I'm not supposed to take the boat either. So yeah, hell yeah! I'd go tonight if we could.' I clamp my hand against the cold aluminium pole behind her head and kiss her. I almost forget we're standing in the middle of the village, when some drunk fella standing outside the cop shop does a loud wolf whistle I'm pretty sure is for us.

Em pulls away. 'I feel weird about going to Mum's Family Day thing tomorrow. It's been looming over me for days now,' she says, glancing towards the drunk lad but looking through him somehow. She's impressively unbothered by his antics.

'Nervous about seeing your mam?'

'A bit, but it's not just that. I know this'll sound strange, but I almost don't want to go back there, to England. Even for a day.'

I can't not smile. 'Ah, here, you don't have to say that …'

'No, seriously. I've managed to keep everyone and everything at a distance these past weeks and the truth is, it's been so much … easier. Thing is, I feel free, but going back, I mean physically being there, feels … I dunno, unsafe maybe.'

'It's only one day, right?'

'Yeah, I guess,' she says, walking on again. 'C'mon, I'm starving,' she orders, before turning around and marching ahead.

'Wait!' We're only yards from the chipper now. 'I'm not sure I can wait until next Friday,' I say, not quite caring that I didn't dress this up better. I'm racing inside just thinking about it. 'I'm off next Tuesday night and I've only an afternoon shift on Wednesday. What do you say?' My brain's whirling inside my skull as I stand there, waiting for her to answer.

'Your enthusiasm is noted.' She laughs. 'It's a date!'

EMERALD
Settling a wobbly glass

I've counted nineteen chairs in our little circle. Dad's sitting on my left and between us, on an empty seat, there's a sticker with *ELIZA* written on it in green marker. I can't work out whether that means Mum is going to sit here or whether they were expecting only one of us. Tea and some sorry-looking biscuits sit on a table at the front, but so far nobody's touched them. The lady three chairs down has begun weeping loudly. There's an Asian guy with a shiny gold necklace tapping one Airmax trainer restlessly, fanning some air around the stuffy room. An older couple on Dad's left appears to be having a wordless row. In the corner a girl, dressed in a long cardigan and well worn UGGs, is biting her nails. She's around my age, I think. Suddenly she gets up and leaves the room. I wonder if anyone actually wants to be here.

'Did Mrs McKenzie get back to you about my results?'

Dad is reading an email on his phone. 'Huh?'

I nudge him. 'My GCSEs. Did she say whether you could collect them for me on the twenty-fourth?'

'Oh, yeah. There was a message on the answering machine,' he says, still staring into his phone. Then he looks up, as though suddenly struck. 'Don't you want to go back to Hollyfield to pick them up? See all your friends?'

'Maybe you could just bring them over?'

He squints back at me, bewildered. I don't know whether it's to do with me not wanting to go back, or something he's read.

The door opens and Nick walks in. It's a striped blue shirt day. He's smiling at everyone and crossing the room in long, purposeful strides. He pulls at the knees of his grey cords before taking his seat by the window. Dad is punching furiously into his BlackBerry again, his forehead looking like a freshly ploughed field. Nick does this little cough. I want to nudge Dad again but he looks too absorbed so I look around and count the still empty chairs, of which there are four.

Eventually Dad looks up. 'Apologies,' he says, slotting the phone into his jacket's breast pocket.

'Thank you.' Nick mouths it from across the room. Dad puts his hand on my knee. I hope it's a signal to say he's ready.

Nick stands up. 'Welcome, everybody, I'd like to thank all of you for coming here today.' He clears his throat in an unnatural sort of way before continuing. 'This is what we call our family-group session. This will start us off before we move into the individual sessions, when some of you will join your loved ones for one-to-ones this afternoon. This may even be the first session for some of you …'

I zone out for a bit now, mostly because Nick has that kind of voice, but it doesn't help that my eyes won't seem to stay open. I stayed up way too late, listening to Liam's music.

Ended up creating a SoundCloud profile just to comment on his songs. I couldn't help myself. Spent ages googling around afterwards to see if I can find any other trace of him online, but I've found nothing. It's not even eleven and I'm ready for lunch.

It's been five weeks since I've seen Mum. Dad said under normal rehab circumstances, if such a thing exists, she'd be out by now. Most people come in here for twenty-eight days but Mum opted for a rehab double whammy. Her decision, apparently. Nick said it was a positive sign that she's 'invested in her recovery' and really wants it to work. I won't allow myself to believe this is true, not yet.

It's so frustrating to think we're here and she's here, some-where, and we can't even see her yet. I pluck out some of Nick's words, but really I'm busy watching the other people in the group. A psychologist would have a field day on the body language in this room.

UGG-boot girl returns. Nick smiles up at her but doesn't miss a beat. 'I'd like to invite you all to introduce yourselves and share, perhaps, how it is you're feeling today.'

For real? I slump down into the chair. UGG-boots folds her arms deliberately across her chest, obviously sharing my enthusiasm level. The crying lady begins to convulse.

'Let's start with you,' says Nick, motioning to Dad with one hand and handing the crying lady more tissues with the other. The room is deathly silent aside from her gentle whimpering, which has just been softened by the clump of Kleenex.

Did he really ask Dad to start? The air in the room changes; suddenly there's not enough of it. I can't figure out whether Nick is just stupid or whether he has way bigger balls than I thought. I feel a bit weak.

'Ah, ehm ...' says Dad, hooking his feet around the legs of the chair with a horrible screeching sound and sitting up straight. Then he *stands* up, which I don't think you're supposed to do. I slide down even further in my seat and try to concentrate on what he's saying but all I can do is panic that it'll be my turn next.

'It's good to be here,' he says, and then he looks around like he's addressing a boardroom. 'I'm sure we're all pleased our ... loved ones are here, and eh ... attending to their issues,' he says, before clapping his hands, which sound like cymbals crashing inside my skull. 'And, yes, that's it. Thank you.' He rubs his palms together one last time and sits back down.

Awkward is not the word.

It's clear from Nick's face that Dad didn't quite get it, whatever it is, but thankfully Dad doesn't seem to notice. I can feel all the eyes in the room land on me. I close my eyes and slide my sweaty palms down the thighs of my jeans.

'Thank you, Jim. Let's move on to you now ... Bev.'

It takes a second for the name to sink in. Only when I hear a lady with a harsh East London accent launch into the horrors of her son's relapse do I breathe out.

It took over half an hour to get around the small room. Airmax guy, Sunil, was a revelation; articulate and wise. Basically, his girlfriend lost her mind on crack cocaine. He's in recovery himself, but it's only been a year and he was really open about how wobbly he feels and how he's

221

frightened of her now, even though he really loves her. He spoke for ages, like he really needed to. I felt Dad shift in his seat for most of it, like he was angry the guy wouldn't shut up. Eventually it was my turn but I froze after I said my name; all the words I'd feverishly planned stuck in my throat and nothing came out. Nick just smiled at me and said, 'Maybe next time,' which I thought was pretty cool.

I'm lying on the grass outside now, looking up at the cartoon blue sky and following a scattering of *Simpsons* clouds sailing slowly by. I begin to feel dizzy so I sit up and stare up at the house that Dad and I pulled away from five weeks ago. It looks different. Just being in England feels different; shapes feel sharper, their shadows more pronounced, like everyone is speaking just that tiny bit too loud, or that weird way you realise your house has an actual smell when you walk in the door from holiday, but then quickly it's gone and you can't get it back again.

I'm almost afraid to look at my phone in case it might somehow announce to my entire address book that I'm back. For the life of me I can't work out whether I've come back to reality or whether I've actually left the real world behind. Being in this place doesn't help.

Someway off in the distance, sleepy-looking people in leisurewear spill out from the main door. It's not long before I spot Mum in the small crowd and my stomach flips. That's how Liam said he feels when I smile, but I hope it's for a very different reason. Dad's been pacing up and down by the rhododendron bushes, waiting. His phone buzzed relentlessly during the session; emails dropping into his inbox like soft, silent bombs. He looks grey from it all.

I watch them come to stand together at the top of the drive. It feels like an eternity before he kisses the top of Mum's head and she dips low, leaning on his chest now so his whole body is taking her weight. I'm waiting for his arms to reach out and hold her but only his right arm moves and she slowly steps back. I stare into the space between them, unsure of quite where to look. Dad's head nods as his voice drones indistinguishably in the distance. His eyes might even be closed but his hands keep gesturing in short, sharp bursts that way they do. I wish I could hear what they're saying. Suddenly they both freeze and their eyes lock. I'm wondering what's happened when I realise the ringing phone I can hear is Dad's. But he's not actually going to answer it. Not now. Is he? Oh God, he is.

He turns and strides up the path. Mum's left standing alone. I want to jump up and rescue her. She looks around the garden and seeing me, lifts her hand to wave. As she approaches I can't help notice her walk, the way her arms move freely by her side. Despite what's just happened she seems looser. Her thick curls are tied back into a low pony-tail. Her hair has grown. I'm about to get up but it's too late, she's already at my feet.

She sits down beside me and steadies her breath deliber-ately, like she is preparing to say something but maybe she's just recovering from that marooning at the top of the drive. 'Thank you,' she says finally, 'for coming.'

Maybe I was expecting something more. Not drama exactly, but fervour perhaps. She's staring straight at the house; we both are, when she turns to look right at me. Her eyes look so clear but she's ghostly pale under the last traces of a suntan. It's sad that I still describe people using Instagram filters, I get that, but it's like she's been rinsed in Reyes, or possibly Sierra: beautiful but totally washed-out.

'It's so good to see you, Em,' she says, placing her soft, cold hand on mine.

It is good to see her. I smile back. 'You too, Mum.' It's the first time I've seen Mum outside the house without make-up. She crosses her legs and takes another long, yogic breath before reaching over and taking my shoulders in her arms.

She holds me there, clumsily. Our bodies are unnaturally twisted and it's really uncomfortable, but still it feels so nice. I've almost synced my breath with hers when she pushes me back and releases me, gently, holding her hands there, a few inches from me, as though waiting for a wobbling glass to settle. Eventually she takes her arms away.

I want to let her know Dad's been distracted like that with me too, and it doesn't mean he doesn't care. 'He's got a lot on.' It spills out clumsily.

'He has, sweetheart.' She says this in a way I can't read.

I want to make her feel better. I desperately want to believe this is going to work and that she really will get well. I want to tell her she's doing great. I want to tell her I love her, but because of how much I do, I can't. It's precisely the fact I want all of this so badly that makes me want to ruin it before there's a chance that she, or anyone else, can.

I nod to the other leisure-wearers, huddled in small groups around the garden. 'Made any new friends?' I ask, clearing my throat in an attempt to distract from the quiver in my voice.

Her lips part to reveal her lovely teeth. 'I have actually.' It's that smile from the photo on my phone, but then quickly it's sadder. She flicks her fringe out of her eyes before closing them to the strong sun. I wonder what more to say to her but I'm scared to let anything I really feel out in case I damage this easiness. I know how fragile it is. I know how quickly this warmth can blow cold.

I feel her turn to me again and I'm suddenly terrified. I say nothing but I know my face betrays me. Mum always said I have a lot going on in my face, which basically means I can't lie. Not that this has ever stopped me, but it makes it hard to hide what's going on in my head from the few people who really do want to see.

'I know you're afraid,' she says, swallowing. Mum and I haven't shared a truthful word like this in weeks, months, possibly even years, and I don't know where to look. 'But I'm really trying to do this, Em.'

I feel all my fear morph into a deep longing, that could, at any moment, sneak out of my eyes and roll down my face.

'I don't want to rush you, darling,' she says. We both sit up and stare back at the house, clearly uncomfortable with this intimacy, but craving it all the while. I notice we're both rocking, out of time. 'I know I've got a lot of making up to do too,' she adds, placing her trembling hand back on mine.

The route back to the airport is the exact journey Dad and I made together five weeks ago, but it's overcast now and not because of the weather. Dad is driving fast, too fast, which is nothing unusual, but it's making me nervous. Whatever is troubling him is making me even more uneasy. There's no music this time: just a stiff, brittle silence I don't know how to break. Whatever happened between Mum and Dad back there after his call, the thick, leaden air has followed him.

'Mum was looking well,' I say, hoping to lift the mood. But nothing; it doesn't even register. 'You OK, Dad?'

All his movements are brusque. 'Fine,' he says.

'It's just …'

'What?' There's no tenderness. 'What is it, Em?'

I fold my arms and legs to stop them shaking. 'It seemed like you didn't want to be there today.'

'I didn't.'

'Dad!'

'Christ, Emerald. I have other things on my mind. OK?'

My whole body freezes. You could choke on the tension. Dad never calls me Emerald. Suddenly he indicates and slips into the slow lane behind a very slow-moving lorry. I knew I shouldn't have said anything. We travel in the shadow of the giant truck. Every passing car rolls by like thunder. My heart is hammering too loud. Why couldn't I keep my mouth shut?

'I'm sorry,' he says finally. 'It's just … I could have done without it today.' He fiddles with some buttons on the dash, before running his fingers under his shirt collar. The AC is on full and the car is almost too cold, but Dad is smouldering under some mysterious heat. I can think of several responses to what he's said about 'doing without today' but

226

none of them are helpful. We continue to tail the back of the lorry in silence.

'I'm in trouble, Em,' he says, without looking at me. I watch as his shoulders slump forward, almost like he's going to fall. I'm surprised by how small his hands look on the steering wheel. For one horrible moment I think he's going to let the car and us, and everything in our life, spin out of control. I lunge at the wheel to grab it but he pulls himself back and brakes. We both try to catch our breath. Then he flicks the indicator left again. I try to catch his eye but he stares ahead blankly, not looking at anything in particular, just locked into the middle distance. We're driving so slowly that the truck is way out in front now and I can't see any slip road ahead. The steady *tock-tic, tock-tic, tock-tic, tock-tic, tock-tic* continues and we stay put in our lane; there is nowhere else to go.

'Dad?'

It takes a few seconds before I realise we're sliding gradually to the left, drifting into the hard shoulder. It takes another long, long minute to come to a gentle stop as we literally run out of road.

'Dad?'

His head falls forward on to the wheel. 'A lot of trouble,' he whispers.

LIAM

A lost wallaby

The call-out for Saturday night scoops has gathered a fine crowd: Kenny, Fiona, Turbo, Murph, Billy and two of Fiona's school friends are all here in Moloney's. Dirty glasses and peanut packets are strewn over the table. Kenny's telling a joke I've heard before. I take my phone out and start typing under the table.

Hope it went OK with your mam today.

Send.

X.

I hit send again, and lean back against the wall, taking in all the sights and sounds around me, then I take my phone back out.

Thanks for the SoundCloud raves btw.

Send.

I'm staring up at a bunch of older lads crowding around

228

the door, all sporting red-raw tans after the day's sun when I feel the phone ring between my legs. It's her.

'Hey!' I'm not sure what I was expecting to be honest, but her sniffling on the end of the line comes as a bit of a shock. 'Emerald?'

'Where are you?'

I stand up. 'Moloney's. Y'OK? Is it your mam? Is she –?'

She takes a deep sigh. I can only imagine what it's like to have to worry about a parent like Emerald has had to. I'm already reaching under Kenny's stool for my jacket. 'Want me to come over?'

'No, I'll be with you in ten minutes.'

I'm sitting on the wall outside Jackie Chan's Chinese, waiting. There's a line of sight all the way to the crossroads but the bang of curry-chips is making me queasy. I'm slinking towards the steps by the ATM when I spot her. Her hair sways lightly in the wind, but her walk is slow and heavy.

Without a word I fold her inside my jacket and hold her there, tightly. 'Y'all right?' I ask, after a minute, but she doesn't answer. I lift her chin. 'Hey?' She sniffles and I can see her sad eyes properly now. 'I take it this isn't about the Johnny Cash track I uploaded?' I ask, gently steering her towards the steps, away from passers-by.

She doesn't even smile. 'You know I told you it's all messed up with Mum? Well, I didn't really cover Dad and all the stuff going on there too,' she says, crouching down by the railings, her head falling into her hands.

I sit down beside her, watching all manner of Saturday night legs file past between the railings in front of us. 'Go on.'

229

'Today went OK. At least I thought it did, even though Dad was being his usual distracted self. But on the way back from the airport' – she turns to look at me – 'he went all weird, Liam.'

'Whatcha mean?'

'Said he's in trouble, serious trouble.' Her breath is shaky. 'And it's all my fault.'

I almost stand. 'He actually said it's all your fault?'

'No!' she pulls at my arm. 'It's not my fault about him being in trouble, but it's my fault I made him lose it. He nearly crashed the car, and I was the one who made him do it,' she says, finally slowing her gallop before sucking in another long breath.

Somewhere in the distance I hear our names being called, but I block it out. 'I don't understand, Em. How could any of this be down to you?'

'D'you remember I told you about his case?' she asks.

'Yeah,' I say. I do. She brought it up the night of Fiona's party.

'All right, lovebirds.' It's Fiona shouting, teetering unsteadily by the ATM. She waves over eagerly, clearly thrilled to have discovered us. I'm not sure we even acknowledge her before turning back to one another.

'There's a pretty good chance he's going to lose. I know it probably sounds stupid, but I never thought Dad would lose at anything.'

'But doesn't that happen?' I say, as the sound of Fiona's precariously clicking heels get progressively louder. 'I mean sometimes lawyers lose. Don't they?' I wave up at Fiona, who is at our feet now and I attempt a discreet point at Em, along with an explanatory shrug, but she doesn't take the hint and just stands there, grinning.

'He's not a lawyer, Liam.' Em whispers. 'He's the one being sued!'

I'm staring at Fiona but my brain's desperately trying to focus on what Em's just said.

'Lads, it's five minutes to last orders. C'mon!' she says, reaching out her hand to Em, who surprises me by taking it.

I shove open the heavy door and together we fall into the warm noise. They're all still there, just more glasses and even more crisp packets. Kenny waves over and I nod back to him.

'Here, what d'you want?' I ask Em as I break off towards the bar. I watch her for a moment considering.

She's not sure whether to follow me, or to answer Fiona's beckoning wave. I can tell. 'Just a Coke,' she shouts back.

She's at the table now. Murph's pulled up a stool for her and she nestles in amongst the girls. Not for the first time she seems like that lost wallaby amongst the native wildlife. When I think back now, to that first night at the shelters, I didn't *meet* Emerald. Emerald *happened*. Emerald Rutherford: the seminal event of this summer and all summers thereafter, Amen.

As is the way in Moloney's at this hour, it takes an age to get served. The bar is two deep. In between attempts to catch one of the barmen's eyes, I stare back at her. She's wangled a beer from somewhere and is sipping it steadily, flanked between Murph and Fiona now, chatting away like she's been there all night. Whether she really feels it or not, she looks content again. She's good at that front of hers.

I spy Kenny out of the corner of my eye. He's waving frantically, then he's up, walking towards me. 'Did you not see me?'

'Wha–?'

'Two Heinos, you walnut?'

'Cool, I got it.'

Finally the youngest Moloney brother clocks me. 'Flynn?' he says, slapping his palm on the counter. I shout my order over the head of some aul fella, Kenny on sentry duty at my side. He's not taking any chances on not getting his beers.

'She all right over there?' I ask, nodding over.

'Yeah, she's grand. They're all blathering about results. My head's wrecked listening to them, to be honest.'

I hand him his pints and we push through the thick crowd together.

I'm about halfway across the crowded bar when I pick out Em's voice above the others. It's her vowels: like herself, they can't help but spring out from the surrounding flatness. She's got her back to me. Her hands are gesturing away to Fiona. What Em clearly hasn't clocked is that the rest of the table is also listening intently, and then suddenly I know.

'I mean he's so talented. Have you heard his SoundCloud stuff? It's … incredible! He just *has* to go for it,' she says. 'There are so many opportunities now –'

I want to shout at her to stop. I want to run over and slam my hand over her mouth to stop the words coming but I know it's too late. I never thought I'd say this but I wish to God she'd shut up. Then her long hair tips back briefly as she drains the last of the beer. I make the rest of the short journey through some kind of treacle. Turbo's looking up at me and I know what's coming. Well, I don't know exactly, but I know something's coming. Everyone goes quiet as I crouch down and their faces move from hers to mine, as one. I'm staring at Turbo, daring him to do whatever it is he's got planned. I can feel the heat of their burning irises. I nudge the sea of empty glasses forward and land the fresh wave of drinks on the table.

Em looks up at me. Has she any idea what she's done? It feels like everyone in the world is looking at me right now. I can't lift my eyes.

'Well, if it's not Hozier himself,' says Turbo, rubbing his hands together.

My head's melted. I've never admitted to anyone that I want to sing or that I write any of that stuff. Those dreams were mine, only mine, and now they're out there for people like Turbo to piss all over. I thought she'd respect that, but it's like she didn't even twig it. No, it's just banter to her, some chatter to tell Fiona and Murph while waiting for me to come back from the bar.

Everybody breaks into ribbons of laughter. A few of the lads sing that bloody song about the church.

What the hell was she thinking?

I've got to get outta here.

EMERALD

Falling, right there in front of you

I watch Liam's broad, black figure, steering the boat expertly into the wind. He's thoroughly absorbed and fixed on our destination. It's not only the cold or the missing sunset that makes this journey to the island so unlike the first. It's us. I hear him take a breath and I hold mine.

He's been quiet like this since we left the pier. We spoke on the phone last night but only when he called to say he wouldn't be joining me to babysit, which, when he's come every other time, I couldn't help but find significant. There've been texts but we haven't actually seen each other since he left Moloney's suddenly on Saturday night, something to do with his little sister, he said, but I'm not convinced. Something is clearly off. After almost seventy-two hours I'm pretty certain he's mad at me.

Although it's only Tuesday, everything before Saturday feels like a lifetime ago. Since seeing Mum, I've felt at sea in every sense. By the time we reached the airport on Saturday evening Dad had bounced back to some strained sense of normality, insisting all will be fine, but I still can't get that image of him, slumped over the wheel, out of my mind. It's as though everything is upside down.

It's hard to believe we're out here on the water again. If the last journey felt dreamy, this one feels wild. The light shifts and my insides churn. I can barely see the look on Liam's face, but I know I don't like it. I wish it wasn't so dark.

'We'll head for the harbour.' He shouts it up the boat, his eyes never leaving the invisible skyline.

He's always said we need to stay clear of that side. 'Aren't we trying *not* to be seen?'

'This easterly is picking up. I can't risk the rocks. Even if we make it, it's too exposed for anchorage overnight. We'll hit the smaller shore north of the harbour. Slip in there. There's no way they're expecting anyone at this time of night.'

'OK.'

I feel him looking at me for the first time. 'It'll be grand,' he says, his hair blowing about his angular face. I might be imagining it from this distance, but his expression appears to soften.

As the white boathouse along the harbour wall comes into view, he turns off the light and we drift in gently towards land.

It was an easier mooring this time, but there's a distinct chill in the air. We start to unload the bags and carry them towards a sheltered cove, just uphill from the tiny shore. It's protected and safe but still I can't relax. The noise of the birds disturbed by our arrival is ear-splitting. I watch Liam crouched down checking the ground to see that it's level.

'You going to Kenny's results party next Friday? Or pre-results as he calls it.' It's my attempt to fill in the silence.

Liam sits down on a large rock and sighs. 'Not sure I feel like celebrating.'

'C'mon.' I'm kneeling in front of him now, trying to catch his eye.

'I'm not punching the air about what's ahead, Em,' he says, getting up with another exaggerated sigh.

'Isn't that the whole idea though? You're celebrating the achievement of being finished and not the actual results?' He doesn't answer. 'Besides, you never know what's going to happen.'

'I do know. And I don't want to,' he says dismissively, brushing past me and unrolling the tent with one great shake.

God, this is irritating! I get up and plod back through the shingle towards the remaining bag but I stop before I reach it and turn back to him, bolstered by some unexpected charge. 'You can't fix what happened to your dad, Liam.'

He spins around and glares at me. It's excruciating. Even as I turn away I feel the weight of his eyes following as I drag the heavy swell of tent poles up the slope to him. I know I should regret opening my mouth, but my blood is rising and I'm not regretting anything at all. In fact, I want to keep going. My tongue is loaded with words I want to let out. Words I've never found with anyone else, and now they've formed I need to set them free.

'You're not responsible. You do know that? I mean, it's not –'

He stops unfolding the tent and approaches me, snatching the other side of the bag. The force of his movements startles me and I stop.

236

Together we hoof the bag up the sand in unbearable silence. It's not long before we reach the cove where he stops dead. 'Listen to you.'

I let go of the bag.

He blows air sharply out of his nose, looking up and shaking his head. 'It's like you suddenly believe talking about shit will make it better,' he says coldly. I'm gripped by a surprising rage. I open my mouth to speak but he's in too quick. 'And, if I don't make it right for Da,' he says, 'who will, eh?' He falls to his knees and spreads the groundsheet out in a circle around him.

'C'mon, Liam. You're not expected to be some sort of family saviour.'

He shoves his fist into the small bag of hooks, searching furiously for something. 'That's how you see it?'

'Yes! You're being ridiculous now.'

'Jesus, Em, say how you really feel.' He finally looks up at me, stands and then draws a pole out roughly from the bag between my legs. 'Getting good at that, aren't you?' His hands are shaking.

'All I meant is it's not your job to fix your parents' problems.'

I don't recognise the look in his eye. I've never seen his chin jut forwards like that. The beautiful geometry of his mouth has shifted, like he's eaten something bitter. I can't believe I've made him look like this.

'You can talk!' he says, returning to grab another pole.

'What's that supposed to mean?'

'So you're telling me your whole flawless front comes out of nowhere, does it?'

237

'Excuse me?'

'So …' he says, waving one arm in the darkness, 'you don't play at being Daddy's darling Scout to compensate for your drunken mother? None of that's related?' he says, tossing something into the sand in front of him. 'I must have read that one wrong.'

I drop the remaining poles at my feet and the bag tumbles down the sandy slope with a heavy clatter. 'Fuck you, Liam!' I have to unclip my life-vest so I can breathe; it's trying to burst from my chest, along with my lungs.

'Fuck me?' he asks, as though he can't believe the words coming out of my mouth either.

'Yes!' I spit. 'I trusted you and now you're throwing that trust back in my face.' I toss the vest towards the tent.

'I'm not throwing anything, Em, but if we're digging up some truths about trust here, then let's do it.' His eyes bore into mine. 'Let's really be honest.'

Jesus Christ. 'You want honest?' My heart is literally thrashing around inside me.

'Yes! Be properly honest with me. Go on,' he says, stepping closer, like he's daring me.

I want to push him away, but I clench my fists into balls and step up to him. 'OK then, say what you like about me, but I'm pretty bloody angry at how you just spoke about my mother. No one has called her a drunk out loud like that and d'you know what? It sounded cruel.' My words are as hard and unsteady as the ground beneath me. I want to cry so badly, but I won't let it happen. 'And … and I'm sorry I embarrassed you in Moloney's last Saturday night, because that's the real truth you're getting at here, isn't it?'

He kicks the sand with his feet and I know I'm right.

'But it's not just your dad holding you back, Liam. It's you! I mean, it's pretty pathetic, when you're as talented as you are, to throw your future away on a career you're not interested in, just to please him.'

'Pathetic?' he says, examining me now with wounded eyes.

I can't look at him. I go to rescue the poles that have stopped in front of a well placed rock. 'Sorry, that came out wrong. I just don't understand why you don't … follow your heart.'

His hands fly into the air but that doesn't stop me.

'I think you're afraid, Liam.'

He swallows hard. 'Afraid?' he asks, aghast.

'Yes.'

'You don't get it. Do you?' He shouts it at me. 'Not everyone gets to "follow their heart". Life's not some fairy tale, Emerald. Not everyone's dreams come true.' He dances around in a circle waving the pole in his hand like he's mocking me.

I hike back up, dragging the heavy bag behind me and dropping it at his feet. 'Don't patronise me. I'm not totally deluded.'

'Perhaps, but you have to accept you're in a very privileged minority?' he says, starting to hammer the last pole into the sand.

'After everything I've told you, you still think I'm … privileged?'

He begins to heave the tent upright. 'Well, yeah! You are. It's bred into you … all that opportunity and possibility, go-after-your-dreams shit.'

'It hurts when you talk like that.'

'Yeah, well, the truth hurts,' he says, hurling a small bag of pegs at me, before crouching down on the opposite side. I crouch too, copying him and I thrust a metal skewer into the ground. We each pull at the tent cover on our side, grappling with each other for canvas.

'Don't be smart-arsed. Not now.'

'I'm not. Clichés make people mad because they're true, Emerald.'

He's right, I am mad. I'm so angry it's terrifying: terrifying and exhilarating. 'I'm not saying it's untrue, but its suits you to look at only one superficial part of my life and that's why I'm mad. Your cliché, Liam, is incomplete.'

I'd storm off now only it matters too much. He matters. I matter. This matters. Nothing in my almost-seventeen-years has mattered like this. 'D'you know something else that's true?' I ask, yanking the tension needlessly tight on my side and shoving my last peg into the hard sand. 'I actually hate you a bit right now.' I stand up and hammer the hook further in with the heel of my shoe. I have to lean against a rock to steady myself. I've never spoken to anyone like this and certainly no one's spoken to me like he just has either.

He's moving towards me and I'm scared my quaking legs will give from under me. He's almost beside me. Our faces are edging closer and I feel that charge again but it's pulsing between us now. I know my nostrils are flaring and I have a horrible feeling I look like my mum.

'Well, I hated you a minute ago,' he says, catching my hand and drawing me gently down to the ground beside him. His heart pulses against my breast. Slowly my splayed ribs settle but the new silence feels dark and endless. I can feel the lingering heat of his breath on my cheek as I try to reorder his words, but my mind is a blender, whisking everything into chaos.

I close my eyes to stop the spinning and then I hear his voice again. 'I don't any more though, not really,' he says, lightly tracing his finger down the length of my face.

I don't want to open my eyes.

'This is messed up,' he says.

'What is?'

'Feeling this mad and being … madly in love at the same time.'

I feel my brain slowly brake and I play the words again inside my head. I know for a fact I've never felt this close to anyone ever. I never knew that closeness like this existed. 'Are you?' I ask, like a child. 'Are you madly in love with me?'

He pulls my elbows from under me and I dissolve on to the ground that is part sand, part tarpaulin. 'Maybe.' He smiles, leaning over me now.

'Maybe?' I roll my head away. 'OK, I am properly mad at you now.'

He gently tilts my face back to his and I can feel his breath again, stronger. I can almost taste him. 'I love you,' he says, slowly, pulling me up towards him and hauling us fully inside the tent. 'There, will that do?' His beautiful full lips beam at me.

I pull him on to me, twining my arms around his neck. 'Say it again.'

He nestles his face into my hair and falls into me. 'I love you,' he whispers. 'But you knew that. The very first night you looked at me, you saw me falling, right there in front of you.'

I want the world to stop so we can stay like this forever. I need to see his eyes so I push his face away, but I find his mouth, open and waiting like the answer to a question I didn't dare ask. I place my lips on his and let his warm tongue fall, full and heavy on to mine. I begin to taste something: like apples at first and then sweet tea, before he pulls away and covers my mouth in small salty kisses. He rolls on to me, plunging again, kissing me deeper. This is no ordinary kissing. He seizes my hands, holding them trapped against our sides. I can feel his thumbs brush my palms and then his fingers move up to my wrists, stroking their insides as I lie completely still and in bliss. Our lips open to each other again and he pulls me hard against him. God, oh God.

'Sorry,' he says, pulling away suddenly. 'We better stop.'

I press myself in to him, refusing to let him go. 'No!'

Mouths open, tongues deep and demanding. What is happening inside me? I can't stop. He leans in to me, heavily, one more time before he pushes himself off. 'I didn't think this would happen,' he says, his stubble rasping at my chin. 'I mean I hoped it might, but I didn't allow myself to believe it. I haven't … I didn't … you know, bring anything.'

I can feel his weight on me and I am full with a longing that is entirely new. 'I have one,' I say.

His eyes go so wide. 'What?'

'In my bag.'

'You carry condoms?' he says, part disbelief, part hilarity, part something else that I don't even want to work out. 'You think you know someone, and then –'

'One! I have one! It's been there since the Fifth Form Ball. Kitty gave it to me … it was a kind of joke. Well, it was to me anyway.'

He swipes a lock of hair from my eyes. 'But are you sure you're sure, Em?'

'Yes, completely.' And it's true; I know I am.

'It's just, I haven't …' He pushes off me and squints into the darkness. 'It's my first –'

'Me too,' I whisper, cutting him off and gripping a fist of hair from the back of his head and drawing him steadily forward.

He kisses me again, soft and willing, before placing a hand on either side of my face and pushing himself up again. 'OK, that helps, you know … that we're in this together. Not gonna lie.' He leans back through the open zip, limbo dancer style and swings my bag into the tent by its long strap. I fumble inside it, rummaging through the make-up and empty Haribo packets in rising panic. He doesn't take his eyes off me. Eventually my fingers find the inside pocket and I undo the popper and slide my hand into the same scented envelope Kitty placed there a couple of months ago.

I place the soft foil packet in Liam's palm and I lie back, writhing clumsily out of my dress. I am naked now: completely naked, open and bare, watching Liam wrestling with his jeans. My face scrunches up into some sort of cringe I know can't look good, but I can't help it. I'm not sure I even care. I'm not embarrassed, but still, I keep my eyes closed until his hips fall on to mine again and I feel him press up firmly against me so that I have the full delicious pressure of him on me now. My nipples harden, which startles me. Everything is startling me. It takes a few tries before he finds me and I allow my hands to explore his back, tearing his sweat soaked T-shirt over his head.

'What if I … ?' he says, stopping again and pressing himself up.

His arms tremble under his weight and I watch his chest rise and fall. 'What if you what?'

'Hurt you.' His breath is urgent and his eyes are glistening now. 'Or, that I get it wrong –'

I raise my face to his without answering and let his lips cover mine again. 'It's OK,' I say, pulling back as my body heaves. His hands are everywhere. Mine too. 'We can't get this wrong, Liam,' I whisper, knowing with utter certainty that this is now true. I feel a small stab of pain somewhere between my legs. I push him back but the sensation has moved to my hips, turning into something extraordinary I don't want to stop, and as we move together now I am nothing but my body, our bodies. I take his head in my hands and kiss him with all my life.

'I never expected this, Emerald,' he whispers, moving inside me now. 'I never, ever expected you.'

I open my eyes to his and it's just us. Liam and me and the Irish Sea. We've shut out the world; all of its sharp edges beautifully blurred.

LIAM

Watching the day become itself

Emerald and me huddle up on the low cliffs, watching a flock of razorbills diving off the rocks and swimming out together in a large circle. The sleek, black bodies disappear in an instant and then, all at once, they rise to the surface: elegant heads first, then dashes of bright, white throats with beaks wide open, expecting what, I don't know. It's like our own good-morning flash-mob. I look up at Emerald to see if she's catching it all, but she's staring out into the sky. My eyes follow hers and together we watch the day become itself.

I nestle my head into her. 'This has got to be my new favourite place.'

'I know. It's so beautiful here.'

'Not the cliff. I mean lying here, on your chest.'

She leans her head over and kisses me upside down.

'We gotta go,' I say, getting up reluctantly. 'There's no holding back that sun.'

We run along the cliff edge and stumble down the rocky path, back to our little base camp. Together we gather up the last of the bags and haul them towards the boat. It's only us and the birds up this early; even the sea looks sleepy. We board the RIB and push away from the shoreline, drifting out into the silky waters. Once we're at a comfortable speed I look back through the binoculars. There's no trace of us on the empty shore and I exhale slowly, deeply, happily.

As we round the cliffs, I spot a line of wallaby tails bouncing out of the bushes. I reach over her seat and point up behind us. 'Look up to your left.' I have to shout it over the roar of the engine. Then I sit back into the helm and watch her, watching. My insides surge with something new and warm, softening the bite of the cold morning air. There is no golden egg-yolk sun this morning, just a pure, white light rising in the shining sky.

'Liam, Liam. I see them!' She goes to stand up but staggers and has to grip the backrest to steady herself. She's pointing like a mad thing and rocking the boat.

'Whoa, whoa, sit down.'

She looks up again, binoculars clamped to her eyes. 'There are four of them. Ohmygod, look!' she squeals with delight.

I need to keep clear of the cliffs and just steering is taking all my concentration. Still, I want her to get a proper look.

'It's like they're whispering to each other,' she says, turning to look at me. I catch a quick glance at her face, wild and alive, and then she starts to laugh: a beautiful peal of inexplicable laughter. 'I can't believe it's true. I can't believe they're really here!'

'Careful!' I call out.

We're riding steadily across the water now so I squint back up for another look. I'm watching the clumps of bushes in the high distance, but I can't see anything. I follow Emerald's eyeline but her gaze is off. She's looking further left, away from our cliff.

'Are there more?' I say. She doesn't turn. I don't know if she's even heard me. 'Did you spot –?'

She spins around and the binoculars tumble down from the strap around her neck. 'There's somebody there, Liam.'

'Where?'

'Up there,' she points in the direction of Deadmaiden's Cove. 'He's watching us.'

'Jaysus.' I stand up, waving her back down the boat towards me. 'C'mere, gimme them,' I shout, reaching.

She dives towards me, slipping between the seats but she manages to hand the binoculars over. I fix them to my face, without letting go of the wheel. There in the distance, Gerry stands with his gun slung over his shoulder, looking like some lonely warlord. I'm staring at what looks like a large brown sack by his feet wondering what on God's earth he's sporting that bloody weapon for at all, when he bends down and swings the heavy brown bulge into the air and over his back. It's only as I spot the thick line of blood that drips from the poor wallaby's body I realise it's not a sack at all. Nobody culls the island wallabies, even I know that. What's more, Gerry knows I know, which is exactly why the bullying bastard's done it!

I tighten my grip on the steering. 'Sit down, Em! Sit down!' I can't believe she nearly saw that. Ducking behind the wheel, I feel for her hand and pull her back towards the cover of the cab. My other hand is all over the dash, grabbing at the dials. I grip the engine throttle and set it at full speed. The boat lurches to port, tossing us forward as the RIB rips through the water. 'Hold on!' I shout, as I regain control. We're doing over thirty knots. Adrenalin and rage shoot through me as we tear in the direction of home. We slice through the water, both of us now drenched in the salty spray.

We're a mile or two out before I reach for the throttle level and slow it to half, which is enough to catch my breath and then we slowly, slowly ease down. As we finally cross over the sandbank, I look over at Em.

She looks back at me. 'That was the gamekeeper, wasn't it?'

I nod. 'Y'OK?'

She nods back. 'D'you think he saw us?'

I want to put my arms around her but we're almost at the marina and I need to navigate the buoys. I don't want Gerry polluting the wonder of all we shared last night. 'Nah. Not without binoculars. I got a fright; that's all.'

There isn't a soul out as we saunter back along the coast road towards Portstrand. It's even too early for the die-hard triathletes who pound this road in any weather. In the pale sunlight everything looks new, like we've earned the morning as truly ours. We follow the path along by High Rock and I can't resist squeezing her hand; she squeezes mine back. We don't need words. How can the world have changed like this in one night?

The first bus of the day fires into life as we pass the terminus. I check my watch; 5.27 a.m. I hold it out for her to see.

'We made it, Captain,' she says, leaning against a pillar by the hotel entrance. She looks up at the sky and she exhales with a shiver. 'There are faces in those clouds,' she says, pointing up. 'Smiling at us.'

I slink towards her but it's as though my clothes have shrunk with me in them and I can just about breathe. She tugs me towards her, kissing me. I've got to get her indoors but this could be our last kiss for hours and I don't want to pull away.

Pushing me slowly off, she plants a final kiss on my mouth. 'You can leave me here,' she says eventually.

'No way. I'll see you up. C'mon!' I say, dragging her hand towards the gates of her grandma's big house.

We're barely a foot through the dark gates when her body stiffens next to mine and I track her eyes up the drive. She stops dead. Light pours out from the downstairs windows. I'm trying to process this when I notice the navy car in the drive. Then I clock its aerials. 'That's a cop car, Em.'

Her eyes flash wide. 'She's called the police?' I take her shaking hand in mine and slowly nod my head. 'What am I gonna do?'

My head's splitting apart, trying to work out what the hell has happened. 'OK, we'll go straight in there. We've got to. She'll be up to ninety,' I say. Em's searching my face in panic but I'm terrified of what she might say in front of the Guards. 'Don't worry – I'll explain it was all my idea. Nothing about the island. I'll say we slept on the beach.' Her eyes career around in their sockets and I'm even more afraid she'll blurt out about stealing the boat and Gerry will slaughter Da like he did the poor wallaby. 'Have you got that, Em?' I turn her face to me and squeeze her fingers in mine. I need eye contact, confirming this is understood. 'This is important,' I say, moving my hands up to her shoulders and squaring them. 'We slept on the beach, OK?' She dips her head back to me.

We begin our march up the long, rose-lined drive, clutching each other's arms. There's a sound of a latch and our eyes fix on the hall door, gradually opening as we get closer. Bit by bit the figure of her grandma is revealed, standing there in her dressing gown. She doesn't look at all like Emerald, but right now they share the same petrified expression.

Emerald begins to run the last few steps, dragging me with her. It's only when I have my sodden shoe inside the hallway door that I see him, Sergeant O'Flaherty, leaning between the hall table and the banisters, clutching a mug of tea. There's another Guard with him; a young, fidgety fella, fresh-out-of-the-box. He's got his eyes fixed on Em, not on me. Without any words, we're ushered deep into the large hall. Emerald is the first to speak.

'Grandma, I'm so sorry,' she says, falling into her arms.

The woman holds Emerald there for a moment; her eyes closed, lips moving like she's praying, then she steps back a few inches and stares up at her face. 'Heaven help us, where have you been all night? What in the name of God were you thinking, Emerald?'

'I'm so sorry. I didn't mean to worry you. Everything's OK. I'm OK,' says Em.

'And everyone's safe, which is the main thing.' It's yer man, Fidget, bouncing up and down on his feet. He's a total bogger.

'Grandma, this is Liam,' Em says, seizing my hand and heaving me forward.

There's no way Em would have found herself in this sort of situation had it not been for me. Me, I'm used to the odd scrape, the occasional brush with some authority or another. I bet she's never even coloured outside the lines. I'm feeling every inch the bad influence that all the gathered stares have decided I am. Where do I even start this apology?

'Hi, eh … Mrs Rutherford,' I say, unsure of what to do with my hands. 'This is all my fault,' I add, but she looks at me without a word. The air is thick with silence. Fidget starts to cough. He's still at it when I glance back around the hall to find all of them gawking at me at once. 'You see, Emerald didn't –'

'It's Byrne,' O'Flaherty's gravelly voice pipes up from the stairs. 'The lady's name is Mrs Byrne, Liam,' he says, shaking his head at me.

I shoot him a stare, confused. His eyes have a mad look I'm not sure I want to decode. He's still shaking his fat, dimpled chin ever so slowly from side to side.

Emerald is hugging her grandma and I glance beyond her head, around Fidget's back and into the kitchen, where my eyes land on a photo of her beside the fridge. She's much younger, wearing earmuffs and holding a man's hand. It's far away but I instantly recognise his face.

My mind turns to fog and I can no longer see straight. I spin back to face O'Flaherty, who sets his mug down on the hall table with a deliberate thud, right beside the old phone. I follow his thick, hairy hand jutting out the end of his coat-sleeve and watch as he tears the top page from a pad of old Post-it notes and hands it to me. My eyes dart from the scrap of blank paper in my hand, to Emerald, and then back to my shaking hand. There's nothing written on it, only a printed logo somewhat faded from the sunlight. I blink a few times but my eyes won't focus. I glare at the letters, willing them to stay still. Then, like some sort of Ouija board formation, the pattern emerges and I can suddenly see the word screaming at me:

HORIZON.

Bile skulks up my throat. I clamp my hand over my mouth, pushing towards the door.

Emerald reaches for me as I pass. 'Liam!'

I start to run.

'Young love, eh,' Fidget announces in the distance but his voice is soon drowned out by the sound of O'Flaherty's heavy boots, which follow me down the drive.

'Get in the car, Flynn,' he shouts, gaining on me.

'Liam!' I hear Em call out again but I can't turn around. I feel O'Flaherty's cold hand on the back of my head as he swings open the door and shoves me into the back seat.

EMERALD
'All this lip!'

Grandma is sorting through paperwork at the kitchen table. She's flicking through bank statements and totting up numbers on an old envelope before punching them into a calculator. Neither of us has been back to bed.

I've left Liam yet another voicemail and I'm going out of my mind. 'You must know something, Grandma – you were with that policeman for hours. I need to know what he said to Liam. Please!'

I'm trying not to be angry with her, but it's hard, because right now she's my only lead. I slam my phone on to the kitchen counter, kind of accidently, mostly on purpose.

'Emerald!' she snaps. I've broken her concentration. 'As you're well aware I barely slept a wink last night and I'd like this behaviour to stop now.'

'I was just asking!' I did mean this to be an apology but it doesn't quite come out like one.

'You've asked plenty and it has to stop – all of it!'

I'm on thin-ice already but I wish she could understand how unbearable this is. 'That awful look on Liam's face, Grandma. If I just knew what was said –'

'God almighty, Emerald. All this lip!'

I've never heard Grandma raise her voice like this. As I turn slowly around she gives a soft, steady sigh. 'I'm sorry,' she says, taking off her glasses and squeezing the bridge of her nose. She rubs at her temples in tiny circles. Her breath is heavy as she clears her throat. 'I'm just finding it hard to believe you stole off into the night, and with him,' she says, shaking her head now, as though trying to let the reality of it all fall out from her brain. 'You've no idea who he is.'

'Yes, I do,' I say, stepping closer. She continues flicking through the papers, without really looking at any of them. 'I know him better than I've known anyone,' I add.

'Trust me,' she says, with her tiny eyes peering at me over the top of her glasses, 'you don't.'

I hate the assurance with which she says this. Like she knows something I don't.

She places her balled-up fist over her mouth and motions towards the chair opposite her with her other hand. I sit down, feeling very much like a child about to be scolded.

'Emerald, you need to talk to your father. D'you hear me?'

'You haven't spoken to him?'

'No.' She whispers it. I'd assumed she'd already done it. In fact, I'm surprised she called the police before calling Dad.

'I'm sorry, Grandma. Really I am. I know you must have been so worried. It was a stupid thing to do, and –'

'Yes, it was,' she interrupts. 'It was stupid and irresponsible. I was up the walls imagining what might have happened to you. And now … well, I hope you haven't got yourself into any trouble with that –'

'Liam. His name is Liam.' I feel a fat tear well up and I open my eyes wide to let it sink back in. 'And it's all even more dreadful because … I love him –'

'Oh, Emerald, please,' she butts in, her face and hand gestures freezing for a second.

'It's true, Grandma, I do.'

She braces her shoulders and tilts her face towards the fridge and away from me. Her body judders at the impossibility of it.

'I know you're terrified … about upsetting Dad, what with everything –' Something in the way her bottom lip quivers stops me from finishing this sentence and I change tack. I'm shaking now and I see she is too. I take a deep breath. 'Yes, he'll be mad at me for sneaking out but he won't be as shocked as you think about me having a boyfriend. I think he'll really like Liam. They've got a lot in common. Even music –'

Her two hands cover her face. 'You need to speak to him,' she says it again, really slowly this time.

'OK! I will.' I want Dad to be happy for me. I want him to like Liam, but now I don't know what's gone on and I can't help thinking of every other phone call I've had with Dad since I've been here, and how impossible it's been to get his attention. I pace the room. 'Might it be better face to face?' I suggest, hoping this might buy me some time to speak to Liam first. 'He'll be at the family session on Sunday. He's meeting me at the airport – can't I tell him when I get to Bristol?'

She bites lightly on the tip of her glasses, considering. 'All right,' she says, pressing her palms on the table and rising up out of her chair. 'Maybe this would be better in person, but you're not to see that Liam again before talking to him.'

I immediately stand. I can't agree to this. 'But Grandma –'

'It's all I ask, Emerald. And you need to tell your father everything,' she says, dusting the leaf of a Busy Lizzie on the window ledge.

Everything: the single, simple word reverberates in my ears and I feel off balance. I crumple back into the chair. Looking around the room I catch Dad's eye, peering out from the photo beside the fridge. I blink a few times, trying to sharpen the blurred images that are now rearranging themselves behind my eyes. At first it's just patches flashing into place before evaporating again.

I close my eyes and suddenly I'm eleven again, back to the Boxing Day, where everything changed. *There she is, my mother, in the corner of this kitchen by the oven. She's younger of course. She hadn't cut her hair into that bob yet and her long, golden-red curls fall loose down her back. She's wearing a tight, blue woollen dress with lots of pretty bracelets jangling at the end of her wrists. There's a smell of mince pies and through the open door I can hear logs spitting in the fireplace. Dad is singing along to the TV in the other room, but then all of a sudden he's not. He's behind me in the kitchen, shouting at Mum. She's telling him I deserved it.*

I let my forehead fall into my palms. The memory is coming in waves now, like a familiar nausea. The unravelling is imminent, but I don't like it. In fact, I want to tie it up into the messy knot it was and kick it out of my head and out of the kitchen window, but I can't stop it rising up from my insides. My hand cups my face and underneath my fingertips I feel the heat of my stinging flesh.

'Why did she hit me, Grandma?'

LIAM
Everything to do with everything

'Liam!' Laura yells it up the stairs for what I sense is not the first time. Thin Lizzy's 'Still in Love with You' is on repeat behind my head and I can just about hear her above the music. How is it Phil Lynott knows exactly what I'm feeling since last Wednesday morning? I look down at the text that I've been trying to write to Em. I've rewritten it at least ten times. I've spent less time writing an entire song.

Actually, it's not a text; it's a bloody essay and I still can't send it. Suddenly the hall door slams and the whole house rattles from the aftershock.

Footsteps hammer on the floorboards outside my bedroom and I stash the phone under the rug just as Kenny's ginger mug pokes around the door.

'All right, man,' he says. Taking the tiny motion of my neck as an invitation, he saunters on in. He stops in the middle of the room and starts doing woeful air guitar all out of time. He's no Gary Moore.

'Wanna write a little song about it?' he says, grinning at me. I aim one of my little Velcro darts at him. 'Ah, I'm only slagging, moody girl. Here,' he says, tossing a Double

Decker into my lap. 'Comfort food, for your period pains.'
He laughs. I catch the chocolate bar and fling it up on to
the bed.

'At the risk of stating the obvious,' he begins, 'you were
missed last night.' He crouches on his skinny legs and budges
up to sit beside me on the floor.

I fire another dart at the felt board above the waste-
paper bin. It hits the little bull's-eye, dead centre, before
slumping straight into the metal bin, which just about sums
up everything I feel right now.

'You gonna say something, Flynn, or are we having a
one-way dialogue here?'

'Monologue.'

'Wha–?'

'That'd be a monologue.'

'Whatever, at least yer talking. So you don't show up to
my party last night, which was only THE party-to-end-all-
parties, the one we've been planning for ten bleeding years,
the one where we toast the ultimate end of our school life
together, just that one. And ...' he says, with his palms out
open like some phoney politician, 'you haven't returned
any of my calls or even tried to explain what in the name
of Jaysus is going on?'

I fire another dart at the wall and watch it plummet
limply to the floor.

'You know your game?' I say, turning to him. 'The one
where you ask me to make a choice?'

'Yeah?' he says, rubbing his hands together with irritating
enthusiasm.

'I have to choose. This time it's for real.'

He's excited. He thinks we're playing now. 'Between what?'

'Between who.'

'All right, so who do you have to choose between?'

'Emerald and Da.'

His legs stop bouncing and he holds them, uncomfortably mid-position. 'What?' His face twists in confusion. 'Why?'

'The Garda, O'Flaherty, yer man who came to the shelters that night –'

'What about him?'

'Said he'll tell Da everything, unless I stop seeing her immediately.'

'Tell him what? What's she got to do with anything?'

I fire the last dart at the board and turn to face him. 'She's Jim Byrne's daughter, Kenny. Only the prick that bankrupted generations of my family's business.'

His jaw drops loose. He goes to say something, but stops. Finally he just blows air from his mouth for a very long time.

'She's got everything to do with everything.' I say it slowly having spent the best part of three days digesting this rancid fact. I hear him sigh again, when suddenly he starts digging me in the ribs, hard.

'What?'

He's pointing under the door.

I swivel around. 'What?'

He keeps pointing, urgently, his brow creased into some kind of alarm. I crawl over to the doorway on my knees, following his finger and slanting my head on the ground to peer into the gap underneath it. The white rubber toes of Laura's Converse come into focus. I reach up for the handle, flinging the door wide open, but she's off down the stairs like a bullet.

'Laura!' I shout, scrambling to the top of the stairs, but the hall door slams shut and the whole house trembles once more.

Kenny is scratching his head when I walk back in the room. 'Whatcha gonna do, man?' he says.

'About Laura?'

He waves his hand dismissively. 'Nah. About Emerald.'

'Dunno.' We sit like this on the floor; Kenny's sighing and I'm just staring ahead, sure of only one thing – that I'm a damned man either way. 'What's mad is I had this sense, you know. Last Saturday night outside Moloney's, something she said about her dad didn't feel right.' Kenny is still slowly shaking his head. 'But I couldn't go there. It was like a piece from a different jigsaw, one I didn't want to see at all.'

Kenny nods softly and I know he gets it. I'm even starting to feel grateful when he begins to noisily unwrap a Twix from inside his pocket. He takes a massive bite. 'And it was insane, by the way, the party. Thanks for asking.'

I'm too depressed to respond. I can't bear the sight of him munching away. It's too normal; eating a Twix is something you'd do if the world weren't falling apart.

'Your aul fella must be peppering about you heading off to Dundalk, excited like,' he says, masticating loudly.

'I don't wanna go.'

He's gawking at me, mouth full of slobbery, brown goo. 'What's that?'

'You heard me.'

He swallows hard, as though all the gunk in his mouth is now concrete. 'Any more bombshells for me today?'

Results in four days. How do I begin to tell Da? I'm standing by the hall door, watching Kenny hurdle the hedges all the way to the end of the street. Then, gritting my teeth, I walk into the living room. He's sitting there, watching telly.

'Thought you'd be doing an island run today?' I say.

'Gerry's away,' he shouts over his shoulder. 'Asked me to come over on Monday instead this week, which means I get to watch the game. Happy days,' he says, rubbing his hands.

I'm suddenly remembering the horrible image of Gerry the wallaby slayer. I've wanted to tell Dad about what he did, but how can I? Besides, I've other bombshells to worry about. Every fibre of my being is quaking, as though the words I'm about to drop will make the walls cave in.

'Anyway,' he says, 'just the man. Sit down. Sit down.' He taps the seat cushion next to him, all keen, but he's still staring at the football on the box. I watch his furrowed face in profile. 'Amn't I only off the phone to the Credit Union,' he says. 'They've agreed your loan.' He steals a happy side-glance at me before turning back to the game. I clear my throat. Da sits up, roused by something happening onscreen. He thumps the side of my leg, playfully. 'We'll go and see John-Joe when I get back Monday afternoon and we'll take a couple of his motors out for a spin. What d'you say?'

John-Joe's got a second-hand car garage up by the airport now. Da's been dying to take me there. Kenny was right; he's peppering with the excitement all right. The way he sees it this September life-plan of mine is actually coming together.

'I need to talk to you, Da.'

His head drops and he takes a deep breath, staring at the ground. Then he picks up the remote and mutes the TV. 'Go on,' he says, settling back into the seat. Da has a look of perpetual concern; it's his beady, blue, cowboy eyes. Grandda had the same, but with even more of a Clint Eastwood squint. Da generally reserves direct eye contact for when it's absolutely necessary, like he somehow understands the power of his stare. Most of the time when he's talking to you, he looks past, or around you, but I can feel the full weight of those eyes now.

The house is completely silent apart from the faint thud of bass coming from Laura's room upstairs. There's not a sound from outside: no car pulling out of its drive, no screechy kids playing, no ice cream van in the distance. All of which gets me wondering how it's anything less than a lifetime ago that we all piled out on to the street queuing for Tangle Twisters and Icebergers.

Da's breath is heavy and I watch his nostrils widening with each exhale. His eyes focus again, piercing mine. It's impossible not to break under this stare; it's the weight of glorious expectation in his eyes. Wish I didn't know him so well. I wish to God I couldn't see all the life-giving hope that's filling his poor head.

'Liamo?' he says, digging my leg.

'Nothing. I'll need to change my shift Monday, that's all.'

EMERALD

Sometimes it takes a little fight

I've decided WH Smith is the best place to kill time in Arrivals at Bristol Airport. Another coffee might tip me over the anxiety cliff and I need some distraction from the daunting task of telling Dad 'everything'. I didn't expect to be this jittery. Liam *still* hasn't been in touch, so I'm not sure how much point there is working myself up to tell Dad I'm in love someone who won't even return my calls. But I need to do it. I also need to ask him about that Christmas with Mum before we get to the clinic. Grandma said Mum's the one to give me some answers but I'm really hoping Dad can shed some light on it first.

I'm scanning *Elle* magazine with one hand and hitting redial with the other. I'm only slightly aware of my foot drumming away involuntarily at the end of my leg as Dad's phone goes straight to voicemail again.

I've moved on to *Glamour* when my pocket starts to vibrate. Thank God!

'You're now officially ...' I take the phone from my ear to check the time, 'twenty-nine minutes late!' I don't hear anything. 'Dad?'

'Emerald, it's Magda.'

I picture her immediately: all silk-blouse and Slavic efficiency. I drop the magazine and it slinks heavily back into the rack.

'Em?' she says again, louder.

I think she's driving. I can see her with that prehistoric Bluetooth thing in her ear. I hear Ed Sheeran playing in the background. I struggle to compose myself. 'Uh huh.' I can't bring myself to be friendly.

'Your father asked me to call you. He's sorry but he's locked in a meeting and it's running over.'

My bag slips from my shoulder on to the floor. 'But it's Saturday!'

'He had hoped it would be finish –'

'He's supposed to be here now. He's supposed to be driving me there.' I'm practically snarling so I force myself to breathe deeply. 'We're supposed to be –'

'I know,' she says, cutting me off. No you don't know, I want to say, but I clamp my mouth shut. 'Don't worry. I've called a car to take you there. It will be outside Arrivals now. The driver will have a board with your name on it. It's on account.'

Magda's Polish accented 'don't worry' is about the least reassuring thing I could hear right now. Slinging my bag back on, I stomp through the crowded terminal, weaving through happy families hugging loved ones over mountains of outsized luggage. 'Is he even coming later?'

'He said he'd call you.'

'When?' I ask, picking out the familiar soft *tick* of an indicator. Ed Sheeran is louder now and I can make out the words; she must have stopped at some lights.

'As soon as he can. Call me back on this phone if there're any problems.'

'OK, fine,' I say. 'Thank you.' I tag it on lamely and hang up, thumping my way through the stiff revolving door and out into the air, which feels anything but fresh.

True to Magda's faultless organisation, the driver is already here. I hop into the back of the car and rest my face against the cool glass. The car meanders to the exit, rocking over speed bumps and jolting to a stop at the zebra crossing to let a trickle of suitcase-draggers pass by.

I open my eyes and stare out at the roads sliding past. Being here and driving through this familiar landscape is like peeling back a dirty old plaster. I wanted to believe the wound underneath might have healed, but no, it's still there: raw flesh and dried blood covered up with a tatty Band Aid that's lost its stick. I feel dizzy. And cross. I hate being here. I hate being alone. I hate being late. I don't want this reality.

When I finally arrive at Foxford Park, a lady with a barely audible voice explains that the family group is already in session. I don't even know what I'm doing here without Dad. The whole trip feels terrifying now. The silent lady starts to physically guide me where to go. I let her but I'm actually calculating whether I have enough cash for a taxi back to the airport when she pushes an enormous, white door wide-open.

A line of faces spins in my direction. It's a much bigger room than the one we were in last time. A woman is talking; Scottish I think. I freeze, unsure of what to do, until I see Nick motioning to me from over by the window. I want to turn around and run really fast in any other direction, but somehow I don't. Instead I follow his hand hypnotically as it gestures for me to take a seat.

As I cross the floor, all eyes in the room weigh heavily on my back. I wish I knew how late I was. The large sash window is open and despite the chill, my cheeks flush. Then I see Mum, sandwiched between the only two empty chairs. I can't help but notice how small she looks. Tugging my flimsy shirt around me I sink down next to her. I'm not ready to look at her.

The Scottish woman is still talking. A man on her right gawks up at her like a dog under the table waiting for scraps. 'Growing up, Stu was our rock. He was like that even when we were wee bairns. He'd look after us all. Always did his best to –'

'Joanne,' Nick interrupts. 'Your regard for your brother is understandable, but as I said earlier, we're focusing today on how our loved one's addiction has impacted on our lives. Please share with us what it was like to live with Stu during his drug use, and how it made you feel.'

She snivels. 'Ach, it's hard, you know …'

'We appreciate that, Joanne, but it's crucial to Stu's recovery that he understands the implications of his behaviour. Please be as specific as possible, like we discussed.'

Nick is on it today. Joanne wipes her nose with her sleeve and looks at him like she understands there's no getting off lightly. 'I guess it was when his wee son got sick, that we knew he was nay in control …'

At this, the guy who must be Stu lets his head crash into his hands, rocking his body back and forth, slowly at first and

267

then more vigorously, before properly howling. Joanne's voice becomes hysterical but I switch off from it in order to quiet the voices in my own head. Mum is staring at me; I can sense her eyes burying into the side of my face. My jaw clenches.

Nick half stands. 'Thank you, Joanne. We'll give Stu a moment to compose himself and we'll return for his response in a few moments.'

The room falls silent and I turn to look at the young guy on Joanne's left, the next lamb up for slaughter. I lean back and stare at the ceiling.

'Emerald? Do you feel ready?' I roll my head around to Nick's chair, but it's empty. He's up, opening another window at the far end, near the door. I glare at him, like another doomed animal in the mouth of the hunter's trap. I scan the door. He sits back into his seat. 'Emerald?'

He's said my name again. I'm so unprepared for this. There are too many questions I haven't asked yet. Why is Dad not here? I can't do this. Not with all these people. My fists ball so tightly my nails pierce my palms. I concentrate on the stinging pain. I notice the girl with the UGGs sitting next to me, picking roughly at a rash on her arms and suddenly I'm itchy too. Something is scratching at me from the inside, trying to get out.

'Would you like to tell us what it was like for you, Emerald?'

I look around and spot Sunil, the guy with the crack addict girlfriend, clearing his throat opposite me.

'Your mum has been preparing for this, so please, don't be afraid,' Nick says as Mum's icy fingers slide across my jeans and grip my knee.

I'm suddenly livid that she's put me in this position. I jerk my leg away and her tiny body recoils into the plastic chair. I swallow hard. 'I don't know,' I say, barely recognising the sounds leaving my mouth.

'What is it you don't know?'

'It's just …' I inhale. Closing my eyes to steady myself, it's like I'm back on the island with Liam, wearing that too tight life-vest and feeling like I might, at any second, explode. 'It's been a long time …' I can't believe the voice I'm hearing is mine. My eyes meet Sunil's and they dazzle me, somehow urging me on. 'Since she's been like my mum.'

Mum straightens, leaning forward in her seat. My heart is hammering against my ribs. All my thoughts are in flux, whirling up inside my head. The pressure is building; it's almost unbearable. I tear at the life-vest, pulling it all the way off.

'It's all about her.'

My mouth is full of words, each of them ready to fire out of me now like bullets. 'It's not even the drunkenness. I hate it of course, but the distance is worse. She has no idea what's going on for me, no idea what's actually happening in my life.'

I can't help but glance back at Nick, as much to check he's still there, that I'm still here and that I'm really saying this stuff. He leans forward so that his arms are folded on his knees.

'She goes to that place behind her wall and I wait, like *her* mother, worrying all the time. ALL the time! I'm always there – ready to clean up the damage. I miss having a mum, but that's how it is. That's how's it's been for

269

years. But I'd like to know why –' I stop and look to Nick again.

'Why what, Emerald?' he asks.

Mum slinks down into her chair beside me but I turn around, looking right at her for the first time. Her eyes are closed but I take in her whole face: the tiny twitches in the half-moons on either side of her mouth and how, as they adjust, they seem to unlock more pieces of the puzzle. I'm overcome with an urge to defy this awful memory. I hate how it hides inside me, lurking, waiting. I can't keep it in any longer. I won't.

'Why she hit me.' It comes out more forcefully than I'd planned and all the tired, leaden heads around the room rouse and turn to me.

I feel the first warm tear slide down my cheek. 'It changed everything, that slap. I've blocked it out for so long, burying it along with other secrets I've had to keep, confusing it with lies I've told to bridge other gaps along the way, but I'm certain now that it all started that Christmas. It's when everything between us became –' I stop to catch my breath – 'broken, I guess.'

Mum raises her hand. 'Stop!' she cries, but she's looking away so I don't know if it's to me or to Nick. 'I know,' she says, louder this time. Her body slumps forward and she starts to sob gently. 'I know why.'

'Eliza, you'll get your turn,' says Nick. 'Let Emerald speak.'

Mum begins fumbling in my lap and clasps my hand tightly in hers. I don't know whether to pull it away or lash back at her. I wrangle out from her grip and look her right in the eye.

'You slapped me across the face, as if I was a man. You told Dad that I deserved it. I heard you.'

Her lips quiver. 'Em,' she says. 'You called me a drunk. You shouted it at me across Annie's kitchen. You were the first ever to say it. It terrified me. You terrified me.'

I lift my face to meet hers and I find my own eyes stare back at me, that way they do when I need it least.

'And you were right. Eleven years old, standing there with your ponytail swaying behind you. You were absolutely right.' She kind of laughs this bit. She looks crazed but slowly tears start to stream down her face and she nods back at me.

Then she falls into my lap. Her body is heaving. I don't know what to do. I sit there frozen as she cries uncontrollably. Mum takes another deep breath and slowly sits up, reaching over to hug me properly but I flinch from her slender arms; I can't help it.

She swallows hard and sits back into the chair, clearing her throat. 'I was drunk, Em, and I was angry. It wasn't me. Of course it was, but it wasn't really. I wasn't angry with you,' she sniffs. 'It wasn't ever you, but you were like a mirror I couldn't face, and since then I've … I've been afraid of looking into it. Truth is, I've been afraid of you.' She blows loudly into the tiny, scrunched-up tissue jammed into the palm of her hand. 'I wanted you to slam that kitchen door in my face, but you didn't. You just stood there, stunned. I mean, of course you were. What kind of mother –' She stops.

I sit on my hands now and begin to rock forward gently with my legs crossed at my feet.

271

'The look on Annie's face as she ran into the kitchen behind you, that look as she dragged you away to safety. Away from me.' Her body judders and she looks to her feet. 'As soon as my hand touched you I collapsed on to that cold kitchen floor and started to grieve, for you, for me, for everything. I immediately wanted to take it all back but I knew I couldn't. I knew it was over,' she says, closing her eyes and raising her trembling hand to her mouth. 'So I just lay there, in front of the Aga, but above my shame, my grief and everything else in the world, d'you know what I wanted? What I really wanted?' She's addressing the whole room now. 'Another drink. Another fucking drink!'

There's another sharp inhale, and she breathes heavily out of her nose before filling up her lungs again. 'After that day I knew I couldn't lie any longer. I tried. I tried for years. I kept trying until six weeks ago, when I couldn't go on.' Her voice is low and guttural now. 'I'm s—sorry,' she says, turning around and addressing only me. Her face is a flood of pain and tears. 'I am so sorry, Emerald, for everything.'

She says the last seven words more slowly than I've ever heard her speak and for a few seconds all I hear is my own breathing, like I'm submerged in a tank.

I feel her hand snake across my lap once more and I don't pull away this time. I close my eyes and grip her hand in mine. I'm chilly suddenly. It takes the smallest second to realise it's not cold I'm feeling, it's something else new and strange. It's like I'm lifting. Someone else starts to talk. It might be to Mum, but their words don't reach me.

I just allow that apology, the one I've waited five and a half years to hear, to seep in and dissolve under my skin.

Mum folds a tissue into itself like some complex piece of origami. It's getting smaller and smaller. I'm swinging my legs on the bench like a child, surveying the garden, peppered with people in uncomfortable clusters like us. My phone rings inside my bag. I look at Mum. 'Dad.'

She gets up, presumably to allow me some privacy, but I kill the call. 'Where is he today anyway?' she asks, turning around.

In all the madness she never asked and I never explained. 'In a meeting. That's why I was late. Magda called when I was at the airport.'

Mum sighs and I watch her chest surge and then fall. She does that strange new laugh again just as my phone beeps with a text. I shade my eyes to read it.

Sorry about earlier. Hope it went OK. Coming to see you for celebrations on the 24th. I'll make it up to you then. Will call later. LOL Dad.

I roll my eyes at more than his crap text-speak.

'Everything OK there?' she asks. I nod but it's unconvincing, even to me.

'Thought I'd see him today, that's all. It'll be another week and a half now. He's bringing my results back to Dublin on the twenty-fourth.'

'You're not going to school to collect them, with Kitty?' I shake my head.

273

Mum is watching me closely. It's been a while since she's looked at me like this. 'Em, what you said in there was true. You were right about all of it. I don't know what's going on for you, and I haven't, not for some time.'

I don't even pretend this isn't true. 'Uh huh.'

'You've always been so competent too. I guess I fooled myself into thinking I didn't have to worry about you, but that was so wrong of me. Jesus, I was numb. It sounds corny, I know, but I've had a lot of help. I'm able to see stuff now that for so long I couldn't. Or, at least, chose not to.'

It's almost too much, but then it's not. I don't know if it'll ever really be too much or too late. I look up into the strong afternoon sun and I feel that lightness again.

I sit back into the bench, watching the other people attempting conversations like ours. How do we change when something has been wrong for so long? Is it even possible for us to really change inside of that room, inside of a day, inside of a summer? When did I stop being me? When did she? When did we stop being the two trembling bodies on her dressing-room floor?

It doesn't matter. Something enormous is happening; something that never could have happened before now.

'D'you know,' Mum says, 'there's this cheesy little picture of a Buddha at the end of my bed here. "When the pupil is ready the teacher will come", it says. I've looked at it for weeks not understanding, but then I realised it's taken sixteen years for me to notice you've been with me this whole time. If only I'd opened my eyes wide enough to see you, standing there all along.' She squeezes my knee tightly. 'I'm ready now, Em. I'm really ready.'

She's so excited. For a moment I'm afraid she doesn't understand, that she still doesn't get it. 'I need a teacher too, Mum. Can't you see that?'

'Exactly!' she says, clamping her hands on my shoulders. 'I'm not here just to learn from you. I've things to teach too, but first I need to learn *about* you. That's what I really want now, Em.'

The Scottish guy, Stu, is sitting on the grass with his sister and a teenage boy who is playing the guitar. The boy looks over and I decide to leap. 'I met somebody,' I say.

'But what about … ?'

She can't even remember his name. 'Rupert,' I say and she nods. 'That nothingness finished before it started.'

'OK …' She draws out the word. 'So tell me then, what's this new boy's name?' She settles in beside me on the bench, clearly encouraged by my new openness.

'He finished with me too.' It hurts to say it out loud. 'At least I think he has,' I add.

She places her hand on the back of my head, smoothing my hair. 'Oh, Em … I'm sorry.'

I cross my stretched-out legs and sigh. 'Liam, that was his name.'

'What happened?' She whispers it.

'That's what I don't know. He stormed out of Grandma's house on Wednesday morning and hasn't returned my calls since.'

'Did you have a row?'

'No! Everything was great. It was perfect. A policeman

said something to him. Actually, I don't think he said a word, but a *thing* happened. I'm sure of it, but nobody will tell me.'

She leans in to me, forcing eye contact.

I pull away. 'It's fine, I don't think he's in any trouble. Otherwise … Oh nothing.'

'Does Annie know him?' She sounds serious.

'She knows something. She's been acting really strange about it. It's one of the reasons I need to talk to —'

'Your dad?'

I nod. 'I can't believe he didn't come today, Mum.' I stop and stare at an older woman over by the pond. She's hugging a man the same age as Dad to her chest. I can tell from how his back vibrates in her arms that he's really crying. God, this place is intense.

'You'll get your chance to talk. Don't worry,' Mum says, bringing me back around. 'But did this Liam actually finish it?'

'Well … no.'

'How do you know it's really over?' she asks.

'He just flipped out and left — it's been radio silence since. I've called him every day. I don't know what's going on, Mum.'

Her face adjusts like she's learned a new expression and I don't know how to read it. She unfolds the tissue and smooths it out on her thigh. 'Mmm …' She sighs. 'You really care about him?' I bow my head, bobbing it gently. She nods hers too, like she understands. 'And does he know how you feel?'

'I thought he loved me too.'

276

'Well …' she says, 'if I've discovered anything these past few weeks, it's that you need to work at love.' My head slumps against her shoulder and settles into the outer pool of her hood. 'Sometimes it's not easy, Em. In fact, sometimes it takes a little fight.'

LIAM
I'm not asking you, I'm telling you

I finally succumbed to *Game of Thrones*; Kenny dropped over the box sets and I'm losing myself in Season Three already. I'm trying to zone out and forget about life but Laura's FaceTiming her friend and they're both shrieking.

'Can you do that in your room?'

'What?' she says, rolling her eyes at me for what must be the fifth time in twenty minutes.

Suddenly there's another screech. At first I think it's the TV, but then I look back to Laura and she's already folded over the couch, peering outside to where Da's van is skidding to a halt inches from the living room window. He gets out and wallops the van door, trudging towards the house with a face like thunder. The hall door slams shut.

'I gotta go,' Laura says, flipping over the iPad cover. We look at each other and I'm wondering whether she knows something I don't. My sister has a sense for these things. I hear Da's feet thump up the hallway and then the door opens and he's standing there before us.

He points to Laura. 'You. Out!'

I automatically stand up. I'm trying to figure out what Laura might have done when I realise Da's nose is practically touching mine.

'What part of "never take that boat out again" wasn't clear to you?' he says. 'Eh?' Specks of his saliva hit my face. He pokes his finger into my shoulder, hard. Jesus Christ!

'I'm sorry, Da.'

'You've no idea how sorry you are, pal.' I've never seen Da this mad. Well, I have, but it was a while ago. He hasn't been mad like this in ages. 'Would you like to be the one to tell your mam …' he says, his voice beginning to crack, 'why I've lost this job?' This last bit struggles out.

I stare at his mouth. I want to push the awful words back in and then I want the carpet at my feet to hoover me up. He's looking around now, anywhere but at me, rubbing his stubbly chin as though smoothing a beard that's not there. 'And,' he starts again, 'that her week on the Shannon, her only holiday in three years, is no longer happening. Would *you* like to tell her that?' he asks.

I don't know what to say or what to do. I just stand there before him, hopelessly shaking my head. 'That prick!' It trips out of my mouth.

'At least I knew Gerry was a prick, Liam. I thought more of you,' he says, pacing up and down in front of the TV. 'I mean, what were you thinking? What in the name of Jaysus were you thinking, son?'

'I'm sorry, Da.'

'So you keep saying.'

He's stomping around the room now and fuming like an angry dragon. It's like he's getting more worked up the more he thinks about it. He fires a look at me, drilling more guilt into my heart. I can't answer him. There is nothing to say. This is the worst ever.

'Did she put you up to it?'

'No!' I can tell he wants me to say yes. At least it might go some way to explain things for him.

'Who is this Emerald anyway?'

How do I answer this? I desperately want to come clean, to tell him how I'm trying to do the right thing by giving her up, but how I can't bring myself to, and how I'm being physically torn apart because of who she is. There's no way I *can* tell him, he'll explode, for sure, but I can't lie to him either. Never could. I'm stuck.

'She's Jim Byrne's daughter.'

I spin around to where Laura is swaying on the door handle, looking revoltingly pleased with herself. Da's staring at her too. I'm still scowling, trying to work out why in the name of God she'd do this, when I feel Da's eyes shift over to me. I know this because his eyes are literally corroding the side of my head somewhere around my temple, but I can't drag my eyes away from Laura.

She gives me this look, as if to say 'what's the big deal?' but then her eyes *ping* back to Da and her face alters. The brazen pout falls away. She knows she's got this wrong.

Out of nowhere, the doorbell goes. The ordinariness of its cheery ring is like a brief pardon from the unfolding nightmare, but nobody speaks; nobody even moves. It rings again: longer now.

BRRRRIIINNNGGG!

'Get the Jaysus door, Laura!' Da shouts and she swings back out of the room. Da's pacing starts again, his jaws and fists clenched even tighter now. He squints his already closed eyes at me. 'OK,' he says slowly, eyes narrowed. 'Tell me –'

'It's her!' Laura hollers from the hallway.

My eyes dart to his, immediately feeling the draught of the open hall door. Neither of us can believe this is happening. He slams his hand to his chest like he's trying to keep it from bursting through his shirt, but still it rises, slowly, fully, like at any second his buttons might pop. Then he exhales, without breaking his stare.

'I've never asked anything of you, son,' he says, stepping closer to me. 'But I'm asking this of you now. In fact, I'm not asking you, I'm telling you. For me, for your grandda, for this whole family, you've got to end it. End it!' he grunts, without opening his teeth.

I gulp down a mouthful of acid and brush past him, out of the room. Laura's still standing by the open hall door, blocking all but the top of Emerald's head.

'I'm sorry, Liam. I'm so sorry,' Laura says, her long arms reaching out for me.

'Go!' I snap at her but she stops and waits there looking terrified until I get closer. Then she swipes off to the side and slinks back up the hall.

I can feel Emerald flinch from the front step, those wide metallic eyes desperately trying to read what's going on. 'Lorcan at the Metro told me where you live. I hope you don't –'

I steal only the briefest glance at her because I can't look into her face knowing what I've got to say. 'You have to leave.'

She shakes her head slowly. 'Liam?'

'You need to go,' I plead, but those beautiful eyes bore into me and I cower behind the closing door. I have to; I am completely helpless to that look.

Em steps forward. There's no armour for the missiles her eyes fire as they scan my face, hunting for clues. 'Aren't you even going to tell me why?'

'End it!' Da hollers from the bottom of the stairs.

'Now!' I beg.

She steps back off the porch, leaning into Da's dirty old van. My body slumps forward and I smack my forehead against the closing door, thumping my fist on the glass as my heart breaks in a line of painful cracks.

EMERALD

Like vultures, they were

I fell back against the van, stunned. Shouts continued from inside the house but still my feet wouldn't move. It was only when I heard a small, soft voice call my name that I came round.

'You didn't choose your da.' Liam's sister, Laura, was leaning perilously from an open upstairs window.

'My dad?' I called back.

'Neither of you did. I'm sorry,' she whispered, before disappearing behind a net curtain. The window shut and she was gone.

My dad? Dad? As I squeezed past the beat-up van in the driveway, I saw the words barely concealed under a thin layer of paint.

FLYNN CONSTRUCTION
BUILDING QUALITY HOMES

I burst into the house.

'Grandma!' I shout out, stomping up both flights of stairs. 'Grandma!' I scream, snatching my laptop off the bed before marching back down to the kitchen. I slam my computer on to the kitchen table and flip it open.

JIM BYRNE, FLYNN CONSTRUCTION, I punch the names into Google.

457,000 results in 0.54 seconds

The page is awash with words wrestling for my attention. I hit the first headline and it expands to an article from the Irish *Business Post*, fourth of July; just days after I arrived in Portstrand! There's a photo of Dad, walking alongside another man on a Dublin street.

Irish taxpayer fronts €35 million bill for Byrne's failed developments.

Pictured outside his Irish solicitor's office today, Jim Byrne, declared bankrupt in the Republic after his bankruptcy attempts in the UK were thrown out of court, is now being charged by HM Revenue and Customs (HMRC) with concealing substantial rents from his Irish portfolio that should go towards his debts in the UK. It's understood that Byrne had been trying to raise funds to restart his building empire in the UK. Along with a substantial UK bank debt, Byrne owes the Irish Revenue Commissioners €1.9 million and his various companies owe debts of €6 million to the National Asset Management Agency.

My head is spinning. I close my eyes but it's chaos. I force my eyes back to the screen, back to the results, and hit another link from the *Irish Times* three years earlier.

Portstrand company, Flynn Construction, goes under with €1.1 million debt.

There's a photo of a dark-haired man in a hard hat and high visibility jacket, standing in front of huge scaffolding. I immediately know it's him. Liam practically bursts through the cracks of his lined face.

ONE of the country's largest property developers, Horizon Holdings, has gone into receivership – putting a number of major construction projects around the country on hold and threatening the future of several significant building businesses. Byrne Developments, which wholly owns the Horizon company, had been liaising with NAMA over a business plan, which was rejected. It is understood the receiver was put in place last night following the collapse of the plan.

Donal Flynn of the North County Dublin family business, Flynn Construction, had been providing the building contract for Jim Byrne's Horizon Holdings at the luxury Bay Road Apartment Complex in Portstrand. Flynn was due to receive €200,000 yesterday out of a total €900,000 owed.

It goes on but I can't. I shove my chair out from the table and pace up and down the kitchen. I can't take it in. Dad? My dad? How could I not know all this? And so many lies!

That's why we haven't come back here. It wasn't just the fight with Mum that changed everything. I shift back towards the table to continue reading but suddenly Grandma is by the back door. Her hair is stuck to her forehead with sweat and her cheeks are flushed.

'There you are, Em,' she says. 'Your dad called earlier, but I couldn't find you. Your mobile was ringing out.'

I shake my head at her. 'How could you not tell me?'

She looks around the room, her eyes darting between me, my laptop and the door. I can see her brain try to put it all together.

'Why did he not tell me?' I'm shouting now.

She drops a little trug on to the countertop and several baby potatoes rattle out on to the floor. She closes her eyes. 'Oh, pet,' she sighs. 'I wanted to –'

'How could you even let me be here?'

'With what happened with your mum … It was so last minute, there wasn't much choice, for anyone.' She drifts off.

I slump back into the chair and drive the laptop further into the bowl of apples in the centre of the table. 'So that's why Liam hates me now? He's discovered I'm the daughter of Jim Byrne – destroyer of entire communities – and only the bloke who bankrupted his father. Jesus!'

'I'm so sorry,' she says. 'I don't think your father knows the extent of the hurt he's caused.'

I can tell from a side glance that her clouded eyes are full of tears. She's not talking about Donal Flynn's hurt, she's not even talking about me. This is about her; this is about her own pain.

She sits in a chair opposite me, straightening herself into its back and lets out a long, deep breath, like she's arrived at a decision. 'I've stopped reading all that stuff,' she says, tapping at my laptop screen. 'When the Bay Road development first collapsed, Father Martin asked everyone at Sunday mass to pray for those families suffering. He didn't mention Jim's name of course, but I could feel the disgust rising from all those bowed heads. I haven't been back since.' Her eyes close and she gently shakes her head. 'God forgive me, but I just can't.'

I reach across the table and take her silky hand in mine. It must have been dreadful for her. I squeeze her hand and her wedding ring feels like a huge, impossible clump amongst her bony fingers.

'You've every right to feel angry, Em,' she says.

I release her frail hand. 'I'm suddenly … numb.'

'It'll come,' she says, undoing the back of the little gardening belt from around her waist and draping it on the chair next to her. 'And when it does, let it, but don't hold on to the anger – it's poison.' She goes to pick up the potatoes that have rolled under the table. I watch her crouch down but it's a struggle so I bend down to help. 'He never meant any of this … you should know that,' she says to me between the table legs.

'And Mum?'

'It's been hard on her too. Obviously, it has.'

'I always thought it was *her*, Grandma. I thought she did the lying. I never, ever, expected this from Dad.'

'He was trying to spare you, love.'

'Did he honestly not expect me to find out?' I ask, rearranging the pile of potatoes. 'Liam's about to throw away his future, so that he can make the business right for his dad – the business my dad ruined. You should hear the way he talks. What it did to his father, and what it did to him and his family. It's no wonder he won't speak to me.'

Grandma pats a small circle into my back before making for the kettle. 'I'll make some tea. You've had a terrible shock.'

'I've just been there. I've just come from his father's house!'

She covers her mouth and I follow her eyes over the bank of geraniums on the window sill and out into the back garden. 'Oh, Emerald,' she says, shaking her head again. 'Of all the families in this town —' She stops and shakes her head. The boiling kettle finally *click*s, startling her. She looks so delicate.

'You shouldn't have had to go through it alone, Grandma. You should have come to live with us in England, years ago.'

We both watch the boiling water slosh into the pot from a height. 'It wouldn't have been right, love. Eliza, and me, we'd had our differences,' she says, setting two cups down on the table. 'We never really recovered from … that incident. It was only a year or so after that Horizon started to collapse. It's taken a long time for me to forgive Eliza for what she …'

'I feel better about that now.' Grandma looks up. 'I mean, I always knew something serious happened that Christmas. I had a horrible sense that something was lost, but I didn't remember what I said to Mum. Isn't that strange?'

Grandma nods gently, her eyes glued to me now.

'I thought Mum … stopped loving me. I realise that now. I think I've been afraid to really open my mouth since in case someone else stopped loving me too. Turns out Mum was scared. Ashamed, I suppose.' Grandma takes my hand. 'I had no idea my words had that kind of power.'

Grandma does a sort of upside-down smile without opening her mouth.

I take a sip of the syrup-like tea. 'How did you face it here, all on your own?'

'Oh goodness, love, I'm all right. It was all over the papers at the time, but sure it's over three years ago now that it all hit the press. Thankfully this recent case is happening in England, so the interest here, if that's what you'd call it, is not as … intense.'

This is a relief.

'Except of course the night you arrived,' she adds. 'Didn't they snap him coming out of that airport hotel the next morning. Cover of the *Irish Times*. Like vultures they were,' she says, with another little shake of her head.

The cup sort of slides out of my fingers and *plunk*s back into its saucer. I'm out of my seat now. 'Do you still have it? The paper?'

'Let me see,' she says, getting up and delving in one of the dresser drawers. 'Yes, here it is,' she says, passing me the folded newspaper, which is now a little crispy. 'I'm sorry for not being truthful with you, Emerald. Your dad wanted to get through this round of meetings here, he'd promised to tell you after that, but then everything happened with your mum …'

'So after he dropped me off here, he didn't go straight back to England?' I cut her off.

'No, love, he didn't.' She looks as relieved as I am to be telling the truth after all this time.

She's going on now about lawyers and all sorts of stresses Dad's been under, but I fade her out as I open the paper out flat on the table. There he is coming through the hotel's revolving door, walking towards the silver hire car

I immediately recognise. Then I see the blonde plait and the tight skirt of the figure, several feet in front of him, carrying his leather overnight bag. 'Magda!'

'What's that?'

'Up to his eyes with meetings –'

'What's that, love?'

I hear her voice but I'm underwater again.

LIAM

Wish I could say she was,
but she wasn't

I'm standing in my hutch lashing coleslaw into a baguette, trying not to think about the CAO offer that arrived from Dundalk earlier, when I see old Whiskers ambling in through the automatic doors. I stack my pyramid of rolls, pretending to prepare for the lunchtime rush when he hauls himself up on to the very stool where Emerald sat only weeks earlier. His face is normally a reassuring sight, but I can't take him sitting there; not today, not with the dicey state of my insides. Waves of pain, like actual grief, have lapped inside me for days now and seeing him there my stomach begins to hurt again, properly.

It takes some effort under the circumstances, but I bow my head by way of salutation and he gives one of his deep nods back. I can almost hear the bones in his neck creak.

'The usual?' I ask, waiting for the rusty neck to jack itself up again, but no, he's squinting at the list of coffees on the wall beside my head.

His eyes dip up and down as he studies each item individually. I return to my heavy thoughts until the *clink* of coins on the countertop snaps me back. I turn around to see his hand smooth over an impressive stack of change. Almost a tenner piled up between his stubby grey fingers.

'Out busking?' I ask, but I can't raise a smile from him today. He's focused, or distracted maybe. I can't tell.

'What are the blended ones like?' he says suddenly. 'Them icy ones, with the syrups.'

I quickly scan the shop floor on Lorcan-watch; he's been on a feverish tip today, buzzing around, ticking boxes, making sure we're all slaving away, but I can't see him, so I lean into the counter and summon Whiskers in closer. 'Wanna try one? For free, like,' I whisper. 'Vanilla is nice – a bit sweet, mind you. You might prefer the almond?'

His glassy eyes shut for a second. 'Ah, it's not for me,' he says.

'Of course you're the tea. Here,' I say, grabbing one of the tiny espresso cups, 'take a little taste out to her if you like. She in the car?'

He shakes his head. 'She's beyond in Mount Pleasant, son. Been buried four years now.' His lips purse, holding in a lifetime of something I can't determine. It's taking a few seconds for his words to sink in. 'Sure, g'wan,' he says. 'We'll try an icy almond so. 'Tis fierce warm out there today.'

I spin around and busily scoop a load of ice into the blender. It's only once the machine fires into life that I allow the quivering breath out of my mouth.

I can't turn back to Whiskers, not yet. I'm afraid to look into his eyes, afraid that I'll start to weep over my freshly baked rolls. What kind of love drives a man to take a daily cappuccino with four sugars and no dust up to his wife's grave? I'm thinking of Da now, of him and Mam.

All sorts of thoughts are swirling around in my head as I try to gather myself to face Whiskers again. I have to count to ten silently.

'It all happened so quick,' he says, seemingly about nothing, but clearly about everything. My fingers drop the straw into the drink and our eyes latch.

So if ya had to choose … It's Kenny's voice now playing between my ears. My best friend might be proud but it's not a decision. It never was. Like Da said, when love pounces on you, there's no real choice involved at all.

The drive is empty when I get home but I still sneak in around the back, buying time to rehearse all I need to say. I've only just started pacing the kitchen when Mum walks in holding Evie on her hip.

I sit down. 'Howrya, Mam?' I say, trying to sound normal.

She smiles at me briskly. 'Hiya, love.'

Evie is in her high chair now, shouting about life, as Mum starts setting the table around me. Mum's moving at a pace I recognise; too fast, in hyper-efficient mode. One, two, three, four glasses crash against the table and cutlery is clattering down all around me. I shift around so she can set the place under my arms. I slide a spoon on to Evie's tray so she can bang that. She babbles at me gratefully, all thrilled with her new toy. I blow some raspberries on her arm. I need to hear her laugh.

'Take off those work things. Your da will be home any minute,' Mum says, without looking at me.

'But –'

'We're having dinner.'

I'm not sure I can do this over a meal. I can't face sitting opposite Da with all the dangerous stuff in my head unsaid. I'll wait till he's eaten. It's self-preservation. 'I'm not really hungry, Mam.'

'We're having dinner,' she repeats. 'All of us!' There's no arguing with her when she's like this. 'Go on!' she says, shooing me out.

I shunt myself up off the chair and stagger towards the door.

I skulk back down the stairs minutes later to find the kitchen door closed. The kitchen door is never closed. Da opens it just as I'm about to knock. He says nothing so I stand there not quite sure what to do, when he pulls it wider, allowing me in. He doesn't look at me as I squeeze past. Laura traipses in a few seconds later, but still, nobody says anything. Mam clinks crockery by the sink while me and Da rearrange our place mats, wondering what these are doing out of the drawer; staring at anything but each other.

I get up and fill Evie's plastic cup from the glass jug for something to do. Mam plonks the large dish in the centre of the table but just as I think she's about to sit down she goes to the fridge and grabs a beer. Laura and I share a look; Da never drinks with his dinner.

'Now,' she says, hooshing her chair in under the table. 'Before we eat your da has something he wants to say.' She leans across to open Da's beer and shoots him one of her don't-forget-who's-really-boss looks.

We all watch as Da pours the fizzy golden liquid to a thick white head at the top of the glass. 'We've all done stupid things, son. You were blindsided, I get that,' he says, setting the bottle down, still without looking at me. Gulp! Laura seems to take this as a sign that my lecture is over and she's up, poking at the large dish of food with her fork.

'What is this?' She prods it like it's roadkill. 'Mam?'

'Fish pie,' Mam says, still glaring at Da.

Laura gives a desperate sigh. 'Eh, hello! I'm vegetarian now!'

Mam slams the stainless steel serving slice on the table. 'That's enough, Laura!' she snaps.

Laura settles back into her chair, only mildly humbled and Mam starts dishing out folds of creamy-looking pie on to each plate. 'What your da meant to say, Liam, is that he forgives you, about the boat business and you know, the other matter. We both do. Isn't that right, Donal?'

OK, this is not what I was expecting.

Da takes a slow swig of his beer and grunts.

'And,' she says, 'he's arranged for you to go up to John-Joe's at the weekend, to take a look at a car.' Good Jesus, I'm totally wrong-footed here. 'He's got a new one with low mileage in. It sounds good, doesn't it, Donal?'

Da nods on Mam's prodding. 'Over the budget though,' he announces. 'But I've got another shift at the depot so I sup-pose we'll be able to manage,' he says, turning back to Mam.

Mam places her hand over her mouth before letting it rest on Da's giant hairy fingers. I watch her squeeze them, smiling at him. 'John-Joe said it's just the one for running you up and down the motorway to Dundalk,' she says, looking across at me.

This couldn't be any worse. My head is spinning and I've to shut my eyes to focus, but when I do all I see is Em:

arms outstretched, twirling around the lamp post under the moonlight. *'If you could be anything in the world, Liam Flynn?'* I'll never forget those words or the surprising anger and excitement that mixed together in my belly as she said them it. It's now or never.

'I want to defer,' I whisper it into my plate.

Nobody says anything so I look up and say it again, louder now. 'Dundalk, I want to defer my place.'

Da puts his fork down and cranes his chin up from his plate. 'But you've only just got in. How –'

'There's this music production course.' My eyes flit between him and Mam, both their jaws hanging in disbelief. I take a sip of water, trying to grasp hold of my thoughts, which are swimming around my head like slippery eels.

'Explains all the sneaky web searching,' Da says, picking at his teeth now with his fingernail. 'Galway, England and everywhere, I saw them.'

'This one's in Dublin. I've got the points. I'll need to show a demo portfolio, but I've got the material. And I'll have to get an interview first of course, but please! I'd just like to … follow my dream.' Holy shit. Did I say that?

Da sits back. 'Dreams?' he says, rolling his eyes. I wish I couldn't see his anger boiling so close to the surface. 'Oh, we've all had those, son,' he says, taking another long, slow slug of beer.

Mam sits forward in her chair. 'In Dublin?'

I nod.

Da shoots her a look. 'Hold on there now!' He sighs shakily and his eyes meet mine but only for a split second before they dart down again. 'Don't be getting ahead of yourselves,' he adds, before stabbing his fork into the pie so fiercely it crashes against the plate underneath. He forks another mouthful of pie into him. 'I was prepared to chalk the other matter up as a mistake. You weren't to know about the Byrne girl, I know that, but –'

Mam taps lightly on Da's forearm. 'It was a terrible shock, that's all,' she says before he can finish.

Da's fork shoots into the air. 'I won't be steamrollered into some notion about a music career.' I swallow the lump in my throat and set my still-clean cutlery back down. 'Not without –'

I don't let him finish. 'She wasn't a mistake, Da.'

All heads roll around to mine, even Evie's. Their disbelief, mixed with the new silence is unbearable. I push my untouched plate out in front. The colour of Da's face changes. Redness is rising up from his neck, making his whole face florid and I'm starting to imagine molten lava bubbling up from his insides. Laura pipes up from the end of the table. 'Seriously, Liam?'

I don't look at her; I keep my eyes on him. 'I wish I could say she was, Da, but she wasn't.' My knees are knocking under the table and I clamp them together to stop the quakes vibrating through the rest of me.

Da closes his eyes and pushes himself out from the table. His chair scrapes against the floor like chalk on a blackboard. He grips the table edge, like he's about to get up, but he doesn't. His eyes snap open. 'Help me out here, Liam. What exactly *are* you saying?'

I suck in some air, gripping it in my lungs and then I release it slowly, the way Kenny does with his inhaler. 'I'm saying she wasn't a mistake. She isn't.'

Mam winces as each of my words clout her from the far side of the table. She can't believe I'm doing this, after everything she's just done to get Da onside. I can't believe it either, but I keep going. 'She's not her father, Da. In the same way that I'm not you and to be honest, right now, I'm really hoping there's a chance of her still being my girlfriend.'

He's staring at me, shaking his head. Mam's elbow thuds on to the table, shielding her eyes from mine, from his too maybe. This is so not what she'd planned, but the fact is I'm in love with Emerald and I'll do whatever I need to to be with her. Surely they, of all people, can understand how this feels?

Dad pushes himself up out of his seat. 'I've tried, Maeve,' he shouts, storming out of the door in a gust of fury. This undoes Mam entirely and she leans back in her chair, eyes closed.

Desperate to do something, anything, I get up and start clearing away the uneaten food. Laura pulls her phone out of her pocket and starts texting. Mam, statue-like, apart from her trembling breaths, raises her glass to her lips and takes a slow sip, without opening her eyes. I walk around and place my hand on her shoulder. 'I'm sorry, Mam.'

I wish I could make it better. I'm thinking what I could say to her to make it right when she reaches up and takes my hand in hers.

'I know you are, love,' she says, squeezing my hand before twisting her neck and silently kissing the back of my palm.

My heart swells and I grip hers tightly, willing the extraordinary rush of love to flow from me into her. I suddenly remember the conversation I had with Em on our first night on the island and how, when she asked whether I get on with my mam like I do with my da, I said she was *just me mam*.

She's not *just* anything. She pats my hand again and gets up, reaching for Laura's untouched plate.

I get there first. 'I've got it.'

Her arm falls away and she tucks her chair back in under the table, nodding to herself before walking through the open door. As soon as she's gone, Laura drops her phone and squeezes herself out of her seat. She snatches our four glasses together with one hand and dumps them noisily in the sink before hoisting herself on to the countertop. 'What was all that about?' she asks, casually swinging her legs and crashing them against the cupboard doors.

I watch her arm contort and disappear into the shelf behind her. Seconds later it reappears brandishing a packet of Jaffa Cakes.

'You know perfectly well what it was about.'

'Yeah,' she says, taking a bite. 'But I don't get why you couldn't just say what he wanted you to say?'

I scrape the scraps into the bin. 'It's not like that, Laura.'

'Why not?' she mumbles through a mouthful of biscuit.

'Da refuses to get that I'm not him.' I say this for me. I don't honestly expect her to understand.

'I didn't mean to land you in it –'

'Well, you made a fine job of it.'

'C'mon, Liam, please?' she says, thumping my arm before rummaging further into the packet.

Despite my best efforts, I'm almost smiling at her. I'll never admit it, but I feel a little better. I never thought I could talk to Da like that and I guess I've Laura to thank for stirring up the whole shitfest.

She shoves another biscuit into her mouth and pushes my shoulder again, 'Liam! I'm sorry.'

'Go on. I'll do this,' I say, nodding towards the dirty dishes in the sink.

She gives me this squinty look, as though to ask 'you feeling all right?'

'Go!'

'Nice one,' she says, hopping down off the counter, grabbing another Jaffa for the road.

I take out my phone. I scroll back through all of the texts Em sent since last Wednesday morning and, for the first time, I take in how they've become shorter and shorter: the last being a simple SORRY on Monday night, after I'd shut the hall door in her face hours earlier. What mad arrogance made me check my phone on the hour these past few days, hoping she'd be in touch to wish me luck or ask about my results when I've responded to not one of her texts. I've left her there, hanging …

Where on earth do I begin?

My thumbs hover over the letters and then I start to type …

EMERALD

And that's just the way it is

meet me
tomorrow night, after work
10
please

These four single texts allowed me a full breath for the first time in days. I didn't stop to think.

I typed back immediately.

I'll be there.

No kiss. Can't kiss back when there was no kiss to start with.

Liam didn't say where. I didn't ask either. I'm on the wall with the stripy kiosk shielding the traffic sounds from the road behind me, watching as small pockets of beach nightlife play out in the new darkness. I look out to the silhouette of the island and think of our little tent there, flooded with sunlight, and knowing, despite how much I want it, we'll never get back to the promise of that first morning.

Suddenly I feel hands squeeze my shoulders and I yank

my headphones off and stand. Liam takes me in his arms, folding me inside his jacket and holds me there. It's such a relief. It's all I can do not to cry.

'I had no idea, Liam,' I muffle it into his chest. He just pulls me closer. 'About any of it.'

He gently pushes me back and shakes out his hair, which I can't help notice is so much longer than when we first stood here so many weeks ago. He looks pale and his face looks leaner. I swear he's an inch taller too. Can that even happen in a week? There's a distance. I can feel it. Everything feels different. I want to take his face in my hands and examine all of the changes.

I'm wondering whether we can ever forget all that we now know when a small gang of girls skips past in a fog of cigarette smoke and perfume: Marc Jacobs' Daisy, the same one Kitty wears. Two of the girls twist back bouncily in our direction. 'Hey, Liam,' they say in stereo.

He calls out a hearty 'howrya' and my heart seizes. It's not jealousy. It's so much deeper. 'Laura's pals,' he explains. 'Let's get out of here.' He grasps my hand.

We're walking along Strand Road. I'm on the outside of the path when a bus rumbles past on my right. Without a word Liam moves to stand between me and the road, which is exactly what he did the first night we walked like this to Fiona's house. I want to say something; not to remind him exactly, but take him back there, take us back there, but we just amble ahead in silence. Somehow we both seem to know where we're going.

Eventually he stops at a familiar dune further up the beach, settling himself down sufficiently far away from the Friday-night shelters crowd.

'I haven't spoken to him yet – my dad,' I say, joining Liam on the sand.

The wind blows his hair about but his face is completely still, like a piece of sculpture. 'Serious?'

'When you … left, on Wednesday morning, Grandma wouldn't tell me anything. She clammed up like a shell, insisting I spoke with Dad. I'd no idea what had happened, and after everything –' I stop here. The way he looks away from me now, I don't need to explain.

He shakes his head like he might understand.

'It was only when I googled him after leaving your house on Monday that I found out. All the horrid detail spewing back at me in countless search results.'

'Jaysus, that's rough.' He puts his arm around me, staring ahead. 'And you still haven't called him?'

'He's left messages, but I can't. I'm so angry, Liam. I've never felt this kind of rage before.'

'He's your da, Em.'

'Not the dad I thought he was. Besides, what I've got to say to him has to be said in person. If we speak on the phone first, he may never come over.' I shiver involuntarily and Liam takes his arm from his jacket and wraps it around me. 'He's been having an affair too. I'm certain of it. I should have seen it ages ago, so on top of everything else I feel like a fool. So much has fallen into place lately. It's an awful picture, but I can't deny all the pieces fit.'

Liam makes an *ouch* kind of sound and we huddle in closer. 'Quite the lad,' he says, hooking a piece of my outgrown fringe behind my ear. 'He had the glad-eye for my

303

mam once. Bet Google didn't tell you that?'

Have I lost track? 'Who?'

'Ah, it was twenty years ago now,' he says. 'But it wasn't just business between him and Da –'

'Are you kidding me?'

Liam's whole body judders. 'Seems your aul fella has always had the glint and the swagger. Jaysus, I'd laugh if I hadn't spent the past ten days in pieces. The whole thing, it's been tearing me apart, Em. When I saw the HORIZON Post-it in O'Flaherty's hand, I thought I was gonna puke on your grandma's carpet. I swear to God. In my worst nightmares I could never have envisaged anything this bad.'

'Laura was right.' I mumble it to myself.

'Laura?'

'I didn't choose my dad. Nor did you. She said it to me out of the window as I left your house. I'm not sure when I would have found out if she hadn't.'

Liam shakes his head in some kind of disbelief before starting to rub his hands together. 'Let's do something fun.'

'Fun?'

'You up for a swim?' he asks, gazing at me. His thumb points towards the sea, but his eyebrows tilt in such a way that I'm guessing this has got to be a joke.

I back away into the long grass, without breaking his stare. 'You can feck off, Liam Flynn, I am not getting in there.'

He creeps towards me, swinging his arms out until I fall backwards and collapse in a heap further up the soft sand. I'm laughing now. I can't help it.

'Listen to the dirty Dublin mouth on you. Course you are,' he says, already undoing his shoes. He peers up at me through his dark fringe; he's serious.

I gaze back into his eyes, which now look black and wild. 'But it's freezing!'

'How d'you know?'

'Well, I'm freezing sitting here, with my clothes on, NOT in the water. So …'

His belt is off and he's opening his jeans.

'Hold on. You mean that kind of swimming?'

'Let's see, shall we?' he says, pushing me further back on to the sand. I can feel the wonderful weight of him on me as he leans into my chest. Our cheeks touch. The cold smell of his skin and the steady determination of his breath. His hips fall into mine and I want to cry out with happiness. I throw my head back and shudder as the relief of his hungry hands on my skin takes hold. With our noses touching, he places one hand behind my back and starts pulling my boots off with the other.

'Liam! Liam, I'm serious!' I say, and I am serious, but about so much more than swimming. I want to swallow him up in kisses, right here.

'And so am I, Lady Emerald of Bath,' he says. 'I'm terrifyingly serious right now. Get your clothes off!' With that he scoops me into his arms, pulling my dress from under me, wrestling it above my head and throwing it into the wind as we run down the dunes.

'Hey! *Agghhhhhh* …'

'Don't scream,' he whispers. '*Shhhh.*' He's laughing again now. 'No one can see us from here but they'll hear us if you're not careful –'

I throw my arms around his neck and he stops. I turn to watch my dress drift away behind us as he carries me in my underwear towards the water. My skin looks even more milky in the moonlight and I try not to think of how heavy I feel in his arms. As we near the shimmering water the far off voices from the shelters recede to the lapping waves. The tide is out; everything around us is still and it's like we're the only things moving on earth. We are nothing; we are everything.

He winces as his feet hit the water and I can feel thousands of tiny bumps that rise on the skin of his upper arms. His grip gets tighter. 'I've got you, I've got you,' he says, wading faster into the waves, running at them furiously until they hit his chest. Suddenly he kneels down and we're underwater. For a second there is no sound, only the wild beating of my heart. Deep stabs of pain shoot up from the bottom of my legs and glugs of salt water come gushing down my nose.

Drawing my head out of the icy water, I inhale deeply. '*H'ahhh!*' I am hyperventilating. '*Haha haha haha.*'

He grasps my waist, pulling me tightly against him and I wrap my arms and legs around him. Every part of us is touching. I feel his rough, brackish lips on mine. His warm tongue hits my mouth and he kisses me. 'I love you, Emerald Rutherford Byrne and I always will. That's just the way it is.'

I've never, EVER, EVER felt this alive.

LIAM
Driving like an Apache

We've just left John-Joe's and I'm powering along the motorway in my new wheels. Well, I'd be hammering it were co-pilot Da not next to me, eyeing over my shoulder, laying out the conditions of my repayment plan whilst insisting on a top speed of seventy kilometres per hour. Really we're tootling along behind a slow-moving caravan while traffic whizzes past on either side. I indicate and cross into the fast lane.

Da rams his work boots into the passenger footwell, slamming his hand against the glove box. 'Holy mother of God, Liam!'

'What?'

'You're driving like an Apache.'

It takes everything I have not to lash back at him. Somehow I manage to keep my eyes fixed on the road ahead. 'I did pass my test, Da, and there's no law on overtaking as far as I'm aware.'

'Still, you haven't stolen the car either,' he says, settling back into his seat. 'Just … would you take it easy!'

I continue to drive on as the rest of the four-wheeled-world steadily passes us. He can't resist the odd sharp glance, but at least we're talking now; well, you know, sort of talking. It's not like before, but I guess neither of us is either. I'm not him and I'll never be how he wants me to be and that's just the way it is.

At least we both know that now. Of course it's hard for him. Maybe one day I'll even understand.

We stop at the Metro on the way back and Da fills the car with petrol as a little pressie for me. I can see him jabbering away to Lorcan by the till. He comes out and throws a packet of Rolos on to the dash. He's got a packet too and he's chewing away something fierce.

'All yap no trousers, that fella,' he says with a nod back towards the shop.

'Lorcan?'

Da nods, picking toffee out of his teeth. 'He's in there, talking up his position, which I've no problem with by the way, don't get me wrong. But then, doesn't he start saying he's got you lined up for a managerial opportunity. I'm not being funny, but did you not tell that useless article what you got in your Leaving Cert?'

'He's only being nice, Da.'

'He's not the full-shilling all the same.'

There's no point in defending poor Lorcan. I pull out of the forecourt and we steer along the twists of the coast road silently, the only sound being the pair of us chewing and some fella on the radio complaining about hospital waiting times. The sun beats down on the water and the golden sand glistens up ahead for miles and miles.

The dog-walkers and middle-aged women are out in force, pounding along Menopause Mile: that stretch of extraordinary coast between the beach and the village.

There are families and day trippers ferrying armfuls of gear in and out of car-boots. Out there in the water, in the midst of all the everyday life, sits the island – Emerald's isle – glittering under a shard of glorious, holy light.

Since lobbing the 'she's not a mistake' grenade last week, I'd be lying if I said father-son relations weren't strained. Still, I have a go. 'We're going to see a film later.' He says nothing. 'Da?'

'What's that?'

'I'm taking Em to the movies. She picked an Irish one, set in the Eighties.'

'Uh huh.'

'About a fella starting a rock 'n' roll band at school ... I've been dying to see it. Didn't think it'd be her cup of tea, but there you go,' I say.

He doesn't flinch. Nothing. He's zoned me out completely.

'It's in Swahili too, which is what I may as well be speaking.'

I thought I'd said this last bit under my breath but he turns around. 'Don't push it, son.'

'Push what?'

'You know bloody well what.'

I swerve to avoid a kamikaze courier who rips up from behind, weaving between my new motor and an oncoming bus, almost nipping my wing mirror with his handlebars as he goes. 'I do?'

'Jaysus, Liam. Watch it!' His thunderous boot slams into the footwell again. He nearly grabs the handbrake. 'John-Joe can't take the car back if you've written the bloody thing off.'

I brake. 'What are you talking about, Da?'

He sucks his teeth, looking out the window now. 'Your mam's been doing the sums,' he says. 'Even with the finance options, we'd have to sell these wheels back to make the enrolment fees. And you'd have to keep up the Metro job at weekends to help out with the remaining instalments.' He's still not doing eye contact.

I slow to a dangerous pace, steering the car into a bus stop on the main road, no mirror checks, no indicator, no nothing. Da doesn't seem to notice. 'If you're saying what I think you're saying, Da, then I'm definitely good with the bus.'

'You better be,' he says, before tapping at the little clock on the dash. 'Get a move on. There's a game on at six.'

I indicate and pull out on to the road again. In all seriousness, they should send Mam into Syria or Gaza or one of those places, such is her diplomatic talent.

'She played me a couple of songs you've got up on that internet,' Da says, unwrapping the Rolo packet the whole way so that all the chocolates spill out on to his lap. 'A bit of Springsteen up there wouldn't hurt,' he says, popping one into his gob. 'Something from the early stuff.'

A surge of gratitude seizes all my wits at once. 'Right,' I say, welling up. I know exactly what it's taken him to get here. I have to blink a few times before I can turn around. 'Thanks, Da.'

He looks at me, eyebrows skewed. 'What's that?'

'I'm saying thanks, that's all.'

He stops chomping and we gawp at each other for a second, his top lip in a sort of snarl. Mine's quivering as I try to hold it together. I'm studying the lines around his eyes when he blinks and reaches over, fixing my left hand back on the wheel.

'Ten o'clock, two o'clock, son, remember! Don't be taking yer hands off that wheel,' he says, before returning to the pile of Rolos in his lap.

I guess that's it, but at least he's heard me.

We pass the iron gates to Emerald's grandma's house. I think Da clocks me rubbernecking up the empty drive, but he says nothing.

EMERALD

This isn't a game

Grandma and I are silently clock-watching. I don't know which of us is more jumpy. I'm nervous about my results, obviously, but I'm even more anxious about seeing Dad.

Grandma is standing by the machine refilling her cup. 'Coffee?'

'I'm OK, thanks.' Nothing tastes right this morning but I'm sure that's to do with what's ahead. There's so much I have to say, so much I need to ask Dad about. Of course I'll have to bring up Magda too, but not in front of Grandma; she's been through enough.

'He must have had an early start,' Grandma says, pressing the button on the frothing machine. It whirrs into life and she clasps her hands together, standing back in admiration.

I say nothing. It's almost eleven o'clock. Kitty and all the girls will have had their results by now. WhatsApps flew around last night, wishing everyone luck, endless chatter and party plans, but the past few hours have been quiet. That I'm still in their WhatsApp groups at all was reassuring, I won't lie.

Kitty called last night. Apparently St Tropez was kind of boring this year because they're putting in a new pool and the place like was a building site, but the results party in Bath is going to be next-level, she says. Byrony and Rupert are still a thing but she also likes some older guy she met in Cornwall. It took over an hour for her to confirm that a) nothing has changed there over the entire summer and b) no one has actually missed me. Listening as she downloaded all her news I felt the full breadth of the Irish Sea between us.

Still, if I'm honest, it was comforting just to hear her voice. I don't think Kitty will ever understand how it feels to love a boy like Liam, or how it feels to wake up on the island and watch the sun rise from its vast horizon and that's OK. I've had sex and my best friend doesn't even know. That's a conversation for another time.

How is it that what once felt like the entire universe is now just one tiny little world orbiting around like a gazillion others? Stupid as it sounds, I never realised how many worlds fit within the one world; worlds as real as the one I left behind. I see now the deep, dark ocean that separates the reality I live and the reality I so desperately wanted. There were times when I thought those waters would take me under; times I thought I'd drown. I can't avoid going back, I know that, but I've found an island now, somewhere I can go, somewhere in the middle that is mine.

I'm digging into my boiled egg and thinking about all of this when my phone starts to buzz gently, lighting up Grandma's newspaper from underneath. Praying it might be Liam, I jump for it: unknown number.

I place the phone to my ear. 'Hello?' Grandma and I exchange glances.

'Emerald?'

It's not Magda, which is an instant relief. 'Who's this?'

There's a shrill laugh I recognise, but can't place. 'It's Mrs McKenzie, Georgina McKenzie. A star in Economics! Bet you're pleased you stuck with it for A Level now.'

My stomach cartwheels. 'Oh, h–hi, Mrs McKenzie,' I stammer. Grandma is standing in front of me now.

'The only girl in the year with that result. It really is quite something.'

I'm pointing to the phone, for Grandma's benefit, I think. 'Really?' It's all my swimming brain can manage.

'Super results. You must be delighted,' she says excitedly. 'Your parents too.'

I'm picturing her now, sitting in her large, oak-panelled office where I stood opposite her on the second-last day of term. I'm not sure what to say; that my parents don't know, that it's just Grandma and me here in Dublin? Does she have any idea about what happened with Mum, or even Dad for that matter?

'Anyway, I'll let you get on with celebrating. I wanted to congratulate you, that's all …'

I don't hear the rest of what she says, I just blurt out, 'What did I get?'

There's a little cough on the other end of the line. 'I'm sorry?'

'Could you tell me my results, please, Miss?'

'Oh, gosh!' She stops. 'I'm so … I assumed that you'd have opened them by now. Your father was here at eight o'clock sharp, one of the first in line. Emerald, I'm terribly –'

314

'I'm in Dublin. Dad's on his way – you may as well tell me. Please!'

'Oh,' she says again. 'Goodness, I don't know what the protocol is on this, but I expect in this case there won't be any complaints …'

I'm about to burst.

'Ah yes, well, Emerald, you attained one A star, 6 As and three Bs.'

I press speaker and hold the phone out again so that Grandma can hear. 'Could you say that again, please?'

She clears her throat, 'One A star, six As and three Bs, Emerald. The As were in English Language and Literature, Maths, Science, History and French,' she says. Grandma grips my arm tight, like she can't believe it either and we both gurn crazily at each other. 'Emerald?'

'Thank you. Thanks again, for everything,' I say and hang up.

Grandma takes me in her arms. The last time she did this was when we sat outside on Granddad's bench after watching *The Fault in our Stars*, me spilling a barrel of buried pain, but now we're both standing, hugging each other properly. It's so lovely I have to close my eyes to feel it more.

Grandma pushes me away, looking me up and down. 'I never knew there was such a thing as an A star,' she says. 'How on earth did you get one of those?' I laugh and she laughs too. 'Well, it's astonishing is what it is.'

I glance up at the clock; it's quarter past. I fumble for my phone to dial Mum but Grandma gently pulls at my hands as we hear the hall door close and the sounds of what must be the taxi pulling away on the drive. Grandma looks shaken.

'Hellooo,' Dad cries out cheerily from the hall.

'In the kitchen,' says Grandma, covering well.

Dad strides into the kitchen, looking dapper in a slim-fit, dark suit. 'Special delivery for Miss Emerald Rutherford Byrne,' he says, handing me the envelope with a wink. Behind the smile he looks exhausted and grey. I grasp it without our hands touching and place it on the counter. His eyes follow my moving arm.

'Would you like some tea, Jim?' Grandma asks, but he doesn't answer. 'Or maybe a coffee?' she suggests in an even smaller voice. Dad still says nothing; he's staring at me, clearly thrown. I stare right back.

'I'm going to pop upstairs a minute,' Grandma says, backing out of the door.

Dad moves further into the room and I take a step back into the corner, by the kettle. He goes to the right and I instinctively move to mine, like a matador in the ring with my bull. Or maybe that should be the other way round.

'Aren't you going to open them?' he asks, inching towards me. I step to the side again and his eyes fly all over my face.

'When Grandma said you were staying in that airport hotel, Dad, I honestly thought she was losing her mind,' I say, slowly shaking my head. 'I mean, there was no way you'd lie to me, about anything. It was the only conclusion I could come to.' His body slumps into a nearby chair. 'How long were you going to keep it all from me?'

He shakes his head silently and lets out a lengthy breath, like one from Mum's yoga DVD. It goes on forever. 'Em.' It's a whisper.

I catch his wounded eyes before they close and despite everything I want to hug him. Gripping the edge of the sink, I anchor myself for strength. I've got to keep going. 'I've lain awake every night trying to work out how long you've been lying to me about your work, about Magda ...' I can't hide the quiver in my voice. 'I've been running over everything in my head relentlessly.'

His eyes open but it's like he doesn't want to see me or anything else. 'I was building our future, your future.'

'By walking away from your debt, a mountain of it, by all accounts? By devastating this town, leaving other families suffering?'

He stands up and walks to the window further up, arranging his suited limbs against the countertop. 'It's not that simple, Em,' he says, reaching for my hand. 'The banks moved in. Most of it was outside of my control. It was a complicated and difficult situation for everyone. Nobody came out of it well, believe me. And then with everything with your mum, I was only trying to protect you, sweetheart.' He reaches for my hand.

I step closer to him. I need to see into his eyes. 'How, Dad?'

'Shielding you from all the court-case stuff, I guess. Allowing you to concentrate on your studies.'

'But how could you leave me here, knowing how everybody here feels about you?'

'I've been so busy, so consumed –' He stops here. Clearly even he knows this answers nothing.

I try to hook his eyes but he won't look at me. 'Busy sleeping with someone who's not Mum?' I say it, just like that. 'Your secretary?'

317

Dad collapses back into the chair. He rubs his furrowed brow, his thumb and index finger meeting in the middle.

What am I doing? I can't believe this is really me talking to him like this, arguing. Nothing is as it should be; it's all wrong, but I can't ignore the fire that's been lit inside me now.

'Magda's a director of the company –'

'One that does your Amazon shopping, one that makes music playlists you pretend to like? One that arranges taxis to ferry your daughter to your wife's rehab sessions when you're tied up?'

He goes to protest but I keep going. 'And while we're at it, I'd like to talk about Mum, who could clearly do with our help right now. Trouble is, I'm not sure how your company director fits in with that plan.'

He shuffles in the seat and his fingers drum on the table, lightly at first but getting louder. Then his foot begins to tap against the table leg and he starts patting his trouser pockets like he's looking for his keys.

'Can I take it Mum found out about Magda around … the end of term?' His eyes close. 'Would that be right, Dad?'

'The timing,' he says, with his hands running roughly through his hair now, 'I know the timing has been rough.'

'That's one way to put it.'

'Sweetheart –'

'I thought it was me, Dad – that I'd driven Mum to it. I still find it hard to convince myself it wasn't something I'd done, or should have done … But clearly –'

'Em, you mustn't –'

'Do you love her more than us?'

Without answering he pushes himself up, walking to the far side of the kitchen and into the laundry room. I follow and find him by the back door, which he flings wide open, drawing a packet of cigarettes from his pocket and putting one to his lips. He looks back. His damp eyes look just like Grandma's. I have to look at him side-on as he stares out into the little orchard beyond. He looks up at the overcast sky.

'It's not like that, Em. It's …' he says, rhythmically clenching and unclenching his right fist as though it might hold the words he's searching for. 'Look, I know it's hard for you to understand, but over these past few months and years I've been to hell and back with the businesses and may very well return there. I'm back in court in London on Friday and who knows what might happen.' In a slow blink the heavy wet drops brimming on his dark lashes break and a pair of tears race down his pale face.

'To be honest, it's all I can do to get out of bed and put on the armour these days,' he says, dragging heavily on the cigarette. 'And Magda, she –' He stops to exhale an impressively long plume of smoke but says nothing more. He couldn't look any more sad.

'But you love her?' I ask, tears streaming from my own eyes now.

His silence says everything.

I swallow my heavy sobs. I know this is my time. I know this is the moment. I open my mouth again and out it fires. 'I have a boyfriend, Dad.'

He spins around, stunned. His eyes blaze wide and he's perfectly still now. Even his jowly cheeks stop wobbling.

For the first time in weeks it feels like I really have his attention.

'I tried to tell you about him before. I was really excited, desperate to share it with you, but each time I'd go to talk to you, like properly talk, you had to go.' I lean against the pantry door, needing its support for what I'm about to say. 'I never thought I'd feel the way I do about him.' Dad turns to me and inhales deeply. He's really listening now. 'You see, Dad,' I take a deep breath, 'I didn't know. Nobody told me I wasn't supposed to fall in love with Liam Flynn.'

Dad's eyes flash open and smoke spills chaotically from his nose and mouth. I can only watch as the blood drains from his face and his Adam's apple drops in his throat as he stares into the middle distance. He flicks the cigarette to the ground.

'Jesus Christ, Emerald!' he says, stepping closer, running his left hand over the stubble on each side of his chin. 'You've got to tell me this is a wind-up.'

It's my turn to shake my head. He registers this and stamps on the discarded cigarette butt with his heel, crushing it into the path. He starts to pace up and down on the gravel. 'I'm taking you home.'

'I don't want to go home, Dad.'

'Now listen to me, Em.' He stops here and I watch him attempt to grab a hold of his temper. 'Give me a few more weeks. I'm going to sort this. You've got to trust me.'

'No.'

In a split second his rage is suspended and his tired eyes skim back up at me on the step. 'No?'

I grit my teeth, but every part of me is shaking. 'No. I won't.'

'No, you won't come home, or no, you won't trust me?'

'Neither, not right now, no.'

He slinks towards me. 'Emerald,' he says, his face wide open; the pain is plain to see. 'Please,' he says ever so slowly, 'tell me what I need to do to make this right.'

My hands find the wall behind me. 'I already know.'

'OK,' he says, tapping another cigarette out of the pack. He flips it up and down on the box as though considering whether or not to light it. Finally he pops it into his mouth. 'Tell me.'

'You need to apologise.'

He spits the unlit cigarette from his lips and reaches out, seizing my hand. 'Sweetheart, I am sorry. I am so sorry,' he cries.

I shake off his grip. Did he really believe it could be that easy? 'Not to me –'

'I've been to see your mum,' he cuts in, reaching for my hand again.

I hold it up to his face, stopping him. He scratches his head and I clear my throat. 'To Donal Flynn.'

There's a low growl as he turns on his well polished heel, walking into the garden past Grandma's little vegetable patch. He takes a right by the shed and disappears amongst the apple trees. Where's he gone? Suddenly he's marching back up the path towards me, each stride faster and more resolute. 'This isn't a game, Emerald,' he barks, waving the unlit cigarette in front of him, a storm raging behind his eyes.

'It's not. And that's why you've got to put it right.'

'How are you proposing I do this?' he says, cupping his hand around the lighter and sparking it too close to his lips.

A vehement trail of smoke spills from his nostrils but my eyes never waver from his. 'A simple sorry, face to face.'

'We're not in the playground now.'

I fan the stinking cloud away. 'That's exactly my point, Dad. This isn't a squabble between boys – this is real!'

'Real?' he says, with a laugh that is horribly hollow.

'Yes!'

Both of his hands fly into the air. 'I am within a hair's breadth of losing everything. Everything!' he roars. 'That's what's bloody real to me right now. All that Horizon stuff was three years ago – water under the bridge. Donal Flynn will always blame me for what happened.' I watch his eyes slowly close, exhausted by his anger. 'I'm damned in his eyes, no matter what I do. That's just the way it is, Scout.'

'You can't call me that any more.' I look down on him from the step, the only time I've towered above Dad in my life. 'Don't you see? Scout's dad was the bravest man alive because he started something he knew was doomed but he stuck with it, in spite of everything, because he knew in his heart it was right.'

Dad blinks, his face a wash of confusion: eyes and mouth, frozen open in stunned surprise. Then he flicks his fag butt behind him with a deflated sigh and slowly shakes his head.

'He had real courage, Dad.'

He looks up at the sky, squinting through a shaft of sunlight that's broken through the heavy grey cloud. 'What do you honestly expect it to achieve, Em?'

'I don't know. I just know it's the right thing to do.'

LIAM
All I came to say

Da doesn't seem to notice my lousy driving the rest of the way home; at least he says nothing. It's not until we pull into the drive that he sits up sharply in his seat, which in this car means his head practically hits the roof.

'Who the f—?' he barks, flinging the door open and clambering out of the car before I've even stopped.

I'm still rolling down the drive when I look up to see Mam standing inside the open door, talking to some man in a suit. Her arms are crossed over her spotty apron. I expect he's selling something. Da's up now, hoofing down the drive towards them. I pull the handbrake up and shove the door to get out. Then I hear him.

'Get out of here,' he roars, slinging at the fella's neck from behind. 'Get out of my house!'

My brain's struggling to compute; it's no salesman.

'Wait, Donal,' the man cries, wrestling free from the grip of Da's giant arm around his neck. He struggles loose and twists around so I see his whole face. It's his hairline, the same grey receding hairline that stood out from the photo in Emerald's grandma's house. Jim Byrne, the shameless scut is standing on our front step, fixing himself. I can't believe what I'm seeing.

Da's giving him a filthy look, looking like his chest is finally about to burst out from under that shirt of his. Mam's one step higher, perched inside the door, nervously tucking her fringe behind her ear. What the Jaysus is going on?

'D'ya hear me, Byrne? Out!' Da shouts, pointing back to the road before pushing his shirtsleeves further up his arm.

Mam pulls Da's hand down. 'Donal, listen to what –'

'I can't, Maeve,' he cuts in, waving his hand violently up the drive again. 'I've had twenty years of his shite. He can't Back-to-the-feckin'-Future himself out of this one. There's no making this better.'

I follow Da's hand to where a little black A-Class Merc is parked up on the road by the bus stop. It's Emerald's grandma's car! I must have missed it driving in but I'm staring at it now, trying to digest all the chaos, when the passenger door opens and Em's head emerges. Decked out in a man's shirt and shorts, her feet *flip flop* down the tarmac drive. Her hair is all tied up on her head and she looks over, her eyes meeting mine. Her face is steely and determined, exactly like it was the night she waded through the icy sea, on to the shore at Deadmaiden's Cove.

I want to run and shield her from the bomb that's about to explode on the porch below.

We all watch as she approaches. I don't want to take my eyes off her but she's staring ahead to Jim and my head has to track from side to side to follow both her and the unfolding showdown. She bows her head in a tiny, stern nod to her own da, who studies her for a second before turning back around to mine.

Next thing I'm watching Jim's hand tentatively extend to Da's and my heart is doing mental things; that's when I feel her body brush up against mine and volts of electricity surge through me.

'I'm sorry,' Jim says to Da.

I look to Da, then to Mam, then to Emerald and then to the back of Jim's head. I don't move; nobody does. We're collectively fixed on him.

'That's all I came to say,' he says, his neck and shoulders hung low. 'It's too late of course, but maybe one day you can forgive me.'

Da's staring at the ground, rocking his head from side to side. His lower jaw juts forward and he's panting like an animal. He sucks in a huge breath. 'Well, you can feck off now you've relieved your conscience,' he shouts at Jim, kicking at the plant pot by his foot.

Jim dips his head and starts to stride back up towards us. I slump as Emerald leaves my side; her force field edging towards their triangle of doom. Seeing her approach, Da steps back beside Mam, like he feels her electricity too. Jim stops and turns around. I can see all their faces now as Em scans each of them in turn.

What's she at? Does she not know what Mam's already been through? That force field of hers won't stand up to Da's red-hot lava. Still she stands, hands on her hips, looking at Da, before she takes a deep, growling breath. He recoils further into the hallway and Mam clamps a cautionary arm on his available limbs.

'I was angry too,' Em says, her voice is small but her words are crystal clear. 'And when I didn't think I could possibly get any more angry, I did. But I couldn't stay that mad,' she says, shaking her head. 'It was eating me up from the inside, like I was drinking poison and expecting the people I'm mad at to drop dead. What's the point in that?' she says, throwing her hands up at the two dumbstruck men. She settles her gaze back on Da. 'You've suffered enough, Mr Flynn. You deserve to be free. Don't do it for him.' She gestures back to Jim. 'Do it for you. For all of you.'

Is this happening? Have we switched galaxy? Something is going on with Da's face. Em's stare is like a dimmer on his cowboy eyes – the longer she looks at him the more their burning light defuses. I'm walking down the drive for a closer look. I stop beside Em and instantly feel her fingers lace into mine. Jim glances up at us, looking tortured. I see Mam's eyes over the top of Jim's head, Da's too, and all six startled peepers dart from one to the other, trying to work out how the world just flipped upside down.

'C'mon, Em. Let's go,' Jim says. The raised veins at the side of his head are bulging.

Emerald squeezes my hand. 'Go on, Dad, I'll follow later,' she says. Her body is shaky against mine and I squeeze her hand back as Jim stands there for what feels like an eternity, eyeballing her. He won't even look at me. I don't think he can. Then his head drops and he trundles back up the drive.

Without Byrne as cover, Da's eyes are fully on me now. It's hard to read his look but I'd hazard a guess at that post-traumatic shell-shock. Emerald twists back up the drive and I spin on my heel. Her body moves with mine and we pivot together like the wheels and pinions on Grandda's old watch, except now our little mechanism is turbocharged.

Together we turn back to Mam and Da, who are motionless on the front step. Da's arms are crossed and Mam's leaning against the door frame on her left. As I take them in, it's not Da's face that shocks me; it's Mam's. She's looking at Em. Actually, it's not so much looking at her as dissecting her. Despite her defensive stance, her eyes are warm and alive. Em stares back and something passes between them, the force of which is making my chest tight.

Perhaps it's Mam's lips that give her away, not smiling as such but slanting a fraction like they mean to.

Who was I kidding? I don't need to shield Emerald Rutherford Byrne from nothing; nobody does.

EMERALD

A bit like Irish college

'That was fun,' I say, thumbing away the remains of my Carmex cherry lip balm from the edge of Liam's mouth. 'I mean it.'

'Your little shelters goodbye party was Kenny's idea. Had I my way I'd have kept you to myself.'

I take in a last lungful of Portstrand's sea air. 'Can't believe I'm going home.'

Liam sighs. 'It's a bit like Irish college.'

'What?'

'Ah, you think it's the worst thing ever, being sent off, but then you're heartbroken to leave there in the end.'

'Um, I think there's a little more to it than that,' I say, kicking him lightly on the shin. 'I was kind of hoping you did too.'

'I do and you know it, but it's a good analogy; trust me.'

'Wanna come in?'

'Better not. Nana Byrne's going to want a piece of you tonight. She's gonna miss you too, I bet.'

I shut Grandma's front door gently behind me and take a second to savour the delicious quiet of the hallway where the steady *tick-clang* of the grandfather clock is the only sound. I think about my first night here eight weeks ago and how everything so familiar now felt anything but. I'm about to set my key down on the hall table when I pick it back up and hang it on the ornate row of gold hooks above the holy water bottle.

'In the kitchen,' Grandma calls out.

I catch a glimpse of my mascara-less eyes and cheeks more freckly than ever and I smile a crooked smile at my smiling-back face. It's like the cracks are merging into some kind of whole.

'Emerald?'

'Coming,' I say, bouncing into the bright kitchen. Grandma is sat at the table, twisting her rings around her finger; a tiny clump of tissue crumpled into her fist. There's no steaming teapot, no china plate of biscuits. I try to swallow.

'Eliza has called several times now.'

I search her face for a lead, instinctively patting down my pockets. 'But I left my phone here.' I walk into the room, closer to her.

'Call her back first, pet?' she says, pressing her lips together and making them go thin.

'She's OK, isn't she? I mean, nothing's happened? They let her out?'

'She's fine,' she cuts in, with a slow nod. 'She's at home but she needs to talk with you.'

I sprint up the stairs, tumbling all the way until I reach the bed. Collapsing on to the floor, I snatch the phone from where I'd left it charging under the side table. Six missed calls from the home phone number, which is some relief.

No message. I hold my breath and stab redial. She picks up immediately. 'Mum? You OK?'

'I'm fine, darling. You?'

I push myself up and sit down on the bed, letting the air cautiously out of my lungs. 'Yes, but –'

'It's your dad.'

'What about him?' I say, curling my feet underneath me.

'They reached a verdict. Well, the first verdict, at least.'

Today of course! I'd somehow let Dad's court case slip my mind. I've been so distracted; so blinkered by all the implications for me that I'd somehow detached from it, fooling myself into believing his punishment was served on the Flynn's driveway last Wednesday. I'm now absolutely sure that was a mistake. 'And?'

'There isn't an easy way to say this, Em.'

'Spit it out, Mum. Please!' I'm sitting up straight again, perched on the edge of the bed.

'He's been served a three-month sentence.'

'Jail?'

'It's hard to believe. No matter how many times I say it myself, it won't seem to sink in. I keep expecting to be told it's just a bad dream.'

'Because of the Bay Road development? For how he pulled out?'

'No, that's part of a wider investigation. He was found guilty of contempt. Failing to cooperate, basically. A receiver was appointed to examine several of his companies and Dad's people seemed to string them along, or, up the garden path, as the judge said. I'm so sorry to have to call you with this, Em. I wanted to tell you myself tomorrow, but I was afraid you'd see it in the papers at the airport.'

I can't think of anything to say. Having read all those stories online, none of this should feel like a shock. But it does. It feels like we're talking about someone else, someone who's not my dad. My skin feels too tight and there's a delicate pattern of bluish rings all the way up my cold legs.

I need a bath. I've a sudden desire to be underwater again.

'D'you want to talk about it?'

'Not now,' I answer, curling back up into a ball. I lay my face against the cool pillow, wondering how a night can swing from such joy to despair inside of an hour.

'It's a lot to take in.'

'I'd like to try and sleep.'

'I hate the idea of you going to bed with this sort of worry.'

'I've had worse, Mum.'

She sighs but neither of us speaks. Jail? Prison? I'm trying to picture him now alongside these words, but no image comes.

'The house feels strange without you,' she says.

'Will they take it? That's what happens, isn't it?'

'They'll take what they can, but –'

'Will I have to leave Hollyfield?'

'You don't need to worry about school. It's your grandmother's gift to you.'

I almost drop the phone. 'Grandma?' I'm sitting bolt upright now, my back stiff against the hard headboard. The bed sways like I'm back on the boat, which makes my head spin and my heart race even faster. I'm picturing her, doing her sums at the kitchen table a couple of weeks ago. Totting up numbers into her ancient calculator, for me. And all I could think about was my broken heart.

'She's agreed to cover you as a boarder for the next two years, if needs be. We've a lot to talk about, but it can wait. You don't need to worry.'

The ground beneath me fixes. I close my eyes as I lower myself back into the pillow and my neck sinks deep into the soft feathers. Mum's waiting for me to say something, but I'm all out of words. My head and heart are full. I can't take any more in.

'I'll let you rest, but I'll see you in Arrivals. I'll be the one with the sign, waving like a madwoman who's just been let out.'

I allow myself a laugh.

'It's gonna be OK, Em.'

Without thinking, I answer. 'I know, Mum. I know, it will.'

LIAM
Say what, Yoda?

The hall door swings open before I even ring the bell.

'Howrya, Mrs Byrne.' I'm trying to play it cool, but it's hard to forget what happened the last time I actually set foot in this house. I slide my sweaty palms back into my pockets, not sure what else to do with them.

'C'mon in,' she says, ushering me inside the old hallway, which without O'Flaherty, Fidget and Emerald to fill it feels even more enormous. Only the giant grandfather clock feels to scale. In fact, I'd say Da'd get another room out of the wasted space on either side; a downstairs loo under those stairs at least. She studies me for way longer than is necessary. The whole staring thing must run in the family.

Her hand taps lightly on my arm. 'G'wan up and give her a hand down with the bag.'

'Sure, Mrs Byrne.'

'Annie,' she says, not overfriendly but there's no edge either. I plod up the long, double flight of stairs with no idea where I'm going, except up. Soon I spot Emerald through an open door. She's kneeling on a huge bag, struggling to get the zip the whole way round.

'*Aghh!*' she groans. 'It's like stuff reproduces while you're away.'

I'm not sure how to read this lack of 'hello'. She was in good form when we said goodbye last night. 'If only travel broadened the bags as well as the mind, eh?' I say, adding my knee to hers.

With a united shove we get the two zips to meet, but she doesn't answer. She buckles back down on the bed, surveying the large, old-fashioned room as though committing every small detail to memory. 'It seems so different now,' she says, sitting up and our eyes meet properly for the first time.

Her shoulders hunch forward. Looking unreliable in her denim shorts, she stands like a newborn calf. Just staring at her is making me feel wobbly. I'm sure it'll be better once I'm out of this house. I steal a look at my phone from inside my pocket. 'Nearly time to go.'

I'm holding the door open, watching her gather the last of her things when she stops in front of me. 'I thought "lump in your throat" was just an expression, something people said. I didn't think it actually happened,' she says, closing the bedroom door softly behind us.

I undo her fingers from around the suitcase handle and we shunt down the stairs without another word. Annie appears at the hall table like a ghost.

'I'll be outside,' I say, sliding the backpack off Em's shoulder and drawing up the handle of the wheelie case and dragging it towards the hall door.

Out on the drive, the warm wind blows hard. I lean against the car and stare over the tops of the tall trees at the unbroken view of the sea. I tell myself it's the angle of the strong, morning sun stopping me from looking straight ahead and keeping my eyes veered south, down towards Howth. But I drag my eyes back and force myself to stare at the hunk of green rock jutting out of the sea, unashamed. The island: it's not sorry about nothing.

Eventually Emerald appears at the door, her hair gusting around her face as she plants a kiss on Annie's forehead. I know it's going to be my goodbye next. I don't want to look.

She takes Annie's hand. 'I won't waste a day of it, Grandma. I promise,' she says, lowering her head on to Annie's shoulder now. 'From the bottom of my heart, thank you.'

Mercifully the rest of her words are muffled. I wish they'd finished this stuff inside; it's making me uneasy. I hear Emerald's footsteps and then I catch Annie's face in the slice of closing door.

'G'wan, you'll be late,' Annie shouts, shooing Emerald off the front step, before putting her tiny hand to her mouth.

We hop into either side of the car. I flick the key in the ignition. 'You know, I've a good mind to get woefully lost and take you to Belfast.'

Em says nothing so I continue my attempt at a three-point-turn on the ungenerous stretch of tarmac between the wall and the rose bushes. It's some scabby driveway for such a big gaff.

'Please, just go,' she says, still holding her hand up to the window at the closing door. You couldn't exactly call it a wave.

Five turns later, I face her, a whole lot sweatier. 'You OK?'

Her hand falls limply back into her lap. 'He's going to jail.'

I heard what she's said, of course I did. It was only four words and I heard them all. I bring the car to a slow stop by the front gates at the junction with the main road. For so long I've wanted Jim Byrne to get his comeuppance, for him to experience the pain and humiliation he's put my family through, but after witnessing him on our step only days ago and looking at Em's face now, I don't know what to feel. My legs turn to jelly and the word jail clangs around inside my skull like a rusty key.

'Contempt of court, twelve weeks.' she continues, staring right through the pram-pushing mother who crosses the footpath in front of us. 'Seems I wasn't the only one to be strung along. Mum said it'll hit all the papers today.'

I pull up the handbrake and drape my arms over the steering wheel. I don't know what to say; nothing seems right. This is not a situation life prepares you for. 'I'm sorry,' I say, taking her hand.

'Thanks,' she says, squeezing mine. 'But it's Grandma I'm worried about. It'll be a long time before I can get back.'

I hate hearing this. 'If you think it would help, I could always, you know … call in and check she's OK?'

Her lips give way to a slow, wide smile. 'Those pink marshmallow biscuits, the ones with the jam?'

'Mikados?'

She nods. 'Bring her some of those, from me?'

'Consider it done.'

Neither of us speaks as I pull out on to the main road. It's a beautiful late-August morning but it's too early for the crowds. We pass the kiosk, but there's no line of greasy beach goers sticky with suncream yet. We drive along the

337

coast road, past the golf club and a family of mallard ducks waddle across by the roundabout, holding up adoring traffic in both directions.

'It's weird,' she says, as our small tailback of cars begins to move again. 'The last two months feel like a dream now, only the opposite.'

The last of the ducklings mosey past. 'Like a nightmare, is that what you're saying?'

She doesn't answer.

'OK, I'll try not to take that personally,' I add, flicking the indicator up roughly.

She reaches over and shoves my shoulder. 'No!' She laughs. 'You don't understand – just the reverse. It's like, instead of falling down the rabbit hole, I seem to have crawled back up it and found some kind of life that's even more …' She stops there and looks out across the marshland. Her eyes are a thousand miles away.

I think about bounding in, insisting she finish, but I decide to leave her sentence hanging there while I imagine how I'd like it to end.

We exit the car-park building and head towards the terminal. I've to cover my eyes from the blinding sun. Crowds of trolley pushers and hassled parents drag luggage and kids in every direction. Like one of the Portstrand ducks, Em stops in the middle of the road unannounced, like she's about the say something but then doesn't. A taxi screeches to a halt, only inches from us. The driver throws his hands in the air. I wave back at him, putting my other arm around Em and pushing her gently towards the kerb.

We hit the first set of sliding doors. I watch her set off towards a bank of departure screens and all I can think is how much I don't want her to go.

'I'm late,' she calls back.

I have to chase after her now, pushing through the summer holiday crowds. We've reached the security gate by the time we turn to face one another again. 'Wait, Em …' She stops and stares right at me. 'I've been thinking …'

She folds her arms now and her mouth twists into a grin. 'Thinking is always a good idea, Watson … go on.'

'I'm serious,' I say, sucking in a breath to slow the rising gallop inside me. I take both of her hands in mine to steady myself. 'Please tell me this wasn't all just … summer?' I can't meet her eyes now. I'm suddenly incapable of looking up from my shoes.

She pulls on my hand and when I glance up she's staring back at me with an entirely new look: the quick grey eyes, that think faster than I'll ever talk, are flecked now with tiny streaks of green, which after my weeks of staring at them, I'm pretty sure are new. 'Liam,' she whispers, 'this wasn't just … anything!'

'Good,' I say, ''cause I'd hate that,' I say, shaking my fringe back over my eyes before they give me away.

'Stop!' she says, tugging my hand back and turning my face to hers. 'I mean it, Liam!' she says, digging my ribs. 'I needed to meet you this summer. I was ready, and … *when the pupil is ready the teacher will come.*'

God knows why, but I laugh; it's nerves, it's everything. 'Say what, Yoda?'

'Oh, nothing,' she says, waving her hand away. 'It's just … there's a whole new voice playing inside my head now.'

I move to let a couple of pristine-looking businessmen file past. 'So will you miss me or this loving new narrator?' I slide my hands into my back pockets and look away across the crowded concourse.

She tugs my arms loose. 'You!' she says and I feel her step closer.

'Really?'

'Liam, when I arrived here eight weeks ago, I made my life look perfect when it was really a mess. Now my life looks a mess, what with Dad going to jail, Mum fresh out of rehab and the fact that I've barely spoken to any of my actual friends in weeks.' She rolls her eyes here like she's catching herself saying all of this aloud. 'But you know what? I feel OK. I feel better. I might even feel pretty good.' She smiles, revealing every pearly tooth in the beautiful moon of her mouth.

I wrap my arms around her waist. Our legs are slotted together with our foreheads touching.

'And when I think of you, of us, I actually feel great.' Her warm breath on my skin feels unbearably good and I close my eyes to make it last. 'Truth is,' she whispers, 'I get you, Liam Flynn, and in some crazy way you seem to get me. I could make it more complicated than that, but I won't.'

Suddenly I feel her trembling lips on mine. I want to absorb as much of her as I have left but she quickly pulls away, glancing at the fancy Swiss clock above our heads. 'I've really got to go,' she says and with a firm squeeze of my hand she hoists her backpack strap on to her shoulder

340

and bounds up to the gate. I watch her hand over her boarding pass.

She doesn't look back.

I stare through the airport official's enormous chest, convincing myself that if it weren't for some small security details and the fact that yer man's a total unit, I'd run after her. I wouldn't hold back. I'd tell her she wasn't the only one ready. Hell, I'd open my mouth and I'd sing it.

EMERALD
Almost four months later ...

Apart from the wind whistling through gaps in the clapped-out windows and distant, excited cries from the corridor, the dorm is strangely quiet. I glance at the clock; we're twenty-one minutes into the Christmas holidays. Everyone is packing up but I'm lying on my bed, daydreaming of months gone by. The longing for summer twists inside me like the vines of bindweed on Grandma's raspberry bushes. At times I think it might choke me from the inside out. I scrunch the duvet up around my chin like it's Liam's sleeping bag and I can't stop myself imagining we're together again, outside our little tent, with his warm, heavy arms wrapped around me. Except he's miles away over the Irish Sea, finishing up his college exams and I'm left with a stack of my own Christmas revision and a particularly ferocious bout of period pain.

It's hard to complain about boarding school when you know your grandma has used her life-savings to pay for it and your dad is spending the same term in an *actual* prison.

In a classic McKenzie move, I arrived back to Hollyfield last September to find myself sharing a room with none other than Ignatia Darcy. As Iggy and I sat in silence opposite each other in the dining room that first night back, I thought about what McKenzie had said to me months earlier about courage being a muscle. Then I thought of Dad's hand, extending into the lonely space between him and Donal Flynn.

I wrote a long letter to Iggy attempting to explain the hold certain friendships once held over me. I went to great lengths to describe the workings of our hierarchical squad dynamics, but mostly I said sorry quite a lot. Iggy corrected my grammar in sparkly green pen and hung the letter on the wall above her desk. She was surprisingly forgiving, but most revelatory of all was how little she seemed to care for the people I thought might have mattered so much to her.

Iggy Darcy, for resolutely giving zero f★★ks, I salute you!

Meanwhile, in another genius McKenzie move, Bryony was put in charge of the new school initiative to promote online etiquette and combat cyber bullying.

Iggy shoves into our room bringing a blast of winter, West Country air in with her. Everything is ninety degrees off. My head is horizontal, gazing up at the picture of Liam and me on the sand dunes after Fiona's party. The photo sits in a silver frame on my bedside locker in front of Grandma's little clock. It took some creative editing but you can actually see our faces now, smiling out from the blackness. I reach up and brush my thumb over his cheekbone and up to his fringe, like I've done a thousand times.

'Eh, what's all this?' Iggy says, taking in my sorry state. With a formidable back-kick she slams the door shut behind her. 'If I don't see a smile soon, I'm going to drop all this crap and come over there and hug you,' she says, dramatically tossing her fencing kit and a mountain of books on to her bed before loping goofily towards me.

In my long history at Hollyfield, I don't remember a term passing this quickly, ever. I thought as a boarder the weeks would drag, but the past four months have whipped by in a not entirely unpleasant haze of school routine, hockey fixtures and the various dorkish activities I've somehow allowed Iggy to enlist me in.

'You *will* cope without me for the next three weeks,' she says, taking in my mournful expression while smoothing her newly short hair off her face. I pick up a tennis ball from beside my bed and fling it at her. She ducks it skilfully before bouncing heavily on to my bed. 'OK, spit it out.'

'I just miss him.'

She leans in closer, elbows on her knees, listening.

'Miss who?' Bryony bursts in; a blizzard of bags and clashing neon accessories. 'Ohmygod, Em! Are you like, crying?'

Actually, I'm not. 'No.'

While it turns out stealth-bitch Bryony *can* actually think beyond 140 characters and is a moderately good friend when she wants to be, compassion is still not a strong point.

Bryony plonks down on Iggy's bed. 'Don't tell me … it's that Irish guy, right?' I look away. 'Seriously, Em, he's like espadrilles, or the rosé my dad buys in France that tastes like vinegar when you get home. Summer stuff doesn't travel – it's a well known fact. You've got to let it go.' She follows my eyes to the photo beside my bed and studies Liam's face for a few seconds, then very slowly she turns it towards the wall. 'So,' she says, leaping back up and rifling dresses out of the wardrobe, 'what's everybody wearing tonight?'

I fling my blankets off like my legs have caught fire and pace the room, consumed with an urgent need to counter every word I've just heard. It happens lately. I look across the room at the two girls staring back at me.

'D'you know what, Bryony? Liam is not some pink wine.' I sit into the chair by the desk and scratch it along the floor, closer to her. 'In fact, I've been thinking about it and if he's anything, he's that vintage dress – the one in, what did you call it … Virgin-of-Mary blue.'

Her mouths gapes open. Iggy's does too.

'The one I *didn't* buy for the Fifth Form Ball.'

Bryony screws up her face. I know she knows. 'The one I said no one would shag you in?' she says almost sheepishly.

'That's the one! It fitted me perfectly. I even liked me in it. But it seemed too easy. I listened to you when I should have trusted myself, and I left it behind, but I never forgot that dress. Not your fault, really. But I won't let it happen again.'

Bryony rolls her eyes, 'You're such a drama queen lately, Em.'

'Look, Liam's not a bloody dress, but there's no one like him anywhere. He wasn't just a chapter is what I'm saying. He was the book.'

Bryony opens her mouth, then clearly thinks better of it and closes it again. I watch as she goes for a second attempt. 'For what it's worth, I really liked that yellow dress.'

I'm almost relieved she's changed the subject. 'It wasn't me though.'

I sigh. I glide past her on my way to the wardrobe and pull the dress out and hand it to her. 'You could totally pull it off.'

She takes the hanger and stands, holding the dress up against her. 'You sure, Em?' she asks, turning from side to side, examining herself in the mirror.

'Take it. It's yours.'

LIAM

'Howrya, Mrs Rutherford,' I say, slinging my stuff into the boot before hopping around into the passenger seat, grateful to be out of the biting cold air and into her lovely, warm car.

She smiles softly. 'It's Eliza, please.' I run my hands roughly down my thighs, pretending to rub away some dirt that's not there. 'You look just like your picture,' she adds, in a slow, hypnotic voice that might be even posher than Emerald's.

It doesn't feel right to look at her too long, but I don't want to seem rude so I give her a stupid-looking grin back. It's mad, 'cause her face is so familiar but then not. It was only a glance but it was enough to catch the same quick eyes, the scaffold of cheekbones and delicately pointed nose I know so well. I turn further around to stare at the airport lights disappearing into the traffic behind us. Good Jesus, what am I doing here?

We hit a huge roundabout and take the first exit, then she does a right off the main road, and then, half a mile later, she nips right again and suddenly we're lost in a knot of never-ending country lanes. Endless hedgerows slink past us, almost tickling the car on either side. I don't know why each of these points feels important, but they do. I don't know how she knows where she's going. There are no signposts anywhere.

Neither of us speaks as we roll down a steep, narrow hill for miles and miles but for some reason the silence isn't awkward. After everything Em confided in me about her mum, I thought I'd have a head start, but from the way Eliza looks at me, I reckon she's got the full skinny on me too. Classical music is playing and she breathes in sync with the strings, like she's forgotten I'm here. Despite everything I'm feeling, it's almost relaxing. Still, I can't stop my right leg from bounding up and down.

'It was really sound of you to pick me up.' I kind of whisper it so as not to disturb her concentration.

I catch her eyes looking across at me and I immediately sit straighter. 'It's the least I could do, Liam.' The way invisible threads between her eyes and mouth inform each other, even the way she moves her hands on and off the wheel, it's like Emerald flows through her. She takes a drink from the large coffee cup between us. 'Besides, I love driving now. Used to hate it, but it's funny how things can change,' she says, as warm breath smokes from her mouth.

Soft, icy flakes dapple the windscreen making everything even more dreamlike. It's not long before a veil of snow covers my side and the view is lost entirely, but soon a huge wiper swoops across the white-out, revealing yet another vast patchwork of hills all around. I never imagined England would be this still and beautiful.

'How've you enjoyed your first term at Uni? Em says you're studying music.'

'Yeah, but it's more technology and production than actual music. There aren't many instruments, like. It's kind of industry focused.'

'You mean you might get a job at the end of it?'

'I better,' I say. 'I've promised my da.'

'Well, good for you,' she says, tucking her hair behind her ear as she laughs. 'Is music something you've always wanted to do?'

I nod. 'I'd never be doing it if it wasn't for Em though. It was her that pushed me.'

Eliza's huge eyes widen. 'How did she manage that?'

Maybe it's her honeyed voice or the fact I'm melting into the soft leather beneath me, but I'm opening my gob again, blabbing away. 'Ah, one night, we were talking about stuff and she just came out with it. Said I was afraid. No one had said that to me before.' Eliza is staring at me but for some reason this just makes even more words spill out. 'At the time I was raging, but only because she was right. Sorry,' I say, finally getting a grip of myself. 'That probably sounds a bit stupid.'

'Not at all,' she sighs. 'Sounds like you guys were really ready to meet.' She takes a long look at me now, communicating something beyond what her mouth has just said. Then her eyes flick back to the road.

When the pupil is ready the teacher will come. I say it to myself but the car slows at the top of the bridge, and each of my words come out so much louder than I intended. Like when you've been singing along to the radio and the music suddenly stops.

Eliza spins around. 'What was that?'

'Something Em said to me last summer. It didn't make sense then, but it does now.' I stop there because we have. The car is completely still now. I realise Eliza is nodding at me, which only compels me to keep talking. 'I want to show her I'm ready. That I'm trying, you know, to push myself. Ah, it's hard to explain, but –'

Eliza places her hand over her mouth and breathes heavily before turning back around to me. 'You explain it perfectly, Liam,' she says slowly. I look at her full-on for the first time. 'You know, I'm still trying too,' she says, sniffling. 'I was a difficult pupil ...' She stops there and begins tapping her hand on my right knee. 'But I'm really trying to be a better teacher,' she adds.

We drive on silently through the dark until we eventually arrive at a set of ancient gates, where a sign reads HOLLYFIELD SCHOOL FOR GIRLS. DAY AND BOARDING. VISITOR'S ENTRANCE. We follow a winding, tree-lined road and in the distance I see a grand house lit up at the end of the drive.

The car has steamed up and I need to see better so I crack a window to let in some air. Gravel crunches loudly under the wheels as we reach the end of the drive. Eliza pulls into a car park space in a small courtyard opposite a large set of doors that sit at the top of a fancy-looking entrance. A couple of girls, younger than Em, file out of the front steps, armed with bags and bundle into waiting cars.

I follow Eliza's eyes through the windscreen. 'Do you know which room is hers? Can you see it from here?'

We both peer out and Eliza jabs her finger on the foggy glass in front of me towards the left of the building. 'That one – three floors up. You want me to go and get her?'

I reach for the door handle. 'You're all right. I just need to grab something from the boot.'

'But you're shaking, Liam. You'll need a warmer –'

'Thanks, but I'm not cold.'

EMERALD

Kitty bursts into the room, her enormous hood covered in tiny white flakes. 'Your mum's here, Em. Her car has just pulled up outside.'

'Is it snowing?' we all cry, crawling over beds and each other to reach the large window that spans the length of our room. I pull back the curtains and look out over the school grounds. It's almost fully dark but the front field is covered in a delicate dusting of white. The lamplight illuminates gazillions of snowflakes in its glare and everything from the old granite gates and beyond is bestowed with a strange and majestic stillness.

'Snow is like the best make-up – everything looks so much better with it on,' says Kitty with alarming conviction, pulling out her phone to take a photo.

I quickly spot the lights of Mum's old silver Volvo parked on the front drive outside. It's taken a while to get used to her doing what she actually said she'd do. I grab my duffel bag from under my bed and start shoving the last unnecessary shoes inside. Kit, meanwhile, joins Bryony in pulling every last item of clothing from our wardrobe on to the floor.

Kitty picks up Iggy's fencing foil and darts towards me. 'Sure I can't change your mind about coming out tonight? C'mon, it'll be fun.'

I shake my head and push Kitty backwards on to Iggy's bed. 'Mum's asked me to come home. Dad gets out next week so it's kind of an odd time.'

Bryony busies herself re-tying the laces of her high-tops, which I see aren't even undone. Talk of my incarcerated father makes her uncomfortable. 'It's been hard for Mum lately,' I add.

Nobody says anything, but I feel Kit's arm around me. She gives me a quick squeeze but soon she's up, prancing around the room and we're all whistling as she hikes the waistband of some gypsy skirt up over her boobs and starts some crazy dance.

Suddenly Bryony stops zipping up my yellow ball dress in front of the mirror and flashes her hand dramatically mid-air. '*Sshh* ...' she shouts. 'Do you hear that?'

'What?' asks Kit, irritated her act has been interrupted.

Bryony cocks her ear towards the window. 'It's coming from –' She stops, shuffles towards the window, wiping the glass with her sleeve. 'Ohmygod!' She leans back and rubs at it again, furiously, pushing her face right up against it now. 'Ohmygod. Oh. My. God.'

'What is it?' asks Kit, shoving past. Me and Iggy climb over the discarded clothes heap and topple over the beds to join them. Next thing we're all lined-up along the heavy mullion windows, all of which have steamed up with the heat of our breath. Bryony and Kit are screeching so much I can't hear a thing. Opening the windows this high up is a number one school no-no, up there with smoking. You just don't do it, or if you do, you make bloody sure you're not caught. Still, I yank down the catch on the old glass pane to a blast of freezing air. It's only then I hear a familiar guitar riff and I'm hit by his voice, all rough and smooth and extraordinary, rising up from the ground, three floors below, walloping me clean in the heart.

'I wish you could see you the way I do,
Your all-knowing look cuts right through …'

Everything behind, above and below me, including Mum, who I see is standing by her car (and even from this distance I can tell might be crying) – everyone around me falls away. All I can see is Liam, his accidental coolness, standing outside my school – my school – with his guitar slung over his shoulder and wearing no coat in December. He's shivering … staring straight ahead, singing to me.

'You see the truth when I've no clue …'

'Liam!' I shout out into the darkness. He stops playing and I watch his eyes scan the building for my voice. Finally his heart-stopping stare hits the glass and our eyes lock. He opens his mouth to sing again, his face exploding into the most insane, nervous smile.

'I just fall deeper and deeper into you.'

There's a thud as Bryony crashes backwards on to the bed,

but I don't even look. I'm watching Liam set his guitar down gently on the ground outside, not looking at anyone but me.

I push off the window and topple over Bryony's various limbs to pull on my boots. I fly through the senior girls' dorm like I'm running through air. I reach the top of the stairs and charge down the three ancient wooden flights before swinging around the enormous Christmas tree twinkling by the fire. As I burst out into the air, tiny flecks of delicious cold snow hit my skin and I tear across the gravel and into his arms.

Clasping his strong, cold hands on either side of my face, he examines it just like he did the night of our first date on the beach in Portstrand, his icy fingertips feeling every part of it, like it really is, to him, some kind of treasure.

'You dared me to dream and I did,' he says quietly, his blue eyes burning into mine so much they close.

The heat of his mouth is a surprise. His soft, slow kisses are like warm waves, surging into every part of me. There, in the snow and the biting December wind, my tongue finds saltwater, cocoa, woodsmoke and the delicious, unmistakeable taste of last summer.

ACKNOWLEDGEMENTS

No Filter would never have made it without the unique magic and infectious passion of my agent, Marianne Gunn O'Connor. Huge, heartfelt thanks for believing in me.

Rebecca McNally, Publishing Director of Children's Books at Bloomsbury, I am indebted to your support. Thank you for welcoming me into the Bloomsbury family. I'm so grateful you took a chance on me. To Hannah Sandford, Commissioning Editor extraordinaire, for being so lovely, for saying so many sensible things so nicely and for simply making this book better. Your notes are a masterclass. To Helen Vick and Lizz Skelly for their guidance and being marvellously good at their jobs.

Author Brian Keaney read this book in its infancy. Thank you for your honesty and for pulling no punches in telling me just how atrocious my grammar was. Your advice was invaluable. To my writer friends John Moloney, Deborah Bee and Alice Smellie for your early enthusiasm and well chosen words of encouragement.

I was lucky enough to be young in the beautiful seaside village of Portmarnock. The view from the Shelters there is forever etched into my heart. Special thanks to all the

Liams I've loved for showing me how kind young men can be. Massive shout-out to all the incredible women in my life on either side of the Irish Sea: you know who you are. I cherish your constant support and madness.

For my dear dad, Paddy, who read this book before he died last year and was generous enough to say he liked it. Thank you for reading me stories. I miss you every day. My wonderful mum, Maura – thank you for being the finest human I know and to Niamh for being a great big sister. To my children, Alfie and Mabel, for your delicious mischief and for always making me laugh. And to our dog, Mildred, without whose steadfast affection I'd have finished this book a whole lot sooner. And finally, to my husband, Alan, without whom this would all still be a dream. I love you.

BC 8/17